Connie Burns was born ～～～～～～～～ degrees in English and ～～～～～～～～～～～～ San Diego State University, as well as a California Teaching Credential. She was recruited by the New South Wales Department of Education to teach in Australia in 1974, and has taught in several high schools in the Sydney area. A committed feminist, she has taken a keen interest in women's affairs and Australian women's writing since her migration to Australia. She has co-written, with Marygai McNamara, four high school English textbooks, including *Literature, A Close Study,* published in 1984, and she and Marygai McNamara are the editors of *Eclipsed: Two Centuries of Australian Women's Fiction,* published in 1988. Married with three children, Connie Burns lives in Sydney.

Marygai McNamara grew up in the highlands of New Guinea. She has a degree in English and History from the University of Sydney and has taught English and History at high schools both in Sydney and London. She has travelled extensively throughout Australia, and especially in the outback. Marygai McNamara has a special interest in women's literature, and has written several plays and short stories. Books published include four English textbooks, written with Connie Burns, and one anthology of Australian women's fiction. She is married, has three daughters, and lives in Harbord, New South Wales.

IMPRINT

FEELING RESTLESS

CONNIE BURNS
MARYGAI McNAMARA

Preface by Drusilla Modjeska

*Collins
Publishers
Australia*

IMPRINT

COLLINS PUBLISHERS AUSTRALIA
First published in 1989 by William Collins Pty Ltd,
55 Clarence Street, Sydney NSW 2000

Copyright © Selection: Connie Burns and Marygai McNamara 1989
© Introduction: Drusilla Modjeska 1989

National Library of Australia
Cataloguing-in-Publication data:
Feeling restless: Australian women's short
stories, 1940–1969.

ISBN 0 7322 2500 0.

1. Short stories, Australian—Women authors.
2. Australian fiction—20th century.
I. Burns, C. J. (Connie Jean). II. McNamara,
Marygai.

A823'.01089287

Typeset in 11pt Times Roman by Midland Typesetters, Victoria
Printed by Globe Press, Victoria

Cover illustration: *Portrait of Betty Paterson* by Esther Paterson

Creative writing programme assisted by the Australia Council,
the Australian government's arts advisory and support organisation.

Arts for
Australians
Australia **Council**

To our mothers, Nora Christine Marchman Burns
and Veronica Josephine Walsh McNamara

ACKNOWLEDGEMENTS

The following pieces were first published in the sources mentioned: 'Mrs James Greene' in *The Little Ghosts*, Angus & Robertson Publishers, Sydney, 1959; 'Marlene' in the *Bulletin*; 'Marriage is for Fools' in *Home*, 20 November 1948; 'The Lottery' in the *Bulletin*; 'The Price' in *ABC Weekly*; 'The Hotel-keeper's Story' in *Southerly*, 1952; 'The White Butterfly' in *Coast to Coast 1961-62*, Angus & Robertson Publishers, Sydney; 'Full Cycle' in *Meanjin*, Vol 9, No 3, 1950; 'Amble' in *Southerly*, 1953; 'First Job' in *Southerly*, 1943; 'The Face of Despair' in *Australia Writes*, F. W. Cheshire (Longman Cheshire Pty Ltd), South Melbourne, 1955; 'The Double Track' in *Coast to Coast 1961-62*, Angus & Robertson Publishers, Sydney; 'Rewards to the Faithful' in *Summer's Tales 1*, Macmillan, Melbourne, 1964; 'Fate' in *In the Sun*, the Australian Medical Publication Company, Sydney, 1943; 'The Lame Duck' in the *Bulletin*; 'The Trap' in the *Bulletin*, 12 July 1950; 'Burning Off' in *Meanjin* and the *Bulletin*; 'Mini-Skirts' in *Chance International*, 1968; 'Other Woman' in *Australia Week-end Book 4*, Ure Smith Pty Ltd, 1945; 'The Procurer' in *An Affair of Clowns*, Angus & Robertson Publishers, Sydney, 1968; 'On the Terrace' in *Summer's Tales 3*, Macmillan, Melbourne, 1966; 'It's Nobody's Business' in the *Bulletin*, 20 May 1953; 'The Travellers' in *Australia, National Journal*, Ure Smith Pty Ltd, Sydney, 1947; 'The Scenery Never Changes' in *Coast to Coast 1961-62*, Angus & Robertson Publishers, Sydney; 'Lance Harper, His Story' in *The Vital Decade, Ten Years of Australian Art and Literature*, Sun Books, Melbourne, 1968; 'A Long Way' in *Coast to Coast 1961-62*, Angus & Robertson Publishers, Sydney; 'A Sense of Mission' in *People in Glass Houses*, Macmillan, Melbourne, 1967; 'The Secret' in *Southerly*, 1968.

The editors and publishers would like to thank the following for permission to use copyright material: Angus & Robertson Publishers for 'Mrs James Greene' by Ethel Anderson, from *Tales of Parramatta and India*, © Bethia Ogden; Angus & Robertson Publishers for 'Marlene' by Katharine Susannah Prichard, from *Happiness*, © Ric Throssel; John Fairfax & Sons Ltd for 'Marriage is for Fools' by Myra Morris; Curtis Brown (Aust) Pty Ltd, Sydney, for 'The Lottery' by Marjorie Barnard; Paris Drake-Brockman for 'The Price' by Henrietta Drake-Brockman; Penguin Books Australia Ltd for 'The Hotel-keeper's Story' by Christina Stead; Helen Helga Wilson for 'The White Butterfly'; Longman Cheshire Pty Ltd for 'The Face of Despair' by Kylie Tennant, from *Australia Writes*; Curtis Brown (Aust) Pty Ltd, Sydney, for 'The Double Track' by Dame Mary Durack; B. S. Jenkins for 'Fate' by Margaret Trist; Gwen Kelly for 'Mini-Skirts'; Thelma Forshaw for 'The Procurer'; Hilary Linstead & Associates Pty Ltd for 'On the Terrace' by Dorothy Hewett; Curtis Brown (Aust) Pty Ltd, Sydney, for 'It's Nobody's Business' by Nancy Keesing; Curtis Brown (Aust) Pty Ltd, Sydney, for 'The Travellers' by Ruth Park, © Kemalde Pty Ltd; Hickson Associates for 'The Scenery Never Changes' by Thea Astley; Angus & Roberston Publishers for 'A Long Way' by Mena Abdullah and Ray Mathew, from *The Time of the Peacock*, © Mena Abdullah and Ray Mathew.

The editors would especially like to thank the staff of the Mitchell Library, New South Wales; the Fisher Library, University of Sydney; and the Rare Books Department of the Fisher Library. Thanks also go to Pan Books (Aust) Pty Ltd for permission to include the extracts from *Yacker* by Candida Baker in the introduction, and to Penguin Books Australia Ltd for permission to quote from *Damned Whores and God's Police; The Colonisation of Women in Australia* by Anne Summers.

Every effort has been made to trace and acknowledge the owners of copyright material in this book. The publishers would be pleased to hear from anyone who can provide them with further information on this material.

Contents

PREFACE

In Christina Stead's 'The Hotel-keeper's Story', first published in 1952 and reprinted here, a Belgian mayor arrives at a small hotel in Switzerland. The hotel keeper tolerates his odd behaviour, at first put down to eccentricity, though her husband is less inclined to be patient, as the mayor writes his mad diatribes against the Germans on the hotel tray cloths, towels and tablecloths. The episode shakes the marriage, the hotel, the other guests. 'But you know,' the hotel keeper says, 'the Germans have left deep marks on everyone's heart and mind in Europe; they have burned themselves in, for better and for worse, and so it will be for a long time.'

And not only in Europe. The stories in this collection, written by Australian women between 1940 and 1969, bear the mark of war. Not many are about war, that is not what I mean, but its shadow is there: the loss and destruction echo in the stories. So do the shock, the slow recovery, and the immobilising aftermath of cold war. Only the stories that come well into the 1960s manage to shake it off entirely, pushing towards the colour and the changes that were to come.

When the stories in *Feeling Restless* were written, women still wore gloves to town, dance halls played Old Time and Modern, and a woman was ashamed to be thirty and single. Before the war women writers had taken on questions of gender as part of a broad social agenda; and in a climate that was economically tougher but politically more variable they were able to expand the terms on which they could write. Modernism was in the air; there was the excitement of urgency in their work. A decade later the possibilities of political and cultural dissent had been undercut by the pervasive conservatism of cold war. Marjorie

Barnard stopped writing fiction, she said, because of the silence that greeted the publication of *Tomorrow and Tomorrow* in 1947, disheartening her more effectively than the war censor who cut pages and paragraphs from it. One of her short stories is in this collection, written at the end of her fiction career. Katharine Susannah Prichard, also in this collection, wrote on into the 1960s, but it could be argued that her best work was written before the war. Christina Stead stayed out of the country. This did not give her immunity from the cold war, but it did provide a more conducive context for a writer who was constitutionally not a social realist.

Knowing this history, I confess I was expecting a certain drabness in this collection, interesting drabness, but drab nonetheless, like the dyed hessian curtains Bohemians hung in their windows. These were the years when Australian writing was said to be dun-coloured realism, and cold war had squashed the life out of everything. But I'm pleased to be able to report that these stories are not drab. Far from it. I was wrong, caught in historical gloom perhaps, or in the prejudice of a generation born as the war ended, and coming to maturity in the late 1960s, just as this collection ends, determined only to look ahead.

True, there is little of the modernism that was beginning in the 1930s, or the formal self-consciousness we've come to expect in writing since 1969. These are *stories*, not the *fictions* of today. They were written when modernism was out of critical favour, when narrative meant story, and story was predominant; and when fiction was used, often consciously, and usually defensively, as a means of political, as well as literary expression in a doggedly conservative society. As a result most of these stories are social realist, and some strike a didactic note we're no longer accustomed to. But by the same token there's plenty of plot and no difficulty turning over the pages. There are old-fashioned pleasures in this collection. There are also some unexpected and impressive stories. The best of them shine through everything that has happened since, and are as fresh and startling today as they would have been when they were first read in magazines and anthologies after the war. It is a mistake to dismiss them as belonging to a low period in Australian writing, lost between the interesting thirties and the flamboyant seventies. Rather, they are a reminder, at their best, of the resilience of writing, and the courage of writers who held their own against considerable discouragement.

For my money the best of them all is Marjorie Barnard's 'The Lottery'. It is a taut account of a husband who hears on the ferry that his wife has won the lottery. I won't spoil it by telling you what happens, only that it is a modest story, and a shocking story; a story that shocks. Its power, it seems to me, lies in the silence of the woman.

The voicing of the social silence of women and the terms of female speech is now commonplace as a way of understanding and discussing women's writing. During the 1950s and 1960s there was no critical or political acknowledgment for such a discussion. These were the years between feminisms: the Menzies era, economic complacency, the triumph of the suburbs. So I was surprised by *Feeling Restless*. I found myself reading the stories as if the feminism that was yet to come was already present. This was not so much because of its absence, which is thorough, but because its antecedents are here, if only as a desire, or a restlessness, not yet a possibility. The noisy voices of my generation didn't come from thin air. We joined a conversation that had started long before we were born. It might have been quietened, put on the defensive, but it wasn't stopped by the disabling rhetoric of cold war. These women, feeling restless for another future, were writing, as women had for generations, not only of the contradictory desires and forces that daily pressed on them, but of the terms on which a woman could speak, and write.

There are many strategies. Like Marjorie Barnard, Helen Wilson uses a masculine point of view, in this case to show the fragility of a woman caught between the desire and desires of two men. In Nancy Cato's sharp-edged story the woman remains enigmatic, seen at a distance in her hut on the beach where the man sets his trap for fish. It is through the silence between them that we understand his attraction, and his anxiety; and her knowledge of the greater and entrapping fear of what isn't and can't be spoken between them.

Myra Morris and Thea Astley take a different tack, writing through the perspective of unmarried women who are facing bleak possibilities at an age when, as Thea Astley says, they're 'not too old, but again, not too young'. The woman in Myra Morris's story considers a marriage which women in the fictions of the 1970s would scoff at. Thea Astley's Sadie Wild suffers the indignities her fictional daughters know all too well, but while they would be angry, she is left silent, nursing an 'ashamed and humiliated heart', and 'moving to her martyrdom like a saint'. These are stories about the vulnerability of feminine existence, but they are not vulnerable stories. On the contrary their meaning, and their politics, lie in the toughness of a narrative voice that is willing to say what its characters wouldn't dream of saying. They are not consenting to a verdict, but offering a judgement.

Dorothy Hewett strikes a more modern, and modernist, note in her story from the early 1960s. Her Emily is not ashamed to walk naked back to her lover's bed 'as the cistern wheezed and gurgled through the flat'. More to the point perhaps, the writing self is not ashamed to take on seduction, betrayal and the sexual desires — and realities — of a woman who will not settle for life defined simply as mother, or mistress. It is this, as well as the story's interior form, that has it straining towards the changes that were coming.

For the most part the accent on sex and sexuality falls elliptically. There was no way Australian women could write explicitly of sexual matters during the 1950s and be published. Helen Wilson relies on a metaphor that is clumsy to our more permissive ears: 'The sweet fructifying smell of wheat and the warm heady yeast of germination.' Charmian Clift refracts seduction and betrayal through the fearful bond that exists between rivals. Gwen Kelly's chilling 'Mini-skirts', another story from the 1960s, slips between an adolescent erotic cruelty, and a mother's self-satisfied preparations for an evening at the club.

Nancy Phelan pushes hopeless longing and desires that exceed social possibility to a painful and comic limit. 'Rewards to the Faithful' is the spinster's dream, the romantic fantasy, when everything Ethel has ever wanted comes true and the boss moves into her house, disgraced, dependent, and at her ministering mercy. ' "Rewards to the faithful," mother used to say. "Everything comes to those who wait." ' This is a parable of class as much as gender, of inequities that divide us even in our dreams and fantasies.

The social resonance of these stories prevents the anxiety about female speech and female existence reducing itself to individual grievance. Perhaps because they are written against a political discourse saturated with immobilising abstractions, and at a time when social realism was still popular with Australian readers, these stories press the critical significance of small individual experiences. In a bald attempt to make one woman stand in for all, Henrietta Drake-Brockman uses grandiose imagery when a mother named Mary hears news of the war and, simultaneously, the excitement in her son's voice as he tells her that at last the price of wheat has gone up. 'In his eagerness for response Dick stepped forward, flinging out his arms. The shadow of a tree darkened his face. A vague shadow, she never knew whether it was there or not, where it began, where it ended — but all at once the shadow falling on Dick, on his lifted arms, was the shadow of a cross.'

Kylie Tennant takes the focus off the individual in a characteristic story of a community caught in a flood. Some people squabble and worry about the carpet; but the vagrant woman is silent, with *the face of despair* that gives the story its title. Katharine Susannah Prichard and Mary Durack, those grand old social realists, take on class, Aboriginality and gender in grand style. These stories seem particularly of their time, perhaps because they address vexed issues in a tone white women can no longer use; perhaps because they are taut with political intention, which is no bad thing. The courage it took to do this in the late 1940s should not be forgotten. They are, and not only for this reason, important stories, in their own way uncompromising.

The fact that women write of their own troubled subjectivity is too often taken to mean that their themes are small. If anyone should wish to argue this, they should consider an anthology like *Feeling Restless* which, with admirable dexterity, puts stories with a small interior focus together with stories that turn their attention outwards to the clattering events of the external world. Not that the two are so easy to distinguish. Ethel Anderson writes of a woman who survives the Indian mutiny in very frightening circumstances. But is this a story about imperialism, the Indian mutiny, or about repressed feminine desires? Is Shirley Hazzard's 'A Sense of Mission' an indictment of a UN mission, or of a woman's loneliness and disappointment? Is Mena Abdullah's story about Pakistan and immigration, or humility and the universal task of being a mother?

There is restlessness in this collection, as the title suggests, as if the stories themselves, as well as the characters who inhabit them, are straining towards some other future. Thelma Forshaw's smart little fifteen-year-old, an avid reader of magazines and a 'priestess of self-improvement', mooching past the dance halls, isn't going to find what she wants in the boy her brother finds for her, or even in her footballer. We know it, the story knows it, but she can't know it, whatever it is, because what she's looking for isn't there yet.

The title for the collection comes from a line in Judith Wright's story 'The Lame Duck'. Lyla is married to Ronnie. They love each other and live a cheerful life in a cluttered and run-down house on the edge of a country town. The only blemish on a happy arrangement is that Lyla is alone a lot, looking out at the bush from her house. When the bank manager's widow builds herself a house on the empty block next door, Lyla is seduced into a view of life that makes her own suddenly shabby, and a little shameful. Curiosity turns to restlessness, restlessness turns in on itself; and, while she was once happy, or happy enough, now she feels her life falls short. Of what, she doesn't know. She doesn't put the question to herself. Instead she tries to smarten up the house, herself, her marriage, to meet the unspoken requirements of a woman who surely embodies all that was objectionable in a culture ruled from the suburbs.

This story is emblematic of the mood of the collection, a restlessness bred in a culture that limits and closes off the options of its women, so that their energies are wasted, or twisted against themselves. It is also emblematic of the best writing in *Feeling Restless*, writing that does not give in to the dun-coloured realities and drab rhetoric it challenges, but speaks through silence to the possibility of another, more fully coloured future.

Drusilla Modjeska
Sydney 1989

INTRODUCTION

In recent years there has been a revival of Australian women's literature.[1] Access to this literature has made it possible for modern women to develop an understanding of their predecessors and to better define themselves.[2] Unfortunately, the recent past, the period from the Second World War to the rise of modern feminism at the beginning of the 1970s, has been largely overlooked in this revival.

1940 to 1969 was a period of great economic prosperity in Australia. It was a time when there was a mass move to the suburbs, an increased birthrate, full employment (for men), increased immigration from southern Europe, and political conservatism. The repression of women in some ways was worse in this period than it had been in previous decades. During the Second World War women experienced a brief period of freedom; they were mobilised into the workforce as part of the war effort and were able to gain work skills and attend university in large numbers. However, when the men came home from the war, women were expected to return to their more traditional roles of wife and mother. They became isolated in suburbia, far removed from the extended family life and close-knit neighbourhoods that existed before the war. The role of homemaker was not as highly skilled and time consuming as it had been, and no longer had the same status in society. Gone were the days of fuel stoves and home-made remedies. Domestic appliances which were readily available after the war made the role of housekeeper appear to be much easier. Women were being told by 'experts' how their job should be done; the role of homemaker now came with doubts and confusion rather than a sense of pride and accomplishment. Pressure to a prescribed role came from the

1

church, the media and the burgeoning advertising industry — and even governments, who made abortion illegal and contraception expensive and difficult to obtain. Anne Summers describes the effects of these pressures in *Damned Whores and God's Police*:[3]

> Family life and suburban life quickly became synonymous and were idealised as the most desirable way to live and the best environment for raising children. With these certainties being so confidently asserted it became difficult for women to express whatever doubts they may have had about restrictions suburban family life had for them. It would have entailed abrogating the security that comes from conforming to a socially approved lifestyle; they would have had to battle against incomprehension and hostility as well as their own self-doubts. 'There must be something wrong with *me*' was the usual reaction of these restless women; as suburban wives and mothers they were embodying the ideal female existence according to the prevailing ideology. Everyone else professed contentment and happiness so the sources of discontent were seen to be purely personal.

The stories included in this anthology were first published during the period beginning with the Second World War and ending with the rise of modern feminism at the end of the 1960s. There has been an expectation that the literature of this period would be mundane and reflect an attitude of complacency. However, the Australian women writers of this period *were feeling restless* and their writing reflects their growing dissatisfaction with society in general and in particular with the sexist role prescribed for them; a dissatisfaction which was to grow into the feminist movement of the 1970s.

By the end of the 1960s these women began to realise that they were not alone in their discontent and they began to unite. One of the earliest indications of this was the first conference of the Women's Movement held in Melbourne in 1970. In 1972–73 organisations such as the Women's Electoral Lobby and Media Women's Action Group were formed. Germaine Greer's *The Female Eunuch*, generally regarded as a landmark in the women's liberation movement, was published in 1971. Women's restlessness was turning to action, marking the end of the period covered by this anthology.

1940 to 1969 was a period when Australian women writers were still finding it difficult to write and to be taken seriously by the publishing world. They faced the usual problems women have when trying to write;[4] as in the past their sexist conditioning was a particularly difficult handicap to overcome. As Christina Stead said of her own upbringing:

> We were brought up to be pretty and catch men. I wasn't pretty and they didn't think I'd catch one — by that I mean go into the suburbs and have children. All I wanted was to find the right man and marry him. I didn't give tuppence about writing![5]

Luckily the man she did find was very supportive of her writing and she was able to become one of the greatest novelists of the twentieth century. The women writers of the time often lacked the self-confidence necessary to write from the women's perspective despite the fact that most of the best prose writers of the immediate past (the 1930s) were women (e.g. Henry Handel Richardson, Miles Franklin, Eleanor Dark, Katharine Susannah Prichard). Thea Astley commented:

> I also grew up in an era where they talked about 'women's' literature. 'It's a *woman's* book,' they'd say, as if there was something wrong with that. So when I was eighteen or nineteen I thought to myself that the only way one could have any sort of validity was to write as a male. It seemed to me that male writers were accepted, and what they said was debated and talked about, whereas women writers were ignored.[6]

Whilst not adopting a male pseudonym as many women of the previous century had done, Thea Astley often wrote from the persona of a male character. Margaret Trist was advised early in her writing career to use a male character as the central character in her stories. 'I tried the male as central character, and thought I'd get away with it, until I received a note from Miles Franklin in which she asked why I'd put my heroine into

3

pants.'[7] Her story 'Fate' is a good example of just how powerful and significant the 'mundane' events of a woman's life can become.

In order to give an overview of women's attitudes and experiences at the time, we selected the short story form. We were particularly interested in the development of fiction, a genre that allows writers to explore possibilities and crystallise experiences, and felt that women's non-fiction, a different and in some ways more confining genre, should be considered in a separate study. We have not used novel excerpts because the short story has the advantage of being complete in itself and excerpts often neither do justice to a writer's skill nor leave the reader with a feeling of satisfaction. Short stories were a popular genre of the period and we had a wealth of good stories from which to choose.

At the beginning of the 1940s literary journals flourished. Not since the 1890s had the short story enjoyed such a creative period. *Southerly* began in 1939, *Meanjin* in 1940, and *Angry Penguins* in 1941. Few women's contributions appeared in the early editions of some of these journals, but later their representation improved. The *Bulletin* as well as many women's magazines contained stories of high quality. Anthologies were popular and many were published regularly such as *Summer's Tales* and *Australian Weekend Book*. Most important to the development of the short story was the establishment of *Coast to Coast* in 1941, which was the most prestigious outlet for stories in the 1940s and 1950s. Many anthologies were conceived and edited by women such as Beatrice Davis, Henrietta Drake-Brockman and Kylie Tennant.

Choosing the short story has unfortunately caused us to omit many of the acknowledged best and most popular writers of the period. Miles Franklin, Dymphna Cusack, Eleanor Dark and Eve Langley are novelists who fit this category. Ernestine Hill and Patsy Adam Smith were primarily writers of non-fiction and their few short stories do not do justice to their range of subject matter or their writing skill.

We selected what we considered to be the most enjoyable and satisfying stories. These included some by the acknowledged greatest fiction writers publishing at the time, as well as writers who were very prolific but have since been eclipsed (e.g. Margaret Trist, Marjorie Robertson, Lyndall Hadow). In addition we chose stories by writers who were not prolific, but whose work was of such high quality that we felt compelled to include them (Helen Meggs and Irene Summy).

We would have liked to have better represented the attitudes and feelings of all Australian women; however, only the work published in the popular short story outlets of the time is represented here. It is hard to say how much the attitudes of the white publishing world limited who was published.[8] It is certainly true that work by Aboriginal writers such as Oodgeroo Noonuccal, Faith Bandler and Monica Clare did not appear until the 1970s; with the notable exception of Mena Abdullah, very few Australian women writers of multicultural backgrounds are represented in the published work of the period.[9] This may possibly have been due to linguistic and cultural barriers.

The women whose work was being published in the 1940s, '50s and '60s form a very homogeneous group. They came from professional, middle-class families, and they were well-educated. Over half of the women included in this anthology attended university. They saw themselves as serious professional writers; writing was not just something to dabble in, but an important part of their lives. Many of these women supported themselves by their writing; while many were full-time journalists, others tended to combine a career as a lower-paid professional, such as a teacher or a librarian, with that of a writer. It is interesting to note that half of the women included either had writers in their immediate family or were married to writers. This suggests that they moved in literary and academic circles. Reflecting Australian population trends, most of these women lived in the capital cities. With the exception of Christina Stead, Shirley Hazzard and Sarah Campion, these women were for most of their lives residents of Australia.

The short stories published by women during this period did vary in subject matter; however, there were some subjects that

5

were obviously more important to them. Like Australian women writers of the past, relationships, particularly between men and women, were the predominant concern. The quality of existing marriages was scrutinised, and the idea that marriage was the only alternative for women was frequently being questioned. The problems of being a single woman were often presented. There were stories about domestic matters, pregnancy, ageing, and the day-to-day details of just trying to survive.

Although these traditional women's areas were a primary interest, the restlessness of women writers extended to broader concerns. Underprivileged groups like the poor and the Aborigines have always been subjects of Australian women's writing and continued to appear. While the writers of the past had been concerned with the problems of English migrants, the women of this period often wrote about the difficulties of the newly arrived southern European migrants struggling to adapt to a new culture. Other topics examined were war, conservation and bureaucracy. This anthology contains stories that reflect this wide range of subject matter.

Stories by Gwen Kelly and Irene Summy, both published at the end of this period, *did* touch on controversial issues; however, subjects like rape, menstruation, lesbianism, and incest did not appear. Women may not have felt free to write about such subjects, or the male-dominated publishing world may not have allowed material on these issues to be published. The appearance of writing about these taboo subjects marks the beginning of the next period of women's writing and the coming of modern feminism.

When we were choosing these stories, we became more and more aware of the superb craftsmanship of these women writers. They understood the power of the written word and were able to use their skill to reconstruct their feelings and experiences. While most of the pieces selected *tell* a story, their styles range from stream of consciousness to straight narrative; from dialogue to description; from satirical to lyrical.

The women writers of this period were concerned, questioning women. It was their restlessness that helped to establish the women's movement of the 1970s as well as initiate other aspects of social reform. Reviving their writing not only helps us to gain a clearer understanding of their ideas and experiences, but it also reaffirms that women's writing has not been fragmented or sporadic, but has been a strong and continuing tradition.

NOTES

1   A range of Australian women's writing can be found in the following:

Burns, C. & McNamara, M. (eds) *Eclipsed: Two Centuries of Australian Women's Fiction*, Collins Publishers Australia, Sydney, 1988.

Giles, F. (ed.) *From the Verandah; Stories of Love and Landscape by Nineteenth-Century Australian Women*, McPhee Gribble/Penguin Books, Fitzroy, Victoria, 1987.

Spender, D. (ed.) *The Penguin Anthology of Australian Women's Writing*, Penguin Books, Ringwood, Victoria, 1988.

Spender, L. (ed.) *Her Selection: Writings by Nineteenth-Century Australian Women*, Penguin Books, Ringwood, Victoria, 1989.

Also helpful:

Adelaide, D. *Australian Women Writers; A Bibliographic Guide*, Pandora Press, Sydney, 1988.

2   For a discussion of the importance of the heritage of Australian women's literature, see:

Spender, D. *Writing a New Word: Two Centuries of Australian Women Writers*, Pandora Press, Sydney, 1988.

3   Summers, A. *Damned Whores and God's Police; The Colonisation of Women in Australia*, Allen Lane/Penguin Books, Ringwood, Victoria, 1975, p. 426.

4   Suggested readings:

Ferrier, C. *Gender, Politics and Fiction: Twentieth-Century Australian Women's Novels*, University of Queensland Press, St Lucia, 1985, pp. 14–16.

Modjeska, D. 'That Still Blue Hour Before the Baby's Cry' from *Exiles at Home*, Angus & Robertson, Sydney, 1981.

Woolf, V. *A Room of One's Own*, Penguin Books, Ringwood, Victoria, 1965.

5   Baker, C. (ed.) Christina Stead in *Yacker: Australian Writers Talk About Their Work*, Picador, Sydney, 1986, p. 22.

6   Astley, T. *ibid.*, pp. 42–43.

7   Lindsay, H. (ed.) Margaret Trist's 'Names on a Splotch of Ink', from *Ink No. 2, 50th Anniversary Edition*, Society of Women's Writers, Sydney, p. 119.

8   Suggested reading:

Russ, J. *How to Suppress Women's Writings*, The Women's Press, London, 1984.

Spender, L. *Intruders on the Rights of Men: Women's Unpublished Heritage*, Pandora Press, Melbourne, 1983.

9   Suggested reading

Gunew, S. & Mahyuddin, J. (eds) *Beyond the Echo: Multicultural Women's Writing*, University of Queensland Press, St Lucia, 1988.

ETHEL ANDERSON
(1883-1958)

Ethel Anderson was born in England to Australian parents and educated at Picton, New South Wales, and later in Sydney. Married to a British Army officer, Anderson spent ten years in India before returning to Australia, where her husband was attached to the governor-general's household. When her husband died in 1949, she became a professional writer.

Although she considered herself a poet and had three volumes of poetry published, she is perhaps best known for her prose. Anderson published two collections of essays and wrote for journals in India, England, America and Australia.

Her best known collection of short stories, *At Parramatta* (1956), was republished in 1985. A discontinuous narrative, it is filled with stories of wit and humour, satirising life in early Parramatta. She also published two collections of stories based on her Indian experiences. 'Mrs James Greene' is based on historical evidence surrounding the Lucknow Uprising. It is a compelling story using contrast and irony to great effect and reveals examples of Anderson's wit and her lyrical, sensuous descriptions.

MRS JAMES GREENE

Mrs James Greene at sixteen was not exactly a bride. She had a daughter three months old. However, she was still so new to the duties of a housekeeper that the cookery-book which her Great-aunt Hannah had given her as a wedding present could, on occasion, absorb her whole attention.

Her husband, Cornet Greene of the Green Bays (as his regiment of irregular cavalry was nicknamed), stooping to kiss his wife good-bye when he was leaving for the usual morning parade in Sitapur barracks, found her less responsive than was her custom to his deft caress. A subaltern's wife who for the first time was to entertain a general, who was to give that very night (3rd June 1857) her first really important dinner party, might be forgiven if a little thing like an after-breakfast kiss—which is mere marital small-change, in any case—had but her half-hearted notice. She was weighing the rival merits of fish soup with croutons—'Jimmy, what are croutons?' she had asked without raising her eyes from the page, and he had told her 'Snippets of toast'—or of the Prince Consort's Favourite Sweet—'Just fancy, Jimmy,' she had murmured as he tweaked her ear, amused at her earnest air, 'milk and rice only!'—and so enthralled was she that for the first time in their fifteen months of married life she had almost allowed her Jimmy to mount and ride away without her customary blandishments—the butterfly kiss and the waving handkerchief.

How glad, how very glad, she was afterwards to remember that, as he put his foot in the stirrup, she had tossed aside her book, rushed to the mounting-block, and flung both arms round his neck—passionately, for she was a passionate young creature—and that, in doing so, she had murmured in his ear, 'You know that I love you better than all the rice puddings and all the generals in the world, don't you, darling?'

Laughing, Jimmy Greene had ridden down the drive, his scarlet jacket, black stock, steel gorget, and braided dolman gleaming brightly in the tropical sunshine. He had waved to her as he was about to turn from the drive into the high-road, where the neem-trees hid him from her sight.

So they parted, never to meet again.

For as Cornet Greene rode onto the parade ground where his regiment—unmounted this morning—was already drawn up in the neat unbroken lines that had been his pride, a *feu de joie* that sounded like paper tearing had ripped along the front line and he and all his officers there assembled fell from their chargers, shot dead by their own men.

The sowars then dispersed to kill every European man, woman, and child that they encountered. Simultaneously in every British cantonment in Oudh the prearranged revolt broke out. On that fatal day the mutineers began to loot, to burn, to torture, to pile into dreadful heaps, living and dead alike.

In the well at Cawnpore where screaming children were tossed alive among the hideously mutilated dead and dying; in the white-washed shambles of Dinapore where (until Lord Curzon obliterated them) stained fingerprints could be seen patterning the skirting-boards (the men's high up, the women's just above the ground); throughout all the provinces of Oudh and Behar black terror stalked the white race suspected, quite unjustly, of forcing Hindus and Moslems alike to bite cartridges greased with pig-fat, to break a rule vital to their religion. Their priests had told them that all ammunition was so greased. The resulting mutiny was, to all Indians who took part in it, a crusade, a holy war; no cruelty, therefore, was considered too revolting to be practised.

Meanwhile, on that first morning of the rising in Sitapur, Mrs James Greene, seated in the cool central room of her house with one foot on the rocker of her child's cradle, turned the pages of her recaptured cookery-book.

'Khuda-Baksh,' she was saying to her cook, 'last night you made an omelette and charged me for eight eggs. This book says that four eggs are the utmost—' So far had she got when shots rang out on the parade ground.

Khuda-Baksh heard them. He had been waiting for them. He leant quickly across the cradle and snatched the book from his young mistress's hand.

Aghast at such unheard-of impertinence, Mrs Greene looked at her swarthy bearded servant, terror growing in her eyes. The man's evil intention was clearly shown in his dark, treacherous looks.

Taking her child in her arms, Mrs Greene backed against the wall.

'Khuda-Baksh,' she cried, trying to keep her voice firm, 'put that book back on the table and leave the room at once! When the sahib comes home—'

'He will never come back!' Khuda-Baksh laughed. 'He and all the sahib-log in India have been killed.'

Shadows blocked the doorway.

Some near neighbours, Sir Harry Johnson and Miss Binnie, with two soldiers' wives, rushed into the room.

The baronet was an old man. The exertion of running had deprived him of breath. He stood panting and speechless while Mary Binnie gasped out, 'The sepoys are murdering all the English in cantonments. They are even killing the children. Oh, what shall we do? Where shall we hide ourselves?'

'In the taikhana!' Mrs Greene exclaimed immediately.

In every house built in the early days of India, either by French, Dutch, or English, there was what was called a taikhana, a set of underground rooms meant to be a refuge from the intense heat of summer. Many were kept secret, and provided with a secret outlet, to be used in time of danger. The Greenes' taikhana had a concealed door opening onto the river-bank nearly a quarter of a mile from the house.

Looking to see what had happened to Khuda-Baksh, Mrs Greene found that he had vanished, intimidated by the sight of Sir Harry, whose feeble, shaking hand held a revolver—a pistol, as it was then called. She guessed that the man would not have gone far, but she hoped that they would be able to gain entrance to the underground rooms before he returned, bringing others with him, as he was certain to do.

'Come through this archway,' she urged her companions. 'Quickly! Quickly! Thank God that Jimmy always makes me carry the key of the taikhana in my pocket. Hold Baby, Mary, while I get it.'

Stooping, Mrs Greene lifted the voluminous shirred flounces of her crinolined skirts and found the pocket sewn into the lining. She fished out the key, unlocked the strong door of solid teak that appeared to be merely the panelled back of a cupboard, and led her trembling friends through it.

The main rooms of this taikhana were lit by fanlights of thick glass let into the ceiling. They were not hollowed out directly under the house, but were situated under the plot of ground between the bungalow and the river, the Surayan, that ran at the foot of the grounds.

'We have no food, so we shall not be able to stay here long, but after dark we might slip through the river door at the end of the tunnel that leads to the ford,' Mrs Greene was explaining, when sounds of running feet and a crackle of musketry sounded faintly far above them.

'The mutineers!' Mary Binnie exclaimed. 'Oh, if they find us we shall be brutally murdered!'

Sobs choked her utterance. Ten minutes earlier she had seen her sister with her infant child and little son hideously massacred. Sir Harry, too, had tears streaming down his furrowed cheeks. His grandson, Ensign Johnson, whom he had come to India to visit, had been shot down and then hacked to pieces in his presence. The two soldiers' wives had seen their husbands decapitated, and all their fellow women killed. They had seen the mutineers march off in triumph with the heads impaled on their bayonets.

Three months later the Viceroy's wife, as she drove along by the waterside at Allahabad, was to see the miserable band of women who were to be the sole survivors of experiences which had entailed unspeakable suffering. She was to write in her diary that night, complacently: 'It shocked me to observe that these wretched females were so insensible to the delicacy of their position.' Lady Canning had not learnt, with Elizabeth Barrett Browning, that 'Hopeless grief is passionless.'

In the initial hours of this ordeal which was to end for all but one of them in a terrible death, Sir Harry, Mary Binnie, and the two soldiers' wives—widows, that is—though they were dissolved in tears, though their irrational gestures of dismay told how deeply their feelings were moved, had still to follow the primal instinct for self-preservation which is inherent in the very nature of man. These poor fugitives wept for those they had so tragically lost; still, they also feared for their own safety, and they clearly showed the terror that overwhelmed them.

Mrs Greene alone was calm. She had her child to care for, and nursing it, her neat bodice unbuttoned, her white, blue-veined bosom partly covered by a lace handkerchief, she sat on the floor of the tunnel apparently unmoved, her child at her breast and a gentle and maternal tenderness lighting up her lovely face.

'We must wait till darkness comes, then we must make a dash for the ford, cross the river, and try to make our way to Lucknow, which is, I think, our nearest British post,' she said to Mary Binnie, who though distracted was slightly more composed than the other three. 'News may reach our people that a mutiny has broken out in Sitapur. They may already be sending men to rescue us.'

She did not guess that in Lucknow, too, regiment after regiment had rebelled and murdered their officers; that a remnant of the surviving English was to stand one of the noblest sieges in history in that unfortified house now known as the Residency.

It was cool in the taikhana.

Even when the mutineers above them burnt the house down (thinking they were hidden in it), the shuddering group far below ground came to no harm, though like all old Dutch bungalows it had a thatched roof which burnt fiercely.

After an hour or two there was silence above the fugitives. It became apparent that the servants had known nothing of the

14

taikhana's existence, and the entrance to it was now concealed in the ruins of the house. Evidently, too, the secret of the passage to the river had been well kept.

'Those glass panes,' Sir Harry said, looking up, 'surely those must have been noticed by your gardeners?'

'No, I think not,' Mrs Greene answered. 'They are deeply set between two pairs of iron gratings. From above they look like the deep drains they are intended to imitate. We are safe for the present.'

The long hours of daylight dragged.

The house above the little company was a heap of ashes and tumbled piles of masonry. It was useless to venture back to such ruins. For all they knew, there was no one left in the cantonment, or in the civil lines adjoining it.

Mrs Greene was a vigorous young woman, robust in faith as well as in body. As she leant back against the wall of the tunnel and hushed her child to sleep, she said to Sir Harry, 'Let us pool our knowledge. I know the surrounding country so little. To get to Lucknow we must cross the river—I know that much! Fortunately the ford is passable; only last evening I watched the coolie women wading across it, and the water barely reached their knees. Yes, it was knee-high, no more.'

'I know the track that leads to Mitauli,' Mary Binnie said. 'Rajah Lone Singh of Mitauli is friendly to Europeans. He was dining in mess with my brother only a week ago.'

'Yes.' Sir Harry spoke thickly; he seemed to have had (as indeed, he had) some sort of stroke that impeded his speech. 'Yes, I met the Rajah of Mitauli the night I dined in mess. He is quite friendly, I think.'

Throughout the day Sir Harry had seemed to be in a sort of coma, his old white head nodding on his chest. He had been inert, not asleep.

'Yes,' Mary Binnie eagerly agreed, 'Rajah Lone Singh is a friend. He will help us. He is a splendid man. My brother admired him immensely. I have often ridden on the other side of the river and passed his house at Mitauli. It is not more than five or six miles away. Oh, do let us try and reach it before daylight tomorrow!'

'Yes', one of the soldiers' wives put in, 'it is better to try and get help from the Rajah than to attempt to make our own way to Lucknow, which is fifty miles away at the least. How can we hope to go safely through a country where our enemies are as thick as flies?'

The other woman agreed with her.

'There is a full moon,' she reminded them. 'We must bolt out of here directly it gets dusk. We'll have to get away before the moon rises.'

'True! Let us go as soon as we can. We might find something to eat, at any rate, though the idea of drinking river water makes me shudder,' the woman who had been a sergeant's wife added in agreement.

Directly daylight faded they crept out of the taikhana by the river door.

They made their way through the long unkempt and half-burnt grass, every few minutes waiting motionless to look about them for some signs of their enemy. There seemed to be no one near, but the darkness made it hard to distinguish objects a few yards away.

The water when they reached the ford ran swiftly, yet it was scarcely knee-high, and by clasping hands they crossed the river safely, though Mrs Greene and Mary Binnie found their floating crinolines a great handicap. It was fortunate for them that the two sturdy soldiers' widows could twist their skirts round their hips and help the two ladies to keep their feet.

Feeling (quite irrationally) more secure when they had once reached the opposite bank of the Surayan, the fugitives rested and drank thirstily, well hidden by the tall sugar-cane which grew there. They picked some stalks of the ripe cane and sucked the sweet juice, which greatly revived them.

The women had been both alarmed and distressed to find that Sir Harry moved with difficulty. They realised that he would be a great drag on their progress, for he stumbled over stones or clumps of cane or scrub as if he could not see the obstacles that lay in his path. It was not so dark but that the black outlines of more solid objects showed still darker in the dusk. Sir Harry, too, fell several times.

They had scarcely got safely into the shadows of the sugar-cane when the moon rose and flooded the whole panorama with light.

The country was flat and, as flat country does, it seemed to magnify the size of everything. Under the brilliant moon the river shone like a sheet of glass, every dark piece of flotsam on it perfectly visible.

They were lucky to have crossed in time.

They were just thinking of moving on their way when pandemonium broke out on the farther side of the bank about sixty yards above their hiding-place. There the Surayan was deeper and could only be crossed by swimming, or in a boat.

Pouring headlong out of the shadows of a bungalow that stood some twenty yards back from the river came a frenzied mob of English people—men, women, and children. The men, it appeared, were trying to shepherd the women and children to some place of safety; they had waited too late. The moonlight had taken them by surprise and made their movements apparent to their foes.

As they ran, many of these poor people were mercilessly shot down by the pursuing sepoys. Others were cut down by the curved swords of the cavalry soldiers, the men of Jimmy Greene's regiment.

Some fugitives reached the river only to sink, wounded, below the turgid waters, churned up now by all the struggling swimmers. Very few reached the opposite bank. Even among these, several were hurt by long shots from the sepoys' muskets. In the end only thirteen or so dodging through the cane seemed to the onlookers to escape, for the time being, the dangers which threatened them.

Mrs Greene and her companions, their faces pale with horror, watching this dreadful massacre of their friends, hurriedly debated whether it would be wiser to turn upstream and join the larger party, or keep to their original plan of throwing themselves on the mercy of Rajah Lone Singh. They decided in the end to make their way to Mitauli. They realised that Sir Harry could make little effort for himself; his feet dragged, and the two soldiers' widows had constantly to support him on either side. Mrs Greene doubted, too, whether with her child to carry and hampered by her long skirts she could make much headway, though the close-knit cane; besides, how could they make certain of finding the other party?

It was after very little discussion that they made up their minds to make their way to the house of that nawab whom they believed to be friendly.

So simply did Sir Harry, Mary Binnie, and the two soldiers' widows—Mrs Simmons and Mrs Pike—make the resolution that was to lead to their deaths. For the party of thirteen which they had seen cross the river, protected by some native police, did, finally, though after many hardships, reach their friends in Lucknow.

Mrs Greene, like Mary Binnie, had often ridden past the village of Mitauli where Rajah Lone Singh had his house. She guided the forlorn little company through the tall sugar-cane which had been their salvation, for it both fed them and hid their movements, and by two o'clock in the morning they had reached their goal, a flat-roofed white two-storeyed building enclosed in a red brick wall which had trees waving over the top of it, like feathers in a casque.

They beat with stones and sticks on the fast-closed gates.

After twenty minutes someone heard them and they were admitted.

Daylight was even now creeping through the rose-flushed sky, palely beautiful in the thick opalescent mists of dawn.

Looking back, as she was in after years so often to look back on these first dreadful days, Mrs Greene, who was to suffer and endure so much, felt always that the moment when she and her four companions stood before Rajah Lone Singh and saw no kindness in him was the worst of many ordeals. She looked at his gloating, oily countenance; she read there no pity, only a treacherous satisfaction; the complacency of the bully who has found fresh victims.

Yes, as she looked at the Rajah when after two hours of waiting he had strolled out of his house to stand with two attendants on either side of him and hear their petition—that he would give them palki-bearers and escort them safely to their own people in Lucknow—she knew immediately that there was no hope for them. She realised that they had delivered themselves into the power of a brutal and implacable enemy.

The light was still faint, for a mist as white as milk hung over everything. The fugitives were grouped under an immense banyan-tree bearded with long roots that sagged down from every branch and made colonnades and pillars as stately as those in any great cathedral. The tree with its far-roving boughs covered quite half an acre of ground, each limb being as thick as the trunk of a well-grown oak, while the earth under the tree was quite bare and ribbed with the main-roots that sometimes rose five or six feet out of the black fertile soil. The leaves of this tree were bigger than a man's palm and of a rich incandescent green; its aerial roots were as thick as thatch.

Standing under it, the Rajah wore a white muslin coat folded across his strong and muscular chest. His wide striped drawers were not drawn round the ankles like jodhpurs but were very full, baggy, and patterned in stripes of green, red and black. His turban was of Dacca muslin, very fine and clean. He wore gauntlet gloves that reached his elbow, because he was a leper and sought in this way to hide his deformity.

Now, Rajah Lone Singh was a great gambler. He had won the estates he at present enjoyed at dicing with his brother, and when he had contemptuously given his guests leave to lie under his banyan-tree and had sent them out a chapati or two and a chatty of drinking water, he dispatched a messenger post-haste to a fellow nawab, a neighbour whose fields he coveted. Mrs Greene and her exhausted companions lying under the banyan-tree heard the beat of departing hooves and trembled; they now felt certain that Rajah Lone Singh intended to betray them.

Cock-fighting is a sport popular with Indian gentlemen. Rajah Lone Singh had a famous cockerel imported by caravan from China, and he had many times longed to pit this bird against an equally famous cockerel belonging to his friend Nawab Allah-ud-din of Surayan, for whom it had won a number of wagers. This nawab played only for high stakes. Rajah Lone Singh, being a miser and the most avaricious of men, had for some months been casting about in his mind to find some tempting stake which he could use in a match between his bird and the Nawab's, and yet risk neither land nor money of his own. In the poor English now claiming his protection he thought he had found what he sought. He would challenge Allah-ud-din to wager his corn fields against the baronet and four Englishwomen.

Sitting under the banyan-tree as morning changed to noon and noon to fiery evening and dark night, Mrs Greene and Mary Binnie, still outwardly more composed than the soldiers' widows, who wept unceasingly—the baronet, apparently, slept all day—judged from the preparations that were being made that the Rajah meant to entertain a large party of friends that evening. There was a general bustle of activity that made it plain to any housewife that a big dinner was in preparation.

Mrs Greene, in spite of her fears, was so much a child that she was interested in all that went on. She watched some twenty chickens being chased, caught, and killed, and fat quail being taken from the quail-pit. A peacock was brought in. Several baskets of fish came up from the river which ran near. Trays of sweetmeats dried in the sun.

Regarding all this, it crossed Mrs Greene's mind that twenty-four hours earlier she herself had been making preparations for a dinner party.

When Rajah Lone Singh early that morning had listened to what the fugitives had got to say he had confined his attention wholly to Sir Harry. He had neither looked at nor spoken to the four women.

Indian men do not admire Englishwomen—white women, that is to say. Their pasty faces, they assert, look anaemic and unwholesome; beside the honey-coloured and flawless skins of Indian beauties they lack brilliance. Their hair, too, seems dull and lustreless in contrast with the satin-sheened oiled and raven tresses of zenana belles. Their figures (they consider) are bad; their heads, hands, and feet are too large. They have, in short, no grace of movement, no subtlety of rhythm in dancing, no charm of expression in their colourless washed-out eyes.

The dust-stained dejected women sitting under the banyan had nothing to fear from Rajah Lone Singh's attentions: had they but known it, he intended to pay them none.

When the red sun had dropped below the sugar-cane, and lavender mist lay like a tablecloth floating a few feet above it, a clatter of galloping hooves and much shouting from his running torchbearers and servants heralded the arrival of Nawab Allah-ud-din.

Stories of the destruction of every Englishman in Sitapur, of the terrible massacres of Cawnpore, Lucknow, Fyzabad, Dinapore; or Delhi, Agra, and Bareilly; tales of the risings in the Central Provinces, in Meerut, Patna, and Lahore, had been eagerly passed from mouth to mouth throughout the length and breadth of Oudh. They had lost nothing in the telling.

It was current gossip that the race of Englishmen was doomed to an ignoble extinction; the glory enjoyed by every rebel who had murdered one or two was the envy of every Indian.

Nawab Allah-ud-din had been unlucky. Directly the sun rose he had ridden post-haste to Sitapur, hoping to take part in the general massacre, but in every case the victims he had selected had fallen to another sword or bayonet. In the five fugitives offered to him as a bait by Rajah Lone Singh he saw a chance to redeem his reputation. He would win them. He would gain much praise by openly insulting them. He would finally murder them with as much cruelty and publicity as possible.

Mrs Greene, her baby in her lap, was seated among the roots of the banyan-tree, which made a comfortable resting-place. Mary

21

Binnie, in an effort to keep the mosquitoes from the child's face, was waving a flowering branch she had broken off from a nearby neem-tree; Mrs Simmons and Mrs Pike were lying asleep on a patch of grass beyond the limits of the tree, when two man-servants carrying lanthorns came out of the house and preceded Rajah Lone Singh and Nawab Allah-ud-din, who were coming out to inspect the prisoners.

Rajah Lone Singh coveted his friend's canefields, yet he was beginning to feel that he would prefer to keep his captives for his own amusement; he thought, 'Perhaps I had better see that my cockerel wins the match; I can win the fields any time.'

There is a certain disarming innocence about youth. Mrs Greene, at sixteen, was young even for that age. She knew nothing of sin or of the tempestuous passions of the human heart.

When Mary Binnie rose, trembling, to her feet as the two men approached her, Mrs Greene rose with her, more to keep the waving neem-branch within reach of her child's face than for any other reason. She stood up quite without any sign of fear and said 'Salaam', the only Hindustani word she knew, by way of greeting.

Mrs Greene had been very proud of being a married woman. Since she had married early, a doting mother and five spinster aunts had constantly impressed upon her the need for dignity in a married woman. She showed dignity now.

Picot-edged frills, ribbons and furbelows—indeed every device known to the Victorian dressmaker's robust imagination—tricked out the many yards of her scarlet tartan dress, and made her voluminous skirts stand out like cumulus clouds. Her plainly fitting tight bodice buttoning up the front with a score of tiny tartan buttons had a white lace collar of the type called 'puritan'. It was fastened with a cameo brooch carved with the elegantly classical theme of Diana teaching Cupid to shoot.

Mrs Greene's pale-gold hair, parted in the centre, was bunched in feathery ringlets on each side of her very Dolly Varden face. She had a firm well-rounded chin, a short retroussé nose, blue eyes set wide apart and made brighter by the dark lashes and arching eyebrows that were a deep fawn colour and very thickly spread. Even in this moment of trial there was a dewy freshness about her that would have charmed the most critical eye, but to the two Indian men she made no appeal.

Both Rajah Lone Singh and Allah-ud-din were brutal men, delighting in cruelty in the way that has hitherto stamped the Eastern mind as uncivilised to Western ideas.

As this helpless girl stood before the two men who held her fate in the hollow of their evil hands, no one knowing of the orgies of butchery that during the past twenty-four hours had gone to stain the pages of Indian history would have guessed that Mrs Greene had one chance in a thousand of surviving the next few hours, or at least the next few days.

A great many lights were now flitting about the courtyard.

Servants carrying the exotic delights that were to furnish the forthcoming banquet hurried to and fro between the kitchen and the house—a two-storeyed stucco structure, more like a Cheltenham villa than the dwelling of an Indian landowner.

It happened that the chuprassy who carried the much-prized white cockerel which Allah-ud-din had brought with him, confined in a wicker cage, had set his burden down beside a brazier, an iron basket filled with burning charcoal which another servant had dumped carelessly down on the ground while he ran to answer a summons from the cook's godown. (The whole courtyard teemed with humanity, and the general excitement was causing a great deal of confusion.)

The two Indians were standing with their backs to the coop, laughing while they discussed their captives—now quite obviously their prisoners, not their guests.

The wicker coop was carpeted with straw, dry after the day's intense heat. Mrs Greene, who had been attracted by the beautiful fighting-cock's plumage, had been watching it idly when suddenly she saw that the straw, ignited by the brazier, was smoking. Without a moment's hesitation she put her child into Mary Binnie's arms and swooped in her brilliant tartan draperies straight across the courtyard.

23

She had unlatched the burning hatch and taken the cockerel in her strong young arms before anyone realised what was happening. There she stood, the coop flaming beside her, the cockerel safe. Behind her the great banyan-tree, garlanded with marigolds—for it was a shrine of some sort—caught the dancing light from the fire and became an unreal stage-like green, while the red flounces on her tartan dress glowed yet more brightly in the blaze that was now shooting showers of sparks upwards towards a starlit sky.

The servants who had left the coop darted up and would have taken the cockerel; but, still gently and firmly clasping the snow-white bird, whose curved tail-feathers flowed out from it, graceful as a playing fountain, Mrs Greene walked towards the spellbound Allah-ud-din.

'This bird is yours, isn't it?' she asked, smiling. 'If I had been an instant slower it would have been burnt to death, poor creature.'

She put the cockerel into its owner's hands.

'It was touch and go, wasn't it?' she added casually, halting a moment before him.

Nawab Allah-ud-din was a small man, active and muscular. He was not ill-looking. He had the hooked nose, the slanting eyes, the high cheekbones of his race, which had in it a Mongolian strain. His white linen coat and jodhpurs were spotless; his turban was a miracle of art, being wound with all its pleats festooned in a direct line with his left eyebrow, which was higher than his right; this gave him a dashing air.

The Nawab's ears were long and weighed down with heavy ear-rings. It may be that the women behind the purdah made a speciality of embroidering shoes for their menfolk. Certainly the Nawab's shoes and those of Rajah Lone Singh were equally resplendent in natty stitchings of silver wire and sequins.

There should have been nothing to alarm Mrs Greene in the quiet figure of the Nawab; but meeting his black, very shallow eyes, she had a moment of real terror. There had been no pity in Allah-ud-din's face. In its relentless cruelty, as in Rajah Lone Singh's, she read the same implacable menace.

24

She took her child from Mary Binnie and stood erect. She would show no fear.

'It's a fighting-cock, that bird, isn't it?' she inquired, carelessly strolling over to Rajah Lone Singh, whose laughter had been quieted by the incident.

'Yes.' He smiled. 'I mean to match my bird against the Nawab's tonight—for a wager.' He and his friend exchanged amused glances. 'You shall watch the fight. Yes. We will let the birds fight out here where you and your companions shall watch them.'

Laughing again, the two Indians went in to the banquet.

During the past half-hour many men had been arriving in doolies and palanquins or riding trotting ponies. An elephant having a magnificent howdah on its back, its tusks encased in gold, had brought an old man and a graceful boy who wore a coat of pale-blue brocade.

Looking from the banyan-tree through the open french windows beyond the veranda arches, it was possible to see into a room with long tables and lines of turbaned guests. With the exception of the white-bearded Talakdar, who had arrived sitting with his grandson in the howdah of the elephant, the men were of little importance, being merely the Indian equivalent of the Irish squireen. They were mostly swashbucklers and landowners of small holdings in the neighbouring villages. Several of them were sowars, soldiers who had been serving with the irregular cavalry which, twenty-four hours earlier, had mutinied and shot down their officers. They could be seen still in their uniforms recounting their triumphs with rowdy abandon.

Looking through the windows at these carousing men, Mary Binnie and the soldiers' widows felt fear knocking afresh at their despairing hearts. They thought that these men, after drinking the arrack and other potent intoxicants in which, against the teaching of their religion, they were indulging, would be capable of any crime; a fear that was to prove only too well founded.

Even Sir Harry, awakened as the women had been by the noise, seemed to realise more poignantly the dangers which surrounded them. He struggled to his feet and with the aid of

25

Mrs Simmons and Mrs Pike, who were strong, buxom women, he moved across to where Mrs Greene was sitting in her old place among the roots of the banyan-tree.

'My dear,' he murmured, feeling difficulty in articulating, 'I fear for you and your poor little child. I still have the pistol which I have hidden in the lining of my coat. I am old. If I were tortured I should not live long, but you and Mary Binnie and these women are young. There may be terrible indignities and suffering before you, and you might not die easily. This is perhaps the one moment left to you to decide whether you will take your own lives, and so evade the terrible future.'

'Oh, sir,' cried Mrs Simmons impulsively, 'these Indian gentlemen might not be so unkind! I'd rather have my own life to live, whatever may come to me, than take a coward's way out.'

Mrs Pike was of the same mind.

Mary Binnie, crying as if her heart was breaking, as indeed it was, sobbed out, 'I know enough Urdu to understand what those men are saying. They mean to make us the stake in the cock-fight they are going to have. If the Nawab wins us from Rajah Lone Singh our fate is sealed. He is a villain. I have heard many tales of his cruelty.'

Before Sir Harry could speak again, the banquet drew to a close. The revellers with shouts of laughter prepared to leave the house. Servants came out and traced a chalk circle on the hard, smooth earth behind the banyan-tree. The two fighting-cocks were brought out and given pills of some drug that was meant to make them more pugnacious. Golden spurs were affixed to their claws.

Chairs were arranged along the fringes of the chalk circle.

Flaming torches were affixed into the poles and baskets intended to hold them. They gave, within the circle, a light as bright as sunlight but less stable. Beyond the circle, however, all was dusk among the heavy foliage of the neighbouring trees.

The two fighting-cocks, perfectly groomed, were being held by the men who tended them when the riotous drunken men

26

crowded out of the house and arranged themselves round the earthen arena. The birds were magnificent creatures. Allah-ud-din's entrant was the white cockerel Mrs Greene had rescued from the burning coop; Rajah Lone Singh's was a leggy orange-coloured bird, imported from China.

The fight began.

There is a monument on the China Bazaar Road, outside Lucknow. It has on the north face the names of ten or twelve soldiers killed within the Residency; on the south face are inscribed the names of Sir Harry Johnson, Mary Binnie, Mrs Simmons and Mrs Pike. Mrs Greene's name companions theirs.

The motto gracing the tomb reads: STRANGER! RESPECT THEIR LONELY RESTING PLACE.

It is true that Sir Harry, Mary Binnie, Mrs Simmons and Mrs Pike lie in that grave. The Nawab Allah-ud-din's bird won the match. The Chinese game-cock was left lying dead within the chalk circle. The exulting Nawab took possession of the prize—the English fugitives.

He forced them, lashed by long whips, to run before his trotting horse. After unspeakable indignities he murdered them in a mango-tope, not far from the place where their grave now stands.

Mrs Greene was not among the Nawab Allah-ud-din's victims. In spite of the inscription on the tomb, she, in reality, escaped their dreadful fate.

It happened that among the soldiers who had been invited to Rajah Lone Singh's banquet there was a young sowar—a cavalry-man—called Mirza Khan. He had been in Jimmy Greene's regiment. When Mrs Greene's child was born this sowar's wife had also given birth to an infant—a son. Mrs Greene had a great many more clothes in her infant daughter's layette than she could possibly need, for she had a number of relatives who took pleasure in making the loveliest garments imaginable for her expected baby, among them being many boy-baby garments with the conventional blue bows. She sent a generous bundle of these to the sowar's wife.

Mirza Khan's wife had been delighted with the gift. They made her child look, she thought, most distinguished; so during the past three months she had constantly asked her husband to tell her any news he could about her benefactress.

It chanced that Mirza Khan on his mettlesome country-bred stallion had ridden into the Rajah's courtyard just at the moment when Mrs Greene had made her dramatic rescue of the white fighting-cock.

Indian men admire above all things bravery in a woman. Many legends of brave women are told in Indian history. Mirza Khan, therefore, being a brave man himself, admired the spirit Mrs Greene had shown. Dismounting, he gave his piebald mount to a groom to hold, and walked closer to where Mrs Greene in her brilliant red tartan dress was standing under the leaves of the banyan-tree. The flames still lighted up her face, so exalted now in its brave endurance of her ordeal. He watched her accept without flinching her captor's insulting words (which she did not understand) and insolent looks (which she perfectly comprehended).

Mirza Khan realised that nothing could save Mrs Greene from the most agonising tortures if she were left in the power of the Nawab Allah-ud-din, and that the leprous Lone Singh would be an equally cruel tyrant. He slipped away, therefore, and sought out old Mosin-ud-Dowlah, the Talakdar who had arrived on the elephant. He was a kind and enlightened man, a well-tried friend of the English, who is now known to have assisted many of them to escape from the mutineers, and whose touching tribute to his friend Wellwood George Mowbray may still be read on the tomb he erected to his memory, in Lucknow.

This Talakdar's well-armed band of fighting retainers, his wealth, and his recognised standing in Oudh prevented the disloyal faction from showing him any hostility. He was too powerful.

Mosin-ud-Dowlah immediately agreed to Mirza Khan's suggestion that he should smuggle Mrs Greene to a place of safety hidden in the howdah of his elephant. He caused his young grandson to divest himself of his blue coat and turban and baggy

28

muslin pyjamas, and leaving the boy to borrow clothes from one of his grooms, the Talakdar gave these others to Mrs Greene.

So great was the excitement over the cock-fight now in progress that Mrs Greene, directed by Mirza Khan, easily slipped away into some tall growths of sunflowers that bordered the Rajah's mango-tope, where, taking off her crinoline and bunching up her curls under the turban, she, like Rosalind, put on a boy's attire. Mirza Khan brought her some coffee with which she stained her face and hands.

When she was ready, Mosin-ud-Dowlah established himself in front of her on the howdah, and together with his grandson and the mahout, they escaped on the swaying elephant through the open and unguarded gateway of Rajah Lone Singh's serai.

Once they were outside, Mirza Khan handed the child up to Mrs Greene, for he had carried it out with him, riding with his usual gallant bearing on his piebald horse, which had blue beads for a necklace, and a saddle chased in silver. Then, his drawn sword in his hand, he rode off in their company.

Mosin-ud-Dowlah at this time kept no harem. So the sowar, Mirza Khan, took Mrs Greene and her child into his house.

Mirza Khan, who was the son of a small landholder, a zemindar, had a house that was a little better than that of most sepoys, or sowars. It stood on the left bank of the Surayan, about three miles south of Sitapur, and it was enclosed in a high mud wall, the top of which was thatched, somewhat after the Wiltshire fashion, in order to keep the rain from dissolving it.

The bungalow itself was small and had a flat roof, and its doors opened out onto several trellised verandas. It contained, in all, seven rooms which opened into a central chamber, in the middle of which lay a large marble catafalque.

The presence of this tomb, a saint's, made it necessary for the sowar to open his house once a year to pilgrims of a sect which paid honour to the buried saint, whose sacred bones were said to lie in this queer sarcophagus.

As is well known, General Martin caused himself to be entombed in the dining-room of his vast mansion, La Martinière, in Lucknow, because he knew that the King of Oudh coveted it and meant to take possession of it after his death; his buried body prevented this robbery. The shrine was probably placed in the sowar's house for the same reason—that is, to protect the rights of the owner of the house.

Mrs Greene found that her kind rescuer's family consisted of his wife, whose child was born the same day as her own; a second inferior woman, whom the wife forced to attend on her husband when he was drunk, which was seldom, for he was a strict Mohammedan and rarely touched wine; and two old aunts of Mirza Khan's, to whom, since they were penniless, he had given asylum.

The sowar's wife received Mrs Greene kindly. For the first three months of her sojourn in this quiet household she was treated as an honoured guest.

In return for all the kindness she received, Mrs Greene taught the sowar's womenfolk the simple arts she had learnt in her English country home; tatting, knitting, the making of peculiarly good cheeses, and of various preserves, comfits, jams, pickles, and sauces, all very rich and unusual, which they sold with profit in the bazaar in Sitapur. She also taught the women to make elaborate patchwork quilts, to paste fish-scales and wind wool on wire into the semblance of the most beautiful flowers, and even birds. A canary holding in its beak a sprig of may-blossom, and having above it an arch of roses and wallflowers, was a favourite design of hers, and always sold very well.

This last pursuit greatly delighted the sowar's two old aunts.

Mrs Greene's child flourished. She was so wrapped up in her daughter's welfare that during those first three months she was not unhappy. News came through of the stand that the English shut up in the Residency were making. She heard from an ayah, who often crept into her room at night, that Sir Colin Campbell was coming to relieve the garrison there. She felt certain that once the revolt was quelled she would be free to return to her own country and her father's house.

The sowar had told her of her husband's death. She mourned

30

him as an inexperienced girl does, with a deep and sincere sorrow, and with only an instinctive understanding of her own wretchedness.

Then, for a reason which she at first did not understand, she felt less free.

At the foot of the sowar's garden there was a summer-house— a chabootra, as it is called—which was set well out from the angle of the enclosing wall which ran alongside the river, here flowing smoothly right against this old red brick wall. The water was deep here, and the river fairly wide, so that it was a cool and sequestered spot, very pleasant to Mrs Greene, since the other women rarely went there. When she wanted to be alone she often sat in this chabootra, watching the paddy-birds in their lovely nuptial plumage, or the fish jumping out of the water after flies.

There were no buildings on the opposite bank of the river; behind the chabootra a grove of mangoes hid it from the house.

During the months she had been under his roof Mrs Greene had seldom seen Mirza Khan. He had taken service with the old Talakdar, Mosin-ud-Dowlah, and she heard him clatter off every morning on his piebald country-bred pony. Sometimes through her lattice she got a glimpse of the resplendent red-and-gold uniform he wore as one of the Talakdar's retainers. It was long after dark each night when he returned.

There was a small enclosed courtyard outside Mrs Greene's window in which she often sat at work. Happening one holy day, when the sowar was at home, to glance out as she sat at her window sewing, she saw him. He was stripped to the waist and wore wrapped round him the dhoti, the muslin garment which all Indian men wear. His turban was discarded and was looped over the bough of a neem-tree nearby. He had a small brass jar from which he was pouring water over his head and over his light-brown glistening torso. He was a magnificent man. He had the strong, thick, youthful neck, the wide chest and narrow hips, the muscular arms of a fine fighting man, and he stood well over six feet in height. Since he was a soldier he took great pride in his appearance. He was meticulously clean. His beard

31

was well oiled and brushed and curled round a string so that it curved in a shining roll from ear to ear, and did not hide the fine lines of his noble masculine throat and shoulders. His hair at this moment was coiled into a topknot on the crown of his shapely head. It was curled like a woman's, and more brown than black. As Mrs Greene instinctively paused to admire him and, fascinated, watched him, a puff of wind blew her curtain to one side, and Mirza Khan, turning at that moment, looked her full in the face with his dark and brilliant eyes.

She was immensely discomposed. She drew back behind her curtains with a scarlet face. How she hated herself! In her looking-glass she saw that her young face was brilliantly alive and that her eyes, usually so blue, were gleaming with a bright orange colour that startled her with its feline sheen. 'I look like a tigress,' she thought, shocked.

It was the memory of this incident—encounter, it might almost be called—that surged up to fill Mrs Greene with shame when, on a still, cool evening late in the summer, Mirza Khan entered the summer-house where she was sitting pasting fish-scales into the semblance of a rose, her child asleep in one of those baskets commonly called a Moses basket.

The lotus in the tank had shrivelled and drooped long ago into the water, the neem-flowers had come and gone, the fruit on the pomegranate was ripe and ready for picking, the corn was already cut.

The evening was very calm. Sunset clouds were drifting incredibly slowly across an infinitely pale sky more green than blue.

'Salaam, Gharib-Purwar,' Mirza Khan began, touching his forehead with his hand in the recognised gesture of salutation, 'I would like permission to speak to the Huzoor.'

'Salaam,' Mrs Greene answered, reddening. As she sat there in her tartan dress she, who had formerly been so self-possessed, was now pitifully self-conscious in her host's presence.

Since that fatal night at Mitauli she had spoken to Mirza Khan on two occasions only: once, when with tears in her eyes

32

she had thanked him for rescuing her from Rajah Lone Singh; a second time, next morning, when she had again to thank him for the return of her clothes, and for some jewellery which, recognising it to be hers, he had taken from a fellow sowar who had stolen it from her house.

The trinkets he had returned to her Mrs Greene, in the happy assurance that she could still do a favour, had given piece by piece to the sowar's wife, who was invariably kind to her.

'Mirza Khan,' Mrs Greene now said, speaking quickly to hide her embarrassment, 'surely the mutiny is over? Surely it would be safe for me to try and reach my friends in Lucknow?'

'Huzoor, not yet,' Mirza Khan said earnestly. 'There are still many bad characters on the roads. As soon as it is safe I will send a letter to Cawnpore—all the mem-sahibs have been taken there; none have been left in Lucknow. When it is safe I will make arrangements to take Gharib-Purwar back to her own people.'

There are still many families in India which can claim descent from the Grecian generals who accompanied Alexander the Great across the Hydaspes—the Jhelum. Mirza Khan claimed to be descended from one of Alexander's generals, and, indeed, as he stood before Mrs Greene he had a very noble Grecian air about him, in spite of his deeply tanned skin.

'But, mem-sahib,' he continued, 'I came to say that tomorrow is the day that the tomb in my house is shown to the pilgrims who come to pay homage to the saint buried in it. The mem-sahib must hide. She must on no account be seen. Rajah Lone Singh and Nawab Allah-ud-din have never given up their search for her. Though the mutiny is put down there are no sahib-log near enough to protect her should these men find her.'

'Oh, Mirza Khan,' Mrs Greene entreated him, trembling and gazing into his face most pitifully, all her embarrassment forgotten, 'you would not give me up to those wicked men?'

'Huzoor,' Mirza Khan replied grimly, 'all that one man can do, I will do.'

He paused an instant, looking at her without speaking and

meeting her eyes with a deep, unsmiling regard. The sky behind his blue-and-gold turban shimmered with an astonishing brilliance as he saluted her gravely and, turning, left the chabootra.

Before it was light next morning the sowar's wife brought Mrs Greene some Indian clothes. She gave her a sari—a full, much-pleated skirt of red cotton, striped round the hem with purple, green, and orange and much braided with tinsel. She brought her a rose-coloured chuddah—the wide sheet which Indian women twist into the waistband of their skirts and fling over their heads. She added a shirt of bright amber muslin, very finely woven and sewn with a gold thread neckband, and a voluminous pair of purple drawers, very full round the waist and fitting tightly round the ankles. A pair of red leather slippers, some glass anklets, and many ropes of turquoise beads carved to resemble flowers completed this outfit. There was also a headband gay with glass rubies and emeralds.

The sowar's wife on lending this dress, said it must be given back—it had been her husband's wedding present to her.

Mrs Greene then stained her face and body with coffee, for her waist above her skirt was bare. She hid her crinoline and her English clothes, and put on the Indian garments.

She covered her fair curls with black horsehair—fly-whisks, in reality—and the headband kept this in place. Mrs Greene thought this disguise complete, for the chuddah veiled her face when she chose to draw it close, and she did not, in any case, intend to leave her room when the house was full of strangers.

From the moment the sun rose, an unbroken line of pilgrims filed through the room in which the tomb stood. Many were very poor, humble people, and they would leave the smallest of copper coins, or a handful of rice, or a few fading marigolds on the grave. Prostrating themselves, they would patter off some unintelligible prayers and petitions (for a petition is to prayer what night is to day—the inevitable sequence) and then they would go on their way, happy.

Coolies, naked but for a loincloth, some shopkeepers, some devotees from other shrines, a few soldiers very ragged but still in their uniforms, though every sepoy now had a price on his head, and some of Mosin-ud-Dowlah's retainers wearing the flamboyant scarlet-and-gold uniforms in which, peeping through her lattice, Mrs Greene was accustomed to see Mirza Khan ride daily away—such were the people who visited the shrine. Late in the day, to Mrs Greene's horror, she saw a contingent of servants from Mitauli enter—she recognised the man who had carried the coop; he was easily identified, for the man had a black patch over one eye.

Though Mrs Greene felt she need have nothing to fear, for no rule in India is so strictly kept as that which preserves the sanctity of the purdah—the entrance to the women's apartments— she shook with alarm as Allah-ud-din himself swaggered in and, making an ostentatious obeisance, laid an offering of many gold pieces beside the relics adorning the sarcophagus: the saint's begging-bowl and his worn flagellant's thong.

Though Mrs Greene for her own safety's sake should have withdrawn immediately from the peep-hole in her curtain (it was a trellis of holes cut out and sewn with thread, which made a lace-like aperture), a dreadful fascination kept her eyes glued to it; she could not tear herself away.

Indian men are perfectly well aware of the lattice, the door with its perforation of peep-holes through which the women in every Indian household peer out at the forbidden world. There is even a certain coquetry about the business. Nawab Allah-ud-din, casting his eyes idly on each aperture in turn, saw, suddenly, Mrs Greene's blue eyes sparkling through the gauze.

Triumph surged through him. He realised that at last he had located the woman who had eluded him for so long.

Aware that he had recognised her—his face plainly showed it—Mrs Greene realised with a rush of terror that her blue eyes must have betrayed her. She did not reason. Her daughter she knew was safe, playing in the zenana with the sowar's children. She ran through the outer door of her room into the trellised courtyard where Mirza Khan stood leaning on his long curved sword as if on guard—as indeed he was.

'Mirza Khan,' she cried, distraught, 'Allah-ud-din is in there! He recognised me as I was peeping through the chink in the curtain. Oh, Mirza Khan, you have been so good—do not let him take me away!'

So great was her fear that Mrs Greene forgot she was not wearing her English dress. She was not used to the management of the chuddah, the veil that should have shielded her. It slipped from her shoulders so that her beautiful body was clearly displayed in bright sunlight through the diaphanous shirt she wore as her only upper garment.

Mirza Khan's sect taught him to practise chastity, temperance, and obedience to a warrior's code; he was as strict an anchorite as any other man who had sworn to conform to an exacting religious ideal.

If Mrs Greene had been attired in her 'foreign' clothes it is doubtful whether Mirza Khan would ever have swerved from his loyal intention of restoring his guest to her friends as soon as it was safe to travel through the still unsettled countryside.

But the sowar's wife, poor woman, in her wish to do her best for Mrs Greene to whom she was deeply attached, had lent her the dress she had worn on her wedding-night—it was as a bride that the lovely English girl now made her frantic appeal to Mirza Khan. Her stained body had no distasteful pallor, her blue eyes were (to him) like those of a goddess, as they besought him, bright with an irresistible and overwhelming brilliance, to save her.

Mirza Khan looked at his suppliant guest. His eyes, soft with that deceptive softness that denotes a tendency to the berserk rages which on occasion can possess men of the Mogul race, dwelt strangely, she thought, on hers. She saw, without understanding, their awakening fires. They were quickly veiled.

'Go back to your room, mem-sahib,' Mirza directed her, quietly. 'I will wait there with you. I know Allah-ud-din. He will act quickly.'

Comforted by Mirza Khan's gentleness and strength, Mrs Greene, returning, had scarcely entered her room where Mirza

Khan took his stand directly to one side of the curtained archway into the larger, central room, when a hand drew the hangings aside, and Allah-ud-din slipped noiselessly through them.

His movements were as swift and menacing as a panther's. He was famous as a huntsman. In each hand he carried one of those squat two-edged knives which Indian men formerly carried stuck through their wide swathed belts. One of these knives he pressed against Mrs Greene's breast as she stood boldly facing him—boldly, but with a fast-beating heart. He kept his right hand free as he darted a snake-like gaze about him. He did not turn when Mirza Khan, stepping in front of him, cut him down with one movement of his long curved sword.

Mirza Khan left Allah-ud-din's body lying where it fell, and, having sent Mrs Greene across to his wife's apartments, he himself rode off across the river to see Mosin-ud-Dowlah, his master, and to acquaint him with all that had happened. Two hours later he returned with some of Mosin-ud-Dowlah's servants and some armed retainers, who carried off the body to their master's serai— a display of friendship and strength which prevented any further trouble.

During the next five months Mrs Greene saw Mirza Khan not at all. On those rare occasions when he was at home she could hear him through her curtains talking to his two old aunts, who adored him, or holding long murmurous conversations with his wife. Mrs Greene he had always treated as he did his two old aunts, with a most exquisite kindness and courtesy; they were his dependants; but now she never saw him to speak to.

In the spring when the mango-trees were in flower and the bees crawled laden with pollen into the orange rosettes of the pomegranates, Mirza Khan's wife, as was her custom, decorated the tiny pleasure-ground that abutted onto her outer door. She hung up on the bough of the big peepul-tree that shaded her lawn a swing with tinsel-bound chains. She decked this with garlands of the fragrant champak-flower that has so overmastering a perfume. On a grassy knoll beside the lotus tank (the lilies were not yet in flower) she spread the couch of love, the ceremonial

37

quilt of neem-flowers and frangipanni, and creamy-flowered scented jasmine boughs.

A parrot in a gilt cage swung from the boughs of a flowering cork-tree nearby; a rich red-and-blue counterpane lay beside it.

Mrs Greene, who spent the best part of her days in the zenana, where she was on friendly and affectionate terms with Mirza Khan's family, particularly with his two old aunts, saw these preparations for the entertainment of Mirza Khan with an aching heart. She had learnt that her letters would always be returned to her, that she could hope for no communication with the outside world, or with her own people. Great kindness had been shown to her, but she lived apart from the warm and vital springs of life that made Mirza Khan's household so happy a community; whenever the god and lawgiver of this little world appeared she was excluded from the circle.

On the rare occasions when by accident they passed one another, he saluted her but did not speak to her; his eyes, she felt without understanding at first their message, seemed to her to be sad, hungry and reproachful.

In the Indian spring there is a musically humming moth that flutters about in the zephyrous night air. The newly opened champak-buds have a sweetness that makes the senses swoon with a languid and overpowering delight. The jasmines, more potent, even, by night than by day, send out an intoxicating fragrance that makes each puff of air as glamorous as Arabia's fabled incense-tree.

It was on the sixth spring of her sojourn under Mirza Khan's roof that Mrs Greene hung up on the bough of her peepul-tree the tinsel swing garlanded with champak-flowers, and spread out on the smooth lawn of her garden the sweet-scented couch of love, the quilt of neem-flowers and jasmines, the neatly arranged rows of frangipanni blossoms, and waited for Mirza Khan to visit her.

Nearly forty years later, a famous traveller, walking through a bazaar in a remote Punjab village, had his attention caught by the vivid blue eyes of an old beggar woman who was leading by the hand a blind old man, a very stately white-bearded figure, soldierly and dignified. This traveller stopped the woman and said to her in English (for he was convinced that she was English), 'Can I help you? Are you not an Englishwoman?'

This traveller said afterwards that the blue-eyed woman was clad in incredibly tattered rags, bespeaking the direst poverty, but that the old man was wearing garments of a much better quality, clean and neatly darned, and that the woman showed a most affecting and touching solicitude for his comfort, brushing the flies away with a whisk when they settled on his closed eyes, telling him in advance of every inequality in the ground, and, when the sound of the Englishman's voice alarmed him, clasping his hand in her own with a warm, reassuring pressure.

Since this woman looked at him in amazement and made no reply to his questions, the traveller repeated them. 'Surely,' he persisted, 'you are an Englishwoman? Tell me—what is your name?'

So strange are the vagaries of the human mind that, hearing for the first time in so many years her mother tongue, this poor woman's mind flashed back to a moment when, standing proudly erect beside her young husband at a hunt ball in the Worcester Assembly Rooms, she had heard, for the first time, the same question addressed to her.

Surprisingly she answered now, as she had answered then, 'Mrs James Greene—spelt with an "e"!'

The traveller could not induce her to leave the old sowar, whose name, he found, was Mirza Khan, and to whom she appeared to be devoted. He was obviously entirely dependent on her.

KATHARINE SUSANNAH PRICHARD
(1883-1969)

Katharine Susannah Prichard was born in Fiji, the daughter of a journalist, and grew up in Melbourne and Tasmania. Prichard wrote from the age of ten, and as a school girl had a short story published by a Melbourne newspaper. A scholarship student at South Melbourne College, she was unable to continue her education at university because she had to nurse her mother. Having worked as a governess and a teacher until 1908, she then travelled to England to study and work as a journalist. On her return she became the social editor of the women's page of the Melbourne *Herald*. Her awareness of the inequalities in society led her to become a Marxist and, in 1919, a founding member of the Australian Communist Party. She also founded support groups for women.

Prichard published eleven novels, five collections of short stories, some uncollected stories, one book for children, a travel book, two books of verse, two plays and some political pamphlets. In 1915 her first novel, *The Pioneers*, was published and won the colonial section of the Hodder & Stoughton novel competition. This drew overseas attention to an Australian writer for the first time since Lawson. *Coonardoo* (1929), which won the 1928 *Bulletin* Novel Prize, was a revolutionary novel exploring with understanding an Aboriginal woman's experience.

Also active in the literary scene, Prichard was elected federal president of the Australian Writers League in 1935, and three years later she helped found the Western Australian branch of the Fellowship of Australian Writers, which later nominated her for a Nobel Prize.

'Marlene', which appeared originally in the *Bulletin*, presents the predicament of people of mixed Aboriginal and European race with vigour and sympathy.

MARLENE

Coming out from the trees, the camp on the hillside was almost invisible. It crouched among rocks and wet undergrowth, with the township lying under mists in the valley below. The wurlies of bark, bagging and matted leaves had taken on the colouring of the rocks and tree-trunks. They were shaped like mounds of earth: crude shells with open mouths. A breath of smoke betrayed them. It hung in the air and drifted away among the trees.

The two women riding along the bush track detected the first humpy, then another and another, until half a dozen were in sight about a rough open space. Dogs flew out, barking fiercely. Two or three children, barelegged, lean, sallow, bright-eyed, with black tousled hair, got up from the wurlies. A man lying beside a fire sat up and glanced at the women.

'Hallo, Benjy,' the elderly woman on a grey horse called. 'Sleeping in this morning? Where's Mollie?'

The man grunted, staring sullenly over the rain-sodden clearing. Men and women appeared at the open mouths of other wurlies, all dressed as they had been sleeping, in faded dungarees and khaki trousers, shirts and skirts grey with grime and grease, threadbare woollen jackets and coats—cast-off clothing of the townspeople.

'Hallo, Mrs Boyd!' some of the women called.

'Miss Allison,' the elder woman explained, introducing the girl on the chestnut colt. 'She's from England; going to write a book about the aborigines. She wanted to see your camp.'

'We're half-castes here—not abos,' a morose, middle-aged man replied.

'And not "at home" so early in the day,' one of the young men added sarcastically. 'It's a hell of a place to see, anyhow.'

One of the women giggled shyly. 'How's y'self, Mrs Boyd?'

'I'm well, Minnie. But you're looking like drowned rats, the

41

lot of you. Why don't you shift camp for the winter, George?'
Mrs Boyd's manner was authoritative but kind and friendly.

'Where'd we shift to?' a fat, youngish woman asked jocosely.
Barefooted she stood, a once-white dress dragged across her heavy
breast and thighs, a youngster slung on one hip. A little laugh
nibbled its way through the crowd.

'This is the only place we're allowed to camp in the district,'
the man who had first spoken said sourly. 'You know that, Mrs
Boyd.'

'The rain's been comin' down steady for two months.' One
of the other women raised a flat, uncomplaining treble.

'How on earth do you manage to get a dry spot in the humpies
or keep your clothes dry?'

'We don't.' The crowd laughed as though that were a good
joke. 'Our clothes are all soakin'.' There's not a dry blanket in
the camp.'

'We ought to be ducks. The rain'd run off our backs then.'

'It's a disgrace you should have to live like this,' Mrs Boyd
declared. 'But what I came about this morning is Mollie. Where
is she?'

The crowd shifted uneasily. Eyes encountered and glanced
aside. A wild crew they looked in their shabby clothes, the women
wearing remnants of finery, a bright scarf or coloured cardigan
over their draggled dresses.

Brown-eyed, black-haired, they all were, but their skin varied
from sickly yellow to weathered bronze. The women were sallow
and tawny, the men darker. On most of the faces, thick noses
and full lips denoted the aboriginal strain; a few others had sharp,
neat features, showing no trace of aboriginal origin except in
their eyes.

'Where is Mollie?' Mrs Boyd demanded. 'I've been letting
Mr Phillip drive her in to the pictures on Saturday nights when
he goes into town himself; but she didn't come back last week.
He waited an hour for her . . .'

'She's fair mad about the pictures, Mollie,' Ruby burbled.

'That's all very well, but it's not very considerate of her to

42

run off like this. She knows how busy we are just now, with all the cows coming in. Mr Phillip and Mr Edward have got their hands full. I had to ride in with the mail myself this morning. And Mollie was very useful, helping with the milking and feeding the poddies.'

'She's a fine kid, Mollie,' Albert declared.

'But where is she? What's the matter?'

The crowd surged. Obviously the question was disturbing: had to be evaded. Exclamations and suggestions clattered. There was no surprise, no consternation, although everybody seemed upset, a little nervous and amused at Mrs Boyd's query.

Mrs Boyd guessed they were hiding Mollie. The child had got a quirk about something: one of those mysterious urges to go bush with her own kind.

'Did y'know Bill Bibblemun took bad with the p'monia and died in hospital Sunday week?' somebody asked.

Others joined in eagerly.

'It was a grand funeral, Mrs Boyd.'

'The Salvation Army captain said Bill'd go straight to glory because he was a good Christian.'

'He was, too. Testified at street meetings and sang hymns— even when he was drunk.'

'They said some beautiful prayers.'

'All about his bein' washed in the blood of the lamb and his sins bein' whiter than snow.'

'And the kids have all had measles,' Ruby boasted.

'What's happened to Wally Williams?' Mrs Boyd inquired, willing to humour them. 'He was to come over and cut fencing-posts for me last month.'

There was a lull in the rattle of voices, eyelids fell, wary glances slid under them. Coughing, a hoarse whispering, filled the pause.

'He's gone up-country,' George said.

'You mean, he's in jail. What's he been up to now?'

'Well, you see, Mrs Boyd, it wasn't hardly Wally's fault,' Minnie Lewis explained. 'Jo Wiggins said some steers had got out of his holding paddocks, and he offered Wally two bob for every steer he could track and bring in. Wally took in a couple of clear-skins. He thought they were Mr Wiggins's steers, natcherly—'

'Naturally—at two bob apiece,' Mrs Boyd agreed.

'But when the mounted trooper found a couple of red poley steer skins in Jo Wiggins's slaughter-yard, Mr Wiggins put the blame on to Wally—and Wally got two years.'

'Everybody knows Jo Wiggins's game,' Mrs Boyd admitted. 'But Wally ought to keep his hands off clear-skins.'

'Oh, he's not like that, Wally, Mrs Boyd. He's a real good stockman. But if he can't get a job he doesn't know what to do with himself. He's jest got to be workin' cattle—'

'I know.' Mrs Boyd laughed good-humouredly. 'I suspect he's worked calves from our back hills before now. We had an epidemic of milkers coming in without calves last year.'

'If a cow drops a calf in the bush, Mrs Boyd, the dingoes are as likely to get it as—'

'Wally! Of course. But my money's on Wally. I reckon Jo Wiggins has had more of our calves than the dingoes.'

Her horse cropping the young grass swung Mrs Boyd sideways. She saw the figure of a man sleeping before a smouldering fire at the entrance to his shack. Steam was rising from the damp blanket that covered him.

'Who's that?' she asked.

'It's Charley,' a woman who had been coughing incessantly said. 'He's not well.'

'Better put that bottle away then,' Mrs Boyd advised. 'If the trooper comes round somebody'll be getting into trouble for selling Charley pinkeye again. Where does he get the money to buy drink, anyhow?'

'The shopkeepers take his drawings for show cards sometimes.'

'He's quite an artist in his own way, Charley,' Mrs Boyd explained to her companion. 'Self-taught. Could you show Miss Allison some of Charley's drawings, Lizzie?'

Charley's wife slipped away, burrowed into the wurley, and

returned with a black exercise-book in her hands. Miss Allison dismounted to look at the drawings, crude outlines of people and animals, a football match, the finish of a race.

Pleasure in Charley's drawings, awed interest and expectancy, animated his friends and relations.

'Well'—Mrs Boyd yanked her horse's head round and straightened her back, smiling but implacable—'have you made up your minds yet to tell me about Mollie?'

The faces about her changed. There was a moment of sombre, unresponsive silence.

Then Minnie Lewis exclaimed delightedly: 'Why, it's Mrs Jackson! She's been bad with the rheumatics; but got up—and put on her hat for the visitors!'

A withered little woman, a neat black hat perched on her head, walked across the clearing, wearing a dingy black dress and frayed grey cardigan, with an air of forlorn propriety.

'Good morning, Myrtle,' Mrs Boyd said. 'I'm sorry to hear you've been having rheumatism.'

'What can you expect, Miss Ann?' The half-caste held herself with some dignity: her faded eyes, ringed like agates, looked up at the pleasantly smiling, healthy, fresh-complexioned woman on the big horse. 'I'm not used to living out of doors.'

'No, of course not,' Mrs Boyd replied.

'You know I was brought up at the mission station. And I've worked in some of the best homes in the district; but now— you wouldn't keep a sow in the place where I've got to live.'

'It's not right, Mrs Boyd,' George muttered.

'No, it's not right,' Mrs Boyd agreed. 'But what can I do about it? Would you go into the Old Women's Home if I could get you in, Myrtle?'

'I've been there. The police took me from the hospital after I had the rheumatic fever. But I ran away—'

'She did, Mrs Boyd!' eager voices chimed.

'She walked near on a hundred and thirty miles till she got here.'

'Cooped up in the city—with a lot of low-down old women

45

treatin' me like dirt. I've always kept myself to myself. I've always been respectable, Miss Ann—'

'Oh, yes, she's terrible respectable, Mrs Boyd,' somebody exclaimed.

'Nobody can't say Mrs Jackson isn't respectable!'

'All I want's to die in my own place—like any respectable person. It *is* my own place, Miss Ann, the house your father gave Tom and me; and Mr Henry had no right to turn us out.'

'She's breaking her heart, like any old abo, for the hunting-grounds of her people,' Albert said cynically. 'They always want to go home to die, but, being half-and-half, it's a roof over her head Mrs Jackson wants, and a bed to lie on.'

'I'll see what I can do about it, Myrtle,' Mrs Boyd promised.

'Funny, isn't it?' Albert's lounging, graceful figure tilted back as he gazed at her. 'You're the granddaughter of one of the early settlers who shot off more blacks than any other man in the country. Mrs Jackson is the granddaughter of one of the few survivors, and related to the best families in the district. But you've got the land and the law on your side. They put the dogs on to her if she goes round the homesteads asking for a bit of tucker or old clothes.'

'And this is the only spot where we're allowed to camp in the district.'

'Something will have to be done about it,' Mrs Boyd declared.

'What?' Albert demanded. 'All the land about has been taken up. It's private property. We're not allowed to work in the mines. We're not allowed to sell the fish we catch—not allowed to shoot or trap. They don't want us on the farms. They won't let us work on the roads. All we're allowed to do is draw rations and rot . . . though there is some talk of packing us off to one of those damned reservations "where the diseased and dying remnants of the native race are permitted to end their days in peace". Excuse me quoting the local rag.'

'You can't say I haven't tried to help you,' Mrs Boyd protested. 'I've always given you work on my farm when I could.'

A wry smile twisted the young man's mouth. 'And paid us less than half you'd have had to pay other workers.'

'Albert!' some of the women objected. 'Don't take any notice of him, Mrs Boyd.'

'You're talking like one of those crazy agitators, Albert,' Mrs Boyd cried hotly. 'If you're not careful you'll find yourself being moved on.'

'I'll remember you said so, Mrs Boyd,' Albert grinned maliciously.

'It's hard on Albert not being able to get work, Mrs Boyd,' Ruby expostulated. 'He's real clever: can read and write as good as any white man. When he went to school he could beat any of the boys.'

'Lot of good it's ever done me,' Albert sneered. 'If I'd been a myall I'd've had a better life. The blacks of any tribe share all they've got with each other. The whites grab all they can for themselves—and let even their own relations starve.'

'Do the aboriginals treat half-castes better?' Miss Allison's voice rose clear and chilly against his wrath.

'They don't treat us like vermin.' Albert might have been admiring the gleam of her hair or the horse she was holding. 'Up in the nor'-west, when I was a kid, I went around with my mother's tribe. Never knew I was any different from the rest. Then my father got interested in me. Sent me down here to school. He died—and I've been trying to get a job ever since.'

'Do you want to go back to your own people?'

Albert's anger resurged. 'My own people!' he jeered. 'Who are they? My father was as fair as you are. I couldn't live in a blacks' camp now—though this is as bad. But I don't belong there. I think differently. We all do. We like soap and clean clothes when we can get them, and books. We want to go to the pictures and football matches. I want to work and have a house to live in, a wife and kids. But this is all I've got. These are my only people—mongrels like myself.'

'You shouldn't talk bitter like that, Albert,' Mrs Jackson reproved. 'It does no good.'

'Nothing does any good.' He flung away from the crowd and stalked off behind the wurlies.

'He's sore because he can't get work and the Protector won't let Penny Carnarvon marry him,' Ruby said. 'Penny's in service, and she's such a good servant they don't want to lose her. But she's fond of Albert. She says she'll learn the Protector.'

'She will, too.'

'Stella did, didn't she?'

'Too right, she did.'

'She dropped a trayload of dishes to get herself the sack because she wanted to marry Bob. But the missus forgave her and took it out of her wages. Stella had to get herself in the family way and make up to the boss before the Protector decided she'd better marry Bob.'

'Penny'll be going for a little holiday soon, Albert says. Then perhaps they can get married and go up north. He's almost sure he can get a job on one of the stations.'

'But where's Mollie?' Mrs Boyd returned to the attack. The crowd closed down on their laughter and gossip. There was a disconcerted shuffling and searching for something to say.

'Mollie?'

'Yes, Mollie. It's no use pretending you don't know where she is. If she's hiding, doesn't want to come home, I'm not going to worry about her. But I'll have to let the department know—'

'Hallo, Mrs Boyd!' A girl in a pink cotton frock stood in the opening of a wurley behind the horses. A pretty little thing, sturdy and self-possessed, but rather pale, she stood there, a small bundle wrapped in a dirty shawl in her arms.

'Mollie!' Mrs Boyd gasped. 'Have you been getting a baby?'

The girl nodded, smiling.

'But you're only a child,' Mrs Boyd cried. 'You're not sixteen.'

'I was sixteen last month,' Mollie replied calmly.

'It's scandalous,' Mrs Boyd exclaimed indignantly. 'Who's the father?'

The girl's eyes smiled back at her. 'I been going with two or three boys in town.'

The little crowd before her quivered to breathless excitement: a sigh, as of relief, and a titter of suppressed mirth escaped.

'You ought to be ashamed of yourself,' Mrs Boyd declared furiously. 'You know I thought better of you, Mollie. I thought you were different from the other girls. You've lived with me so many years, and I trusted you to behave yourself.'

'Don't be angry,' the girl said quietly. 'I couldn't help it . . . and I like the baby.'

'When did it happen?'

'Last night.'

Mrs Boyd stared at the girl. She looked a little wan, but quite well.

'Is she all right?' she asked the crone who had come out of the hut behind Mollie. 'Had I better get the doctor to come out and see her, or arrange for her to go into hospital?'

'I've never felt better in my life,' Mollie said. 'Aunty May can look after me.'

'No need to bother,' the old half-caste beside Mollie mumbled soothingly. 'She hadn't a bad time. I'd have sent her to the hospital—but everything happened in such a hurry.'

'Let me see the child,' Mrs Boyd demanded: turned her horse and rode to Mollie.

'She's very little and red,' Mollie apologised, tenderly lifting the dirty shawl that covered the baby.

Mrs Boyd leaned down from her saddle. It was the ugliest scrap of humanity she had ever seen; but there was something vaguely familiar in its tiny crumpled face. Cicely Allison dragged her horse over the grass to look at the baby, too.

'Ra-ther sweet, isn't she?' she murmured mechanically. 'What are you going to call her?'

Mollie drew the shawl over the baby's face again.

'Marlene,' she said happily.

The rain descended in a gusty squall, driving the half-castes into their wurlies, the horsewomen back among the trees. As they rode, the older woman sagged in her saddle, curiously aged and grim.

'The sooner they're cleared out of the district the better,' she said viciously. 'They're an immoral lot, these half-castes.'

'What about the whites who are responsible for them?' the girl on the chestnut colt asked.

She wondered whether it was a tragedy or a comedy she had been witnessing. These people might live like dogs in their rotten wurlies, with the dark bush behind them and the prosperous little township spread in sunshine at their feet; but their aspirations were all towards standards of the white race. The exotic film star and that baby in this dump of outcasts. What an indictment! And yet Miss Allison suspected they had tried to spare the baby's grandmother, with simple kindness, knowing the truth behind Mollie's bravado. Had they altogether succeeded?

The camp on the hillside was moved on before the end of the month.

MYRA MORRIS
(1893-1966)

Myra Morris was born and brought up in the Mallee district of Victoria. She became a freelance writer, and her short stories and articles appeared in many newspapers and magazines. She published two collections of verse, mostly about outdoor life, which were very successful in the 1920s and 1930s. Though she also published two novels, her real talent was in the short story. In her collection, *The Township* (1947), Morris writes about domestic situations with vivid realism, irony and a clever use of detail. Using an idiomatic style, she usually writes from a woman's point of view.

'Marriage is for Fools', which appeared in *Home* magazine in 1948, questions many of the values and attitudes common in this period; marriage was considered the only acceptable and fulfilling occupation for a woman and a woman who worked in a profession did it only because she had been passed by in the marriage market, not because it was her choice to do so.

MARRIAGE IS FOR FOOLS

Eustace was talking in his slightly pained, slightly pompous voice. 'You see, Dorothy, this stick of mine! What would you say it was made of? Cherry wood? Ha-ha, no! It's Brazilian jacaranda which is rosewood. Now when I mention jacaranda I may as well tell you —'

Georgie listened to Eustace talking. There he was again, the old goat, delivering his niggling little lectures, being a Mine of Information, being a Priceless Bore. She sat back in the chair, her legs spread out in a characteristic attitude. She was smoking as usual from a long scarlet holder, and she had the feeling of mingled emptiness and relief that settles in at the end of a successful party.

The party was over now. All the guests had gone save Dorothy who was waiting for her young husband to pick her up, and Eustace who had never learned to know the exact moment when a social function could be considered dead and finished. Everybody had had a good time . . . 'A lovely party, darling,' they had said . . . 'Marvellous,' they had said, 'such fun darling!' . . . 'And you're wonderful, Georgie, how do you do it with your job?'

They had said all these, and now, hurrying down Collins Street, scattering for trams and buses, they would be saying with little neighs of kindly laughter—'Dear old Georgie! Isn't it frantic that she's never been able to hook a man for keeps?' . . . 'Poor Georgie, such a *battler*!'

Georgie, winking down her long scarlet holder, could hear them at it. She got up abruptly. In a moment, Dorothy, who with her fair flying hair and fluttering hands always looked as if she were posing for a picture of distracted Motherhood, would begin braying about her children . . .

Firmly Georgie led the way out onto the landing.

'Let's go down,' she said in her crisp matter-of-fact voice. 'You'll be all ready then when Otto pulls up.'

They went down the solid, old-fashioned stairs that led from Georgie's flat to the front door of the building—a block of doctors' rooms and residential chambers. Georgie felt suddenly happy. She wanted to turn and run up the stairs, to be back in her room again, drifting round, picking up things, thinking of the party, chewing over the fact that Eustace had asked her out to dinner (for the following night) and she couldn't go with him because she had promised Dorothy first.

She glanced at Eustace stealthily as he stood settling his chin down into his collar. Eustace with his prematurely chalk-white hair, his round pink face and grey eyes that swam behind his thick-lensed glasses like little fish in an aquarium tank. Eustace who looked so exactly what he was, a middle-aged chartered accountant with a room at a comfortable hotel, no past, a cosy future unclouded by any matrimonial considerations (or so it seemed) and a praiseworthy interest in art shows and symphony orchestras.

'There's Otto now,' she cried, pushing her way through the crowd on the pavement. 'He's pulling in at the kerb lower down. Hurry up, get in both of you.'

Eustace hung back on the edge of the gutter.

'I'm sorry you're not free tomorrow night, Georgie,' he said wistfully. 'I had hoped to take you to a new little fish-place that I've discovered. They serve excellent trout there. Faintly pink in the flesh, but the trout as you know bears some resemblance to the salmon. Now the common river trout—'

'Oh, but Georgie's promised *me*,' trilled Dorothy, breaking in relentlessly and speaking backwards through wisps of fair, wavering hair. 'Just a happy little domestic party—Otto and Georgie and I and the teenies in bed . . . Oh Otto, there you are and so dreadfully late! Couldn't you have managed—there's nothing worse than departing guests that hang about on doorsteps . . . Bye-bye Georgie, a marvellous party darling—'

A tall young man with a concave chest had unwound himself

from the little cream car by the kerb, and given a surly nod all round. He was now tucking his wife into the front seat, treating her delicately as though she were a bundle of cobwebs that might disintegrate any moment under a touch. For a second Dorothy seemed to be lost between two fussing men—Eustace, to whom they were giving a lift, and Otto the devoted husband.

Georgie banged into the sitting-room and sat down with her legs sprawling. Her happiness, her peace of mind, had gone, dispersed suddenly by the sight of Dorothy being fussed over in the car. And it was because Dorothy stood for Cherished Womanhood that the spectacle had been so unbearable.

What's come over me? she thought disgustedly. She went with her long strides to the mirror on the wall, and studied herself dispassionately. She was thirty-six, but she didn't look it. Her hair, swept up in an irregular pompadour, shone like black lacquer, and her dark eyes with their upward slant gave her broad face an attractiveness that was almost Oriental.

Satisfied with what she saw, Georgie turned away and began picking up glasses and ash-trays. The room had a comfortable lived-in look together with a sly arti-craftiness due to the dyed hessian curtains. The chairs were deep and easy, the carpet rich in tone and texture. Pictures on the cream-coloured walls were discreetly framed—some good modern French prints, a landscape or two of ghost-white gums. A small wood fire burned in the dull red cave of the fireplace.

Georgie carried the dishes out to the tiny kitchenette, came back and carefully removed the wet rings from the cedar tables and the little worms of cigarette ash from the floor. Sherry parties always left their signs, she thought grimly. Why did she bother to give them? Why did she so expend herself on other people? For love of them, perhaps, but wasn't it just a sort of bravado— an answer to those charming ratbags who said so nicely—'Darling Georgie—but isn't it a pity? *One* is such a jolly awkward number to fit in'?

Odd, unattended, a superfluous woman, a spinster in spite of her charm! Georgie washed up with the eternal cigarette sticking

54

out of the corner of her mouth. Fools the lot of them! Why, she had the best end of the stick every time. She was a free woman with her own business—a library right down in the heart of the city—and her life was full. She had had her silly dreams, of course—that handsome radio announcer and that man from Malaya with the leathery skin and the long yellow teeth of a camel, whose character had been suspect, possibly because she had read too much Somerset Maugham. Left only Eustace, solid and safe as a house, as a bank—as a eunuch. And as unmarriageable . . .

Purposefully she settled herself in front of the fire to work with a catalogue of new books under her fingers. She worked for a while, but tonight she could not settle. The thought of silly Dorothy fawned on by a silly, doting husband nagged at her. Presently she gave up trying to concentrate and went to bed, where she lay awake listening to the rats among the dust-bins below, and the long-drawn incantations of alley-cats.

She was ashamed of her foolishness the next morning as she walked down Collins Street, hatless and self-assured.

Her three young uniformed assistants greeted her with the usual deferential smiles, and she sat back at her desk content. This was her world and she was queen of it. Crisply she interviewed new subscribers, placated dissatisfied readers who had made unwise selections, catalogued, indexed, and went out to lunch with a disillusioned young divorcee who flatteringly asked her advice.

It was a successful day and it was not till near the end of the afternoon that she began to think wistfully of Eustace and his invitation. She had been a fool to promise Dorothy. After all, their friendship, begun years before at a business college, was beginning to wear thin, and Dorothy had no more brains than a bird.

Going out in the tram towards Dorothy's fine house in Malvern, she was more than ever aware of her reluctance, and aware of her reason for that reluctance. Dorothy and Otto! Husband and wife. So boring, those two, enclosed in the cocoon of their exclusive happiness. She would be irritated by that spectacle of domestic bliss in which she could have no share. She would be stabbed with envy all over again. And it was always cold at Dorothy's.

Tonight as usual a sulky little fire burned in the grate that was too small for the large, high-ceilinged drawing-room, and there were charcoal smears on Dorothy's thin, ineffectual hands.

'I never *can* fix fires, darling, and Otto won't bring up the wood. That wretched daily girl that I've got went home early because it's her mother's birthday, and I'm all behind with the dinner. You don't mind a teeny, weeny wait, darling, do you?'

No, Georgie didn't mind waiting. She sat in front of the sulky fire politely trying to conceal her shivers and to refrain from kicking Dorothy's Pekinese, who was feeling stealthily around her ankles.

'Fifi's a darling, really,' gasped Dorothy, coming into the room with a bundle of sticks. 'She doesn't bite. Pekinese don't.'

'Pekinese descended from the breed which originally belonged to the Imperial Palace of Pekin,' chanted Georgie, laughing at Dorothy's wooden face. 'It's all right. I'm only quoting that dreadful Eustace, the world's champion bore . . . Look, sweet, can't I help you?'

'No, it's all right,' Dorothy looked harassed as a wailing cry came from the end of the hall. 'That's Susan! She's got earache again. Otto is bringing some stuff from the chemist, but as usual he's late.'

It was Otto's lateness that was responsible for everything Georgie could see—Dorothy's dithering, the cold room, the tinny clashes of sound that came at intervals from the back regions of the house. Striding out into the kitchen she surprised Dorothy in the act of wiping away a tear.

'Good heavens, Dorothy—'

'It's the fourth time this week,' snapped Dorothy with a vindictive little laugh. 'He says he's kept at the office—but it's always the Club. How I curse that Club! More than once he's been tight and I've had to put him to bed.'

Dorothy, pushing away her straying hair, bent over the stove

56

like a sorrowing priestess, and Georgie, watching her, felt not so much shocked by the scandalous revelations of Otto's character as shocked by the bald way they had been given her.

She looked at the sharpened contours of Dorothy's face, and it seemed that Dorothy was changing there under her eyes.

'It'll all blow over,' she said soothingly. 'Do let me finish laying the table, Dorothy.'

'It's done,' said Dorothy, in a cold voice. 'All but the forks.'

The forks were in place, the Jacobean chairs drawn up to the Jacobean table, when Otto made his appearance. His thin face was flushed and his eyes had a puffy look.

'Did you bring that bottle of ear stuff?' Dorothy asked menacingly.

'What ear stuff? Good lord, I clean forgot.' Otto, who had given a cheerful nod in Georgie's direction, became sunk in gloom.

'I might have known.' Dorothy laughed that high, vindictive laugh. 'It's nothing to you that little Susan is in agony. Your own child—'

'Oh, for heaven's sake, woman, stop nagging! Nag, nag, nag—'

Georgie listened with the discomfort of anyone witnessing a domestic brawl and tried to look as if she were not there. Otto and Dorothy quarrelling! Dorothy and Otto of all people! . . . She smothered a little flare of malicious joy.

'We can't wait for drinks now,' wailed Dorothy. 'Anyhow, the dinner's ruined. The casserole dish is burnt black as hell.'

'Better a dish of herbs where love is,' quoted Otto with his right eyebrow lifted.

'Oh, shut up!'

Dorothy tottered out into the kitchen pushing the hair back off her shiny forehead, and Otto sat down heavily, shooting out his neck.

It was a pathetic meal. The food was dried up and tasteless and Dorothy sullen and archly bright by turn. Georgie talked of the latest Osbert Sitwell in a hard, racing voice and prayed that she could take her leave early without drawing fire from anyone.

There was no protest when she rose to go, and Otto, who had half-heartedly suggested taking the car out of the garage, sank back with obvious relief when she protested. Dorothy accompanied her to the door, switching off the porch-light swiftly.

'He's crazily mean about lights,' she explained in a hard voice. 'That's another thing!' She turned her head as the wailing cry of a child came from the middle of the house. 'Oh dear, that's *Mary* this time!' She kissed Georgie in a sort of frenzy. 'Good-bye, darling! So good of you to come. But it's been awful! That coffee! Thick as mud—no, don't deny it, darling—it was stone-cold, too. Oh, Georgie,' she cried, 'I wish I could have my time all over again! I had the best days of my life when I was working in Frater's office. I was a fool to marry Otto. You're the lucky one! You're free!'

Georgie laughed cheerfully. She could afford to laugh. In five minutes she would be in the tram. In less than half an hour she would be in her own comfortable room, not giving a hang for anyone. She was six years older than Dorothy, but tonight Dorothy looked as if she could have been her elder sister. Marriage, thought Georgie jubilantly. Marriage! Who'd be such a fool? I wouldn't have a husband if he were handed to me on a platter . . .

At the door of her building Eustace was waiting with an air of patient suffering.

'I was just hanging around—alone and palely loitering, you know—in case you came home early,' he said.

Georgie stared at him, hiding her surprise. It wasn't like old Eustace to take a chance for nothing.

'I thought we might go along to a little place and have some coffee,' said Eustace. 'It's up here at the top of the street.'

They walked along under the trees in silence until Eustace, with a little snorting laugh, fished a narrow red box from under his overcoat.

'Oh, chocs!' Georgie took the box awkwardly, surprised all over again because Eustace never bought unnecessarily.

'Chocolate-*coated*,' corrected Eustace. 'They call them truffles.

Absurd name. Everybody knows that truffles are a subterranean fungus collected in Southern Europe by—'

'Oh, Eustace, of course.'

They sat at a little table with lace mats under the glass top, and looked at each other warily. The wariness was still there button-holed round Eustace's mouth while he talked.

'Well, Georgie, you know what it's all leading up to, don't you? I've been thinking things over, and I have probably been in love with you for a considerable period of time . . . I am asking you to marry me, my dear.'

Georgie sat stunned. Eustace proposing, actually proposing . . . It was screamingly funny—but oddly enough she did not want to laugh. She felt shocked and elated and queerly *grateful* all together . . . To be married . . . married . . . married.

'My mother left me a little house in South Yarra,' Eustace was saying steadily. 'Small, but livable. It has one of those old slate roofs—quite attractive . . . My income is not large, but it will suffice for two . . . Of course, I would want you to give up the library.'

'Of course,' agreed Georgie, thinking fast. The library—well, what was it after all? Just a sort of bolt-hole—a substitute . . . Already it belonged to the past . . . There was only her future now—her *married* future . . .

She looked at Eustace idiotically, seeing him not as he was, but as she wanted to see him.

'Oh, Eustace,' she said, 'you're rather a darling, Eustace.'

MARJORIE BARNARD
(1897–1987)

Marjorie Barnard was born in Sydney and was educated at Sydney Girls High School and the University of Sydney, where she received the University Medal in History. Although she was offered a scholarship to Oxford, she was unable to attend due to her father's disapproval. She worked as a librarian at Sydney Technical College until 1935, when she resigned in order to devote herself to her writing.

With Flora Eldershaw, whom she had met at university, Barnard wrote five novels, three historical studies and some literary criticism under the pseudonym M. Barnard Eldershaw. Their first novel, *A House is Built* (1929), shared first place with *Coonardoo* by Prichard in the first *Bulletin* novel competition. Their last book, *Tomorrow and Tomorrow* (1947), was heavily censored when it was first published, because of its apocalyptic view of Australia's future. It was not published in its uncensored form and with its full title, *Tomorrow and Tomorrow and Tomorrow* until 1983, when it won the Patrick White Award.

Independently, Barnard published two history books, historical articles, literary criticism, children's stories and many short stories. A collection of these, *The Persimmon Tree and Other Stories* (1943), demonstrates her skill in the short story form. The stories are brief and carefully structured, with urban settings. Barnard often uses irony to highlight the vulnerability of women. Though 'The Lottery' is told from the husband's point of view, it is his self-absorption which highlights his lack of understanding of his wife's unhappiness.

THE LOTTERY

The first that Ted Bilborough knew of his wife's good fortune was when one of his friends, an elderly wag, shook his hand with mock gravity and murmured a few words of manly but inappropriate sympathy. Ted didn't know what to make of it. He had just stepped from the stairway onto the upper deck of the 6.15 p.m. ferry from town. Fred Lewis seemed to have been waiting for him, and as he looked about he got the impression of newspapers and grins and a little flutter of half-derisive excitement, all focused on himself. Everything seemed to bulge towards him. It must be some sort of leg pull. He felt his assurance threatened, and the corner of his mouth twitched uncomfortably in his fat cheek, as he tried to assume a hard-boiled manner.

'Keep the change, laddie,' he said.

'He doesn't know, actually he doesn't know.'

'Your wife's won the lottery!'

'He won't believe you. Show him the paper. There it is as plain as my nose. Mrs Grace Bilborough, 52 Cuthbert Street.' A thick, stained forefinger pointed to the words. 'First prize £5000 Last Hope Syndicate.'

'He's taking it very hard,' said Fred Lewis, shaking his head.

They began thumping him on the back. He had travelled on that ferry every weekday for the last ten years, barring a fortnight's holiday in January, and he knew nearly everyone. Even those he didn't know entered into the spirit of it. Ted filled his pipe nonchalantly but with unsteady fingers. He was keeping that odd unsteadiness, that seemed to begin somewhere deep in his chest, to himself. It was a wonder that fellows in the office hadn't got hold of this, but they had been busy today in the hot loft under the chromium pipes of the pneumatic system, sending down change and checking up on credit accounts. Sale time. Grace might have let him know. She could have rung up from Thompson's. Bill was always borrowing the lawn-mower and the step-ladder, so it would hardly be asking a favour in the circumstances. But that was Grace all over.

'If I can't have it myself, you're the man I like to see get it.'

They meant it too. Everyone liked Ted in a kind sort of way. He was a good fellow in both senses of the word. Not namby-pamby, always ready for a joke but a good citizen too, a good husband and father. He wasn't the sort that refused to wheel the perambulator. He flourished the perambulator. His wife could hold up her head, they payed their bills weekly and he even put something away, not much but something, and that was a triumph the way things were, the ten per cent knocked off his salary in the depression not restored yet, and one thing and another. And always cheerful, with a joke for everyone. All this was vaguely present in Ted's mind. He'd always expected in a trusting sort of way to be rewarded, but not through Grace.

'What are you going to do with it, Ted?'

'You won't see him for a week, he's going on a jag.' This was very funny because Ted never did, not even on Anzac Day.

A voice with a grievance said, not for the first time, 'I've had shares in a ticket every week since it started, and I've never won a cent.' No one was interested.

'You'll be going off for a trip somewhere?'

'They'll make you president of the Tennis Club and you'll have to donate a silver cup.'

They were flattering him underneath the jokes.

'I expect Mrs Bilborough will want to put some of it away for the children's future,' he said. It was almost as if he were giving an interview to the press, and he was pleased with himself for saying the right thing. He always referred to Grace in public as Mrs Bilborough. He had too nice a social sense to say 'the Missus'.

Ted let them talk, and looked out of the window. He wasn't interested in the news in the paper tonight. The little boat vibrated fussily, and left a long wake like moulded glass in the quiet river. The evening was drawing in. The sun was sinking into a bank of grey cloud, soft and formless as mist. The air was dusky, so that its light was closed into itself and it was easy to look at, a thick golden disc more like a moon rising through smoke than the sun. It threw a single column of orange light on the river, the ripples from the ferry fanned out into it, and their tiny shadows truncated it. The bank, rising steeply from the river and closing it in till it looked like a lake, was already bloomed with shadows. The shapes of two churches and a broken frieze of pine trees stood out against the gentle sky, not sharply, but with a soft arresting grace. The slopes, wooded and scattered with houses, were dim and sunk in idyllic peace. The river showed thinly bright against the dark land. Ted could see that the smooth water was really a pale tawny gold with patches, roughened by the turning tide, of frosty blue. It was only when you stared at it and concentrated your attention that you realised the colours. Turning to look down stream away from the sunset, the water gleamed silvery grey with dark clear scrabblings upon it. There were two worlds, one looking towards the sunset with the dark land against it dreaming and still, and the other looking down stream over the silvery river to the other bank, on which all the light concentrated. Houses with windows of orange fire, black trees, a great silver gasometer, white oil tanks with the look of clumsy mushrooms, buildings serrating the sky, even a suggestion seen or imagined of red roofs, showing up miraculously in that airy light.

Five thousand pounds, he thought. Five thousand pounds. Five thousand pounds at five per cent, five thousand pounds stewing gently in its interest, making old age safe. He could do almost anything he could think of with five thousand pounds. It gave his mind a stretched sort of feeling, just thinking of it. It was hard to connect five thousand pounds with Grace. She might have let him know. And where had the five and threepence to buy the ticket come from? He couldn't help wondering about that. When you budgeted as carefully as they did there wasn't five and threepence over. If there had been, well, it wouldn't have been over at all, he would have put it in the bank. He hadn't noticed any difference in the housekeeping, and he prided himself he noticed everything. Surely she hadn't been running up bills to buy lottery tickets. His mind darted here and there suspiciously. There was something secretive in Grace, and he'd thought she told him everything. He'd taken it for granted, only, of course, in the ordinary run there was nothing to tell. He consciously relaxed the knot in his mind. After all, Grace had won the five thousand pounds. He remembered charitably that she had always been a good wife to him. As he thought that he had a vision of the patch on his shirt, his newly washed cream trousers laid out for tennis, the children's neatness, the tidy house. That was being a good wife. And he had been a good husband, always brought his money home and never looked at another woman. Theirs was a model home, everyone acknowledged it, but—well—somehow he found it easier to be cheerful in other people's homes than in his own. It was Grace's fault. She wasn't cheery and easy-going. Something moody about her now. Woody. He'd worn better than Grace, anyone could see that, and yet it was he who had had the hard time. All she had to do was to stay at home and look after the house and the children. Nothing much in that. She always seemed to be working, but he couldn't see what there was to do that could take her so long. Just a touch of woman's perversity. It wasn't that Grace had aged. Ten years married and with two children, there was still something girlish about her—raw, hard girlishness that had never mellowed. Grace was—Grace, for better or for worse. Maybe she'd be a bit brighter now. He could not help wondering how she had managed the five and three. If she could shower five and threes about like that, he'd been giving her too much for the housekeeping. And why did she want to give it that damnfool name 'Last Hope'? That meant there had been others, didn't it? It probably didn't mean at thing, just a lucky tag.

A girl on the seat opposite was sewing lace on silkies for

her trousseau, working intently in the bad light. Another one starting out, Ted thought.

'What about it?' said the man beside him.

Ted hadn't been listening.

The ferry had tied up at his landing stage and Ted got off. He tried not to show in his walk that his wife had won five thousand pounds. He felt jaunty and tired at once. He walked up the hill with a bunch of other men, his neighbours. They were still teasing him about the money, they didn't know how to stop. It was a very still, warm evening. As the sun descended into the misty bank on the horizon it picked out the delicate shapes of clouds invisibly sunk in the mass, outlining them with a fine thread of gold.

One by one the men dropped out, turning into side streets or opening garden gates till Ted was alone with a single companion, a man who lived in a semi-detached cottage at the end of the street. They were suddenly very quiet and sober. Ted felt the ache round his mouth where he'd been smiling and smiling.

'I'm awfully glad you've had this bit of luck.'

'I'm sure you are, Eric,' Ted answered in a subdued voice.

'There's nobody I'd sooner see have it.'

'That's very decent of you.'

'I mean it.'

'Well, well, I wasn't looking for it.'

'We could do with a bit of luck like that in our house.'

'I bet you could.'

'There's an instalment on the house due next month, and Nellie's got to come home again. Bob can't get anything to do. Seems as if we'd hardly done paying for the wedding.'

'That's bad.'

'She's expecting, so I suppose Mum and Dad will be let in for all that too.'

'It seems only the other day Nellie was a kid getting round on a scooter.'

'They grow up,' Eric agreed. 'It's the instalment that's the rub. First of next month. They expect it on the nail too. If we hadn't that hanging over us it wouldn't matter about Nellie coming home. She's our girl, and it'll be nice to have her about the place again.'

'You'll be as proud as a cow with two tails when you're a grandpa.'

'I suppose so.'

They stood mutely by Eric's gate. An idea began to flicker in Ted's mind, and with it came a feeling of sweetness and happiness and power such as he had never expected to feel.

'I won't see you stuck, old man,' he said.

'That's awfully decent of you.'

'I mean it.'

They shook hands as they parted. Ted had only a few steps more and he took them slowly. Very warm and dry, he thought. The garden will need watering. Now he was at his gate. There was no one in sight. He stood for a moment looking about him. It was as if he saw the house he had lived in for ten years for the first time. He saw that it had a mean, narrow-chested appearance. The roof tiles were discoloured, the woodwork needed painting, the crazy pavement that he had laid with such zeal had an unpleasant flirtatious look. The revolutionary thought formed in his mind. 'We might leave here.' Measured against the possibilities that lay before him, it looked small and mean. Even the name, 'Emoh Ruo', seemed wrong, poky.

Ted was reluctant to go in. It was so long since anything of the least importance had happened between him and Grace, that it made him shy. He did not know how she would take it. Would she be all in a dither and no dinner ready? He hoped so but feared not.

He went into the hall, hung up his hat and shouted in a big bluff voice, 'Well, well, well, and where's my rich wife?'

Grace was in the kitchen dishing dinner.

'You're late,' she said. 'The dinner's spoiling.'

The children were quiet but restless, anxious to leave the table and go out to play. 'I got rid of the reporters,' Grace said in a flat voice. Grace had character, trust her to handle a couple

66

of cub reporters. She didn't seem to want to talk about it to her husband either. He felt himself, his voice, his stature dwindling. He looked at her with hard eyes. Where did she get the money? he wondered again, but more sharply.

Presently they were alone. There was a pause. Grace began to clear the table. Ted felt that he must do something. He took her awkwardly into his arms. 'Gracie, aren't you pleased?'

She stared at him a second then her face seemed to fall together, a sort of spasm, something worse than tears. But she twitched away from him. 'Yes,' she said, picking up a pile of crockery and making for the kitchen. He followed her.

'You're a dark horse, never telling me a word about it.'

She's like a Red Indian, he thought. She moved about the kitchen with quick nervous movements. After a moment she answered what was in his mind:

'I sold mother's ring and chain. A man came to the door buying old gold. I bought a ticket every week till the money was gone.'

'Oh,' he said. Grace had sold her mother's wedding ring to buy a lottery ticket.

'It was my money.'

'I didn't say it wasn't.'

'No, you didn't.'

The plates chattered in her hands. She was evidently feeling something, and feeling it strongly. But Ted didn't know what. He couldn't make her out.

She came and stood in front of him, her back to the littered table, her whole body taut. 'I suppose you're wondering what I'm going to do? I'll tell you. I'm going away. By myself. Before it is too late. I'm going tomorrow.'

He didn't seem to be taking it in.

'Beattie will come and look after you and the children. She'll be glad to. It won't cost you a penny more than it does now,' she added.

He stood staring at her, his flaccid hands hanging down, his face sagging.

67

'Then you meant what it said in the paper, "Last Hope"?' he said.

'Yes,' she answered.

HENRIETTA DRAKE-BROCKMAN
(1901-1968)

Henrietta Drake-Brockman was born in Perth, and educated first in Western Australia and then at boarding school in Scotland and at Frensham, Mittagong, New South Wales. Her mother was the first medical inspector of Western Australian state schools, and Drake-Brockman travelled extensively with her throughout the state. She then studied English and French literature at university. After her marriage in 1921 to Geoffrey Drake-Brockman, who worked in Aboriginal affairs, she continued her travels in the outback.

Her knowledge of the country and the people of the bush was demonstrated in her stories written for the *West Australian*, under the pseudonym of Henry Drake. With her first novel, *Blue North* (1934), she started to use her own name. Five of her novels were published and one collection of short stories. She was also a successful dramatist, and her play, *Men Without Wives: a North Australian Play in Three Acts* (1938), won the New South Wales sesquicentenary literary competition of 1938.

A prominent figure in the Western Australian literary community for many years, Drake-Brockman helped establish the state branch of the Fellowship of Australian Writers in 1938. She also served for a long period on the advisory committee of *Westerly*.

'The Price', which appeared in the *ABC Weekly* and *Coast to Coast, 1940*, looks at the hardships endured by people on the land and the first impact of the war.

THE PRICE

The moon hung over the valley like a sovereign glowing from the mould.

She hadn't set eyes on a sovereign for a quarter of a century. Queer, when you came to think how her dad used to treat 'em casually as the kids used to treat ha'pennies. More or less—well, anyhow, he'd always carried a funny round sovereign-case snapped on to his watch-chain, days he went into town. The case'd had a spring bottom, you could push the pretty little gold coins snugly in, and snap 'em out easily—her dad had a knack of spinning 'em down with a fine satisfying chink.

It was years since she'd thought of sovereigns. Gold. You heard enough about it! But you never saw any. All you ever saw to remind you such coins as sovereigns still existed, stacked up in banks, was the moon where it hung, like now, over the valley: full, round, not long risen.

Mary drew in her breath.

The wheat (a bumper crop with any luck), green-silvered by the white light, rippled up the hillside and lost itself, a silver mist, in the shadow of a jam-tree belt. The darkness of the trees—after that sharp black edge of the clearing—itself melted, dissolved, misted away in silver to the silver-blue sky.

From where she leaned on the twelve-acre fence, Mary could see right down the valley.

Flaring out like a pub or something, Hodson's lights were; all on, showing off the plant they'd put in since young Bill Hodson drew second in the lottery. Electric lights: bright spots even in the full moonlight. Ran an iron and a washing-machine and a refrigerator, not to mention the separator! Ken, he reckoned they were mad. Should've put the cash back into the land. But she wasn't so sure. Why not get a bit of comfort? She was sick of the smell of kerosene, and flat irons were fierce in the summer-time!

That little light bobbing around outside like a firefly was Mum Hodson going down the yard to see her turkey chicks were safe from foxes. Old Mum meant to keep her eye on the Christmas market, electric lights or not.

Fireflies! Mary's hand closed round the jarrah fencepost till the splintery wood of it jagged her thickened skin. Fat lot of sense comparing an old hurricane to a firefly! Fat lot she knew what fireflies looked like, anyhow.

'Your trouble, missus,' Ken would fetch her up short, time and again, 'your trouble is imaginitis!'

It always had been her trouble! Like now, comparing fireflies which she'd never seen—only Ken, when he first came back from the war, used to say how they danced in clusters and festoons (like fairy-lights at a fete, only tiny) in and out, through palm-trees along the road to Mandalay. No, no, there she was again, not Mandalay (lovely word!) but the roads round Ceylon, where the troopships called—so that here all these years after, when she ought to know better, she was imagining Mum Hodson's lantern looked like something she'd never seen, and wasn't likely to.

Well, perhaps that didn't matter now! At forty-five it was time you got over fretting for travel. Ken had long stopped talking about the Sphinx and the Wells of Beersheba and all the places he'd someday show her—Paris and London, say. No good fretting. It wasn't as if the valley wasn't beautiful enough for anybody. That first time she and Ken drove out in a sulky to look the property over, she'd cried instantly: 'Yes! Yes! Let's get it. I love it. We could make a tennis-court right there, along by the house. For the boys when they get big.'

She could see Ken's grin now, on his round smooth face. 'Hold hard, missus. I'm more interested in how many bushels to the acre she'll go, and what water we're likely to find, supposing I try for a stud flock.'

His dream. One he'd carted round for the best years of his life, spent mostly in Egypt and Palestine. What Ken wanted was a property where he could set out to breed the best sheep in the district and grow the best crops. And he reckoned *she* was the only one suffering from imaginitis!

He'd tried, anyhow. Tried till the flesh fell away from his cheery round face and his eyes sank back in their sockets. They'd taken on the place, she and Ken, mortgage and all. And she'd been glad. Ken was happy—even if there weren't any conveniences and the house wasn't much. She'd reckoned she could manage along till Ken made a do of it.

She'd been managing for eighteen years! It'd been right enough at first, quite all right that every bean should go back into the land. The bank has got to be considered. You couldn't expect a bank to list house-comfort under improvements. They'd advance what you liked on tractors and fences, but women in the country could manage along with any old makeshift. She hadn't minded. She was young. And strong. Her turn would come. When the boys grew up she'd be able to have this and that, Ken wouldn't need help, so she could get it, hire a girl, seeing they only had the boys and no girl of their own . . .

Heavens, how lovely tonight was! Kind, the moonlight. Out here, looking down the valley, you'd think everything in the garden was lovely! She hadn't any garden now . . .

Eighteen years solid—and the place in worse repair than when they took it on, and wheat a bob a bushel!

Inside, Ken would be reading the paper. He'd got so bitter he'd given over talking. He wouldn't mention the crop or prospects. At first he'd said, too right, this year sure he had the best crop in the district. If the season went on as well as it had started, they'd damn near average thirty bushels to the acre. At a bob! He couldn't talk about it!

Mary struck her hand on the fencepost.

If she didn't go back inside soon, Dick would be out to look for her. Tuesday night—he'd been fiddling for an hour with his wireless set, specially so she could listen in to a sponsored session she liked: Great German Composers. Lovely music. She couldn't tell Dick that tonight the 'Moonlight Sonata', supposing they played it, would just kill her. She couldn't, *tonight*, listen to that— and then hear some announcer in his highfalutin' voice, telling her summer was coming (as if she didn't realise it!) and she ought to get busy buying a refrigerator (like Hodson's, eh!), or else saying that Christmas was only three months off and it was time to start, right now, working the old man up to give the family a new-model baby car, handy for shopping and 'going places', all-steel body, safest for the children!

It was so lovely. And so still. There should be peace in her heart, not this bruising anger. A bob a bushel!

Mum Hodson was coming back up the yard. Some people's Christmas dinners were safe for another night! Down in the creek even the frogs sang. Then, quite close, out of the blue, the little birds that always greeted spring nights: 'Pretty-sweet, pretty-sweet . . .'

She couldn't stand it!

The first time she'd heard those birds at night, to remember, she and Ken had stood together, gazing down the valley. Eighteen years ago. They'd left little Phil and Wally asleep in cots, and gone wandering out to look over the property. At first they'd made plans, like young people do. Ken'd talked a lot about the years he'd wasted fighting, about the big things he'd do now to catch up. Then they'd fallen silent. Silenced by just such a night as this. The stillness. The peace. But they were young then! The beauty of the night demanded more than passive admiration. Ken's arms were already round her before she heard the song of the birds. Then had come the short quick laugh of a man deeply moved, and his own tongue echoing close to her lips: 'Pretty-sweet, pretty-sweet . . .'

The shadows of the trees had been like velvet. And the scent of crushed grass clean and right. Her eyes had seen the shapes of leaves trembling, and the bright points of stars, up beyond the shape of Ken's head. She'd hoped never to have any more children. Two were enough. But she'd never regretted that night— or Dick.

Not until now. Now, what chance was there of giving Dick or Phil or Wally even half of the things she'd bullocked for?

When she went back inside out of the moonlight, Mary saw just what she'd expected. Ken sagged down in his chair, so weary he'd gone to sleep over the *Weekly Mail*—they'd given up the daily long ago. Ken's hands hanging heavy on the paper. The miserable lamp-light making great grooves on Ken's cheeks.

Dick looked up from where he was fiddling.

'Mum,' his reproach met her, 'you're a beaut! Where've you been? It came over first-class tonight—they played that moonlight piece you like, too. I sang out—didn't you hear me?'

She said, 'Sorry, son' lightly, her eyes passing him to where Phil sprawled half-asleep on the blanket-covered stretcher they used for couch. Phil's arm was up over his eyes. It might have been Ken, eighteen years ago—only Ken had never sprawled like that, tired out.

Wally came in from the veranda muffled in Ken's everlasting old great-coat, a couple of new rabbit-traps dangling in his hand. He gave a jab at Phil.

'Here, you lazy cow, who was feeding-up tonight? If y'don't get a move on, we'll miss the bunnies.'

Phil grunted. Mary said, 'Let him alone. He's been ploughing all day.'

'And what've I been doing?' demanded Wally. 'I like that!'

'All right, I'm coming.' Phil stretched his long arms. Looking at Phil and Wally, at their size and strength, it seemed strange to Mary that these men had drawn their life from her. Something like fear prickled her skin. They were so big, so hard, so—so careless in their male pride! She shrugged away the prickle. She'd got a bad attack of imaginitis, and no mistake!

Phil fetched his rifle. 'Might see a fox,' he said. 'Skin's worth more than scalps, these days. Reckon I'll get one dressed for you, mum. Do for Christmas.'

Mary smiled. 'Where'd I wear it?'

'Wait and see,' put in Wally, grinning. 'To the races. Winning the lottery, I am. I got a quid's worth of tickets.'

74

'Wally, you haven't!' Mary's voice—she could feel it—had a jagged edge to it.

'Too right I have. Don't see why Hodsons should have it go all their way.'

'But—a quid's worth! You need new boots.'

'And I'll get 'em. 'S many's you like. After I win—God, I'm tired!' He yawned.

Mary said, soft again, 'Can't you give it a miss, tonight?'

'Not on your life—Captain's in the cart now, waiting. Reckon we'll trap fifty pair tonight, if we're lucky and keep going.'

'If we'd got more traps, you mean,' stuck in Phil.

'Fifty pair—that's twenty-five bob. Not bad.' Wally swung the traps.

A night's work on top of a day's work! Sleeping cold on rugs on the earth and cleaning rabbits' insides as the sun got up! Mary shivered. She'd done it often enough in the past herself. But it wasn't what you'd call a life! Yet she couldn't stop them. It was the only bit of spare cash they got. Besides, they were men. She couldn't go on arguing as if they were still kids.

'Coming, young 'un?' Wally used the top of his boot on Dick.

'Cut that out, you'll wreck this —'

'Coming?'

'Where?' Dick's ears were deaf to all sound not picked out of the air. 'Oh—rabbits. No. Listen to this—I reckon this is Berlin— Oh, hell, it's gone! A new battery, that's what I need . . .'

'Well, you won't get the price sitting on your tail here,' Wally shrugged.

Dick rose and dusted his pants. 'All right then, I'll come. I say—Phil?'

Mary knew what was coming. So did Phil. So did Wally, and Wally waded right in: 'Aw, hell, if you can't guts your own rabbits—'

'Leave him alone, Wal. I'll do it, young 'un. But you can damn well feed the team for a week.'

Dick went out to get into his coat without another word.

'What d'you give in t'him for?' demanded Wally, disgusted.

'I'd knock some sense int' him, I would.'

'You'd be a long time trying,' retorted Phil. 'And you couldn't anyhow. He was born that way. Wasn't he, mum?'

Mary smiled, a bit uncertain, feeling as if they were blaming her because Dick wouldn't gut his rabbits. Unjust blame. Pair after pair she'd done herself to buy them clothes and school books in the days she'd done the round of the traps with Ken, helping him. But she'd hated it—hated watching the sun come up and all the world stir with life, and her own hands sticky-wet with blood . . .

Dick came back to the door. 'Get a move on, will you?' he said to his brothers. Now he was going, he wanted to get it over.

Mary stood at the window and watched her sons walk to the stables.

Not good enough! It wasn't good enough she should have fetched them into the world, spent so much hope, so much love and work and care—and all the world had to give Ken and her for their pains was a bob a bushel . . . Why should Dick have to trap rabbits if he didn't want to? 'They cry, mum,' he'd whispered to her when he was a little kid and the others poked fun. 'They cry when they're caught—and they're little.' The big boys could sling off as much as they liked—why should Dick have to trap rabbits if he didn't want to?

Ken's paper fell on the floor and she turned from the window. 'I must've dropped off,' he said. 'Where's the boys got to?'

'Gone trapping.'

'Dick too?'

'Yes.'

Ken let out a laugh: 'I bet he's done a deal with Phil over cleaning rabbits!'

Mary didn't answer. Ken stared at her, she felt the weight of curious eyes, there where she stood by the window. 'Queer kid, Dick,' he said slowly. 'Your kid. Suffers from imaginitis.'

'My kid? They're all my sons, Ken.' She tried to keep that edge out of her voice. 'And yours.'

Ken grinned. 'I've never doubted that, missus. You know very

76

well what I mean about Dick—there's a sort of a bond—' He got suddenly serious. 'Don't you remember—' He started, but he didn't finish. She was glad he thought better of it—she didn't want any more reminding, not tonight! He drew himself up out of the old chair and it creaked as he rose. He stretched like Wally, like Wally he said: 'God, I'm tired!'

His foot rustled the paper. He kicked it aside as if it were dirt, with a kind of venom.

'Go to bed,' she said. The sag of his shoulders made her soft. She could have stroked his cheek.

'Reckon I will. Coming?'

'In a minute—'

Ken drew up short on his way to the bedroom. 'Look here, missus, you're not to go fixing food and laying the fire at this time of night—'

'Just in case they come in, Ken. It'll be sharp outside tonight.'

'They're big enough and ugly enough to look after themselves,' he said. 'You've been at it all day.'

'Speak for yourself,' she retorted. 'Go on, I won't be long.'

But he didn't go. Instead, he went outside to fetch kindling, and laid the fire whilst she put food and cups on the table. 'Spoilt young b's,' he muttered, but with no rancour to it.

That was on Tuesday. Sunday, September the third, Dick couldn't get his wireless to work at all, so Ken and Phil and Wally went over to Hodson's to listen in. Mary wouldn't.

She knew what had happened the minute they came back. Ken's mouth was set and he'd got a dogged look in his eye, but for all that he'd straightened up his shoulders and walked with a swing she'd not seen for years. Straight off, Phil went and got out his militia uniform, to see its condition, and Wally started to swear because he'd used up his military boots in the paddocks and would have to spend rabbit-money buying new ones.

They sat up to midnight, talking, listening to Ken, who got going on the last war. In the end, Mary left them to it, and went to bed alone. She felt so cold she had to pile Ken's old great-coat on top of the thin blankets.

Monday night was the same. The three of them set off for Hodson's the minute tea was done. Even Ken's offer to dry the dishes wasn't meant to be accepted; she could see easily enough he expected her to understand he'd got to hear what was doing. Dick, even, got straight on to his wireless. He was mad, he reckoned, because they had to go out sucking up to Hodson's for news. He'd an idea he knew what was wrong. By the time they got back, he promised them they'd have the latest laid on at home. 'Direct from Daventry,' he shouted after them.

'Hope you're right, kid,' Phil shouted back. 'But I'm taking no chances.'

When she'd finished the dishes, Mary went out. She couldn't stay, watching Dick fiddle round.

She went the old familiar track, a foot-pad grown over with pink everlastings that whispered round her feet. Everlastings! They were frail as chaff, gone like chaff in a high wind . . . The old familiar way, up to the twelve-acre fence, where spring after spring she'd watched the valley grow green with promise, and every year drawn in her breath at the beauty of September . . .

The moon was up. A dying moon, there was no glamour left in the light of it, the valley looked dim and old beneath the fantastic thin light of it, that false light of a waning moon. There were shadows everywhere.

When she reached the fence, she realised how tired she was. So tired she could scarcely think. Well, she didn't want to think.

A shout from the house came up to her. 'Mum, where are you, mum?'

It was Dick. He sounded excited, a thrill in his voice like a youngster promised a treat. Her own heart leapt to meet it. Perhaps—perhaps—

Dick raced up the hill. Breathless he came, glowing, his eyes bright even in the sick light.

'I got her going,' he burst out. 'First-class. And mum—mum— you'll never guess the first bit of news I heard come over. The best bit ever—'

Her lips were too dry to ask him to hurry, she had to let him run on.

'Listen—are you listening? Wheat has doubled its price. Two bob already. What d' you know about that?'

He paused triumphantly. She couldn't answer. He was taken aback at her silence.

'That's not all,' he ran on, 'not by a long shot. The chap advised no one to sell. Hang on, he said. It's going to rise. Home on the pig's back we are—talk about a merry Christmas!'

Still she couldn't answer him. In his eagerness for response Dick stepped forward, flinging out his arms. The shadow of a tree darkened his face. A vague shadow, she never knew whether it were there or not, where it began, where it ended—but all at once the shadow falling on Dick, on his lifted arms, was the shadow of a cross.

Her name was Mary! Everywhere in the world were hundreds of women called Mary—thousands of sons like Dick. How long, oh Lord, how long?

'Why, mum,' said Dick. 'What's up with you? Aren't you glad?'

She began to laugh. She couldn't help it. She couldn't stop it. Not even the shock in Dick's eyes, who'd never heard her laugh like that, could make her stop. Her laughter rang down the valley. A ripple of wind caught up her laugh and blew it over the paddocks. As the wind passed, the wheat shuddered.

CHRISTINA STEAD
(1902–1983)

Christina Stead was born in Rockdale, New South Wales, the only child of her father's first marriage. Her father remarried and had six more children, for whom Stead took much responsibility. Her childhood figures prominently in much of her writing. Educated at St George's Girls High School, Sydney Girls High School and Sydney Teachers College, Stead taught and worked in various jobs until she saved enough to travel to London. There she met her husband, novelist and economist William Blake, who helped her get her first works published. After living for extended periods in Paris, the United States, Belgium and other countries in Europe, Stead settled in England, where she lived until her husband's death in 1968. She returned to Australia to live in 1974.

When it was first published, Stead's work was highly acclaimed overseas, but it was allowed to go out of print until the mid-1960s. Her work was not published in Australia until 1965. She was nominated for an Australian literature award in 1967, but was ruled ineligible due to her extended residence overseas. However, in 1974 she won the first Patrick White Award, and in 1982 the New South Wales Premier's Literary Award. In the same year she was elected an Honorary Member of the American Academy and Institute of Arts and Letters.

Stead published eleven novels and two collections of short stories from 1934 to 1976. Her novel, *The Man Who Loved Children* (1940) is considered a masterpiece. In her distinctive style Stead seems to explore rather than manipulate her characters and events as she exposes the intricacies of human interactions. *The Salzburg Tales* (1934) demonstrates her skill as a writer of short stories in both her range of subject matter and her versatility of style. Many of her uncollected stories were published posthumously in *Ocean of Story* (1985). 'The Hotel-keeper's Story' first appeared in *Southerly* in 1952 and was eventually rewritten to become the much longer opening chapter of *The Little Hotel* (1973). The story is typical of Stead's unique style; it has a rambling structure, no clear beginning and no obvious hero or villain. The gossipy first-person narration provides us with a fragment of life with many unanswered questions.

THE HOTEL-KEEPER'S STORY

If I knew how to write, I would write a book about what happens in the hotel every day. Not a day passes without something happening; some days too much happens. Yesterday afternoon a woman rang me up from Geneva and told me her daughter-in-law died, died yesterday. The woman stayed here twice and came to see me several times. We became friendly and she confided in me although I always felt I didn't know the truth about her, whether she was divorced and remarried, or otherwise. I knew her before her son was married and I always felt she had a secret or trouble, for she used to telephone me crying and saying she must talk to a friend and I was so good to her. I was looking for a friend too and I still am; for I never had one since I lost my girlhood friend who married a German exile and is now living in Berlin; but this woman was not really my friend. We did not tell everything to each other. My girlfriend Elsa and I never had any secrets; we laughed and we talked—and when her parents put her out of the house because of her affair with the German, she came to my place and had her baby there: and that was the happiest time of my married life; but of course she was in trouble then, and had other things to think of. When you grow up and marry there is a shadow over everything, you can never be happy again. How happy you are as a girl, going out with your friends and always laughing! Besides, you understand I have the hotel to manage, the marketing to supervise, I do most of it myself; I have the menus to type out, the servants to manage; I have to settle all the troubles with the guests; and then I must talk to them all; anyone who comes here and stays for a few months or for the winter season, feels that we are his friends. Still, if anyone needs me I must talk to them mustn't I? This woman used to telephone me every day during her son's engagement and early married days when he left the house for his bride's house, and then for a few months I almost forgot about them. Then she telephoned me and said that her son and daughter-in-law had moved in with her, and she was laughing and crying, nothing so tragic and so beautiful had ever happened to her; and then she began to telephone me every day again, telling me all that went on with the young couple in the house. I don't know what went on; she would be laughing and crying, and it was never clear except that she talked so much about unhappiness and happiness, love and misunderstanding; and I began to try to miss her telephone call. It is not only the accounts but my little boy takes up my time; I must go out in the evenings with Roger when he goes on drinking parties; and then I am obliged to study French and English; and then I felt it was all useless, I had not the time and I felt there was something weighing on her which she could not tell me. Yesterday, when I heard her voice I felt a blow on my heart; she was crying and she said something terrible had happened and she must tell me the end of it before she called the police. It was very confused for she was sobbing and exclaiming and yet she said it had to come to that and I think she said that her daughter-in-law was dead and her son had gone away and left her. But it may have been that her son was dead too, or that her son was dead because she had killed her daughter-in-law; and for a moment I thought she said that her son had killed his wife. But I kept hearing, 'This horror, this abomination'—and what was it? It occurred to me afterwards that it sounded more like an accident or that her daughter-in-law had committed suicide. She spoke in French so hurriedly and my French is not very good. I have not had time to look in the paper this morning; and then I have always had a suspicion that I don't know her real name now. You can see how close we get to people and yet we stay right outside of their lives. We know everything and very little. We don't enquire too far and we keep silent on many things we guess. The police are there to do their job; we do ours: we work together and respect each other, because each keeps to his function. The police are our friends and we need their help.

Yesterday morning I had trouble with that dark fat man you may have noticed the whole of last week in the dining-room. He took double helpings at all his meals and had three decilitres of wine with each meal and his breakfast in the bedroom. He came last Thursday and asked for a room. I quoted him four francs fifty, the usual price which is written up over the gate, and yesterday gave him his bill, at twelve francs fifty complete pension plus the wine he had drunk and service extra, the usual thing; but he said I had quoted four francs fifty all-in and he would only pay thirty-one francs without even the service extra. Besides he said he had no more money except for his fare on to Berne where he has to go for business. 'I don't care about that,' I said, 'you must pay for your meals and wine. Besides I know you have much more money than you say; you probably have two or three hundred francs in your wallet.' You see we get used to sizing people up. I had already thought I would have some kind of trouble with this man although he was quite quiet; but I felt sure he had some money and we can do nothing until it is time to present the bill. I was ready for him you might say. He spent two hours arguing and took his wallet out to show me he had only fifty or sixty francs; he called me a robber, a thief, a liar and said he would send for the police. 'Send for the police, I shall be glad of that,' I said. But I had already sent Jenny for the police. It is a good thing, a blessing for me that they are only just down the street: they come in four or five minutes any time I send for them. They haven't much to do and they like the excitement, too. Well, they made him pay and sure enough he had over two hundred francs in his pocket! They went over his papers, and there were some details he didn't want known—that, however, is neither here nor there—and he went away quite quietly in the end to the bus-stop with the gendarme who put him on the bus for the station.

As for that short fat man who is always on the stairs, and who is at present in numbers five and six, he is the Mayor of B., the Belgian city. He is a funny customer, I never had one like him. He makes us all laugh and he is a little hard to handle but so good-natured that I don't mind; besides he keeps the servants in good humour. He came on Tuesday two weeks ago in a Belgian limousine with a liveried chauffeur who put him down with two leather bags and a shopping-bag outside the hotel and drove off. He was quite negligently dressed, in old sports clothes and a worn felt hat just as you have seen him. He said he stopped at our hotel because of its name, Hotel Swiss-Touring, he wanted a hotel, he was in Switzerland and he was on tour; and he laughed. He said he must have the best room in the house, but there was only a small one vacant then on the second landing where the best rooms are, so I said he could have that and take the large double room as soon as the Russian family moved out. It was then he told us that he was the Mayor of B. and that he had come here for treatment because he had been over-worked and been having too good a time after work; high living and high thinking, he said. Then he said he had got very nervous under the Germans and that as he was in his fifties now he could not stand things the way he could when younger. He not only filled out all the required details on his police paper but he wrote in, 'So-and-So, Mayor of B., Belgium,' and made several additions, things not required by our officials. 'Perhaps they require that in Belgium,' I said to Roger. But Roger said no. 'Well,' I added, 'perhaps the Germans required that and he has got it on his mind; for he keeps talking about the Germans.' But Roger coloured and declared that the Germans did not make people fill out nonsense. The Germans are a modern, orderly people whose only object was to bring backward countries up-to-date and to prevent the disorder malignantly stirred up by the communists. Roger at one time worked in Germany, and has pleasant memories of the Nazi days, for he was butler to one of Hitler's generals at one time. I can't help teasing him about it; 'You're French and you're Swiss,' I say, 'and you love the Germans, while I'm German Swiss and I hate them. Why is that, Roger? Because I understand them.' And I can't help telling him that his father was only a farmer, while mine was a government official and that I always lived in the thick of such discussions and so I know what has been going on all the time. 'Isn't it a shame to have the chance of being neutral?' I ask Roger, partly teasing and partly serious. 'A shame to be a partisan and of such wicked people as the Nazis?' This makes him very angry and upset; the first time I said it in the first year of our married life, he left me and went away for three weeks without giving any sign of life. It's a strange thing how this insults him, for underneath, at heart, Roger is a decent man and reasonable. But you know the Germans have left deep marks on everyone's heart and mind in Europe; they have burned themselves in, for better and for worse, and so it will be for a long time. Well, I get too much of it, and I can't help giving some of it back, though I am very good-natured and in my business cannot offend people.

At first the Mayor took his meals in the dining-room and was very affable. He went from table to table making friends and talking about the weather, even inviting people to his room to have champagne, but after a few days he began to complain about Germans in the hotel. One evening he had just begun his meal when our two Dutch ladies walked in; and he got up and came straight to me in the office with his serviette in his hand and quite loudly and rudely said he must finish his meal in his room, that he refused to sit down with Germans. I explained that they were Dutch and came to us every year. But he has eaten his meals upstairs ever since. I cannot make up my mind whether he objected to the Germans in his country; or whether he had too much to do with them. He twits us and harps upon the subject and I wonder if he does not do it to get a rise out of me too; for he must know from my way of speaking French that I am German Swiss. Then, for instance, he came upon me speaking German to Jenny and he said to me, 'Who is that German woman?' I was quite firm with him. 'She is a Swiss girl and my housekeeper,' I said.

And what did he do? I had to laugh even so. Lina and I laughed together. Lina the chambermaid, not the kitchenmaid, came down laughing you see, and saying, 'Here is an official communication from the Mayor of B.' It was a little cotton hand-towel with our name embroidered on it in red, *Hotel Swiss-Touring Ouchy*. He had written all round the border and then on the towel and in such a way as to keep on including the embroidered name in his message:

> It is no wonder that the guests of the Hotel Swiss-Touring Ouchy use your skinny little hand-towels for writing notes to the management of the Hotel Swiss-Touring Ouchy and letters to their friends, for in your German starvation hotel you do not provide good writing paper for the guests of the Hotel Swiss-Touring Ouchy and they are going to be always obliged to inscribe their letters, papers, documents, bills, receipts, memoranda, diaries and last will and testaments on your little skinny hand-towels. Take notice for if you do not I am going to do my writing on your hand-towels, wash-cloths, floorcloths, mops, window curtains and bed-sheets; and I shall even use the counterpane. Notice to the German Hotel-keepers! Provide paper for guests, even in the little back room. Document Two. So-and-so, the Mayor of B.

You can imagine I kept it; and of course I charged it in the bill, as well as the cost of a tablecloth and a traycloth which he likewise wrote complaints upon and sent down to the office to me, numbered like all the rest of his written statements. You see his police paper was Document One. There was no nonsense about him, he understood everything and was very witty, saucy, sarcastic about things. He has his wits about him; and I'm quite sure he has been someone important all his life and is used to doing just as he pleases. I expressed this idea to Roger but Roger was still furious about the German question and he replied that he was just like all Belgians and now I could see how necessary it was for the Germans to walk in and bring up-to-date this old-fashioned, medieval, fantastic society. 'Well, then, we must invade all other countries and teach them hotel-keeping, banking and how to make watches,' I said laughing. But at that Roger shut his mouth tight and went out into the town to join his drinking friends. Well, that is a thing that used to make me cry and gave me headaches but now for the most part I laugh and I am getting to like my life. In fact, this is my life, the hotel, my little boy, and Roger and I look back to the days when I was a girl and think, 'How did I get on without all this? What did I do all day?'

The Mayor's other documents were all kinds of things, postcards of the lake which he gave me to post in dozens; and some which he posted himself to me. One of them is so funny that I kept it to show people. It is addressed to me, Madame Bonnard, Proprietress, Hotel Swiss-Touring etc., and has a number like all of them, Document 89. I do not know if it is really 89. He says he keeps the more important documents, his own notes and his diaries himself. It is written all over in a very good hand,

Madame Bonnard, my damn Bonnard, bonart, bon-narr, bonnarrish, anyone who wants to visit your hotel can apply to me, the Mayor of B., and I will recommend this hotel, like all the Germans it contains, sweet little Germans, sweet dirty Germs, down with Germs, down with Germans, why do you have Dutch-Germans and Swiss-Germans in your hotel? Your hot-hot-hot-hotel, not-hot-hotel, down with Germanisms, down with Hotelism. Madame Bonnard is a very good German, a, b, c, d, e, f, ach-german, boo-german, cousin-german, down with german, and the german, foul german, germ-man. Come and drink champagne with me, germadam! Document 89. Sgd. Mayor So-and-So of B. Belgium.

And after that every day, every hour, the maids and the servants brought me messages from the Mayor. And what do you think is the latest! He has numbered all his clothes. He took them all out and spread them about the floor, the towel-rack and the bed with a number pinned to each one and he has given chances in the lottery to every one of the servants. The guests have refused them; but he went out at night and posted a numbered piece of paper to each one of the guests; and the Dutch ladies and Jenny the housekeeper and myself got two each because we are Germans, he says; the Germans know how to strip people better than others and so we have two chances in the lottery; then he will be naked, and he will have to stay all day in his room and drink champagne. That is what he says. In the meantime, he goes of course to the specialist who is giving him shock-treatment so he tells me, of one thousand volts a time; a little more, says

88

he, only one thousand and two volts and he would fall down dead. He needs the champagne as a pick-up after the treatments. And besides this he has taken a season ticket to Zurich and another to Geneva. He actually does go to those places. I have seen lawyer's letters from Geneva and Zurich addressed to him, So-and-so, Mayor of B.; and one came to So-and-so, Mayor of L. I said to him, 'But you can't also be Mayor of L.' He said, 'L. is a fortress city, it is built to stand against the dirty Germans and next time the Germans come visiting I am going to be Mayor of L. and I will show them tricks.' All this is rather strange, I know; and yet the man is doing business here and I suppose it is just the result of his nervous breakdown and his champagne. He crosses the frontier for example nearly every day and brings back champagne from France. He does not even hide it. I suppose he gives some to the frontier guards. And then he buys it here and offers it to everyone; and he said to me,

'Madame German, I have brought you a whole crate of champagne and we will toast the regime in it,' but it was only a toy crate of liqueur chocolates in the shape of bottles, you know, so I was able to accept it. In all he does, he shows a very good heart; and he pays his bills not only promptly but generously; and gives presents to all the servants. Naturally I have had to stop them drinking champagne. All this gives them something to think about. They are much more cheerful at present. I should not mind at all his little jabs at me, if it were not that he touches on this very sore point of nationality; for I have more than my hands full with a Swiss-French cook who thinks very highly of himself because his grandfather worked for the La Harpes who as you know were at the Russian Court; an Italian kitchenmaid who came here almost barefoot from her mountain village, and a German-Swiss housekeeper, to mention only three of them. All these dislike each other. The cook is nervous like all cooks and really would love to poison the others. The Italian maid feels she's despised, and Jenny is a poison-pen writer and when things don't suit her, she goes on the rampage and drinks vermouth in her room. Still I know more than I used to and when they are too troublesome I threaten to send for the police. That dampens their spirits; they all go quietly back to work.

Well, as for the Mayor, I suppose he will settle down. He intends to live here in Switzerland. He is negotiating the purchase of several large properties in Geneva, some businesses in Zurich, and he is just about to buy the Hotel Lake-Leman, the one with the palms near the casino you know. I had no idea it was for sale. But the Mayor found out immediately. He has been over there for the past week, has inspected it from top to bottom and he is ready to conclude the deal. If he buys the hotel I suppose he will settle down in this town. You see he has taken a great fancy to my little son, Adrian, even though he is only three years old. Adrian is very forward for his age I know and very engaging, naturally charming like his grandfather. He spoke and walked much earlier than most children and has a wonderful gift of doing imitations. Perhaps he will be an actor when he grows up. All you have to do is give him a piece of lace or a shawl and he will spend hours, the whole afternoon, talking to himself and impersonating things. Sometimes he is a lady, or a dancer, or the Mayor, or Mrs Trollope or a fisherman; and all with a scarf, a piece of string! Mrs Trollope's husband, Mr Wilkins, told me that in his experience, hotel children are very bright because they are brought up in mixed society from the very beginning and have none of that shyness which is at the bottom just uncouthness. The Mayor of B. says he will stay with us, then; and he is giving the Hotel Lake-Leman to Adrian because he has fallen so much in love with him. Naturally, I refused and so did Roger; but the Mayor is very pressing and has already given me a document promising the hotel to Adrian. We cannot take it—how can we take property of that value? And I pointed this out to the Mayor. I even said, 'What will your heirs think? What will they say?' 'Then,' he said, 'since you are so scrupulous, so honourable and so businesslike, I will just give you the hotel in trust for Adrian, or for myself, and you shall draw the benefits and I will pay you a management fee, and I will retain the property in my name. Will that suit you?' But we still have not decided; for it does look strange, when we have known him such a short time. Roger even wonders if the funds are his and insists that we must employ a detective to discover the origin of the funds; for he does not believe that the Mayor is simply good-hearted and has fallen in love with Adrian as I do. But the Mayor told me himself that he is so happy here and we are so good to him that he wants to live here forever and never go back. He says he is very tired, he has lived his life and now he wants to retire and live forever in heaven on our beautiful lake. There is nothing uncommon in this. So many people do it. In our hotel there are half a dozen retired people who want to do just that. 'Very well!' says Roger, 'but he mixes up the Germans too much in his story and we must find out where he got those funds and what right he has to them; and whether he has not simply absconded with funds; perhaps he is an embezzler, a thief.' And Mrs Trollope, who is very sharp in money matters, said to me: 'Telephone to B. If he is such a well-known person nothing could be easier. Telephone to the Town Hall, X.B., or let Mr Wilkins.' But we have not done it yet. We have no right to meddle in our guests' affairs. Let him stay here I say and do his deals which have nothing to do with us, and if he presses the Hotel Lake-Leman upon us, we will get a lawyer to look into it. If a lawyer says it is all right, we are safe from legal pursuit.

I was walking over to the movies only last night with Mrs Trollope when we passed the Mayor of B. outside the Hotel Lake-Leman, he was there without a hat and in a very unconventional costume as usual, for that is how he goes everywhere even to France and Geneva. He saw me and came up excitedly, not even noticing Mrs Trollope, and he said: 'It's done, it's done, just as I told you. It was all fixed up, signed, sealed and delivered forty minutes ago; aren't you glad of that?' So I smiled at him and talked with him a while and went on to the movies with Mrs Trollope, for it was getting late. 'Who is that?' she said. She had not seen him at first and lately he has been eating in his room. In the intermission I told her all about him. She listened to me eagerly; but she said, 'I suppose he drank and made merry with the Germans and now he has gone mad.'

91

HELEN HELGA WILSON
(1902-   )

Helen Helga Wilson was born in Zeehan, Tasmania, but grew up on the goldfields of Western Australia. She was educated at the Methodist Ladies College, Perth, and the University of Western Australia.

Her historical articles have appeared in Australian newspapers and journals and she has published five novels, two Australiana books, and three books of verse.

Her short stories have appeared in numerous anthologies, have been translated into many languages and have won or been commended in fifteen competitions. Some of her stories have been collected in *A Show of Colours* (1970) and *The Skedule and Other Australian Short Stories* (1979). In 1980 Wilson became an Officer of the Order of Australia for services to literature.

In 'The White Butterfly', which appeared in *Coast to Coast, 1961-62*, Wilson examines the intense competition between two brothers and uses a powerful image to present the magnetism that can develop between a man and a woman.

THE WHITE BUTTERFLY

Nicholas Caldwell flung open the front door of the homestead of Lalirra and looked expectantly down the road. He glanced at his watch. Nearly four o'clock. Any time now Joyce would come.

The woolly smell of late wattles hung richly in the air, and a light breeze washed the golden spume of their blossoms as far as the steps.

Nicholas wanted to sing, to whistle, to gambol as senselessly as the new lambs in the hill paddocks. Anything to give expression to his joy. The thought of his elder brother, Brett, dozing on the other side of the veranda, deterred him. Brett's heavy chiselled lips would curve as they did so often when he spoke to his youngest brother. Patronising. Tolerant at best. Sometimes faintly contemptuous. Brett could do all the things on a farm that Nicholas could not do, and do them well. There was not a horse he could not break, a machine he could not mend, a man he could not bend.

A movement below caught Nick's eye. He loked over the edge of the veranda. In the shade of the giant oleander bush sat Brett's half-Persian she-cat, licking and preening herself with a too-obvious absorption. On either side of her, some four feet away, crouched two rangy tom-cats, their lashing tails making a dry frou-frou over the fallen leaves. Their eyes were savage slits, and from their snarling throats came a half-moaning, half-crooning sound.

Further away, where the asparagus fern frothed greenly over a trellis, sat his own cat, Silvanus, watching. Many years ago he had chosen Silvanus from a litter of kittens and Brett had 'fixed' it, as he had 'fixed' so many male animals on the farm. Sometimes Nick wondered uneasily whether Silvanus ever

93

mourned its lost masculinity. He thought not. It was so contented, so superbly conscious of its own magnificence. So now it watched the courting cats indifferently, one paw raised delicately, the sunlight making a faint platinum nimbus round its body.

Suddenly a white butterfly fluttered from the angle of fern. It hovered motionless, as though basking suspended in a ray of the late spring sunshine. The cat made an upward swoop with its claws, but the insect tacked with a negligent grace.

For a few minutes Nicholas stood watching the by-play, whilst the steady hum of the approaching car filled his whole body with a rising tide of excitement and delight.

Then he was aware of his brother at his side, yawning carvernously, hitching his trousers up round a waist already losing its youthful slimness. For a few seconds he stood there, lounging against the railing, lax with a deceptive passivity. Then, without warning, he picked up a small flower pot containing a withered cactus stalk, and, with the effortless grace of a bowler, flung it down between the courting cats. For a second their eyes spat fear, fury and hatred. Teeth were bared, tails rigid. They sprang into the air, then fell apart like a well-scattered wicket.

Brett burst out laughing, and Nick could see the watermelon red of his mouth against the strong whiteness of his teeth. The silver cat scattered with the others, then paused in the shade, looking around with a gentle bewilderment.

'Poor bastard,' commented Brett idly, as he watched it. Then added: 'Thought I'd better break up the party before your girl-friend arrived.' As Nick made no reply he went on: 'Being a school teacher, I guess she's not used to the crudities of farm life.'

'There are cats in towns,' returned Nick patiently. Brett was so obvious he told himself. But he felt his fingers clenching as they always did when his brother was near. He fought against the sensation of shrinking, his muscles taut, his face almost wizened. In some curious way, the mere presence of his brother seemed to sap his vitality, a reaction he'd had to fight since childhood. He kept telling himself that it was only natural, since

94

Brett was ten years older, and had always been bigger and stronger. Desperately Nicholas had always wanted to be like Brett; he refused even to think that he might end up like their father instead—shrivelled, vague and futile.

Brett's wife, Jean, had left him years ago, after a whirlwind wartime wedding. Brett had pretended he did not care, and had made no effort to obtain a divorce. But Nick had always known that, deep down inside, there was the raw chafed wound of his pride. The sudden death of their mother at about this time had overshadowed the departure of Jean, whom he could only remember as a brisk, plump army nurse who looked as though she had been drafted into her uniform. Whenever he thought about it later, it had seemed incomprehensible that any girl should have left a man as handsome and popular as his brother.

But the past was finished. Now there was only Joyce turning her car through the gates. And with her, the beginning of a new life. After they were married, they would live in the township three miles distant, and later, as his work demanded, move right away, from Lalirra and from Brett.

The small cream car spattered the gravel as it drew up in front of the porch, and a girl leant over the wheel, laughing up at him. Nick's heart seemed to fill his whole body. He ran down the steps to greet her.

'Hullo, Joyce . . .' His eyes took in every detail of her face. There was nothing he would have changed. The sea-green eyes under dark straight brows, the faint gold skin, the rippling hair, brown-gold like wheat at harvesting, the smooth red, red lips, velvet like geranium petals. To the young man, all the gold of sun and fields had been meshed in her hair and shimmered about her.

He opened the car door and took both her hands.

'You see, Nick, I found the way quite easily. Three miles is nothing.' She smiled up at him and he was armed with a new pride. Here, at last, was something Brett could never have.

Despite the girl's outward self-possession, Nicholas sensed she was uneasy, uncertain of her welcome. She was looking over

95

his shoulder and he knew that Brett was coming down the steps. And that his own hands were slowly clenching again. He forced himself to smile.

'Joyce, my brother Brett.'

'How do you do, Mr Caldwell?' Her voice was polite but distant. Nick felt himself relax. He had been dreading this moment for months—that was why he had delayed so long in bringing the girl to meet the remaining member of his family. He had decided to arrange the meeting out here, to emphasise that Lalirra was as much his as Brett's, that he was host and not merely a visitor like herself, though he did live in town most of the time. Again and again he had assured himself he was not afraid of Brett any longer, but he had never really believed it.

'So you're Joyce?' Brett put out a large firm hand and grasped the girl's, though she had not offered it. 'Nick's talked of you so much,' he added, inaccurately, 'that I feel I know you already.'

'Then we can dispense with formalities.' The girl smiled faintly in return and withdrew her hand. To Nick's anxious ears her voice sounded slightly shaken.

'That'll suit me,' drawled Brett. He searched her face with his dark eyes, which gave him a slightly hooded look with a hint of mystery which Nick felt flattered him. There was nothing mysterious about Brett, he told himself resentfully. He was simply a fine, well-built, intelligent animal, who knew what he wanted and took it. The old anger began to rise in him like an insidious fever he was powerless to check. Something like a recurrence of malaria, he thought, but I've no quinine tablets. Only self-control. Whatever happened, Joyce must not suspect.

'Shall we go inside?' Brett was saying. 'Mrs Cowan, the housekeeper, has had the kettle boiling for at least an hour.'

Joyce smiled dutifully and, as though anticipating the offer of Brett's arm to assist her up the steps, slipped her hand through Nick's. Quite unperturbed, Brett took the other arm, saying apologetically: 'They made steps pretty steep in the old days, didn't they?'

For a moment Nick had the impulse to snatch the girl away.

Then restrained himself. They couldn't begin fighting over her like those damned cats. He would ignore Brett. After all, he would not have invited the girl out had he not been sure of her.

During afternoon tea, Brett acted as host to both of them. Damn him, thought Nick, simmering, watching how Brett handed round plates with the disarming clumsiness of a man long disused to womenfolk.

As soon as they had finished, Brett rose to his feet.

'Come along, Joyce, and I'll show you around. Nick, nip up and put the dog on the chain will you? He'll drive us crazy besides spoiling Joyce's frock with his muddy paws.'

For an instant the younger brother hesitated, rebellion darkening his face, tingling all over him until he thought the girl must notice. You chain up Nippa, he fancied himself saying to Brett in a clear determined voice. He's your dog. Joyce is *my* visitor, I'm showing her around.

Instead, he found himself walking stiffly away towards the kennel, his stomach sick with self-contempt.

When he returned, Brett was guiding the girl round the garden.

'Used to be a show place, once,' he was saying a little sadly, enlisting her sympathy and understanding. 'But, since Mother died, and Nick joined the bank . . . well, one man can't do everything on the place, can he?'

Joyce Carey was looking around with delight, tinged with awe.

'Why, it must have been marvellous,' she cried. 'How could you bear to leave a place like this, Nicky?'

He winced at the implied reproof. She was turning against him already, blaming him for the neglect in the garden. If it hadn't been for him, it would have reverted to bush long ago. Brett would never have raised a hand.

'I did keep it going until I went to work in town, Joyce. A garden like this is a full-time job, you know.'

She only gazed about her wistfully, pulling down a spray of yellow climbing roses to smell.

'It's all so very lovely. What a shame to let it go . . .'

97

'We've an old pensioner living in that camp over there. He does what he can.'

'A garden has to be loved to make it flourish,' the girl was saying dreamily. 'Like people . . .'

For a frightening minute Nick saw how clearly this girl fitted into the garden and the old rambling homestead, as though born there. A golden girl blending into the mellowness of the distant wattle trees, the yellow roses, the deep cream stonework of the homestead, Lalirra, which the black people long ago had named for the sun.

'Come and see the crops,' Brett was suggesting in a half-proprietorial manner. 'They'll be pretty good this year, if we get finishing rains.'

The crops did look good this year, Nick admitted, almost reluctantly, repressing a wish that he had not given up his life here. Then reason intervened. He could never have existed with Brett. Never. Escape was the only way to retain any individuality. Yet the feeling of loss persisted.

They clambered through the nearest fence where there was a little cart track running through the wheat.

'Jove, it *is* good!' Nick found himself exclaiming with a genuine pleasure, forgetting for the moment it was Brett who had ploughed and planted. 'It must be nearly five feet.'

'Yes. More in places. Should go twelve bags.' Brett's voice was laconic, telling the girl that anything he had planted could not be otherwise than excellent.

As they walked along the rutted track, the walls of wheat shut them in a rustling green world, so that even their flesh was tinged with green. The tallest, most arrogant heads of wheat grew some distance from the track and Brett strode purposefully towards them, stalks bowing as he passed. Nick followed close behind, but the stalks flung back from the two in front, stinging his bare arms, admonishing him to respect their master. And all around, pressing in upon him, bearded heads of wheat waved and whispered in the slight wind. Below them, between the furrows, pale golden dandelion faces looked up, even as Joyce looked

98

up with trust and innocence at Brett, who was explaining how he had seeded with the opening rains, gambling on there being good follow-up ones to help the earth make the young crop.

Angrily Nick swung his gaze away from the two figures, across the wide waving fields to where the trees on the uncleared land made a faint grey smudge in the distance, and the sky itself was a pale screen across which lazy clouds drifted, trailing their shadows over the undulating crops below, the dark green of wheat and the silver green of barley.

A robin skimmed past in a blur of scarlet and brown and Nick's eyes followed it involuntarily, wondering whether it was the same one he had seen so often near the shearing shed. But for Brett and the girl, nothing else mattered but this moment, filled with the sweet fructifying smell of wheat and the warm heady yeast of germination. He saw the two in front of him stop, whilst his brother pointed out a nest of field mice amongst the wheat stalks; quite naturally he dropped a hand on her shoulder, and she looked up at him as he spoke, with his slow deep countryman's voice explaining how the mice usually moved their young long before the rumble of tractors announced that harvesting was upon them. To the younger man's imagination the girl seemed to sway gracefully towards his brother, with the same compliance as the rich green wheat to the casual wind.

Brett stood there, brown and ruddy, with the brown of the earth on his thick shoes and its colour in his dark eyes, his vigour and strong male sweat seeming part of the primitive forces of the soil. The girl grew giddy with the throbbing power of the life forces around her and was afraid: she straightened suddenly, pushed her hair back from her forehead and said, looking around her:

'Where are you, Nicky? I feel a little faint . . . I must be allergic to wheat pollen, I guess.'

She tried to laugh and forget the breathless moment which had hung between herself and Brett, to brush it off as casually as she had brushed off his hand upon her shoulder.

All the way back to the homestead she laughed and chattered, reminding Nick of the play they were in together, of the dance that would wind up the golf season. Nick understood that she was seeking to exclude Brett from that other world in which they had come to know and love each other and in which they expected to live the rest of their lives. He knew she was trying also to make up for that moment she and Brett had shared amongst the quivering wheat, when he had stood apart from them both, watching.

When it was time to leave, she kissed him lovingly in front of Brett and he felt the freshness of her skin and the softness of her hair against his mouth. And, suddenly, Nicholas sensed in her something not there before, a faint gust of passion, the sweet fecundity of ripening wheat.

He looked across her shoulder and saw his brother watching. And hated him, because he knew that Brett knew also: Brett, the farmer, who had planted the seed and knew with a certainty what to expect at the harvest.

LYNDALL HADOW
(1903-1976)

Lyndall Hadow was born in Kalgoorlie, Western Australia, into a literary family. Her mother was a journalist and the organiser of the first Women's Labour League on the goldfields. Her father edited a socialist journal and her brother, Donald Stuart, also became a writer. Hadow worked as a commercial traveller and was matron of a government native settlement before starting her career as a writer. As well as editing the magazine *Our Women*, she wrote numerous short stories, reviews and critical articles. The Western Australian branch of the Fellowship of Australian Writers created the Lyndall Hadow Award for short stories in 1977 in her honour. Some of her stories are collected in *Full Cycle and Other Stories* (1969). In these stories Hadow writes with sympathy about the assimilation of southern European migrants into Australia, the problems of the Aborigines, and relationships between men and women.

'Full Cycle' first appeared in *Meanjin* in 1950. It is a poignant story of a woman's helplessness and dependence upon men.

FULL CYCLE

Maria Mostachetti was married on Easter Monday. It was a full wedding with two bridesmaids, her cousins Fanni and Lenie and her younger sister, Rosie, for matron-of-honour. The reception at home was a hearty affair. Old Mosta, the richest vigneron in the Wannanup district, made sure that this last giving in marriage from his house should be as generously festive as the other three had been. Perhaps there was mingled with his generosity a feeling of guilt as he looked at his eldest daughter in her bridal finery, tall and spare, her face under its make-up flushed with the knowledge that this time she wore the veil and not the sober attire of the woman of the house organising its hospitality in a younger sister's honour. Four times in the twenty years since Mama Mosta had died, Maria had stood with the old man to receive the guests; three times she had remained to manage the Mostachetti household: this time she would leave the bungalow, no longer concerned with its routine—a routine she'd carried on in Mama's way; a routine dictated by the law that Papa's comfort came first because Papa was the man who made the living for them all; and by the seasonal nature of the vineyard's bounty. Last season Maria and the Genucchi girl had fed the six pickers on the side veranda, three times a day and twice in the field. Not for old Mosta the squalid batching in their huts; he had long since proved that seasonal workers who existed on cold, tinned food didn't get the crop through in such good time as those who fed on Maria's meat pies, rich with gravy, walled by juicy greens; and more, old Mosta liked everyone on his place to be warm and happy.

Warm and happy. Certainly all the guests at Maria's wedding were so; talking, laughing, dancing, drinking, eating and drinking again. The old man looked furtively at his eldest daughter, forty-year-old Maria, and the guilt feeling grew. At his side the Genucchi

102

girl, soon to be his wife, smiled boldly and very sure of herself. Next season wouldn't see her feeding the pickers on the veranda and she'd said as much; but old Mosta, savouring again the firmness of her shapely leg under his exploring fingers, and remembering her masterly handling of the situation, thought 'No matter about the seasonal men. Fix all that later.' Now the Genucchi girl, in a voice in which triumph was concealed with care, said in his ear, 'Papa, Maria is going to change now. Soon she will be gone.' Looking into each other's eyes, desire answering desire, Papa Mostachetti and the Genucchi girl both knew that Maria's going would be final. The guilt feeling that had nagged at her father since her marriage had first been arranged, died with her disappearance from the Mosta home.

Maria and Toni Gaspari went to a city hotel for what remained of the night. Next morning they left for Toni's farm.

Toni had come to Western Australia to work on the woodline up on the goldfields. As soon as he could say in English to a pannikin boss, 'Here is ten pound; I want-a da job on your mine', he began work as a bogger, underground, at sixteen-and-ten a shift. When he could say, 'Here is twenty pound' the pannikin boss knew he wanted a machine; and he got one. Then his fortnightly pay envelopes held twenty and thirty pounds. When he married Lucy, the daughter of his friend the boss, he turned in the mining game and opened a workshop where he made domestic furniture for a shop in Hannans Street—the cabinet-making being his trade that he'd learnt at home in his own country. Lucy died and Toni went on making furniture and putting his money on the horses with little profit. When the war came, because he hated the fascisti who had made life miserable for his own old people, he worked like two men in the Civil Construction Corps, up north; when it was over he came down to Perth with £2000 in the bank and a houseful of solid furniture made by his own skilled hands. With this as his capital, Toni made it known to his community in the city that he wanted a farm on the coast—something mixed. Not vines—he knew nothing about vines—something with a citrus grove and spare land for sheep.

His father had had sheep, back home, and his father before him. Also, he wouldn't mind if there were some uncleared acres; heavy jarrah where he could sell the timber rights and clear the land and sow down clover for dairy cattle. Also he wanted a wife.

At the National Club where he went each day, they offered him vineyards and dairy farms and market gardens and poultry farms. He met the Genucchi girl on a moonlight river picnic in aid of Southern European war orphans. He enquired about her, but the girl was looking for someone of her own age or better still, someone nearer the grave; someone in either case with more than Toni Gaspari had to offer. Toni Gaspari, forty-five, strong, virile, with a £2000 farm and a houseful of furniture, savoured of a long life of hard work; and the Genucchi girl, one of a family of ten reared on a Spearwood market-garden, joined the Mostachetti establishment as general help to Maria. Now, at eighteen, she saw in Toni the ideal husband for Maria; and Maria, forty, tall, spare, angular and with a hare-lip that had never been attended to, saw the writing on the wall.

Toni bought a place in the Lower Bindering valley: two hundred acres, a small citrus grove and pastures. There was also good garden land. His next-door neighbour had made £1000 clear on the Singapore market with dry cabbage, the season before. Toni flexed his magnificent muscles and said what others could do, he could do. Maria said she was a good cook and would see that he and his men were well fed, always.

They arrived at the farm in the late morning. Maria had seen the house once, when she and Toni and some of the Mosta cousins and the Genucchi girl had come up to measure the floors for covers and the windows for curtains: and to drink Toni's wine. The furniture had been sent up and all the wedding presents and Maria's store of linen that she'd been collecting since her mother gave her the first bedspread of drawn-thread work when she turned fourteen. Absorbed in the arranging of her home, Maria had been on the place for a couple of days before she realised there were no men there; and a week had passed before she knew that their absence was a permanency. To work these acres

104

there were but two pairs of hands—her husband's and her own.

In May, Maria knew she was having a baby. She told her husband and he laughed boisterously. 'That's a' right. Make-a da strong boy . . . help on da farm.'

Maria wanted to hear him say he would get her some help in the paddocks—someone to milk the cow for the house; someone, even, to gather the firewood in the wheelbarrow after Toni had cut it; someone to water the kitchen garden; someone to carry the heavy buckets of mash to the fowls. After the first week, when nothing had been said of relieving her of any of these duties, she waited for him to say he would get a girl to help her in the house—a young girl, perhaps a child of their community who had no mother, who needed training in the art of good housewifery. She could teach her to make the risotto and the ravioli and the minestrone that hard-working men needed; and the chicken pies with liver; she had a way with rabbits done in wine that the girl could learn; and the Australian grilled steak with onions. Any girl who followed her through the processes of laundering the great linen sheets and the bedspreads and the table linen that was her pride would know how these treasures should be cared for in a good home. Yes, any girl who learned from Maria would go to her own home some day, richly dowered with the art of keeping house; she would be a lucky girl. Maria waited from day to day to hear her husband say he would get such a girl for her. After the second week she knew there would be no help.

In June Toni, who understood how to go about such matters, received his licence to plant potatoes. He had applied for three acres and he was allowed two. Maria heard him ordering a ton of seed and a ton of potato manure from the carrier who brought the superphosphate for the clover paddocks. Maria had never seen potatoes planted before; in the vine country where she had lived all her forty years, people made enough money from dried fruits and wine grapes without bothering about so humble a crop. Toni, seeing her surprise, said angrily, 'Da Board she pay da good price for da potatoes. She is da good way to make-a da money, quick. I get da twenty ton.'

The seed arrived and was stacked in the open shed—twenty bags of it stacked next to the potato manure. 'When does it have to be planted?' she asked. Toni said, 'Plant 'im right-away.' He ripped open a bag and the seed spilled out—round, small, clean new potatoes. 'But da first,' he grumbled as he slit another, 'first cut-a da big ones.'

Next morning as Maria went to the sink to wash the breakfast dishes—his plate with its rime of thick bacon fat and egg yolk, her cup of half-touched tea, Toni said, 'You leave-a da dishes, Maria. You make-a da start on da potatoes.' She stared at him without moving. He went to the door and threw his heavy jacket over his shoulder. 'Dat-a paddock, I plough 'im last-a week. Now I cultivate 'im and put-a da dam harrows on 'im. You cut-a da seed; I plant 'im tomorrow.' Still she stared stupidly. 'You not know how to cut-a da potato seed, eh? You come, see your Toni, see him cut-a da seed.'

For a week she cut potatoes. The bags were too heavy for her to move so she half-emptied them by hand and then spilled the rest on the bench, folding the bag neatly and stacking it with the super and chaff sacks, for Toni reminded her that bags cost a shilling each and must be saved. She sat at the bench and cut mechanically; every piece must have two eyes; it must be sound. The cut pieces she spread on the cement floor and left them to callous; daily she collected them and threw them into a bin, ready for Toni to take to the paddock in bags, when they had begun to sprout. Sometimes the smell of the unsound pieces which she put aside in a bucket grew so heavy that her head swam and she would feel so nauseated that she would have to leave the bench and go into the house; but there the sight of unmade beds and unwashed dishes brought such a feeling of desolation and helplessness that she would return to her job in the shed.

They lived on tinned meat and boiled eggs during that week. Toni said he didn't care what he ate so long as he was able to get the land ready and the crop in; he'd worked harder on less, sometimes, in the C.C.C. But tinned meat made Maria's stomach turn and after the first few days she took time off to bake a pie. Toni ate it but he roared that such things were a waste of time and Maria should stay up that night and finish the job. She finished it at midnight and crawled into bed without a bath and without undoing the plaits that coiled on her aching head. Toni came to bed later, after a long tussle with a hand plough he hoped to use for digging furrows, but by that time she was asleep and snoring.

It was early June and the Lower Bindering valley still retained some of the warmth of autumn. Toni's potato paddock lay on a hillside, over the rise from the house. Across the scrub it faced westward to the line of distant hills that marked the coast—the scrub and the dunes that hourly changed in colour and form, it seemed, as morning mist, midday sun and afternoon cloud swept over them. In the banksia groves that edged the paddock, wood pigeons flirted and minahs chattered companionably; an occasional flash of colour was a redbreast, incredibly dainty in a scene so virile. On the slope above the paddock, acres of ringbarked jarrahs stood statuesque in their grey immobility, home of the joyous magpie and night-hooting owl; and the blackboy grass-trees added their grotesquerie to the scene. Nothing of the beauty of Toni's potato paddock touched Maria. For her the trellised acres, flat and unvistaed, of her father's vineyard, his ordered house, its warmth and comfort; the companionship of the small community which centred around him—his men and their womenfolk and their children; field-hands, packers, truck-drivers and the seasonal hands. Now here—herself and her deep, silent husband and a paddock in the bush.

Two acres to be planted in rows two feet apart; each row to be three-hundred feet from end to end. 'I plant-a da one-hundred-and-fifty rows,' Toni said as they stood on the headland that first morning. Maria looked at the ploughed field uncomprehendingly. Under a Christmas tree he had dumped the bags of seed and a supply of potato manure; eighteen bags there were of the superphosphate, each weighing 200 pounds. Little Bess had carted it all in the rubber-tyred farm cart, up and over the ironstone rise from the house, following the track that the plough and cultivator had cut a week before. Three trips Little Bess had made in the day and she was tired already from her work in the implements with Brownie. Brownie was a medium draught and used to farm work, while Little Bess had never done anything more than take the cart in to the siding on Saturdays, before Toni bought her. She found it as much as her strength would stand to pull with Brownie in the plough; Maria had watched one day. While Toni took four puffs of his cigarette at the end of each furrow and the big horse chewed capeweed on the headland, Little Bess stood with head down, sides panting, distressed with over-exertion. So when the seed and super had to be carted, Maria had asked, 'Couldn't Brownie take that load?' Toni had replied, 'I'm-a da horse-boss round here. Dat Brown, he no good for da cart, anyway. Kick-a da bloody shafts out.' So the mare carted the super and seed and Toni distributed the bags around the field on the headlands, ready for use on that first day. 'I plant-a one hundred and fifty rows.'

Maria asked, 'What do I have to do?'

Toni said, 'I dig-a da trench; you plant-a da potato; you put-a da super in da trench; I put-a da dirt back in da trench. She easy.'

Maria put the seed in. Once, years ago, when the red mite had ruined the green crops of the Spearwood district and only the potatoes remained to bring in a living for the market gardeners there, Maria had heard of the wives and daughters helping in the field. She had heard them laughing about it, later. 'It's easy. You sling a bag over your shoulders and walk along the rows and drop the spuds in.' Maria remembered this as she started off along the first furrow behind her husband as he dug it. 'What-a you do, silly bitch-a?' Toni stopped in his grunting progress with the long-handled shovel. 'What-a you t'ink? Da potato, she is not-a da stone. She is put in dis-a way.' He knelt on the ground, and placed a piece of seed carefully in the trench, cut surfaces to the earth, the outer skin only exposed. Maria realised that each piece needed individual planting; there were 150 rows, each

300 feet long, and the seed was planted fifteen inches apart.

The days passed. Maria walked and knelt and slung a bag with seed in it, in front of her; she found that imposed a strain on her shoulders, so she changed the seed to a kerosene tin. She spread superphosphate in the trenches; she filled in the trenches; she took turn at all but the digging. At the end of the first week she worked, slept and ate without thinking of what she did, her mind a turmoil of hatred for her husband, fear for her baby and plans for escape. Hating Toni affected their daily lives little. During the day he worked mechanically, scarcely speaking except to tally the rows; at night he slept in the room off the back veranda; Maria, he said, snored too loudly and disturbed him with her tossing. Fear for her baby seemed groundless; apart from muscular tiredness, she had to admit she had no symptoms that a forty-year-old expectant mother should not have. As for escape plans—she knew there was no escape: the Genucchi girl barred the only way.

The work was not going fast enough for Toni. One morning he decided to hasten the trenching by using the single furrow mouldboard plough he had at last reconditioned. Maria was too tired to make any comment when he put Little Bess in and started off behind her. She stopped in her work when she heard him bellowing at the mare: Little Bess's first furrow was as crooked as a kangaroo's hind leg, and in the middle of it, she'd jibbed. Toni searched for a stick in the headland and went back and beat the animal, slowly, dispassionately. Maria dropped her tin of potatoes and ran down the paddock. 'Stop, Stop it.' She felt every blow he gave the patient beast. 'Stop it, Toni. Stop it, I say.' Toni dropped the stick, punched Little Bess on the nose so she whinnied with sick pain. He turned to his wife. 'You get-a back to da work.' The horse moved on but the furrowing was not a success, and Toni went back to the spade.

That night Maria crept out while Toni slept. She went to the stable with a can of oats and, petting Little Bess, wept on her shoulder.

Before the last rows were in, the weather changed. Winter

came to the valley. Toni worked mechanically but Maria had to make a conscious effort to battle against the wind and rain. The wind blew the superphosphate into her eyes and hair; the rain caked it in the tin and made it difficult to handle; the wet, heavy earth clogged her hands and her shoes; dry candlewood branches were tossed across her path as she walked in the morning through a wind squall to the potato field; the house was cold and cheerless when they returned at night. Vehemently she cursed the valley, the rain, the wind, her husband, her father and the Genucchi girl.

When the last potato was safely covered in, Toni looked at his paddock from the rise. 'Next year, I plant-a four acres.' Maria looked with sick loathing at the long, even rows of hilled earth. 'Never again,' she said to herself. 'Never again. Not another potato will I ever help to plant.'

The baby was born in midsummer. Maria, remembering her age and the old wives' tales expected there would be pain; she brought forth a strong, lusty child with more agony of spirit and body than even Mama Mostachetti had prepared her for; and Mama had borne six. Maria shuddered at the thought as she looked back on the hours just past; and that her first. How could a woman's life be the same after that experience? How could a woman face a second or a third childbearing? 'Perhaps they're stronger than I am. Perhaps they're not so old. Mama was only as old as I am now, when she died.' Her mind was harassed with her thoughts. Perhaps she hadn't prayed long enough, hard enough? She would talk to the matron, the doctor; she would talk to Toni—and the priest. Whatever they said or did or told her to say or do, she made a vow to herself, there would never be another for Maria Gaspari.

Toni said to the matron, when she took him to the nursery to see his daughter, 'She is-a da fine Australian, yes; but she is-a no use for da farm. Next time I make-a da boy.'

Autumn came again over the Lower Bindering valley in warm, still days with never a hint of winter cold or rain in their sunny hours; flowering red gums massed with blossom, white like clouds

110

against the cloudless sky, were vibrant with the comings and goings of honey bees; the slow, still autumn days went on and the nights were bright with stars. On the Gaspari farm, Toni sowed clover and pruned citrus trees and mended and repaired. Maria swept and polished and cooked and laundered and sewed and watched the baby in the sunshine. The potato crop had been successful; they'd had two weeks at the sea in late summer; and Toni had promised her a girl to help her in the house.

It was after the dinner dishes had been put away one night and the fire drawn, that Maria took her knitting to the back veranda and settled in the early dusk to rest. Toni came in from the horse paddock. He was angry, surly; she could see it in his face and hear it in the short, sharp stamp of his heavy feet as he came up the steps. 'Dat Bess. I take-a da cheek out-a dat bitch. Tomorrow she go in-a da plough.'

'Where are you ploughing now, Toni?' She wasn't interested. She hoped he wouldn't waken the baby with his stamping, but it was as well to ask.

'Where you t'ink I plough? I tell-a you today. Four acres I got for da potatoes. That-a girl from the Orphans' Home— she come up next week. You help-a cut da potato and help-a plant 'im.' He walked into the room he had used since the baby was born. She heard him throw himself on the bed. She put her knitting down. It would be a pleasant change from the house to work in the field; the weather was lovely out-of-doors. A pleasant change.

The baby stirred and she went to calm it. A lovely girl, sunbrowned and with eyes as black as Toni's, hair in tight little curls like his, and a perfect mouth. A beautiful girl . . .

She passed Toni's door. In the dusk the room was blurred but she could smell the man smell of him, hear his heavy breathing. 'Come here, Maria,' he called. 'Tonight we have-a da try for da boy, eh?' 'Yes, Toni, yes,' she agreed, and closed the door.

'SARAH CAMPION'
(MARY ROSE COULTON)
(1906-)

'Sarah Campion' was born in England and worked as a teacher in England, Canada and Germany. She lived in Australia for only three years (1938-1940) before marrying a New Zealand writer and settling in New Zealand.

Though Campion wrote many novels, only her trilogy, beginning with *Mo Burdekin* (1941), has an Australian setting. It was an impressive and detailed account of the Australian countryside and way of life.

Stories by Campion were published in *Southerly* in 1952 and 1953. 'Amble' is about domestic servants in an Australian household and, while it does not demonstrate Campion's skill in describing landscape, it does show her skill as a satirist.

AMBLE

We of the Servants' Hall are not so much superior to the great ones beyond the green baize door as a race apart. We eat different food, off different crocks, with different tools, and at different hours of the day: when the great ones have finished nourishing themselves in the dining-room we do not, as is popularly supposed, fall-to like wolves upon their broken meats, but eat in our own good time our own specially cooked dishes, taking care to be as leisurely as we wish. Underline the leisure: it is our prerogative. The Big Chief, or Old Jellybags as Amble calls our employer, may be at the mercy of any caller with an axe to grind, a plaint to make, or a bee in the bonnet needing release: but we are not. When such a caller calls at mealtimes and is ushered into the study by Amble, Old Jellybags must rise from his seat, wipe his mouth, and leave his dinner to cool while he listens to the reason for the visit. His is a public ear, he's paid for the use of it: and the public see to it that the cash is earned. But we of the Servants' Hall—we live as best we can on the meagre wage which dribbles from Jellybags' pocket, and are by no means too proud to make sure that we have leisure for our meals. When, at these mealtimes, Jellybags' piping organ-note of need comes wistfully down the hall towards the green baize door—when Amble hears our employer bleating 'Amb-ool!'—he does not immediately rise from his food. Not he. With a shrug and a good-natured obscenity or two he stays just where he is: and after ten years or so of this (since the English mind is slower than the Australian to accept inevitables) Old Jellybags will realise the futility of calling for his butler at that butler's mealtimes.

This Amble is my solace, he is so steadily himself. Most of us are undecided, either uneasily English or furtively 'continental'; but Amble has no scruples whatever about being a dinkum Aussie.

Lean, stringy, with tufted sandy hair and a roving sardonical blue eye, he has also a pleasingly irreverent tongue. His humour spares no one, neither our employers, Jellybags and Momma: nor our difficult and forever-on-the-point-of-giving-notice house-parlourmaid, Gertrud: nor even me, the precious Cooky. I may be conscious, as I sweat my way through a seventy-two hour week for a two-pound wage, that I am the thirteenth cook this household has had in five years, and that I shall do nothing to prevent its having a fourteenth, so soon as I have found myself somewhere better to go: while everyone else in the Servants' Hall knows how precious I am and treats me with careful tenderness lest I up and leave them in a huff. But Amble is held in by none of these considerations. He subjects me to that easy flow of blistering comment and affectionate contempt which he pours on everyone but his little English wife: and if I don't like it I can do the other thing.

Amble will do no placating. Mrs Amble treats me delicately and calls me 'Miss' Campion, a courtesy which has only so far been extended to the fourth cook of the line, a Lady Chef who was in the habit of leaving her dentures grinning overnight on the kitchen table: but Amble knows it is not he who will have to go out and comb the agencies of Melbourne if Cooky goes, and, even if it were he, he still would not forego for one moment the sharp pleasure of his tongue.

So, I get the weight of it: a Pommy is always fair game for an Aussie. It is Amble who incites the butcher's lad to march straight into the kitchen, slap a bleeding, naked sirloin on the kitchen table, and go through the motions of a smacking kiss while crying 'It's all for you, Sweetheart!' This is a bracer for my watery Old World democracy: Amble will have me a true democrat before I leave. It is Amble who comments at least once a day on my freckles, thus disciplining vanity: Amble is a noted taker-down of females. It is Amble, finally, who adds pithy comments to my little daily list for Momma headed 'Kitchen Wants', thus:

114

SR flour
B. powder
grd. ginger
LOVE,

the last in Amble's hand, embellished with a few pierced hearts, arrows of affliction, and other symbols of erotic yearning.

It's true, our kitchen and our Cooky both lack love—but only Amble would be cheerfully cruel enough to point this out.

He spares none, least of all those distinguished guests for whom our state dinners are given. The whole establishment east of the green baize door will be in an uproar for days, humming with preparations for feeding a governor-general, a lord, or an archbishop's widow: the frigidaire will bulge unseemly with chickens, oysters, Norwegian creams made by me in despair and blind-eyed sleepiness the night before; the whole floor will bloom with enamel bowls containing water and French beans, it being Mrs Amble's vain but pious hope that the vegetables will thus remain crisp: the smell of scorching linen will blue the air while Gertrud irons her seen and unseen smalls: but still, in this female bedlam, Amble keeps far crisper, cooler than the beans. The women can fret themselves to a frazzle if they will, he contains himself in easy contempt till the night itself, there and then to use all his powers to garner everything he can for our lewd entertainment. Which is the only reward we shall ever get for hours of overtime, lost nightly sleep, and a general feeling, on the day after, of having been put through the mangle.

See Amble, then, on one such gala night. It is the night upon which we jointly lay our fancy for the Melbourne Cup, and I can see it all as clearly now, and smell it, almost, as if I were back there on an antipodean evening, with the drizzle plopping from the Moreton Bay fig-trees outside the window, the smell of drenched lemons wafting in from the kitchen-garden through the door we have opened to let out steamy kitchen heat and let in steamy winter air—I can see it all so clearly, and Amble at the head of the table pluming himself in full rig.

115

We are discussing the dinner-party he has just successfully brought to the coffee-and-brandy stage beyond the green baize door. Amble, as always on these occasions, strikes the eye as remarkably fine: his bosom glinting like a skating rink, his sandy hair stunned into smoothness by Vicar's Violet Pomatum, his blacks extravagantly black.

It is his night. The ladies hang upon his lightest quip—Bessy the little outback parlourmaid, flushed from handing round vegetables and sweets while holding her unworthy breath (an exercise, this, demanded from all her parlourmaids by Momma)— Gertrud the housemaid with her dark Swiss countenance and her bristling Swiss moustache—Cooky smouldering as warmly as her own oven—and an anonymous lady, all ears, known to us as 'The Occasional'. To these, and with relish, Amble is describing the person of the chief guest, a brigadier's relict.

'Looks too young to be the Ma of that great gawpy galoot she brought along—musta had her face lifted. Dress wanted lifting, too—when I handed her the entree I hardly knew where to put me eyes. Old Jellybags did, though; his was poppin' like organ stops. He'd have ordered her outa the house if she'd bin a Nobody— comin' here dressed like that, gapin' all the way down to Glory. Cripes, you shoulda seen Aggie, too: skipped her bath again, the young weasel, and only washed half of her neck, and that in a hurry.'

Gales of giggles from the ladies. Amble, very much the gentleman, leans back, lights one of Jellybags' cigars, lounges there puffing it and carelessly ignoring the eye of Mrs A. She, suddenly intimidated by his shirt front, changes the intended glare for a smirk of wifely pride; and basks awhile, with a hazy expression, in the reflected glory of her man.

'However,' continues the hero, 'let joy be unconfined, let giddy merriment be you-know-what, for the Honourable Mrs has expressed herself in a Honorarium. Order what you like, ladies, order what you like: it's on the house.'

And he holds up a coin. It is a florin.

Being somewhat new to the strict Trades Union rules of the

Servants' Hall, and altogether new to Australia, I am about to say that I think this is rather nice of the Honorable Mrs, when the slow flush on Mrs Amble's cheek checks me. Mrs Amble has a face like a bee's, all proboscis and brooding darkness: if you can imagine a bee blushing, you have Mrs A to perfection during this awkward moment. She not only reddens in spite of herself, but she must also allow tears of outrage to soften the serpent steadiness of her eyes.

'The Jezebel gave you that—for all of us?' says Mrs Amble at last.

'Don't take it so hard, ole girl, she meant well. I've spent a considerable time working it out,' adds her spouse with heavy haste, 'and it comes to fourpence apiece.'

'We can put it on an 'orse,' cries Gertrud suddenly, her face aglow. But for the fatal lure of Tattersall's, poor Gertrud would have got home to Zurich many years before.

Mrs Amble plunges from the table and stumps about in the butler's pantry, slapping all the wineglasses and tumblers onto the wrong shelves. She always does this in a crisis, and lovely is the calm with which Amble puts them all back again, next day.

Our heads are hung together over the evening paper, while Amble jabs a black-nailed forefinger down the column.

'Sum Bust!' he crows, 'Sum Bust! That's it! What a name eh, what a name! And, though I'm not allowed to talk about it (Mrs A being fussy as you know) I wish you'd all of seen it for yourselves, acres and acres of it, with the Mongdayseer powder lying on it in drifts like the snows on Mt Kosciusko! Sum Bust, I'll say it was! That's the horse for us.'

Unfortunately, no; for Sum Bust proved its name too nearly, suffering at the beginning of the race a form of lackadaisical stupor which just allowed it to bring its head as far as the starting tapes, no more. Amble explained this disaster in great technical detail and a wealth of horsy anecdote; but most of us agreed with Mrs Amble that it served us right. We shouldn't have soiled ourselves by taking the money, in the first place.

MARJORIE ROBERTSON
(1908–1956)

Marjorie Robertson, the daughter of a mining engineer, was born in Western Australia but grew up in Sydney. When her marriage dissolved in the 1930s, she became an editor for a firm of legal and medical publishers. In collaboration with a barrister, Mary Cecil Woods, she wrote *Leaves from a Woman Lawyer's Casebook* (1947) using the pseudonym Marjorie Woodson. In 1946 she transferred to her firm's London office, and she lived in England for the rest of her life.

Robertson published one novel, *To Ripen or to Kill* (1953). Her short stories appeared in *Southerly, Coast to Coast* and *Modern Australian Short Stories*, and were collected in *In One Town* (1946). Most of her stories are set in Sydney and deal with domestic situations. Robertson develops the inner life of her characters and there is little action in her stories.

'First Job' is the story of a young woman exercising for the first time her right to make an important decision regarding her own life. Robertson skilfully and with subtlety presents the central character's vulnerability and the self-protective, almost deliberate isolation of her parents.

FIRST JOB

It had been an advertisement, just an advertisement in the daily paper, and she had answered it. Her mother had said: 'The best thing you can do, my girl, is to get yourself a job . . . moping round the house all day, no use to me or anyone else, as far as I can see . . .' And her father had looked vague when he had been told at dinner, 'The best thing Else can do is to get herself a job, that's what I said to her today. The best thing you can do, my girl, is to get yourself a job . . . moping round the house all day . . . Don't you agree, father?'

She had called him 'father', secretly and shyly, before Else was born. 'Good-bye, father,' she would whisper to him in the mornings when he was leaving to go to work, with a world of meaning in the 'father', and he would kiss her fondly and go down the street with his shoulders squared ready to face the world, ready and eager to wrest a living from it for his own family. But down the years, the 'father', that shy and secret joke between them, had worn itself into a thin, deep groove of habit, and now there was no humour in it, no deference, no urgent need of protection to make her subtle.

Else sat there between the two of them, and her father looked at her with a transient unhappiness stirring in his heart. An unfamiliar feeling this. Usually he went about with an air of silently stealing through the world, not wanting to give trouble to anyone, not wanting anyone to be put out by his being on earth. He escaped notice and he escaped deep feeling in that way. He seemed to have said to emotion, 'I'm not worth troubling about . . . don't you worry about me . . . I'll just hang about.' And emotion had long ago decided that he was not worth powder and shot.

Now he looked at Else, at the dark fine hair, long and silky, hanging low on her neck, at the dark line of lashes hiding the dark eyes, at the fine, sallow skin flushing slightly as her mother talked. He could remember her as a tiny thing, dressing up, playing the fine lady calling on him. She would come knocking at the front door, dressed in a ridiculous old coat that her mother had worn on her honeymoon, shaped well in at the waist and flaring out in exaggerated billows round her thin thighs. Else would stand there solemnly, tilting up her head at him to peer with grave dignity from under the brim of a huge hat with a bedraggled feather curling round the crown. He would invite her to come in and they would sit stiffly in the best room and talk about the weather and his wife's health and his little girl. Then she would get up and, swaying across the room to him, she would shake hands and go as gravely as she had come.

Was she happy now, he wondered? What was she thinking about, now, this moment? He didn't, he realised, know her very well. And peering short-sightedly at his wife, he wondered what she was thinking. He didn't, he thought, with a sense of shock, know her very well, either. Grown-up people didn't know each other very well, he decided, and he trembled for a moment on the brink of sentiment. He nearly tried to get to know them both, to gather them to him, to love and protect and understand them. That shy, defenceless look on Else's face, that unlined, unmoulded softness that looked as though it would bruise so easily, stirred his imagination. He only had to take that softness between finger and thumb, he felt, and it would mark. He should do something about it. He knew he should do something.

With gratitude he heard his wife's voice start again and he was able to stop thinking. 'I said to her, when I was your age, I was earning . . . sixteen shillings a week, too, which was a lot for a young girl in those days. You just get the paper in the mornings, my girl, I said, and we'll see what's doing.'

In bed that night, just as he was sinking deeper and deeper into the softness of the mattress with the feeling of being absorbed into a huge nothingness creeping through him, his wife's voice floated, reassuringly familiar, over and above the nothingness, helping him to slide unobtrusively into sleep. 'I said to her, now you take care of yourself, my girl, now that you're going out into the world. There's not to be any carryings-on, mind you. Men will take advantage of you, if you give them any encouragement, my girl. Men, I said, are like that. You keep yourself to yourself, my girl, and see that you're treated with proper respect. No one, Henry, even though I do say so, no one can say I haven't done my best for that girl. Even you, Henry,' she said, building him up in her mind into a critical, carping monster of a man, 'even you, Henry, must admit . . .' And then Henry was completely absorbed into nothingness and became one with its silence.

'Now this,' said her mother the next morning, placing her finger firmly over a tiny advertisement down near the end of the long column, 'now this sounds the very thing.' The advertisement read 'Young girl, artistic, learn retouching, small salary to begin,' and the address of a photographer.

'Now that's just the very thing for you, Else. Why, when I was a young girl, I was always considered the artistic one of the family . . . real talented, if only I'd had the opportunity . . . why, the lovely flowers and things . . .'

'What,' said Else, in a firm small voice, 'what is retouching?' And she looked up into her mother's face to find that it had become completely expressionless like a pond that a sudden wind, rising and dying, has smoothed to blankness. Then life and expression came back to it. 'That's just what you're going to be taught, my girl. You can't expect to know these things without learning them. Now off you go . . . and remember, Mr Sayley will give you a reference. A reference from a clergyman is always such a help, I do think. I was speaking to him yesterday and I told him what I'd said to you, "Now the thing for you to do, my girl, is to get a job . . ."'

Else gazed at herself in the blurred mirror in the tiny front hall, straightened her hat, and swallowed an uncomfortable feeling in her throat as though a tiny fish-bone had lodged there . . . but they hadn't had fish for breakfast, not for weeks had they had fish. Then she picked up her handbag and the paper and went slowly, slowly to the train.

They were long, dim, musty stairs leading up to Floor 3, Room 27, Brook's Building—stairs with indefinable grime ground and packed into the cracks and smeared along the once cream walls; stairs that seemed intolerably weary of being stairs, of being used, day in day out, by men going about their strange occupations, getting excited, getting angry, tramping, shouting, stealing along, whispering, unspeakable things in husky voices, threatening, blustering, being smooth and suave and persuasive. Else found her knees trembling long before she stepped onto the landing of Floor 3, and stood on the little square of brown, orange-mottled carpet that seemed to have settled just outside the door of Room 27 a long while ago.

The door was half open, so she took a deeper breath and knocked, and waited. Interminable ages dragged slowly past, her life going with them, until she was standing there watching herself being slowly carried away on a thick oily stream, with no power to rescue herself. Then a thick voice, that seemed like the voice of the stream, said 'Come in . . . go on, come in,' and she took another deep breath and went in.

She sat down opposite him at the huge desk littered with tumbling piles of photographs, hundreds of photographs of cricket teams, and smiling small girls, and tragic-looking big girls, and queer-shaped vases each holding a single rose.

He asked her questions in abrupt gruff spurts of talk, and sat silent in between these efforts. She would answer the questions, and then wait and watch his large dark hands with the black hairs curling stiffly on their backs, watch his hands playing with a tube of paste, jabbing at some green blotting paper with a sharp little knife. He would look up and remember another question, and the question would come jabbing at her, and he would eye her with heavy dark eyes and then look judicially down his great thick nose while he waited moodily for her answer. 'You might do . . . yes, I think you might do . . .' He became abstracted again and started squeezing the tube of paste. Out of the longest silence, he said, 'Look here,' and with sudden energy, he thrust in front of her a large photograph, brown and cream,

122

of a marble pool with a fountain in the middle and trees growing thickly round the far edge. 'Look here, you take this now, take it to the table over there, there near the window . . . and fill in the white spots, carefully, like this . . . fill them in with this . . . I'll be back, I'll be back in, say, oh, say fifteen minutes . . . I'll come back then, and we'll see.' And he was gone.

She heard his feet go thud thudding down the stairs, heard them for a long while until the thuds were small, protesting echoes, muffled, and then silent.

She made idle dabs at the hundreds of white spots for a few minutes. Then she gazed out of the window and then around the room. She stood up and crept stealthily over to a door, stood listening, then breathlessly pushed it open. The room in there was all white walls and cameras and black cloth draped over the tall backs of throne-like chairs. It was very lonely, very cold and very still. The whole place, she felt, as she carefully shut the door, was lonely, and so quiet that she could hear her breath skipping away from her.

She went back to making idle dabs at the white spots for a few more minutes, hundreds and thousands of little white spots spoiling the beautiful smooth brownness of the photograph. Her eyes fluttered away from the spots to another door, and again she crept over the worn grey carpet and opened the door. She hadn't expected anything, hadn't thought of what the room might be or where the door might lead. But this dim, drab room, with its stretcher bed with the grey blankets pulled carelessly over the crumpled sheets, the still dented and crumpled pillow, the old brown chair with the day's paper tossed across it, and a pair of braces lying limply over the back, the battered chest of drawers with brushes and cigarettes and collars and ties and a little pair of scissors in an untidy jumble among the dust . . . this she just stood and looked at, and then she shut the door and went quietly back to the window and the white spots.

It had frightened her, that room, so unexpected, so out of place, so masculine. She thought again of the large, strong hands with the coarse skin and dark hairs, of the dark eyes in the dark-

123

skinned face with its great heavy nose, and she saw that dark face against the crumpled pillow with the drab grey blankets close under the chin.

Steps came thud thudding up the stairs, heavy steps. She stood up and was half-way across the room to meet him as he came in. 'I don't think I would suit, thank you,' she said with a set, stubborn little dignity in the whole of her sallow, small face, and the dark line of her lashes smudged her cheeks with shadow as she looked down and away from him. 'I don't think I would like it . . . I don't think I would like the work at all.' And she slipped past him and out the door and away down the long, dim stairs, her feet just skimming them like two seagulls skimming the waves as they swooped downwards in their flight.

The three of them sat at dinner that night, caught together, held together for the moment, by the pale yellow light, and her mother's voice came dropping into the yellow light like small stones dropping into a pool and disturbing its serenity.

'There's no need to be down-hearted, no need to sulk, just because you've been turned down once, just because you don't suit. There's just as good fish in the sea . . . Why, when I was a girl it took more than one setback to worry me. So tomorrow morning, I said to her, we'll get the paper again and see what's doing. I think,' and she eyed Else with a ruminative look, the look of a man who has been persuaded to buy a horse, 'I think a dressmaker's the thing, just to start with she could help and learn the trade. I think that's just about the thing. When I was a young girl I always was good with my fingers . . . "Give that girl a piece of muslin," Mum used to say, "give her a piece of muslin and a ribbon, and it's a wonder what she can do with them . . . a model!" '

Else flashed one naked glance at her mother's face and then the dark lashes shadowed the cheeks, and Henry, peering at her, felt vaguely unhappy about her again. What was she thinking now, this moment? He didn't know her very well. But he didn't feel again the impulse to get to know her. Watching her, he was faintly puzzled by a difference. That defenceless, easily bruised youngness had altered, and a stubborn, guarded look moulded the lines of the face into firmness. No, he thought, he didn't know her well, not very well; but then, grown-up people didn't know each other well.

KYLIE TENNANT
(1912–1988)

Kylie Tennant was born in Manly, New South Wales, and studied at the University of Sydney. Her many jobs included book reviewer, journalist, assistant publicity officer for the ABC, publisher's literary adviser and editor.

She often tried to live among the people she wrote about, mainly the poor and dispossessed. During the 1930s Depression she took to the roads with the unemployed to collect material for her novel *The Battlers* (1941). For the novel, *Joyful Condemned* (1953), she disguised herself, pretended she was drunk so that she would be arrested and was sent to gaol. She lived in Sydney slums, lived with Aboriginal people and even travelled with itinerant beekeepers to collect material for other novels.

She published nine novels, two books of short stories, a travel book, three books of Australian history and three books for children. Two of her novels, *Tiburon* (1935) and *The Battlers* (1941), won the S. H. Prior Memorial Prize. The latter also won the Australian Literature Society's Gold Medal.

A lecturer for the Commonwealth Literary Fund at universities in Armidale, Canberra, Adelaide and Perth, Tennant was appointed to the Advisory Board of the Fund in 1961. She was a life patron of the Fellowship of Australian Writers and in 1980 was made an Officer of the Order of Australia.

While Tennant has written about many of the underprivileged groups in Australian society, she is not so much preaching political or social reform as presenting the variety and humour of humanity. Her novels are more descriptive than dramatic.

'The Face of Despair', which appeared in the anthology *Australia Writes* (1955), shows Tennant's writing at its best: full of humour and understanding, and presenting a wide range of people and activities.

THE FACE OF DESPAIR

When the waters of the first flood went down, the town of Narbethong emerged with a reputation for heroism. 'Brave but encircled Narbethong holds out,' a city paper announced, and a haze of self-conscious sacrifice like a spiritual rainbow shone over everyone. Women who would ordinarily have used harsh words if a husband came home late to his tea, were cooking for thirty on a spirit stove with the greatest cheerfulness. Families who made a fuss when a guest stayed for the weekend, walked unceremoniously across the bodies of complete strangers lying in rows on their upper landing. The most popular men in the town were the policemen who in an army Duck worked night and day evacuating grateful families. When they could safely descend into the mud, the residents swapped anecdotes and photographs while comparing the height of the water-marks on their wallpaper. There was a feeling abroad that Narbethong had defeated the flood single-handed.

The water receded only gradually. It lurked in backwaters and billabongs that had not been full since the great flood of '98. Below Paddy's Bend there was a new channel which led to lawsuits and trouble over fences. As the river retreated, it scattered its loot, tree-trunks, haystacks, buggy wheels, the carcases of sheep. Neighbours returned any chattels found in their backyards, if they were recognisable. The librarian moved down the thousands of books which had been moved up so hastily that they had to be catalogued all over again. Strong men grunted and cursed as they strove to shift a sideboard or bed which one small housewife in a panic had been able to drag up all by herself.

The farmers, ruined as usual, were trying to find corrugated iron, barbed wire, food for the survivor pigs. Somehow they felt they should live up to the high valour of the flood and hang

127

on until the next cheque came in. Men who had put off painting the house decided they must do something about it. Wives demanded new covers and curtains. Furniture was hosed down; the awful decayed smell lessened a little. The piles of blackened and stinking water hyacinth were carted away. Where silt had formed a deep inlay in the woodwork, owners went over the carving with a clothes-brush. Refrigerators and radios were repaired. 'Look!' the town seemed to say. 'We've come through.' And the editor of the local paper closed his columns to any letter which mentioned silt, afforestation or erosion.

Presently, mile after mile unfolded the heart-lifting green of young oats, potatoes, lucerne. The river, like a silver snake, wriggled back into its bed, coiling along deep below the level leafage so that strangers asked: 'But where *is* the river?' It twisted humbly past the town's backyards collecting the old tins and bottles as usual, forgotten in its deep soil ditch.

The new paint was shining on the houses, most of the elderly people had recovered from their lumbago, the bronchitis epidemic was over; and then, out of all reason, the rain began again. The silver snake down below swelled, took on a new mottled brown skin. In the evenings there were people walking along the path just looking at the river. They said very little. When the rain stopped, even the trees seemed to sigh with relief; but the clerks in the courthouse were already taking their records away in trucks.

Then the river was racing, powerful, hideous. It was over the banks below South Narbethong; it had crept round and taken the town in the rear, cutting the main road so that the buses roared through a foot of water; it came slowly down the gutters of the back streets leaving the embankments still reassuringly dry, but joining puddle to puddle like a miser making an investment. The librarians at the city library set about stripping the shelves of books again and cursed small, ladylike curses.

'It won't come any higher,' old Doctor Riley announced, when his daughter wanted to move the furniture upstairs. He was always gruff and positive and, before he retired, the more a patient failed to respond to treatment, the more positive Dr Riley became. 'I know what I'm talking about. Leave the furniture alone.'

At four o'clock the clouds parted, the sun shone over a landscape of mauve water with the delicate pale green of willows smudging the distance. Here and there what might otherwise have been a rather flat and monotonous expanse was lifted by a pleasing touch of scarlet where a house roof just showed above the waves. In the older part of the town, cars were being loaded, revved up, and raced to higher ground in the new town or the heights towards the gaol. The railway station was an island connected to the mainland by an overhead bridge. And the water began to pour over Dr Riley's doorstep. In half an hour it was a foot deep in the front hall.

'Look at it!' his daughter shouted—she was usually a meek and forbearing woman. 'Not a thing saved.' And she spoke of her father in wrath and bitterness.

The doctor took no notice. He waded into his study and tucked under one arm a supply of cigars, under the other the stuffed trout in its glass case, a trout he had caught in Lake Neish on his trip home to Ireland.

'They say that the dam may break.' His daughter spoke as though this were a judgment on her father.

'Let it,' he grunted, and went upstairs to bed where he stayed smoking philosophically.

Down the main road came sailing a traffic of great clumps of water hyacinth. They swirled straight along the middle of the road importantly passing and repassing each other. The road was now navigable and the current running strong. The police began to go round in their Duck rescuing the inhabitants, but a strong resistance movement was developing. They refused to be rescued. They had had one flood—that was enough.

'But there's a crack in the wall of the dam,' the constable in charge of the Duck explained. 'You could have twenty feet of water down on top of you.'

'If the dam's going to bust,' one householder argued, 'it ain't much use ferryin' us up to the new town. If the dam goes, that'll go too.'

'You get in this boat,' his preserver snarled. 'Come on now.'

Nobody went to bed. In the minds of the townspeople was a picture of a huge grey wall slowly crumbling outwards over the treetops, but they all had a dumb, mutinous feeling that just by staying put they were defying the water to do its worst. They wouldn't shift, no they wouldn't shift, even though they might be swept away. The rain came down as though it was being baled out of the clouds in large celestial buckets, and it looked as though the darkness and the rain were to be the death-watch of Narbethong. But in the face of this renewed malice there was no heroism, only a grim indignation and a kind of dignity.

At the little private maternity home, Annabelle, who did all the cooking and housekeeping for Nurse Aarons, went down into the kitchen to make a cup of tea. 'Never again,' Nurse was saying. 'All these years and the stairs so bad, up and down those stairs keeping the place open, taking up trays and sometimes bad cases, little babies . . . oh dear . . . and their mothers. And now we've had all the walls repapered and new linoleum . . . no, Annabelle, I can't stand it. I can't bear to think of it. The mud . . . it's too much work with my rheumatism. I'll shut the place. I can't start again. I won't. No, not again.'

Meanwhile she continued to tend four mothers and four newly born babies while Annabelle, splashing about in a pair of fisherman's waterproof boots, cooked all she could until the water poured over the stove top.

When Nurse's two brothers came to rescue her in a rowing boat, they opened the front door, and the grandfather clock floated out to meet them like a large and elaborate coffin. They pushed the clock inside again, shut the door and went round the back. Nurse and Annabelle leaned over the balcony rail like two princesses in a tower.

'No, indeed, Charlie,' Nurse said, 'I couldn't leave.'

'But the dam may go.'

'I can't help that. I'm not responsible for the dam. Last time,' Nurse said darkly, 'that linen bedspread floated away and when I went to a bridge party at Mrs Smith's there it was as large as life made into a tablecloth and serviettes. She said it was buried in the mud and not claimed.'

The police came and took the patients off. The police did not seem to realise that they were now identified with the flood, were part of it and shared the feelings it aroused. One of them stood to lift down the patients and lower them while he balanced in the rocking boat. He tried to make one lie down in the bottom of the boat. The woman glared at him. 'How perfectly ridiculous,' she said shortly. 'The idea!' She sat up straight and continued to snort and mutter. None of the patients was pleased about being rescued. They wanted to stay with Nurse. The last to descend, wrapped in a fur coat curiously distended, really threw the young constable into a state of panic.

'Be careful, madam,' he urged. 'Be very careful.'

From the front of the fur coat emerged the striving head of Nurse's cat. He too hated to be rescued.

In the old manse at the end of River Road the wife of Harry Scott, the town's solicitor, was preparing for the siege. They had bought this dilapidated house because Peg was an artist and could see its possibilities. They had done all the repairs themselves, and though there were still part of the bannisters flapping like a rag and a new set of leaks after every shower, the Scotts were proud of their home. Peg had moved up to the attics all the antique bits of furniture picked up cheap at sales, the walnut writing desk, the carved bed, the big mirror from the mantelpiece in the front room. She was plump and jolly and efficient; her husband and small daughter were safe with her upstairs playing rummy and eating sardines. They had plenty of food.

'I want you to remember everything about this, Winnie,' Peg ordered. 'You'll be able to tell your grandchildren. Dad used to tell me how in '98 the boat he was in was nearly shipwrecked in the awning over the chemist's shop.'

From farther up River Road came a raucous chant of boatmen outside the house of a lady of no reputation. 'Come on, Rosie,' they yelled. 'There's eight of us out here waiting for you, Rosie.' But Rosie had already left.

'Mummy,' Winnie observed sedately, 'if the dam breaks I mightn't have any grandchildren.'

'There!' Peg raised her eyebrows dramatically at her husband. 'She takes after you. Always looking on the bright side.'

Their neighbour had seen the patrol boat approaching. 'Wait till I open the gate for you,' he cried hospitably, then gave a startled howl as he stepped into deep water. Peg hoped Winnie would not remember some of the things he was saying.

The boat approached the Scotts' lamplit window. Its own quite dazzling light shone over the dark water and disturbed the ducks sleeping in the wistaria on top of the pergola. The ducks had had a wonderful time eating all kinds of foods, frogs, insects and pieces of soaked pumpkin. Perhaps, Peg thought, it would be too fantastic to paint a picture entitled 'Ducks and Wistaria'. With those orange pumpkins floating in the foreground and the peculiar mauve shade of the water when the sunlight had struck it . . . but, no, no one would believe it.

'Come on, all out,' a dark figure ordered.

'Oh,' Peg groaned with disappointment, 'they can't *make* us go.'

'I think we had better, dear,' Harry Scott apologised. 'After all, the water is level with the veranda roof.' Peg wanted to argue about it. 'I heard they plunge hypodermics in people who refuse to go,' Harry urged. 'Besides, there's Winnie.'

'I won't go without Jessamine,' Winnie said stoutly. Jessamine was her baby doll, complete with bonnet and bootees.

Peg gave in. 'Here,' she said viciously, 'catch!' and flung Jessamine out of the window. The policeman in charge, seeing what he took to be a baby whirling through the air, decided the woman had gone mad. With a yelp of horror he flung himself forward on his knees on the veranda roof and made the catch of a lifetime. He had his revenge a minute later when the efficiently clad Peg in her plaid skirt climbed out the window and found herself suspended from a stout nail. Delicately averting his face the policeman set about freeing her while Harry carried Winnie down. The Scotts sat in dignified silence until their preservers set them ashore on the steps of the Town Hall.

'You'd better take Winnie round to your mother's,' Peg said coldly. 'I'll go to Jane's flat.'

In looks Jane was as unlike her sister Peg as possible. She was frail, beautiful and willowy with a voice that rose to a delicate shriek and long slim hands that she waved vaguely. But both of them were strong as barbed wire. When Peg burst in, Jane had just finished explaining to her husband how she carried all the furniture upstairs again single-handed, and she and Mervyn were arguing over the wall to wall carpet.

'No,' Mervyn said desperately, 'I won't do it. It's too hard to put down again. You know it shrunk last time.' Their flat consisted of a kitchen, the back stairs and two servants' rooms of what had been a great house.

'Too hard to put down!' Jane cried. '*You* never lifted a hand. Mother and I put it down.' She turned to her sister. 'He's only just come in. Never a word as to where he has been all day.'

'I walked over the railway bridge to the heights.'

'What on earth for?'

Mervyn looked confused. He glanced round his home which was furnished with one hard chair. A candle stood on top of a box. 'Had to go somewhere,' he muttered.

'But what did you do all day.'

'I was helping dig a grave,' Mervyn said angrily.

'Whose grave was it?'

'I don't know. For God's sake, Jane! I haven't had anything to eat either.'

Jane immediately became a ministering angel and flew upstairs to find food. While Peg told them her news, Mervyn sat morosely eating bread and hardboiled egg and contemplating in his mind's eye that grave full of water, the red clay, the sucking noise as they pushed in their spades.

Harry Scott came in quietly from bestowing his daughter and reassuring his mother. 'Where do we sleep, Jane?' he asked.

'Oh, anywhere, Harry,' Jane said. 'You might be able to dig out an armchair.'

At least the water was no higher by breakfast time. 'You girls stay home,' Mervyn ordered, as he took Harry off with him to reconnoitre. But the girls could not stay home. Restlessness seized them. There was nowhere to sit, nothing to do. They prowled out, down the main street to the water's edge, meeting little groups who walked to and fro as uneasy as they.

'This is the finish,' one man said to another, looking at the brown lapping flood. His neighbour nodded almost without emotion. 'That's right,' he said. 'The stone finish.' He looked across to where his farm had been, the crops which would have cleared his debts from the first flood, flattened and gulped down; the sodden pumpkins knocking against the back door where nobody was at home, the windows darkened by great piles of water hyacinth crowding its snaky flesh strands against the glass to blur out the light. Then he looked down at his boots, solid boots for solid ground. A froth of yellow soapy bubble piled up about them, an unhealthy froth like that on the glasses of mineral water in the window of a refreshment room. This spume tossed ashore wherever there was a backwater. The farmer kicked at it; some of it flattened, some of it clung to his boot. He wiped it off on the grass, disgusted.

'Let's go across,' Peg said suddenly, 'to the heights.'

The rain was coming down again, beating on their eyelids, running down their necks. But over there beyond the old town the heights were carrying on a normal life. It would be better than standing like this on the edge of a nightmare unable to come or go, standing fascinated in the squalid foam. Occasionally a boat battled across from the new town to the heights, and presently a motor-boat came by with two policemen, one of them the young man who had rescued Peg not so many hours before.

When they reached the heights the passengers disembarked on the steps of a garage and went leaping and scrambling out with the help of their umbrellas. There remained in the boat only Peg, Jane, the two policemen and a little wretched old woman with blue lips. Her feet were bare. She shivered continually sitting huddled up.

'Oh, her poor feet,' Jane whispered. The boat headed towards the gaol. 'But you're not taking her *there*!' Jane cried. 'Oh no. What a shame! All she wants is a good cup of tea. You let her come home with me.'

'She'll be all right,' the policeman assured his indignant passenger. 'Vagrant, see? Got no place to sleep, doesn't belong to anyone.' The little old woman sat dumb. 'Come along, flower,' the young constable said gently, hooking his big hand under her elbow. He walked her ashore, considerately suiting his slow stride to her weak and tottering walk.

But we're all vagrants, Peg thought. We haven't anywhere to go.

'Oh her poor feet,' Jane whispered again. She said no more. Her husband had looked in the face of despair, and for him it had been a hole in the clay filling with muddy water. For the farmer in the thick boots it was the foam in which he had wiped his feet; but for the two women silently watching that little procession stumbling towards the gaol, the tall constable, the poor half-dazed old bit of humanity, the face of despair had blue lips. Despair does not cry out or behave itself unseemly, despair is humble. Its face does not writhe in agony. There is no pain left in it, because it is what the farmer said it was—'the stone finish'.

The rain began again, and now they were over the other side of the flooded town there was nothing to do, nowhere to go.

'We'd better be getting back,' Peg suggested. But the difficulty was to find anyone going over.

'Mervyn and Harry are going to be so mad about this,' Jane sighed. It was getting dark and the lights of the new town came over the waters in a very comfortable and reassuring way. There was a wonderful sunset.

Finally a boat took them off and carried them over to the Town Hall steps. The current seemed not quite so fierce. They hurried up the darkened street and clattered in the back door.

'Where have you been?' Mervyn was so angry that he swore at them. 'Quick! Upstairs. Get upstairs.'

'But we couldn't help it, Mervyn. We're sorry.'

'Sorry? Sorry! We've nearly gone mad. Word's just come through the dam's going any minute. Get upstairs. It's the *dam*, I tell you.'

'Oh dear,' Jane said wretchedly. 'The carpet! I knew we should have taken up the carpet.'

MARY DURACK
(1913–   )

Mary Durack was born in Adelaide and spent the first years of her life in the Kimberley district of Western Australia, where her father was general manager of a large pastoral company. After her education at the Loreto Convent, Perth, she returned to the Kimberleys, where she and her sister, Elizabeth, helped to run the company properties during the Depression. They also collaborated on books about station life.

In 1937 Durack returned to Perth where she worked as a journalist for WA Newspapers Ltd, writing a column for country women and children. From 1938 she worked as a freelance journalist and, after her marriage in the same year, returned to the north. It was then that she wrote *Keep Him My Country* (1955), a novel about a relationship between a white man and an Aboriginal woman, which links Aboriginal and female oppression. It is one of Durack's most significant literary works. Other important works narrate her family's history.

Durack published one adult novel, eight children's stories (illustrated by her sister Elizabeth), eleven works of non-fiction, an opera libretto, a play and some articles and critical works. She was made an Officer of the Order of the British Empire in 1966, and in 1978 was appointed a Dame Commander of the Order of the British Empire and awarded an honorary DLitt from the University of Western Australia.

'The Double Track' shows Durack's understanding and sympathy for Aboriginal people, which is an important theme in her work.

THE DOUBLE TRACK

'My old daddy had seven wives,' Simeon said, 'but there's no doubt about where he went. The mission people got him at the end, put him fair on that straight road to Paradise. Me—I only had the two women all my life, but nobody in the whole world knows where I'll end up.'

Sometimes he looked back on his life, remembering the simple one-road of his youth in which the world was neatly divided into two compartments, Christian and pagan. He, of course, had been confidently established in the former, where he might well have remained had he not taken that one step against his own heart to gain the Grace of God. Although he would not have had it otherwise, he would sometimes think how easy life might have been for him had he done just as he wanted from the start. As it was he had met disapproval on both sides, and had been led at last into the singular situation of having to travel through life by two separate tracks.

It had started that day at the mission when the word got around that Pat Grogan wanted his daughter home again. The letter was on Brother Matthew's desk and one of the girls had read it while tidying his room. Grogan said that Biddy should have completed her education, and he wanted her sent back, with a good, useful half-caste husband. Whispering and giggling had gone on all the time Brother Matthew was making his discreet enquiries. First, he had approached the girl herself to find out whether there was anyone she fancied. Biddy had been too shy to say anything, but he had heard from others that she liked young Ambrose, the good-looking half-caste boy. Ambrose, however, did not share the attraction, and none of the other coloured boys, each approached with what Brother Matthew thought to be the utmost privacy and tact, showed any interest

138

whatever in the stolid, heavy-limbed girl with the coarse-grained yellow skin and the speech impediment. The missionary had been forced to come down to the full-blood boys. One by one they had turned away with embarrassed smiles. Simeon was the last to be approached, and he had pitied the missionary with the lean features and the intense grey eyes. It would be hard for Brother Matthew to have to send the girl away unmarried. Not only would the Irishman be angry but the girl would assuredly lose her soul out in the harsh un-Christian world. She would go on that down-road to hell fire so vividly illustrated in the pictures shown on Sunday nights. More even than the missionary Simeon had pitied the girl. Nobody wanted her, and that, Simeon thought, was a terrible thing to happen to any human being.

Then he had thought of Annabelle with her smooth black skin, soft eyes and slim, graceful body. When she turned sixteen he had meant to go to Brother Matthew and ask him to marry them, for although they had not spoken much he knew by her eyes that she would consent to be his woman. He had shaken his head when asked about Biddy, but that night Brother Matthew had preached about sacrifice and the great strength of Grace that came as a result of it, and it seemed suddenly that the Lord was speaking to him direct: 'You marry that poor girl, Simeon. You make this sacrifice and I will give you more strength than you ever had before.'

When he came next day to tell the Superintendent of his decision he clung to the last hope that Biddy might refuse him, and that he would still have gained the strength of Grace from his good intention. His sacrifice, however, was accepted. The wedding took place. They went in a truck that took them, with a load of stones, the long miles to Dingo Creek.

When they arrived at the dilapidated iron shack where Grogan lived the old man came out to welcome them. He stood with thumbs in his belt under the bulge of stomach, peering through dark-lensed spectacles attached to his ears by loops of string.

'So that's the best ye could do fer yeself! A girl of Patrick O'Grogan of the O'Grogans, and to marry a black fellow!'

139

Biddy hung her head and said nothing and Simeon, five paces behind, smiled and nodded shyly.

'Thas right, sir.'

'I was not addressing myself to you,' Grogan said. 'Ye can wait till ye're spoken to. Did they not get the letter I was at so much trouble to write?'

The girl nodded mutely.

'Can't ye spake, girl? Where's the tongue in yere head?'

The heavy lips parted and began to twitch, the muscles of the brown young throat contracted. The only sound was the breathy hiss of a frightened animal.

'Biddy still got that little bit speaking trouble, sir,' the boy explained. 'Only when she get nervous like. She get over it d'rectly when she settle down.'

'What's the good of them at that mission at all?' Grogan roared. 'Wasn't it fer that I was sending her, to learn to spake up and help her poor old father in his old age?'

'Biddy's a good girl,' Simeon said. 'She know how to cook and sew and keep a place nice and clean.'

'Is that all they learned her?'

'She can read and write and she know the Bible and can sing hymns.'

'I told them get her a husband—not a black fellow.'

'We been married all right, sir,' Simeon told him. 'Brother Matthew send you this letter, explain everything.'

He gave Grogan the envelope. The Irishman tore it open, turned the sheet this way and that, and thrust it towards his daughter.

''Ere,' he said, 'you cut out that stammering, and read it out. I'm so blind now I can hardly see the hand before my face.'

Biddy stared inarticulately at the letter, her throat muscles working convulsively.

'Give her time,' Simeon said.

'And what about yerself with all the talk in the world?' Grogan snapped. 'Did they learn yer ride a horse?'

'I reckon I can learn to ride d'rectly,' the boy said. 'I learned

140

a bit of carpentry, and then I been in the store, keeping the lists and that.'

'What the hell's the use of that to a station man?'

'I can soon learn that stock work, sir.'

Grogan gave a snort of disgust.

'It takes stockmen of long experience to muster the heathen cattle on this property. I've a mind to send ye back, and tell them find me another man. Don't ye go sleepin' with her now, getting her in the family way. How long ye been married, anyway?'

'Five, six days, sir. That truck got stuck up couple of times. We been on the track three days, three nights.'

Grogan moaned. 'Then they'll be telling me be all the laws of nature it's too late.' He paused. 'What was that ye said ye was keeping lists? What sort of lists?'

'Aw, just keeping the record, like—writing down who was getting the stores and that.'

'Writing eh!' Grogan said. 'Does that mean ye can read?'

'I can read,' Simeon said, 'nuf to get on.'

'Holy snakes!' Grogan exclaimed. 'They'll be learnin' the kangaroos next!'

Simeon chuckled. That kangaroos should be taught to read and write was comical, he thought, but not impossible. It was a good joke. He thought he would like old Grogan by and by.

'See what ye make of this letter then,' the old man said.

Simeon took it from his wife's nervous fingers. Brother Matthew's handwriting was familiar to him:

> I regret that we were not able to marry Biddy to a half-caste boy as you wished and as is our policy. You will understand, however, that such matters are not always simple to arrange as the feelings of the young people themselves must be consulted.
>
> Biddy and Simeon have made this decision themselves and I am sure you will find Simeon a good boy and a willing worker. Both are faithful Christians, and I trust will send their children to the mission when the time comes.

Dismissed at last, the bride and groom were escorted to their quarters by a lean black woman in a dress the colour of the earth. With their rolled blankets and a single suitcase, they crossed the dusty yard to a brushwood hut furnished with a depressed array of battered saddles, bridles and packs. The couple dumped their gear and stood together awkwardly, looking out across the hot plain to the winding smudge of trees that marked the creek and the miserable camps of Grogan's blacks. Neither had any words for the loneliness engulfing them like the desolate breath of the willy-willy that swept around and past them, leaving its residue of dried leaves and grass and horse dung.

'We can't . . . stay here,' the girl said at last.

Simeon shrugged. 'We get used to it soon,' he said gently. 'That's a shock for a white man—find he got a black fellow for a son-in-law, but he get over it by and by. I like him all right, that daddy.'

Biddy's black mother was dead, and she had little in common with her relatives in the Dingo Creek camp, but the boy's friendly, open nature soon broke down the suspicious prejudice of his countrymen. They could not accept him wholeheartedly for he was not a 'proper man' in the tribal sense. He had never undergone even the first stage of initiation, and his marriage to Biddy could only be forgiven on the grounds of his ignorance of the law. They had been at Dingo Creek less than a day when they were made aware of the grave nature of their offence. Simeon had married his tribal mother-in-law.

'Pagan nonsense!' he had told Biddy consolingly, although the girl was not perturbed. She had been only six years old when she went to the mission, and remembered nothing of her tribal infancy, cared nothing for the fact that, ignoring the white side of her parentage, her mother's people had clearly defined her position in the tribal marriage system. Simeon remembered his tribal names, if not their significance, and had announced them with the frankness of his innocence. The revelation had been a shock to the community, but, although still disapproving, they had grown tolerant.

Simeon proved himself adaptable to the cattle camp and

companionable to the rough old Irishman who longed not only for a listener but for someone to write his letters and read to him from his battered collection of Irish writers. Simeon's reading improved with practice, and Grogan was less often provoked to vehement abuse of the ignorance of the black race. It could not long escape even so simple a fellow as Simeon that the old man's near-blindness did not inconvenience him when he was threading a saddler's needle or looking for cleanskin calves on his neighbours' boundaries. The boy soon realised that Grogan did not know one letter from another.

Simeon, however, gave no indication that he had guessed. It would be a terrible thing, he thought, for a white man, especially a station owner, to have to admit that a poor, stupid black fellow had more learning than himself. The boy kept the old man's secret, and tried to please him by reading with as much feeling as possible the long recitative of Ireland's wrongs of which he understood scarcely a word:

> I come of the seed of the people, the people of sorrow,
> That have no treasure but hope,
> No riches laid up but a memory
> Of an ancient glory . . .
> I am flesh of these lowly, I am bone of their bone,
> I have never submitted . . .

Simeon had been happy on the mission, but here, for the first time, he had the sense of filling a useful niche. His heart was full of pitying affection for the lonely old expatriate, and the bedraggled black people he professed to despise but collected around him and clung to jealously. Biddy, on the other hand, found no consolation in life at Dingo Creek. A few weeks before her baby was due she said she must return to the mission or die.

'Let her go!' Grogan said. 'What's the use of her anyway?'

Simeon tried to explain that according to his mission teaching a husband and wife must stick together. If Biddy went back he should go with her.

'Stuff and nonsense,' Grogan scoffed. 'She can come back later if she likes, but right now your place is here in the mustering camp with me.'

Weeks later Simeon heard of the birth of his son. Biddy would be back as soon as she was strong enough to travel, he was assured, but months passed, and he heard at last from a traveller that she had got a job in town and was living with some derelict white man. This Simeon kept from her father, who appeared to have forgotten that he ever had a daughter. The blacks had heard of it, and in their sympathy drew him unobtrusively closer into their lives.

One day when riding after scrub cattle around the foothills of a sandstone range one of the men had taken him up to the entrance of a cave.

'Place belong Ngarangarni,' his companion said, and motioned him inside, where he gazed at the strange paintings and imprints of human hands on the rock face. He noticed that there were skulls and bones in the rock niches, and stacks of long objects wrapped in bark propped against the walls. This, he was told, was one of the few sacred places not yet discovered and desecrated by the white man. Old Grogan knew about it, but had agreed to tell no one so long as his blacks stuck by him. They considered it safe enough as a storage place for the *Tjuringas*, or sacred boards.

Simeon had noticed some tracks at the cave's entrance which were identified to him as those of Wauweri, a man whose name was sometimes whispered in the Dingo Creek camp. Wauweri had grown up on a station. It had been a bad place for black fellows and Wauweri decided he would never work for a white man. He went bush. Ever since he had been trying to keep the old law alive, performing the sacred rituals and ceremonies, secretly visiting the scattered station groups and keeping them in touch with those still uncommitted to the white man's way of life.

Not long afterwards the old warrior himself came into the camp at night to give a message about some forthcoming ceremony. Simeon observed that he was tall and gaunt, and that his eyes burned with some of the zealous intensity of Brother Matthew's. Believing himself unnoticed in the background, the boy had been startled to find the power of the elder's gaze turned suddenly upon himself. Questioned about his name and tribal standing, the boy also remembered what he had been taught about standing up for his faith. He said that he was a Christian and knew nothing of black-fellow rites, but was ashamed that he could feel so little real pride in his avowal. He felt Brother Matthew would have expected him to speak up more forcefully and perhaps sow the seeds of conversion in these pagan countrymen. The words would not come. Sitting back like an outcast, he had listened to the talk of his people, his heart heavy and sad. They spoke of things he had never heard of or thought about and of which he knew too little of the language to follow properly. Then Wauweri had leapt up with his arms raised, the firelight fierce in his deep-set eyes, the words pouring like hot coals from his lips, and Simeon knew he was speaking of the past of old tribes, of the wrongs and sorrows that had come upon them, and of his own defiance, and the words he had so often read without understanding were suddenly illumined in the boy's mind:

I come of the seed of the people, the people of sorrow . . .
I am flesh of the flesh of these lowly . . .
I have never submitted.

He realised at last that Wauweri was trying to rouse his people to walk again with pride and dignity. He was telling them that they had only to hold firm to the law, and the day would come when they would no longer be under the white man's foot:

Beware of the thing that is coming, beware of the risen people,
Who shall take what ye would not give. Did ye think to conquer the people,
Or that Law is stronger than life and than man's desire to be free?

Simeon had never felt he was a slave or that he had any grievance against the white race. He did not believe that the old law could ever be restored to the black people of the scattered and dwindling tribes, but he wanted for the first time to learn of it and of the secret and intriguing world of *Ungud* on the outer boundaries of time.

When the wet season came he applied to Grogan for a holiday. He went off into the sandstones where a number of youths and tribal elders had gathered for initiation rites.

'This is pagan business,' he reminded himself, 'not for Christian man. I only want to find out, that's all.'

But he swayed as he sat in the heady smoke of the ceremonial fires, his every nerve tingling under the ancient, insistent power of the ritual chant, and he had gone at last like a man in a dream to Wauweri.

'Old man,' he said, 'I want you to make me a proper man now.'

The pain of the burning coals and the cutting knife seemed to Simeon the pain of his dividing spirit, but the wounds healed quickly and, to any meeting him, he appeared the same simple, docile fellow who had left the mission two years before. Only Simeon knew the opening of his mind to new vistas of experience, knew the hardening of his will. He returned unafraid to the mission to claim Annabelle as his rightful tribal wife. Even his pity for Brother Matthew did not prevent his taking her.

'What terrible work has the devil wrought in you, my son?' the missionary asked, mourning the ruin and degradation of one whom he had thought the staunchest of his flock.

Simeon had no reply to the question. He knew that he would walk without shame in the two worlds of his spirit, and at peace in the one world of his heart.

NANCY PHELAN
(1913-   )

Nancy Phelan was born in Sydney, and educated at the Conservatorium of Music and the University of Sydney. She was the niece of writers Amy and Louise Mack. *A Kingdom by the Sea* (1968) is an account of her childhood on the north shore of Sydney. Phelan lived in England for several years and has travelled extensively in Australia, the Pacific Islands, Europe, Asia and the Middle East. Her travels provided her with the material for six books of non-fiction, of which *The Swift Foot of Time* (1983) won the Braille Book of the Year Award. One of her three novels, *The Voice Beyond the Trees*, won a prize in the *Sydney Morning Herald* novel competition in 1950 but was not published until 1985. Her short stories and articles have appeared in various magazines and newspapers as well as in *Coast to Coast* and other anthologies. Since 1970 she has been a regular reviewer for the *Sydney Morning Herald* and the Melbourne *Age*.

'Rewards to the Faithful' won a prize in a competition conducted by the *Adelaide Advertiser* in 1963. Phelan creates characters that evoke our sympathy in a moving story about vulnerability and disillusionment.

REWARDS TO THE FAITHFUL

When the postman came that morning Ethel was standing at the front door shaking out the mat. Old, rather bald like an ageing wire-haired terrier, it hung suspended from her hand as they exchanged greetings.

'Busy today Miss Allsop, eh?' said the postman, pushing an envelope into the letter-box at the gate. 'Off to an early start, eh?'

'Yes.' She smiled, though she knew he had brought only a bill. 'Yes. My boarder moves in today.'

'Ah.' The postman briefly exposed his tea-coloured teeth. 'Ah well, you'll have a house full now, won't you, eh?'

She nodded, ready to prolong the conversation, but he had to get along, he said.

'You know how it is . . . First of the month . . . Bills going out, eh?' and he added that this sort of thing wouldn't buy the baby a new bonnet.

'Bye-bye,' she called brightly, and with his whistle and buckles and straps and bag jangling and creaking he nodded and was off, loping down the street on his sponge-rubber soles.

Ethel watched him for a minute, then she laid the old wire-haired terrier in its accustomed place and ventured down the short, salmon-pink drive to the letter-box. On one side was a small square lawn of thin couch grass, bordered with earth beds, where, spaced out with precision, Iceland poppies grew, aloof . . . genteel; on the other side a fence held off the next-door house. During Mother's lifetime a lattice had been erected above this fence, for Mother was a great one for privacy, and a dark-green small-leafed creeper trained to grow upon it; but this protection stretched only to the level of the front door, at the side of the house. Beyond that point a high creepered fence might be taken

148

as offensive, stand-offish or stuck-up. It even suggested there was something furtive, shameful about the comings and goings of one's visitors.

There had been few enough visitors coming and going for a long time now. Apart from Ethel's own movements the little house remained undisturbed, silent, often empty. But all that would be changed now, as the postman had said; and glancing triumphantly at an orange gerbera on its long stem—for her plants rather ran to one flower on the end of a lonely stalk—she took the telephone account from the letter-box and thrust it carelessly into her pocket.

At the gate she looked out, and up and down the street. Long, flat and featureless it stretched into infinity, house upon house, square upon square of couch grass, stalk upon stalk of gerbera and Iceland poppy. The district was poorish, decent, respectable, colourless. Not rich enough for individuality, not poor enough for crowding, the street was so wide that the houses on the other side seemed to lean backwards, far away in a sunset haze. Though it was wide enough to divide into strips—white cement footpath, grass border, tarmac road, grass border, white cement footpath— the adjoining houses stood very close to each other. Lawn in front, yard at back, drive at the left side, neighbour's drive on the right, they stood meekly, like little buildings made of children's blocks.

'Well,' thought Ethel. 'It's a nice day anyway.' She looked at her watch and calculated. Eight o'clock. Four and a half hours before she need leave for the hospital, and everything just about ready. Floors polished, bed prepared, lounge-room dusted, glass and silver polished, pictures cleaned, bird-cage swept, clean paper in the drawers and wardrobe. All she really need do was set the table and prepare the meal so they could eat as soon as they got in. He would be tired, on his first day out of hospital, and glad of his dinner—it was always dinner to her at one o'clock, no matter how cold or frugal—he'd just want a few minutes to settle himself ... wash his hands and so on. She thought suddenly that she would have to explain to him about the bath-

149

heater, for surely he had never seen one like hers, and a slow dark stain spread up her neck and over her face at the thought of a man in her bathroom, of herself alone in the bathroom with him, of herself alone in the house with him, sleeping under the same roof. He was no longer young, he was weak and helpless, but he was still a man, a man only a few years older than herself.

Her hands trembled for a second. She tried to calm herself, wondering if she should cut some flowers for the lounge-room; but they looked so bright in the garden, they made such a nice show and flowers in the house were a nuisance, always needing changing and dropping their petals everywhere. She turned to go inside, her agitation forgotten.

After the spring sunlight she was temporarily blind in the little dark hell. Frigid, its air unchanged for years, undisturbed by breeze or sunlight, for the blinds were always down to save the carpet, the house smelt of moth-balls, bygone chops, and, faintly, of feet. It was so strong, so cold a smell that a stranger might have stifled, but Ethel, used to it from birth, noticed nothing. She moved through the cluttered hall to the dim breakfast-room where blinds, adjusted in line with each other, curtains hanging stiff and still, excluded light, life and warmth.

She regarded it with satisfaction. This was home; all hers; her very own, not a penny owing. How glad she was that she had battled, struggled to pay, hung on when it would have been so much easier to give up. Sometimes there had seemed little sense in it, especially after Mother went, a Great House all to herself; but now her hardships were justified, her struggles rewarded.

'Rewards to the faithful,' Mother used to say. 'Everything comes to those who wait.'

As she peeled potatoes and immersed them in a saucepan of water against her return from hospital, she let her mind wander; but her daydream was a familiar one, more of a plan for action than idle fantasy.

This time next year, for it didn't do to rush things, she might be a married woman . . . Mrs Jefferson, wife of the brilliant, once rich and powerful Andrew Jefferson, founder and owner of Jefferson Enterprises. For thirty-five years she had been dreaming this dream as the faithful might dream of heaven, but now it had become feasible, imminent, no longer fantastic and remote. For thirty-five years, since she first went to work for him as his book-keeper, she had loved him selflessly, single-mindedly and apparently hopelessly. She had watched him grow from a penniless young engineer to the owner of a building empire; she had watched his three marriages come and go, his children grow up and finally his empire collapse in ruins. She was his oldest and most trusted aide, always in the background, unseen behind the elegant wives, the beautiful secretaries, the pretty typists. She had let herself be pushed aside by his more socially acceptable associates but she had hung on, doggedly, as she had hung on to her little house, determined not to be dislodged. He had been the focus of her life, her mission and responsibility. She knew all his business secrets. She had survived rows, scorn, storms of abuse, threats of dismissal, for he was a violent man, knowing they counted little beside her real value and importance to him. He needed her; and some day, she always knew if she waited long enough, she would get him for herself. The others came and went, dazzling, exciting, fickle; but she, the little grey mouse in the wainscoting, waited, biding her time and keeping her heart up with the vision of a future when, ill, ruined and abandoned, he would turn to her and realise how much he needed her.

And now the time had come. When disaster struck, when the empire crumbled, when the adulation turned to abuse, she was there. The wives, friends, hangers-on, admirers all were gone, the splendid offices shut, the great house up for sale. Nothing remained but a sick and ageing man and his little old grey book-keeper; yet to her this was the real purpose of the whole charade.

'He had to learn by suffering,' she told herself. 'He had to learn through grief and loss.' Now he had learnt, she was waiting to reward him.

The potatoes peeled, their eyes gouged out like poor Gloucester's, she took a pinkish cloth and spread it on the imitation oak refectory table. Upon the slippery rayon surface she set cream-coloured plates and teacups bordered with autumn leaves, ladies with salt and pepper in their crinolines, a bread-board and knife and two vase-shaped amber glasses from her Water Set. From the chromium arch over the butter-dish dangled a chromium knife, a petrified sardine; on the jam-jar lid two life-sized purple strawberries gleamed.

In the kitchen she laid out plates and opened tins in a quietly bustling manner. On an oblong autumn-foliaged dish she set a grey-faced cylinder of meat-loaf, its edges smoothed with fragments of pale uterine jelly, its ends still bearing the concentric impress of the tin. In two amber vessels, like swollen egg-cups, she piled spoonfuls of a hectic tinned fruit-salad; in a saucepan she emptied a can of bloated chartreuse peas.

Now all was ready. The evening meal was also prepared. With hospital routine and early nights in mind she had sliced up cucumber and tomato, opened cans of salmon and beetroot. There was no doubt tinned food solved housekeeping problems. Since Mother's death it had provided all she needed, except for a weekly fried chump chop. Food, after all, was only fuel.

Towards ten o'clock, after a quick flip round with the duster, she sat down for a leisurely cup of tea and a sweet biscuit. She took them to the back veranda where, glassed-in and screened from sunlight by brown holland blinds, Mother had lived out much of her life. The place still bore the impress of her niggling, whining personality. Her ugly crochet rug, her hassock still were there, with the old chaise-lounge, a yellow cane affair spotted like a leopard with red-hot-poker marks. Ethel had livened up the doors and window-frames with strong red paint and covered the floor with variegated linoleum. She spent most of her time there now, it saved the house, and sitting with the teacup she thought of the days ahead when Andrew would lie at peace on the chaise-lounge, enjoying his convalescence.

Somehow the future was never too clear beyond his convalescence. What will be, will be, she liked to say; but the truth was that unacknowledged to herself she did not really want

152

him to be anything more than helpless, weak, entirely dependent on her. Her passion for service and sacrifice, so amply fulfilled during Mother's life, must now find another outlet; and the collapse of Jefferson Enterprises could not have been better timed, assuming that it had to come at all.

She saw nothing strange or selfish in such thoughts. With the single-mindedness and dedication of fanatics, saints and lunatics she knew nothing mattered but that she could now serve him openly, no longer the grey anonymous form behind the ledger, the self-effacing squirrel who hoarded away her salary against this very future, refusing to be led astray by pretty clothes or a smarter way of life. As her salary had increased with the prosperity of the company she had stowed away more, she had bought annuities. Now, when everyone else from Jefferson Enterprises was on the breadline, deep in debt and looking desperately for jobs, she could retire in comfort, free of the need to work again.

'Why don't you take a trip?' the girls in the office had sometimes said; but she did not care for travelling. Change bothered her, she disliked oily food, foreigners were immoral and foreign places dirty.

'One day,' she thought. 'Now I'm not alone, I might—*we* might—take a trip, to Canberra, or perhaps along the coast by ship,' and she smiled at the thought of surprising Andrew with this suggestion.

Eleven o'clock! Still another hour and a half, and everything done. She walked through the house making adjustments, stretching up to straighten a picture hoisted level with the picture-rail. She looked into Andrew's room—it had been Mother's—the best room in the house, facing the street, and made sure that all was right. Here a new and unfamiliar piece of furniture took her attention for a moment, a light oak bookcase she had bought last week. She wasn't much of a reader herself; apart from a Bible, a prayer-book and a *Pears Cyclopaedia* there were no books in the house. She had taken the *Reader's Digest* while Mother was alive—it made an interest—and there were still many copies piled up in the garage, but books indoors, she knew, just harboured dust.

Andrew had claimed in his extravagant way that he could not live without them. Well, she had heard him say the same of champagne, lovely women and cigars. You live and learn. But the bookcase was a nice piece of furniture. She had not grudged it.

'Ethel!' she could hear him say. 'You bought it just for me!' She glowed, imagining the fond rebuke in his voice.

Eleven fifteen! Heavens, she must fly . . . get out the car . . . clean herself up . . . call at the cake shop for something for tea . . . She went to the garage, folded back the doors and gingerly, with many little backward leaps and rushes, navigated the high narrow vehicle towards the gates. The tank was full of petrol, the inside had been brushed, there were cushions and a rug all ready on the back seat for his comfort. Nothing to do now but to dress herself and go.

She went to her room, took off her skirt and in a wine-dark flannel dressing-gown stood hesitating. On the bed her grey suit and the bottle-green jumper she had knitted lay ready, her hat and shoes nearby. Why did she hesitate? Why not proceed at once to the bathroom, where germicidal soap and lukewarm water from the temperamental heater awaited her? She glanced at herself in the dressing-table glass and saw that she was pale, her hair, still in rollers, dragged back to reveal a tiny pallid face, the face of a frightened bird.

Frightened? What nonsense! Why should she be frightened? Afraid perhaps that something might go wrong at the last minute? But nothing could go wrong; no one could interfere, nobody cared enough to bother. That was not the answer; and suddenly, staring at the white diminished face, she was frightened because nothing could go wrong, because the long-awaited moment was upon her now, at last, and nothing could stop it; because after today life would be changed forever.

'It's what I *want*!' she whispered desperately. 'It's what I've wanted all my life!' But the fear remained, remained, increased until it verged on panic.

154

'It's only that I'm tired . . . It's after all the strain and worry
. . .' All those weeks of plodding daily to the hospital, of waiting,
hoping, cheering, trying to bring him back to life. He had had
no intention of living; he had despaired when angry doctors
dragged him back from death and kept him breathing. His body
had survived but most of his spirit had gone, leaving a feeble,
bewildered creature, who finally, for want of strength to resist,
had accepted her proposals.

'Listen,' she had said in her urgent little voice. 'Come to my
place. I've got a home . . . a car . . . an independent income . . .'
how happy she had been at the astonishment, the respect on
his face . . . 'You can stay as long as you like. No obligation.
I'll be glad to have you . . . you'll be doing me a favour. I've
been lonely since Mother went . . .' this for his pride . . . and
she added craftily, 'You'll be able to get the pension later on
and if it makes you feel any better you could pay me something,
like a boarder.' '*And I'll bank it for him,*' she thought with a
thrill of pleasure.

He was too tired to struggle. He agreed to everything. He
could not stay in hospital forever. Already they were agitating
for his bed. Would-be suicides, ruined tycoons could not claim
much sympathy. He must go somewhere and there was nowhere
else to go. Ethel, with her years of dedicated service and fanatical
loyalty had seemed the solution. During his illness, when he lay
alone and shipwrecked she had been there all the time, helping,
encouraging, even doing a little nursing, for the staff had soon
lost interest. Without her he did not know what he would have
done, and in his weakness and loneliness had found comfort in
her devotion. He had even grown fond of her little grey face,
had mildly teased her so that she went pink with pleasure and
embarrassment.

She was a decent soul, a loyal faithful slave; and he did not
care about anything more. If she would let him lie in the sun
and regain his strength in peace he would do anything she liked.

She knew her victory came through his defeat, but she had
closed her mind to the thought, as she had to his occasional

half-hearted talks of starting again. Time enough for that when it happened, she told herself, thinking of his damaged heart. The thing was to get him home, home to her loving care.

And that was just exactly what she would be doing in an hour from now. Why, then, was she nervous, frightened, full of jitters?

'We're strangers,' she thought with a devastating flash of honesty. 'I don't know anything about him really, not outside the office. He knows nothing of my life, he's never even seen my home . . . *his* home now . . . It's natural to be a little shy . . . a little nervous. That's all it is . . . I'm just not used to living with a man.'

She went red, then white again, with the same dizziness she had felt, picturing him in her bathroom. Living with a man . . . that usually meant . . . But they were both too old. She was fifty-five and he was over sixty. No, no, nothing of that sort now. Besides, he was still an invalid. But later, when he recovered . . . later, when they . . . when they married, as she meant them to do in time, would he expect—? Oh, this was awful. Awful and ridiculous.

'I must get going,' she said aloud, and moved towards the bathroom.

The doorbell rang, jangling through the silent house. She started and stood trembling, nerves and muscles tensed. Immersed in thought, she had heard no step approach. She was expecting nothing, no one.

The harsh sound came again as a determined hand turned at the little key.

'A hawker!' she muttered angrily. 'Or someone collecting,' and without further thought she pattered to the door and pulled it open.

A man in a peaked cap stood on the doorstep.

'This Miss Allsop's house?'

'Yes. What is it?'

'It's all right—just checking the number. Passenger for you, Miss Allsop, but I couldn't bring him to your door because there's a car in the drive.'

156

'Passenger? What passenger?' said Ethel blankly. 'I can't see anyone just now. I'm getting ready to go out—I'm in a hurry.'

'Yes, passenger for you. This is the address. A Mr Jefferson from the District Hospital.'

'Oh no!' cried Ethel, frozen, petrified with shock. 'It can't be! It's a mistake. I'm just about to go and bring him here . . .' She spoke with desperate urgency, as though force could turn words into tangible weapons of defence.

'Ah well . . . it's saved you the trouble,' said the hire-car driver. 'He got me to bring him over. I'll just give him a hand with his things . . .' He turned away.

'But he can't . . . I'm not ready . . . the cakes . . .' cried Ethel wildly. She clutched at her pallid face, at her hair in its curlers, and was about to slam the door and lock it, but the driver was already down the path and out the gate.

'Oh no . . . he can't! He can't find me like this!' she cried, dragging madly at her curlers. 'Not in this dressing-gown . . . Not like this!'

She ran to her room and tore out the curlers, overlooking three at the back of her head. Her hands were trembling, her breath so short she felt that she would choke. She started to pull off her dressing-gown, then stopped, confused with panic and despair, and as she stood she heard them coming up the path, the driver, kind and reassuring, saying, 'Steady . . . Take it easy,' and the other voice, the dear familiar voice, so much less robust than it had sounded in the hospital room.

'Ethel? Are you there, Ethel?' It seemed a thin and quavering cry. 'It's me. I've arrived.'

She forgot her appearance, her shock and alarm, and rushed to help him in; and Jefferson, giddy with exhaustion, shattered by the sight of his future home, limped weakly into view.

Somehow she got him in, into an armchair, while the driver carried in the bags and parcels. In the suit he had worn to hospital he sat trembling, feeling close to tears.

'Give me a drink,' he said. 'A brandy.'

She looked at him, dismayed.

157

'I haven't got any brandy,' she said. 'I don't keep spirits in the house. But I'll make you a cup of tea.'

Oh God! No brandy! Trying to control his voice he said, 'All right then; tea,' and lay back, breathing heavily.

Confusion and panic flooded her again. She ran to the kitchen and lit the gas, then to her room to finish dressing; then, unable to concentrate, to control her fumbling fingers, to the kitchen again to make tea. But the kettle had not boiled, so back she went, to stand all shaking at the dressing-table.

'Oh,' she wept. 'It's too unfair. To take me on the hop like this!'

A thin desperate whistle rose, and dragging on her dark-green sweater she ran, still in bedroom slippers, to the kitchen where the kettle's steam and fury filled the air.

'What must he *think?*' she wondered in despair. 'To catch me like this . . . as though I were the sort of woman who went about all day in slippers and curlers. Oh, my God!'—as her hand discovered those she had overlooked. 'Oh God!'

But finally the tea was made, the curlers out, the hair-brush plied, the slippers replaced by lace-up shoes. No cakes, but then of course it wasn't teatime. How confused she was.

When she came in with the tea he was sitting in his armchair. Mother's chair . . . sunk in weakness. Depression, reaction, realisation of his rashness threatened to swamp him. He shivered in the frigid atmosphere, he choked with the smell of moth-balls, he craved for light and air and warmth; but seeing her distressed expression he pulled himself together. Poor thing, how terrible she was; and this appalling house, this stuffy darkened cell, those monstrous pictures brushing against the ceiling . . . Courageously he forced a smile and said, 'Thank you, Ethel. That's just what I need.'

She poured his tea—too weak, too sugary—and while he drank it watched him like a Spanish beggar-child. He forced it down and though it sickened him the heat was stimulating.

'Feeling better?' she asked anxiously, and something of her devotion and concern penetrated his depression and self-pity.

158

'Much better.'

'More tea?'

'No . . . no. No more, thanks. That was . . . wonderful.'

A silence fell. He really felt he might be going to faint unless he got some brandy. If only he'd thought to bring . . .

'Why did you come like this?' she asked. 'I said I'd come and fetch you.'

'I thought I'd save you the trouble,' he said. 'You've been so good. And then I wanted to surprise you.' No need to tell her his bed had been taken at ten o'clock that morning and he could not face waiting in the hall.

'Dinner is ready,' she began, but he said suddenly, with surprising strength, 'What am I thinking of? I quite forgot. I've brought the lunch. We stopped at the shops on the way here—the driver got the things for me. He was most kind.'

'What things?' She was suddenly rather sharp, on the defensive.

'Oh, nothing much. Just a few odd things. I thought perhaps we'd celebrate.'

'But dinner's ready,' she said, even more sharply. 'I've got everything. It's ready, all except the potatoes.'

'Well, let's jut pust it in the fridge and keep it for to-night,' he said. 'I've got some special things there, in that paper carrier.'

She was deeply insulted. How typical! Just as he had been in the old days, sweeping aside everyone's plans because his own were better.

'I have prepared our tea for tonight as well,' she said coldly.

'We can have it tomorrow,' he said carelessly, unconscious of her displeasure. 'Give me the bag, Ethel, and I'll show you what I brought.'

Hypnotised, resentful, she obeyed him, all her new-found authority and confidence dissolved.

He lifted the bag to his knees and began to extract the contents. He was excited.

'To have some really decent food after that institutional diet,' he said. 'I've almost forgotten the taste of things. Ah!' . . . he dragged out a parcel . . . 'Here you are, my dear. Just put that in the fridge.'

'What is it?' she said suspiciously, feeling a hard cold surface through the paper.

'Champagne.' He looked pleased.

She stared at him blankly.

'What?'

'Champagne,' he said a little impatiently. 'For our lunch.'

'Champagne? I never drink champagne. I never touch it.'

'You don't? Well, it's time you started. You're going to have some today . . . to celebrate.'

'I don't like it,' she said. 'And you . . . you oughtn't to be drinking.'

He laughed with decreasing patience.

'My dear Ethel, champagne is given to the sick and dying. As for you . . . how do you know you don't like it if you've never tasted it?'

Her face was red with nerves and anger. How dared he ridicule her in this way? How dared he dismiss her plans, her preparations?

He was pulling out more parcels.

'*Prosciutto!* Melon! Red caviar! A beautiful chicken . . .'

'Chicken!' She seized on the only familiar word in this terrifying list. 'Chicken? There isn't time to cook a chicken!'

'It's cooked already. Feel . . . it's still warm. Barbecued.' He thrust the tin-foil bag into her hand. 'Just put it in the oven to keep warm while we have our *hors d'oeuvres*.'

She began to feel quite faint. What was he talking about? Where did he think he was?

'Put the champagne on the ice, there's a good girl,' he said, though the frigid temperature of the room could do it little harm. 'And then I thought we'd have a salad . . . just a green salad . . .'

'We're having salad for tonight,' she said. 'Salmon.'

'Good. Well, here's the lettuce for our lunch. Just make us a French dressing, you know—oil and lemon juice; and perhaps chop up some parsley . . . But careful with the garlic . . .'

She was vainly trying to speak, to interrupt the cataract, but he talked on, over-excited, slightly hectic.

'. . . and then I thought, just cheese. And here we are!' He pulled out a reeking parcel. 'Here's a lovely smelly Port Salut, and a Camembert. Oh, and I forgot the black olives.'

'Phew!' she cried in disgust. 'Take that stinking stuff away. I won't have it in the house.'

He looked startled, as though not sure if he should laugh or shout with rage; then he controlled himself.

'Ethel,' he said laboriously, 'I brought these things as a treat for us both. I've been living on garbage for weeks. I haven't had any decent food since God knows when. I thought we'd both enjoy a lovely meal together . . . to celebrate my . . . my recovery.' And he added dolefully, 'My last burst. My final fling.'

She was shaking with rage, insult and hurt feelings, aggravated by the dreadful sense of inferiority that had always assailed her in the past when the lovely wives and secretaries had glanced at her in their kindly patronising way. She could not see his gesture as a spontaneous offering to them both; she saw it only as a reflection on her hospitality, an inference that what she had to offer was not good enough.

'If you think I can live at that rate,' she said, overcome with angry loyalty to her despised meat-loaf, 'you're very much mistaken. And neither can you. You can't afford these things. Not any more. Why, what you spent on this . . . this *stuff* would keep a family for a week.' She began to calculate aloud. 'How much did the chicken cost? A *pound*? You're crazy! And the champagne . . .? I suppose you've spent all that money I brought you . . .'

He was appalled by her brutal rejection of his gesture. He had a vision of a grey pinched future and suddenly he shouted at her in his old manner.

'Shut up, shut up! Do you have to spoil *everything*? Do you have to remind me of my position? Haven't you enough female sympathy and understanding to realise how I might be feeling?' And shaking and exhausted he began to weep tears of weakness and despair.

There were apologies, remorse, offers of more tea, and then a compromise. A glass of champagne to bring him round, and afterwards the lunch she had prepared. The chicken would do cold tomorrow. It would save getting anything in.

Tired and dispirited, he gave in, only insisting forlornly on a chicken leg. It was so long since he had tasted such a young and tender bird.

He sat at the table while she brought in the lunch. He had not thought about glasses and somehow champagne out of amber tumblers was not quite the same. Having ascertained that the *prosciutto*, melon and caviar would keep, Ethel took them to the kitchen and with an expression of extreme distaste and suspicion put them in the refrigerator. The cheese, well wrapped in newspapers, she put in an empty cake-tin.

With a martyred air of impartiality she carried the chicken to the table, but though she had always regarded poultry as a lavish treat she could not be induced to eat any.

'No . . . I prefer this, really I do!' she said brightly, carving herself a genteel slice of the mole-coloured cylinder.

He refused the warmed-up peas . . . she had let the potatoes go . . . and to her secret distress picked up his chicken-bone and ate it in his fingers.

'Ah well, fingers were made before forks,' she said gaily, understandingly, and handed him a little paper napkin. He tried to smile back but his despair was heavy. How in God's name had he ever got himself into this hideous and monstrous situation? Illness and desperation had betrayed him. He drank his champagne thirstily, hoping it might restore his courage.

'No really . . . no really,' she protested when he tried to make her drink. She pecked at the edge of her glass like a wary sparrow suspecting a trap. She did not like what she tasted . . . she did not like the bubbles, the flavour or the associations of the drink, but she tried hard and her determined efforts, her grim endurance depressed him far more than her original protests. To bolster himself up and to prevent her serving flat champagne next day—for after his first glass she had proposed keeping the rest for

162

Sunday lunch—he drank the whole bottle himself and soon became so sleepy and confused that mercifully he did not even see the tinned fruit-salad in its amber chalice.

'Sorry,' he mumbled. 'I'm worn out. Too much for me . . . exertion . . . excitement . . .' and with a few incoherent remarks about the future . . . starting again . . . building up a new project . . . he had reeled away to his bedroom and fallen upon the bed, too drunk to see or care about his surroundings. He roused himself to snarl at her suggestion of unpacking for him, and then sank back into sleep.

Surprisingly, next morning he was better. Taking in a cup of tea she found him awake, reading. She averted her eyes from the tousled hair, the lids still puffed with sleep, the unfamiliar, almost frightening intimacy of an unshaved male face seen in such a setting. He showed no sign of embarrassment nor disposition to apologise. He took the tea and thanked her and began, almost absently, to talk of the book he was reading.

Poetry! At this hour of the morning! But then he always had been queer that way. A weird mixture, very complicated. Not just a clever engineer and businessman but really fond of Art and that. His house had been full of pictures of *All Kinds*, sold now, or taken by his last deserting wife.

He saw the lack of comprehension on her face and shut the book regretfully. If only she could give him some companionship, he could accept the fearful house, the food, the pinched grey way of life, the dismal future. He sighed, longing for his old vigour and vitality. Would it ever come back? Would he ever have the strength to start again, to get away from this impossible haven; or was this to be his fate from now on? Grey, grey, grey, like the dreadful cardigan she wore, the dreadful street outside the shrouded windows.

'Well, I must get a move on,' she said suddenly, flushing slightly, feeling uncomfortable. He had dragged his things from the bags and they were strewn about . . . men's brushes, lotions, colognes, electric razor . . . luxurious objects unaffected by their owner's changed condition ... silk pyjamas that disturbingly revealed his chest, so different from the rigid hospital uniform; a silk dressing-gown and soft red leather slippers. It was ... it was somehow *indecent*, she felt, somehow shocking here in Mother's room, in her spinster house, a kind of ... invasion; something, something *sexy*—what a painful word—an assumption, a tacit admission of a frightening state of intimacy.

'All right. I'll get up,' he said, throwing back the bedclothes, but retreating, panic-stricken at the half-glimpsed outline in the silk pyjamas, she cried. 'No, no! Don't get up yet. I'll bring your breakfast in to you. Don't get up yet. Besides, you don't know how to work the heater.'

He looked at her in surprise. With a man's indifference to his own dishabille, accustomed to dressing and undressing before women, and more recently to the constant handling of nurses, he could not comprehend what was wrong; but instinct told him to return to bed, which he was glad enough to do, while Ethel, still a-tremble, went to the kitchen to prepare the breakfast he had ordered.

Omelette, coffee, toast and marmalade ... She had never made an omelette but she had scrambled many an egg for Mother; toast and marmalade were no problem nor was coffee, which she poured ready-made from a bottle, half a teaspoon to a cup of milk. With her hands engaged in these rites, in setting the tray and bringing in the paper, she gradually calmed down, though panic still lurked at the back of her mind, ready to pounce at any minute.

'Poor thing, she is a real old maid,' thought Jefferson. It was hard to believe such beings still existed; and gazing at the ceiling where a nacreous basin hung, inverted, on three chains, he pondered on the strangeness and the tragedy. Under her grey exterior, her dried-up little form, Miss Allsop still remained a timid woodland nymph, chaste and virginal. How sad it was that these qualities, so charming in a pretty girl, became grotesque when their possessor's youthful grace had gone. Strange, how immutable things like chastity and virginal shyness could be reflected in the external appearance and behaviour of the being they inhabited. How sad it was; how sad and how repulsive.

'I'll light the heater for you,' she said later, taking away the grey untasted fluid in the coffee cup, the untouched scrambled egg on soggy toast. (*'Sorry . . . I haven't got my appetite back yet. Awfully sorry.'*) 'Then I must show you how, so you can manage it yourself.'

Frightening, frightening. Why was she so frightened? He wouldn't hurt her; anyone could see how weak he was. No, it was nothing so simple as a physical encounter that she feared; it was something more intangible.

'But this is what I've wanted, all my life,' she reminded herself as she cleaned up the kitchen and prepared the back veranda for his comfort. 'Thirty-five years I've waited just for this.' But she was still uneasy, still disturbed in that strange way she could not understand.

'It takes some getting used to, having a man in the place,' she thought. 'It makes a change.'

It certainly did. Weak though he was, it was like having a coiled spring in the house, one that could fly open suddenly and destroy her world.

'He's unpredictable,' she thought. 'You never know where you are with him.'

He came at last from the bedroom, shaved and bathed, wearing a shirt and trousers under his dressing-gown. The dressing-gown upset her somehow. It hinted of sin and other women, of invisible clinging arms. What sights it must have seen . . . She pushed her thoughts back angrily and bustled about with Mother's crochet rug.

'No no . . . I like to have the sun,' he protested as she carefully adjusted the brown holland blinds in line with each other, and reluctantly she pulled them up an inch or two. Her compassion for his weakness, his pity for her ugliness and gaucherie weighed heavily upon them, making each one anxious to avoid a repetition of the previous day. Stilted, polite, ill-at-ease, they skirmished. Gone was the intimacy of his hospital days, bred of his dependence and their isolation among strangers; gone the illusion that each had changed. Neither had changed at all; only circumstances were different. Deprived of common interests . . . the washing she had done for him, the need to buy new handkerchiefs, to get him books and stamps and papers; and further back the bond of work together . . . they had not a word to say to each other; nothing that was not forced, that could be said without that fearful bright politeness.

'We'll have your chicken cold for dinner,' she said brightly, bravely; then, thinking of the salmon waiting since last night, 'or would you prefer the salmon?'

'Oh, let's have the salmon,' he said, even more brightly, with even more braveness. 'I adore salmon'—remembering thin slices of *saumon fumé*. 'Keep the chicken for tomorrow.'

'No no . . . Only if you'd *rather* have the salmon. It's as you like . . .'

'No, as *you* like. After all, you're the boss here.' Oh God!

'All right. Then you could have your . . . your smelly cheese too, if you like,' she said with formidable generosity.

'All right. I'll eat it out of doors.' He laughed, and the sound echoed hollowly in his heart, like a long, deserted room recalling a distant voice.

'This is what I've wanted all my life,' she told herself desperately as she went out to collect the post. 'Him, here in my house, dependent on me. On my back veranda, lying on Mother's lounge, reading while I do the house.' She took the circulars from the box and stood, reluctant to return to him. Only yesterday, on the threshold of fulfilment, she had stood in this same place, her heart alive with hope and expectation. What was wrong with her? How silly it all was. She must buck up and realise her good fortune.

She shook herself and began to walk slowly to the house, then turned and went back to the gate. She looked at the little houses fainting away across the road, at the long grey vista stretching into the distance, and suddenly a sob came to her throat.

Nothing had turned out as she had expected. Somehow it

was all different and all wrong. 'Oh dear . . .' she patted her sleeves in search of her handkerchief. 'Oh dear!' How cruel life could be. It gave and at the same time it gave not. She had him now, the man she had loved and served and given her whole life to; he was hers for the taking and it was too late . . . too late . . . too late.

'He's a stranger,' she moaned, holding her forehead. 'A stranger. I don't know about him and it's all too late. What can I do. What can I *do*?'

Shaken with sobs, she pushed up her glasses, inserting the edge of a handkerchief to absorb the tears.

'I don't know what to do with him!' she thought with sudden clarity, and in that recognised the origin of all her fears. 'I've got him and I don't know what to do with him! Oh God!' she pushed her hair back, sniffing hard. 'Oh God,' she thought, scrubbing with desolation at her nose. 'Oh God, what shall I do?'

MARGARET TRIST
(1914–1986)

Margaret Trist was born and brought up in south-west Queensland.
At seventeen she moved to Sydney where she worked for the
ABC. Her writing first appeared in the *Bulletin*. Trist published
three novels and two collections of short stories, *In the Sun* (1943)
and *What Else Is There* (1946). Writing with insight and realism,
Trist concentrates primarily on women's problems. Her stories
appeared in many anthologies and journals including *Southerly*
and *Coast to Coast*. While her stories often contain humour and
irony, she was equally capable of handling a more serious
approach, as she demonstrates in 'Fate'.

FATE

The woman held her baby tightly in her arms. It was a tiny
scrap of a baby wrapped mummy fashion in a shrunken yellow
shawl. It was a bare fortnight old. By the woman's side a four-
year-old boy struggled with a small suitcase. A smaller boy
plodded manfully in the rear, hauling a nappy bag. The woman
was scarcely conscious of them. If one had fallen or been
swallowed by the crowd, she could not have raised a hand to
help him. It seemed as if this third child had drained all strength
from her body. Her head was clouded and thick. It took every
atom of willpower to make her realise she must catch the train.
The train would take her home. Not that she wanted to go home.
Not that she wanted to go anywhere. She wanted to sink down
where she was and not move any more. Sink down and down
and down. Only for the train she could have done that. But she
must catch the train. She must walk on and on, dragging one
heavy foot after the other, holding the weight of the baby against
the hot tightness of her breasts. Her back ached persistently, her
stomach dragged downward. She was conscious of it only as
part of the general torture.

She stopped suddenly. The children stopped with her. The
three of them looked upward. They had come to a flight of stairs,
a long, seemingly interminable flight that must be climbed before
they could get to the train. People swept past them, making a
grumbling detour round them. Several times the woman was
bumped. She was too weak to make any sound. Beads of
perspiration came out on her forehead. The colour drained from
her lips. At the top of the steps was the train. She must catch
the train. She started off resolutely, carefully lifting one foot after
the other. Sometimes her foot did not quite reach the step level.
She would stumble, jarring her body. The boys walked beside

169

her, lifting their feet in their heavy black boots high. The stairs went on and on. A constant stream of people went up them, people as unreal as a string of hurrying posts. As far as she was concerned there were no people, only a series of obstacles which fate had set down at odd intervals for her to knock against. She was alone in the whole torture-ridden world. She was a concentrated mass of the world's suffering. She could not think any more, she endured. The stairs went up and up. She lifted her foot carefully, her back ached, her stomach dragged, the step slid about then came to rest under her foot. She lifted her other foot. She must catch the train.

At the top of the steps there was an expanse of platform. She set out to cross it, carried along by the triumph of having overcome the stairs. Instinct guided her to the main platform. The lights and the crowd and the noise caused her to blink. She hesitated and for the first time looked back for the children. They were behind her, straining at the heavy bags.

'Out of the way, there,' called a voice.

She looked up quickly as the pocket-size motor car with a luggage trailer bore down on her. She stumbled out of its path, the children staggering after her. They stood watching after it doggedly. A fresh wave of people carried them on again.

At the indicator the woman stood looking upward a long time, trying to figure things out in the dull place that was her brain. She must catch the train . . . the train . . . Ah, number seven, of course it was number seven. It always went from number seven. She moved on, dragging her heavy feet. Now that the goal was in sight she felt her head getting light. Her body was heavy and her head was light. It started to spin—slowly first, then more quickly. A man with a suitcase cannoned into her. The agony of her body restored her senses. She felt the strain on every bone in her body. Her feet continued to move, one after the other. If they stopped now they would not go again. She would never catch the train. The perspiration slid down her white face.

She shuffled through the turnstile, the children following.

The ticket collector shouted at her. She turned and looked at him dumbly.

'You got a ticket?' he asked, not unkindly.

Mechanically she withdrew an arm from around the baby and opened her hand. On her palm lay a grubby piece of cardboard. She stared at it, surprised to see it. It filled her with relief to find it there. He let her go.

The train had pulled into the platform. It was early. Even the second class carriages were almost empty. She selected one at random and got in. The children followed, assisting each other as best they could.

She had caught the train. She could sit still now and sink down into nothingness. It was good to sit down, but somehow her body pained and tortured her more than it had done as she walked along. Her trembling racked her whole body. She felt milk gush into her breasts, making them sting and ache. She woke from her apathy to a sense of dull anger. Anger at some monstrous shapeless devil she vaguely termed fate. The devil that had given her a poverty-stricken childhood. The devil that had given her hard work and little money in her girlhood. The devil that had shifted her from a crowded slum to a three-roomed weatherboard cottage in the near-country. Still more work. Still less money. Poverty always. The devil that when she felt ill with the babies gave her a slice of bread and dripping instead of a cool, crisp lettuce leaf—pale green on a pale blue plate; a cup of stewed tea instead of a glass of milk, cold with shattered ice. Her anger was a little thing against the all-omnipotence of this devil. It seemed that she had been singled out for special attention. He dogged her footsteps always—always would.

She was too tired for sustained anger. It ebbed from her, leaving her apathetic again, even to the pain of her body. She leant back and closed her eyes. The train whistle blew. The wheels began to turn. She had caught the train.

JUDITH WRIGHT
(1915-   )

Judith Wright was born in Armidale, New South Wales, into a prominent pastoralist family, and grew up on the family property near the town. She studied at the University of Sydney, visited England and Europe, and then settled in Sydney. At the beginning of the Second World War she returned to Armidale to help on the family property because of the shortage of labour. This return to the countryside of her childhood led to a very creative period, which produced her first volume of poetry, *The Moving Image* (1946). Her poetry was enthusiastically received by the literary world and since then, in volume after volume, she has consolidated her place as one of Australia's greatest poets. Among her awards for poetry are the Grace Leven Prize for poetry (1949 and 1972), the *Encyclopaedia Britannica* Prize (1964), the Robert Frost Memorial Award (1976) and the Asan World Prize for Poetry (1984). Five universities have awarded her honorary doctorates.

Wright is not just known as a poet. She has been a literary critic, an editor, a fiction writer, an historian, an essayist and a university lecturer. She is well known for her work in conservation and Aboriginal rights.

A prolific and extremely talented short story writer, she has had short stories published in journals and anthologies, and some were collected in *The Nature of Love* (1966). In 'The Lame Duck', which first appeared in the *Bulletin*, Wright examines the power of social position. She skilfully exposes the internal and external pressures placed on the individual to conform.

THE LAME DUCK

The allotment beside the Browns' house had been a tangle of dodder, lantana and low scrub, with a few old boots and useless bits of timber thrown over the fence by Ronnie Brown from time to time. Lyla Brown leaned on her doorpost, looking across at it with a new interest, a slice of bread and jam in her hand. The busy bulldozer worked across and across, piling up the scrub and the lantana in driftwood lines, exposing the raw white clay, smoothing away whatever had been wild and secret there, ready for the builder and his measuring tape.

The cottage was to be built for a widow from the town, they said; the bank-manager's widow, who would have to move from the bank residence. Lyla and Ronnie watched her there when she came out with old Sly the builder, energetically walking here and there, checking the survey-pegs, pointing out this and that to be done. 'Looks a bit of a battle-axe, doesn't she?' Ronnie said, leaning against the kitchen window-sill with one arm over Lyla's neck. 'Oh, I don't know,' said Lyla. She liked people, she liked company. It would be a change.

For of course she had to be alone a lot. Ronnie worked in the big boat-builder's in town on the river, two miles away. Sometimes there was overtime, and he'd be late back, or work Saturdays; sometimes things were slack and he'd be put on three days a week and have to go out in his brother's fishing-boat to keep the money coming in.

Not much—not a lot. Neither Ronnie nor Lyla wanted a lot. Enough to live on, to keep up the payments on Ronnie's bike and on the radiogram, and to have their Saturday party; that was enough. What else did they want? There were no children yet, and Lyla was all Ronnie wanted, Ronnie all that Lyla thought of. When they clung together in the big iron bed with the slightly

173

grimy sheets, they already had more than either of them had thought possible.

The widow's cottage grew, first into a red-boned skeleton of timber framework, then into the semblance of a real house. It fascinated Lyla to watch the carpenters and conjecture what would happen next, and what this or that bodiless enclosure, later to be a room, was meant for. She stared at it through the kitchen window as she washed up, or over her shoulder as she pretended to work in the neglected garden. Soon she came to know the carpenters well enough to carry them cups of tea and scones now and then, call jokes over the fence and ask about their wives and families.

After the floor went down, they asked her over to walk through the house and admire what was done. She looked at the blueprint pinned on a stud, the built-in cupboards, the smart new knobs and handles and arrangements. She grew attached to that house, possessive as though in some sense it were her own. The Browns' house was old—it had belonged to Ronnie's people, dead now ('thank goodness', Lyla often found herself thinking). It had been built in the days when a house was a place no more important than another, a place to be skimped, non-competitive, not for showing off to the neighbours; and Ronnie seldom mended the cracks in the walls, the broken steps, the leaks in the galvanised-iron water-tanks or the creaking floorboards.

Sometimes on Sundays the widow, Mrs Hamilton, came to look through the house that Lyla knew better than she did herself, and to scribble curt notes to the carpenters— 'Window won't shut. Please attend to this'; or 'Nailheads not flush with timber here.' On Mondays Lyla would carry over the teapot and share the notes with the carpenters, giggling as they grumbled at the way the old bag shoved them about.

She shared all this with Ronnie at nights. It was coming to be more important than her own house to her, during the week— the house next door. Except on Saturdays, which were party days, and Sundays, when Ronnie slouched round in shorts and read the paper, or they went fishing together in the Bay, she hadn't much else to think of.

On the carpenters' last Friday, when the house was standing at last ready for the painters and only the last touches were to be done, she went across and asked them to come to the Saturday party and bring their wives. It was a sort of farewell party; and Lyla felt, as she sniffed the exciting, somehow nostalgic, smell of new wood and tile-board that the house exhaled, and flirted a little with young Joe the carpenters' assistant, really as though something was coming to an end; a part of her life, tied up with the hot summer days and the friendly sound of sawing and hammering that had been their accompaniment as much as the sound of cicadas in the garden fig-trees.

She would miss that noise, the small excitement of having the men next door, and knowing their eyes were on her as she went about her daily jobs with a bit more lipstick than usual, a dress a little gayer than she would have worn if they hadn't been there.

Since the carpenters and their wives were strangers to her own friends and Ronnie's, she went to no end of trouble over the party, with flowers in all the vases and the curtains washed and ironed. Everyone mixed well and the party was a success. Lyla played the guitar afterwards, though she was getting so out of practice, and they all sang—'Harvest Moon' and 'Bye Bye Blackbird' and the hit-parade tunes that were popular just then; and Lyla sang the songs she had sung on the Radio Amateur Hour, the time she had come second in the voting and might have gone to the city for good, only of course she married Ronnie.

Next week the painters came; but they were gone again in a few days, and Lyla had scarcely had time to get to know them, though she took them cups of tea in order to find out what colours the rooms were to be. She and the painters agreed that there was no doubt these modern colours made a place look gay, though they weren't to everybody's taste. But after the carpenters, the painters seemed somehow intruders. Lyla missed the noise of hammers and saws and young Joe's modest admiration.

Soon the widow would be moving in, and though Lyla looked forward to that as another piece of excitement, she felt vaguely jealous about the house; as though she herself ought to be the owner, and Mrs Hamilton was an interloper.

The first van came with the furniture on Monday morning early, so that Ronnie was able to watch it with her. Two more vanloads came during the day, and at night she and Ronnie had plenty to talk about—the colours and the quality of the furniture, where everything had probably been bought and what it must have cost. Lyla went through all the furniture advertisements in the piles of old newspapers under the laundry shelf, and added up prices on paper. She still felt restless, somehow forlorn; she decided to buy half a gallon of paint in that pretty pink and do up the kitchen a bit, out of Ron's next pay. There was no doubt the house was looking shabby.

Next day Mrs Hamilton drove up in a taxi with her suitcases and boxes and another woman, it might have been her sister, who must have come to help her get things to rights. Lyla shifted her ironing-board closer to the window and watched them pay off the driver and walk up the path and through the polished cypress-pine door with the little diamond-shaped pane that Lyla so much liked the look of.

Starched, Mrs Hamilton was, Lyla thought—how many bones she had in her girdle you couldn't give a guess. She imagined to herself where all the furniture was going, what the rooms must look like now. She'd had some good jokes in that house, with the carpenters; she knew every wall and corner and window. Oh well, at least she had a neighbour now; it would be someone to talk to.

When she finished the ironing she fetched a chair to the window and sat there with her cup of tea and her piece of bread and jam. She kept an eye on the house; but someone had put up Venetian blinds over the windows already, and after a few minutes Mrs Hamilton came to the windows and let them all down quite sharply. As though she was a Peeping Tom, thought Lyla, and she moved away from the window at once. When Ronnie came, she told him all the day's news, except that. That shamed her, somehow.

The next morning, when Mrs Hamilton was measuring and pegging out the ravaged clay round the house for garden-beds, and Lyla came out to feed the few hens she kept in a tumbledown netting yard at the back, Mrs Hamilton greeted her in quite a friendly way.

'You're Mrs Brown, aren't you? What a little thing to be called Mrs! Would you like to come over here and help me get these measurements straight, dear? I'm sure you've got a better eye for this kind of thing than I have.'

And Lyla found herself holding the end of a string and knocking in pegs for Mrs Hamilton and talking away as though they had been friends a long time. It felt quite right and natural, somehow, to be doing things for that house, for that garden.

And Mrs Hamilton was so kind, so interested. 'I never had a daughter of my own, but if I had she'd be about your age, dear, so please don't mind if I talk to you now and then. I do hope we'll be friends.' Lyla couldn't help feeling flattered.

Yes, it was really a new kind of life that Lyla was beginning. She hurried through her own housework in the mornings, to go over to Mrs Hamilton and help her unpack, move the furniture about, hang pictures, put down carpets. Mrs Hamilton was a great gardener; but since she seemed to have plenty of money, she got a man out from town twice a week to dig the new beds and clear up the mess around the house and lay the lawn. It was old Jim Harrison, whom Lyla had seen round the town since she was a little girl, and had often passed the time of day with.

But Lyla noticed that when Mrs Hamilton made him a cup of tea in the mornings, she left it in the kitchen and had her own in the sitting-room, or over with Lyla. Lyla wondered at that, and once she even asked, 'Shan't I get Mr Harrison over to have his tea here?' He certainly looked glum, stuck over there in the blue-tiled kitchen all alone.

But Mrs Hamilton looked taken aback. 'He's the gardener, Lyla,' was all she said.

Still, she didn't seem to mind Lyla's run-down house, or her not knowing the right way to do things. She told Lyla she was really getting fond of her. 'You're such a pretty little kitten to be here all by yourself.' And Lyla enjoyed that. She liked being liked, and she had begun to feel quite fond of Mrs Hamilton, herself.

'What happened to your little foot, dear?' she asked once, when Lyla was moving round the kitchen with her light dragging step, getting Mrs Hamilton a bit of lunch. (It was so hot, and Mrs Hamilton had given herself a headache, painting the patio chairs.)

Lyla told her the whole story; how when she and Ronnie were not even thinking of getting married, the time when she had just come second in the Amateur Hour, Ronnie had taken her out fishing in the motor-boat that belonged to his brother, and how she had slipped on the jetty just as she was getting out of the boat, and her foot had caught between the gunwale and the jetty-piles, and before Ronnie could push the boat off her foot had gone scrunch—like that. The bones were broken, and when she had come out of hospital after all those weeks she was still lame, and the doctors said she always would be.

But it ended happily, for she and Ronnie were married now, and everyone said it had been for the best after all. Only of course she could never have gone to the city and got a job singing and dancing, as she had meant to do before she fell in love with Ronnie. Still it didn't matter, it didn't keep her from doing all she wanted to do, and since she had Ronnie now she didn't want to go to the city anyway.

Mrs Hamilton listened with as much interest as even Lyla could expect, though the story never failed to seem to her romantic. She made Lyla take down her guitar from the case on top of the wardrobe, and play to her.

'Why, that's beautiful, Lyla. Yes, you're really an artist. A little lame artist—a dancer who can't dance. Such a pretty voice you have. No doubt about it, your Ronnie is lucky, isn't he? Just think of all you might have been doing! Perhaps you might have gone abroad—done as well as that girl—what's her name?—the one who broke into television in London. You might, you know, with that voice and those pretty looks. Yes—I hope he knows how lucky he is to have you, so far away from all the excitement you might have had, out here at Chinaman's Creek of all places! Do play me that again—I just loved it.'

Even sometimes when Ronnie came home at nights—a time they had always had quite to themselves, since they had never before had a close neighbour—Mrs Hamilton would drop in for a few minutes, or call Lyla over to help her with something, or to show her a new ornament or a flower just come into bloom. Ronnie bore it patiently at first; but after a while he began to grumble now and then, when dinner was late because Mrs Hamilton had wanted Lyla to come over.

'We get along all right without a dining-room carpet, or a dining-room either,' he said one night when Lyla came back with a bruised thumb after helping with the tack-hammer. 'Why can't she do her own jobs herself and leave us alone? Why, it's past six o'clock!' But Lyla put both arms round his neck and apologised for being late, and even consented to call Mrs Hamilton a selfish old so-and-so, for his sake.

Indeed, she hadn't at all wanted to tack down that carpet. But it was hard to say no to the poor old girl, all alone over there—and really very kind to Lyla, whatever Ronnie thought of her.

Somehow they hadn't had so many of the Saturday parties lately, either. But that week it happened that they were having a really big one, for once; Ronnie's sister was up from the city on holiday, Lyla's cousins were staying in town. There would be twenty people at least. Lyla half-thought of asking Mrs Hamilton over—poor old thing. But she decided against it, almost without having to consider. The idea of Mrs Hamilton, in her black corded taffeta suit with the frilled white shirt-front, with her precise voice and her white hair so quietly waved, simply didn't go with the easy good-humoured crowd that would fill Lyla's kitchen and living-room and overflow onto the sagging veranda—with the keg of beer on the kitchen table, the glasses leaving rings everywhere, the shirt-sleeves and the women in their cotton frocks and synthetic jewellery.

She was glad she hadn't asked her, since for some reason the party was a remarkably noisy one; Ronnie's brother had brought a few extra men and the men had brought a few extra bottles. Mrs Hamilton's light went out early, and the windows and shutters on the side of her house that faced the Browns' were closed. Lyla thought they were probably locked. And on Sunday she went out early and caught the church bus, and didn't come back all day.

Lyla couldn't help feeling self-conscious on Monday morning, as she hung out the wash and took a peep over her shoulder once or twice to see if Mrs Hamilton was there. She was surprised to find that she felt the way she used to when she hadn't done her homework properly, and the teacher—Miss Goodridge whom she used to have such a crush on, and who wore such pretty clothes and spoke so nicely—looked at her and said, 'Oh, Lyla, and you could be top of the class if you only tried!'

Yes, it was just that feeling. She laughed herself out of it. What business was it of the old girl's if she and Ronnie wanted to have a good noisy party once in a while? Lyla was a married woman and old enough to know what she wanted, wasn't she? And she wanted what Ronnie wanted, and other people could just mind their own business.

But Mrs Hamilton was just as usual, to Lyla's relief. She called out and asked Lyla to come to afternoon tea, because she'd been over to her sister's place yesterday and brought back some things her sister had been minding for her till she got the house to right. Lyla might like to see them.

Lyla went over after changing into a clean dress—one of her best it was—and so tight round the waist, since her figure had begun to grow plumper, that she hardly ever bothered to put it on nowadays. 'Bread and jam,' she said to herself crossly in the mirror, drawing in her stomach.

Mrs Hamilton gave her tea in the sitting-room, where Lyla

had helped to hang the brocade curtains and put down the coffee-coloured wall-to-wall carpet. Tea was in the very best white fluted cups; it wasn't like a Monday afternoon at all. Mrs Hamilton showed her the linen her grandmother had embroidered long ago, and the old pieces of jewellery, and then she set up a screen and a little projector, and showed her colour-slides of her sister's house and her sister's daughter and her husband and the children. The children were neat and pretty and well-dressed, with a pony and two Labrador dogs. They lived in a northern suburb in Sydney, and the two little girls went to a fashionable school there.

Lyla was uncomfortable in her tight dress, but the photographs were worth it. They were nearly as good as Hollywood.

Gradually Lyla began to smarten up the house a bit. If Ronnie put a cup of tea down without the saucer, she'd say, 'Mind the paint, Ron. I only got that done a few days ago and I don't want it spoilt straightaway.' And instead of sitting on the veranda after tea, with their arms round each other, watching the river and talking, she set him to mending the catch of the kitchen window, or fixing a loose board somewhere. Ronnie seldom protested, but his mouth went down at the corners and he worked in silence.

'Don't you want things to look decent?' she said once or twice. But he only said, 'Yair, I suppose so.'

And Lyla's feelings went on confusing her; sometimes she felt guilty towards Ronnie, sometimes towards Mrs Hamilton, and she could never quite tell why. It made her snappy sometimes, the way Ronnie never *said* anything.

She had begun to work hard in the garden too, clearing the weeds and the old cat's claw creeper away, putting in a few plants—things that Mrs Hamilton gave her. Mrs Hamilton showed her how to strike cuttings in flower pots, and Lyla got Ronnie to mow the grass, in hopes that it would turn into a lawn. But it never looked half as nice as Mrs Hamilton's was beginning to.

Of course, her garden had been put in properly from the start, not just patched up like the Browns', and with Jim Harrison coming out twice a week, it was soon looking really wonderful. Lyla could hardly remember the time when there had just been the Browns' straggling picket-fence, and the scrub and lantana and the birds singing there in the early mornings. But sometimes she stood and looked across there, trying to remember, and she was surprised to feel a small dragging pain as she thought of it, a sense of loss.

It was Ronnie. He wasn't the same somehow, she decided. Once he had come straight back from work; now he sometimes stayed for a game of pool or a beer or two, or even stopped back at the firm and did a bit of overtime. He had usually got out of overtime, on one excuse or other, when they were first married.

Still, she had Mrs Hamilton there now, so she didn't miss him as she would have done before. And Mrs Hamilton was always ready to slip over for a talk, to lend Lyla copies of *Vogue*, to advise her about colours for dresses or curtains, and to listen to her playing and singing. She even gave her some sheet-music and song albums—too arty, Ronnie called them, but Lyla practised them just the same.

Quite often, too, Mrs Hamilton had her own friends out from town for an afternoon's bridge, and sometimes she asked Lyla across. Lyla didn't like to say she didn't care for bridge, so she pretended she couldn't play, and it usually ended in her setting the tray for afternoon tea and handing round the cups and clearing up afterwards. Mrs Hamilton's sister, too, took a great fancy to her. 'I quite miss you, when you don't come over to Eileen's parties,' she told her. 'I often say to Eileen, now where is your dear little lame duck today? You mustn't be offended, dear, it's just my way. After all, you *are* a duck, you know—a perfect little duck.' And Lyla smiled agreeably, not knowing whether she was offended or not.

Mrs Hamilton often spent her weekends with her sister; but at last the sister came to stay with her instead. Lyla grew worried, and tried to explain to Ronnie that this weekend the Saturday party really ought to be a bit quieter. 'After all, it's different

182

now we've got neighbours. We mustn't disturb the old things too much. So do try and keep the Lister boys from making too much noise, Ronnie; and don't put the keg on the kitchen table, because that new paint marks badly.'

And she tried to make the party a bit more formal, so that they'd all know they were expected to behave well. She wore her new dress that Mrs Hamilton had helped her make—a sort of heavy dark satiny stuff, with a little cocktail hat to match. Vera and Marlie and Shirley admired it ecstatically.

But somehow the party was a flop. Everyone left rather early; and though Lyla told herself she had wanted that to happen, it made an empty end to the evening. And Ronnie wasn't in a good temper, either.

He went off early next morning, down to the jetty, with some excuse or other about having to do a job on his brother's launch. He'd taken sandwiches with him, but Lyla didn't believe he would stay away from her for Sunday dinner, and cooked it just the same. When he wasn't home by half-past one, she didn't feel like eating, but let the food dry out in the shut-off oven, and sat limply on the veranda with stinging eyes. Perhaps she *had* been on his neck a bit these last weeks—making him mow the lawn, fix the back steps, build her a rockery. She knew quite well that Vera and the rest thought she was getting too big for her boots—a cocktail hat at a Saturday party! Well, let them think. Wasn't it right to make the place look decent, to wear the right thing, to try to get on a bit?

She sat there until Mrs Hamilton came home from seeing her sister off in the bus, and asked her over for a cup of tea.

Lyla knew that Mrs Hamilton knew there was something wrong that afternoon; and Mrs Hamilton's considerate refusal to show that she did know it, her acting as though it was the same as any other day, made Lyla's troubles a dozen times more real to her. Mrs Hamilton never mentioned Ronnie, or wondered why he wasn't home this fine Sunday afternoon, but seemed to take it for granted that Lyla should be alone and needing company. That was what hurt.

So when Ronnie came home at five o'clock, warm and good-tempered again and ready to apologise if necessary, she pushed him away and told him off. That night they slept back to back, resentful, not touching. It had never been like that before.

All the week they were strained and uneasy with each other, either snappy or unnaturally polite. But on Friday, Ronnie came home with a parcel in his hand, and tiptoed into the kitchen where she was peeling potatoes, and kissed the back of her neck like he used to do. Lyla looked up, half-sullen, half-yielding.

'Let's ring them all up and put off the party, Ly,' he said. 'Let's have a weekend down the Bay like we used to. I've got a boat for the two days, and we'll camp at the Point. Look here.'

He undid the parcel. There was a new nylon line for her fishing-rod, and a cute new peaky cotton cap like the ones they were advertising in town. She tried it on, pulling it down over one eye; it made her look like a wicked little girl. My word, Ronnie said, it did suit her!

She hugged him. It was just what she'd wanted, she said, a weekend down the Bay. 'I'm sick of the old house, and the smell of paint. I do believe that's why I've been so cross lately. Wasn't I silly?'

The good spots in the Bay were full of boats at anchor, and the holiday-makers and their wives all knew Ronnie and Lyla. The little waves broke blue and white, the boats rocked all together, and the fishermen shouted to each other and joked and compared catches. On the Point that night there were camp-fires and tents, and the mosquitoes pinged in the moonlight. Lyla rested her head on Ronnie's shoulder and played her guitar, and everyone gathered round their tent and sang—all the pops, all the hits, all the old favourites.

On Sunday a westerly wind got up, and the Bay was cold and choppy. One by one the boats went back, and at last they had to follow. Lyla's nose was sunburnt, and Ronnie ran a hook under his thumbnail. They had engine trouble, and had to row the last part of the way back to the jetty, and Lyla felt a blister coming. 'Here, you can row by yourself, can't you, even if you

184

have got a sore thumb? The sun's giving me a headache.'

They pulled the boat up and tied her, and started home with the bundles of gear, Ronnie bent under the weight of the tent and blankets. After a while they stopped and sat down for a rest. Lyla in her smart peaked cap looked petulant and a little swollen. Sunburn always made her nose swell, and she couldn't help squinting down it.

'There isn't enough brim to this cap,' she said, moving crossly away as Ronnie put his arm across her sore shoulders. 'And I'm going to town on Tuesday to help Mrs Hamilton shop, and she's giving me tea at the hotel. I bet I'll be peeling by that time.'

Ronnie was hurt. 'Damn Mrs Hamilton and the hotel too.'

It all began over again. They sat miserably on their bundles, their throats aching with resentment. What if Ronnie did leave his bike on top of the new garden-bed with the carnation-cuttings, last Tuesday? How was he to know they were there? What if Lyla did keep after him about that hinge on the garden gate? Wasn't it for Ronnie's comfort just as much as her own to get things fixed? And why shouldn't they have a nice place just as much as anyone else? That was all very well, but who was going to have to do the work—dig the garden and paint the roof and pay for the new china and the stuff for the curtains, and the new carpet? What were they doing getting a new carpet, anyway, when the bike wasn't even paid for yet? Oh, money, money, money! Lyla was sick of money—sick of not having any, that is. Maybe she could go to town and earn some for herself if Ronnie couldn't manage to. Well, why not, anyway? Mrs Hamilton said she was just as good as a lot of these popular entertainers— even if she did have a lame foot, and whose fault was that, anyway?

At that Ronnie turned a strange colour and walked away. Lyla burst into tears. 'Oh, I'm sorry, Ronnie, I never meant to throw that up at you, ever. I don't know what's come over us lately.'

'Well, I do,' said Ronnie, stopping for a moment, 'it's that old bitch over the fence. I bet she said something like that to you, or it never would have come into your head. I don't know why you've taken to her like you have. She's too stuck-up for words.'

'Well, that's a nice way to take an apology!' Lyla sobbed. 'She's got nothing to do with it. She just happens to be our neighbour and I've got to be neighbourly, haven't I? It's all very well for you, you don't have to stay round the house all day, stuck away out in the bush a mile from the shops or the pictures. You don't stop to think what it's like for me, alone all day and with nobody to talk to. You're just jealous; you don't want me to know anybody or have anything other people have. And Mrs Hamilton's been real nice to me, and you too. I don't know why you've got to pick on her.'

'Oh, come on,' said Ronnie sulkily. 'I'm sure I don't want to argue any more. Let's get back and have some tea. I'm sick of this and I'm hungry.'

They picked up the bundles that seemed so much heavier than they had been. Ronnie stalked ahead without speaking, and though Lyla had to walk fast to keep up with him, she would not ask him to go slower. Nevertheless, she limped more and more, and almost took a pleasure in it.

Mrs Hamilton, working in her garden in the cool of the evening, said good-night pleasantly as they passed, one behind the other, and watched with her eyebrows up as they went through the garden gate that no longer dragged as Ronnie opened it. Another quarrel? Oh well, it was the way of things. She would hear about it all in good time.

NANCY CATO
(1917–   )

Nancy Cato was born and educated in Adelaide, where she began her literary career as a journalist and art critic for the Adelaide *News*. Her best-known work, *All the Rivers Run*, a trilogy of historical novels, was first published in the late 1950s and early 1960s and was set against the background of the Murray River. In 1978 a rewritten, combined version of the trilogy was published. It became a best-seller in Australia, England and the United States, and was later made into a successful television production.

Cato has published eight other works of fiction, four works of non-fiction and two volumes of poetry. The editor of several anthologies, she has been an active member of the South Australian branch of the Fellowship of Australian Writers and of the Australian Society of Authors. In 1984 she was made a Member of the Order of Australia.

'The Trap', which first appeared in the *Bulletin* in 1950, is a tightly structured story. In it Cato effectively uses the symbol of the trap to depict the relationship between a man and a woman.

THE TRAP

Almost opposite the lonely shack on the road to the Point, the fish-trap, built ingeniously of airstrip mesh, its stout criss-cross wires rusted to a warm orange by the sea, stretched out into the shallow waters of the bay—wind-rippled and turquoise blue in the Dry, smooth as silver satin in the Wet.

Just now it was the Dry, and the curving beach of yellow sand shimmered and almost smoked in the sun's heat, concentrated by the blue burning-glass of the sky. The tide was far out, leaving bare the mud of the mangrove-swamps beyond the Point, exposing sandpits and shoals where the soldier-crabs marched and turned. Only a few shallow pools were left about the far end of the fish-trap. The long entrance-ways of the trap and the two enclosures to which they led (the farther one almost a hundred yards from the shoreline at high tide), looked like a long jetty abandoned by the sea.

There was nothing to keep the fish in, but once they entered the shoreward openings they were lost, their obstinate urge to make for deep water leading them to press on, instead of turning back before the water went down and it was too late.

Over the soft coarse sand beyond the reach of the tides, and the low sandhills covered with purple-flowered convolvulus, a roll of airstrip mesh had been laid. Tracks turning from the road showed that it was often used.

The sound of an engine, the rattling of loose parts over the corrugated road, and a cloud of bright red dust, marked the approach of a vehicle. Soon a khaki-painted utility bounced over the sandhills to the beach. At the same moment a woman's figure appeared on the front landing of the house, which had a flight of wooden steps and was perched on twelve-foot-high stilts, yet

188

only just cleared the growth of rank grass and shrubs surrounding it on three sides.

The utility drove onto firm, wet sand. An Australian Air Force man, dressed casually in khaki shorts and an open tunic over a bare chest, jumped down and went into the first of the maze-like openings through which the fish could not escape.

He came out with a shrug and a spreading of the hands expressive of 'no luck'. From the outer enclosure he emerged with the same gesture.

When he came back, the driver, a young RAAF officer in a peaked cap and a buttoned tunic, leant with one sun-browned forearm on the steering wheel, and pushed the cap to the back of his head. The two men turned and stared at the shack. The woman could now be seen moving about underneath it.

'There hasn't been a fish in the trap since they came here, blast them!' said the young officer, wiping with the back of his hand at the sweat beading his upper lip.

'We've never actually caught them at it.'

'No, but her tracks are always on the beach, leading down into the wet sand. I reckon he sends the woman down because he thinks we'd be soft with her.'

It was still early, but they had met the husband's truck on the road to town, going hell-for-leather over the corrugations to avoid their jarring bumps. He left early to work on the dam, and usually did not return before dusk.

The young officer adjusted the dark glasses on his sharp, square-cut nose. He had weak eyes and the glasses covered spectacles; he had an idea they made him look like General MacArthur. He hadn't the general's imposing physique, but his stocky figure was solid-looking, his chin was firm, and his mouth straight.

He looked back again at the shack. A white sheet was blowing from the line strung between the porch and the palm-tree in front.

'I'm going to tackle her about it now,' he said and turned the utility.

Bumping over the sand ridges he felt his heart beginning to bump a little too, and silently cursed himself for a fool. He had noticed the woman appreciatively, of course—they all had—flaunting about in her bright skirt, with her long dark hair and slim brown legs. Once, driving past to the deserted station on the Point, he had glimpsed a white figure flitting for shelter from the open shower under the house.

He left the utility on the road and walked over the flattened grass, giving a purposeful hitch to his shorts. The woman was still under the house, washing clothes in some improvised tubs on the ground. She stood up, wiping her hands on the full skirt, which was banded horizontally and dazzlingly in purple, green, yellow, red, and white.

She smiled inquiringly. He noticed that she had a lovely mouth, wide but finely cut, and that her long dark-fringed eyes were blue. He was surprised; he'd been prepared to find that, like most of the women in this northern outpost at the end of the war, she had 'a touch of the tarbrush' about her.

He kept his mouth straight and adjusted his dark glasses sternly.

'Good morning. Ah . . . the fish have been disappearing from our trap lately. Have you seen anyone interfering with it?'

She opened her clear eyes wide and shook her head, still smiling. He felt a half-angry urge to make her speak. Her charm would disappear as soon as she opened her mouth, no doubt. 'Your husband not about?'

A smiling shake of the head, accompanied by the lift of one eyebrow.

Curse her, he thought. She went back to one of the tubs and crouched beside it, rubbing at the clothes within. He watched, fascinated, the soap-bubbles clinging to her smooth brown arms.

'The RAAF built the trap, you know,' he said. 'It cost us a lot of work and we count on it to vary the diet a bit. M and V gets pretty monotonous, especially in a stinking hole like this.' He let all his hatred of the heat, all his nostalgia for his distant home get into the last words.

The woman—she was only a girl really, he saw now, not

190

more than twenty or so—twisted a soapy shirt and with a dexterous movement flung it into a bowl of clean water with a splash.

'I like it,' she said quietly. 'Perhaps because I'm used to it.' She had the sallow complexion of a woman who has lived long in the tropics.

He groaned inwardly. There was nothing wrong with her voice!

Unthinkingly he squatted down on his heels, in the comfortable pose which camp life had taught him, with his arms between his knees. He poked at a stray green ant with a piece of stick.

'I come from Melbourne. God, how I'd love to feel a good, cold, sleety wind blowing down Collins Street.' He scratched with the stick in the hard ground under the house. The drops of sweat fell off his nose and chin onto the ground. He stared at her from under his dark brows, and then from the corner of his eye he saw his man beginning to climb out of the utility. He stood up abruptly.

'Well, I wish you'd keep a look-out when the tide is out, if we're not here; and tell me if you see anyone ratting our trap. They'd better look out,' he added darkly.

She replied only with her enigmatic smile.

That night, lying under the stifling sandfly net on the hard straw palliasse, he could not get her out of his mind. He thought fiercely of his fiancée in Melbourne, of Flora's fresh pink cheeks and dark eyes, but instead he saw the unknown girl: the coloured stripes of her skirt, the white silk jumper covering her small breasts, the dark fluff of her hair, her long blue eyes and mocking smile; and as soon as he fell asleep he dreamed that there was a big fish in the trap, and when he went to get it it was the girl, smiling at him with her red lips . . .

Though the low tide came early in the morning now, he saw her several times on the beach, wandering about on the sand-flats in a brief sun-suit.

Then came the dodge tides, and it was dark when they inspected the trap. They found a few fish in it. One morning there was a small long-tom wedged high up in one of the enclosures, where it had swum half through the mesh and got stuck. It was higher than his head, showing where the tide had been up to in the night.

The girl was coming down to the beach as they drove up, and he handed the small fish to her.

'Here, it's not enough for our mess. You might as well have it.'

She smiled. 'Thanks. M and V does get a bit monotonous, doesn't it?'

For the first time he allowed himself to smile back at her, showing his even white teeth. He had suspected her unjustly. Perhaps it was that big sea-eagle sitting on the post out there, with his buff wings and white breast, who was to blame; yet he couldn't pull big fish through the wire. But hermit-crabs? He'd seen fish nearly eaten away by crabs.

'What I really miss most is fresh milk,' she said.

'Milk? I can get you some. We've got a herd of cows inland a bit, though they don't give much milk in the Dry. I'll bring you some tomorrow.'

She was not on the beach next morning He and his two passengers rushed excitedly to the outer trap to see the big fish there, but it was only a ground shark. The tide was already on the turn, and the water was making about the outer trap. He stepped carefully past the patch of quicksand.

A ripple came at his foot with a little menacing rush. Though he was not unduly imaginative, he shivered. There was something inexorable about the daily movement of the sea. Tide waits for no one ... No, what was it? Time and tide wait for no man.

The morning was misty and pungent with the smoke of grass-fires burning across the bay. He parked the utility in the road and took a carefully wrapped lemonade bottle of milk up to the house. The men sat and jeered at him. He took no notice but climbed the wooden steps and handed her the bottle through the open door.

She did not invite him in. He sat on the landing, in the shade of the palm-tree fronds which clacked in the dry wind, and talked to her through the open door. He told her that he had taken the milk off the ice, and she drank some from

192

a thick enamel mug while he watched her with a pleased air.

But he was nervous, and could not sit still. He strode up and down the landing, talking through the doorway and the open louvres, speaking jerkily, adjusting his dark glasses and wiping the sweat from his clean-shaven upper lip. She drank the milk slowly, appreciatively, still preserving the air of calm and secret amusement. She was conscious, conscious all the time of her attraction for these men starved for a white woman's company, bored by routine now that the war was over. He knew it and in a way hated her for it, yet it added to her attractiveness. She had the conscious grace of a cat that knows it is being watched, and will even lick its hind legs with a flourish.

For a week there were no fish in the trap, night or day; but one morning there was an early fisherman on the rocks farther along the beach, and he strolled up to the utility.

'That trap's bin done already, mate. Fine big barramundi they got out there this mornin'.'

'They? Who? This trap's ours.'

'Yours? Thought it belonged to the shack up there.'

The young officer's mouth became a hard line. He looked along the beach to where the girl was gathering driftwood, the backwash of war with which the sand was strewn.

'You go up to the shack and have a look round,' he said to the two aircraftmen with him, 'and I'll keep her talking.'

He found it easy to talk to her, but hard to keep his eyes from the length of neat limb exposed by the mannish white shirt and khaki shorts she wore. Glancing restlessly back at the shack, he saw the men come out from underneath it with something long and shining between them. Still talking, he led her back over the sand-ridges. They walked over the rusted iron mesh, across the red dusty road, and were confronted by the triumphant men bearing a three-foot barramundi.

'Well?' He turned to look at her sternly. 'That bloke down there told us a barramundi was taken out of the trap this morning.'

She turned wide blue eyes upon them. 'Wherever did you find that?'

'Under a tub, under the house there.'

'Well, I can't think how it got there.'

'Perhaps it swam!' he said sarcastically, and turned on his heel.

They trooped to the utility and got in. Before he drove off he turned to look at the house. The girl had disappeared up the steps.

'It beats me,' he said, 'how anyone with eyes like that can be such a damned liar.'

Next day there was quite a good haul of medium-sized fish in the trap. The welcome change in diet, with fried fish instead of tinned-dog on the menu, only whetted their appetites for more. They drove out to the beach with renewed eagerness. On the second day they found two big barramundi, one in each trap. The house among the long grass appeared deserted.

'Maybe they've left,' said the young officer, glancing up at the shack and wondering why he felt a sense of desolation. 'Her husband must have been taking the fish into town and selling it. They've obviously been getting good hauls.'

'I heard that he isn't her husband. They say she's been drifting round the North for years, taking up with different men. She'd probably have taken a Jap on if they'd got here.'

The other scowled. 'Oh, I dunno . . . she doesn't look such a hard case.'

The next day there were no fish in the trap, and the next and the next. At first they took it as a natural turn of the luck, but after two weeks of drawing blanks they were ready to give it away. The morning low tide was at five now, uncomfortably early, and five in the afternoon was an awkward time, and extremely hot.

On the fifteenth day in succession, coming down in the heat of the afternoon, they found nothing in the trap. Nor was there any sign of the girl's figure, though today her bright skirt flapped on the line with some other clothes, in the dry trade-wind.

Inexplicably irritated by one absence as much as the other, the young officer snapped, 'To hell with the fish. Let 'em have them. It's not worth coming all this bloody way for nothing; I've had it.'

'We ought to set a trap for *them*, the b——s,' said somebody darkly. 'Wait behind a sandhill with a revolver, and when they come down for the fish—'

'Ar, it's not worthwhile. We'd only catch the girl, anyway.' His eyes narrowed behind the dark glasses, and he added, roaring up the engine so that it almost drowned his words, 'I've a good mind to make her pay for them, though.'

'How're you going to make her pay for fish she has already? She'd only pull a tale about having no money.'

He set his teeth as he bungled a change of gear.

'She can pay in kind, can't she?'

The next day he came rattling over the red corrugations, alone. It was late afternoon. He had wanted to come all day, but had invented various duties to keep him at headquarters.

He stopped the utility and looked along the beach. No sign of her. The shack looked deserted, too. He walked up the twelve wooden steps and entered for the first time. His feet echoed loudly on the bare floor. The one big room was neatly swept, but the bunks were unmade. A cloth spread on a table under the windows was decorated with a pile of shells and coral, and some food lay under a net. He went through to the tiny kitchen. No one.

From the landing he shaded his eyes against the glare of the westering sun on the water, and looked along the beach. Only the heat-shimmer moved on the sand, and a sea-eagle sat on a post near the end of the trap. The flat, still sea was slowly retreating, until the end of the trap was almost dry. There might be a fish in it. Well! He'd trick her this time, go down before the water had gone, when she'd be scared to enter the trap . . . or would she?

He ran down the steps, half-relieved not to have found her at home. He drove onto the wet sand and got out. Yes, there was something big in the end enclosure—it looked like something big. As he moved forward a thought checked him. It might be a crocodile.

But no, he could see it more clearly now. It was big all right, some coloured tropical fish, striped and banded like . . . God! Like that girl's skirt.

He ran forward clumsily. His feet sucked in the wet sand. His heart had begun to thud, his mouth was dry, his palms sweated. Yes, there was no doubt it was the striped skirt, floating wetly, its colours darkened by water. Beside it lay what looked like a bunch of brown seaweed.

He wound his way into the trap and snatched her up, but the stiff body seemed suddenly to resist him. One hand was clenched round an upright. He struggled to unflex the fingers. Still he could not raise her. One leg was caught by the ankle beneath a stanchion, which fixed the wires firmly into the yielding sand.

He ran to the utility for a crowbar, and levered up the wires. The flesh was rubbed raw about her ankle, cut deeply with her struggles to be free. Her hands were scratched, the fingernails broken and filled with sand, showing how frantically she had dug only a few hours before.

He shuddered and leant against the wires a moment, feeling sick. If he had been any later . . . if he hadn't come this afternoon . . . the sea-eagle, and then the crabs . . .

His imagination presented to his shrinking mind the image of her lonely death: the first panic at the yielding sand, the struggles making the foot sink deeper, the frantic efforts to free it giving way to a more philosophical wait for the help that must come. How she must have been even a little embarrassed, waiting for the RAAF men to come and catch her red-handed in their fish-trap.

And then the cold fear growing, growing, as the first little ripples made their innocent-ugly rushes about her feet, and the water deepened inexorably, and no one came.

If he had not struggled with himself so long, if he had come earlier as he had wanted to, and found her in time; what might or might not have happened? Strangely, under all the horror of the moment, he felt a new lightness, as though a heavy weight had been lifted; he felt free.

The fish which she had come to get, and which had died hours before her, trapped in the tides of air, lay neglected in the shallow water that remained.

He picked up the girl's cold form. Artificial respiration? He would try, but it was obviously too late. He averted his eyes from the pinched, blue face—she was no longer pretty now—and carried the body up the beach.

HELEN MEGGS
(c. 1920–   )

Helen Meggs was born in Victoria, but grew up and was educated in Tasmania, first at Hobart High School and then at the University of Tasmania and Hobart Technical College. She taught at Launceston High School, and later took an arts degree at Melbourne University. For several years Meggs worked as a librarian, and in the late 1960s she became a nursery gardener at Kingslake, Victoria.

A few of her short stories appeared in the *Bulletin* in the 1940s and 1950s. 'Burning Off' was published in *Meanjin*, the *Bulletin* and *Coast to Coast, 1948* as well as in other collections of short stories. Meggs portrays the careless white male attitude towards the environment with such accuracy and humour that the story continues to appear in contemporary Australian anthologies.

BURNING OFF

Aunt Emily was always inviting me to Rock Mountain. 'And come in autumn,' she would say. 'It is so pretty then.' So towards the end of March I found myself in the rather battered Rock Mountain bus, leaning back against the hard leather, and indulging in pleasant day-dreams—lying in a hammock under the tall golden poplars, watching birds and wallabies in the bush, or floating lazily in the placid, if somewhat muddy, dam.

And that's just the way it was, the first day. I had a swim in the dam, then I took a book under the poplars, and after lunch I took my camera to Uncle Jim's ten-acre block of uncleared bush and managed to snap a wallaby, staring with soft-eyed surprise at me over a log.

When I went in to dinner Uncle Jim was back from town, where he had been to take down a load of timber.

'I see you've cut quite a lot of trees since I was here last,' I said as we sat down.

'Yair,' replied Uncle Jim. 'Reckon the logs I took down today'll be the last, though. I've got just about everything worthwhile outer that there block.'

'Oh, well,' I said philosophically. 'Some of the larger ones still there should be worth a bit in another five years.'

'Huh!' was all Uncle Jim said.

'I hope we won't be here in another five years,' said Aunt Emily. 'This place is all right at this time of the year, if there's no fires about and the snakes aren't too bad, though the flies are always awful, but in winter it's always rain, rain, rain and mud up to your knees all the time. It gets me down something awful.'

'When did you have a bushfire in your trees last?' I asked. 'I noticed a good many had been killed.'

'Huh?' Uncle Jim looked puzzled as he shovelled in a huge mouthful of corned beef. 'We 'aven't 'ad any bushfires 'ere since 1939. Two or three years ago I put a fire through that block meself, but it wasn't a bushfire. Just burnin' orf.'

'Oh,' I said. 'It must have been a pretty fierce blaze judging by the tall trees that were killed.'

'Aw, I dunno,' mumbled Uncle Jim, through half a potato. 'Didn't do no 'arm. One or two big fellas looked as though they was dead, so I cut 'em straight away. The fire did get away in the end, though. Burnt a few of me own fence-posts and got into Ted Angus's cow-paddock and burnt a lot of 'is grass.'

'Was Ted Angus annoyed?' I asked.

'Aw, no,' sighed Uncle Jim, as he spread his knife and fork across his plate to indicate that he had finished that course. ''E knew it was an accident. 'E 'elped me put in new fence-posts, an' I let 'is cow come an' eat the weeds down on the paddock that I wasn't using that year. Trouble was I should 'a' burnt orf that scrub sooner. It was too thick. Time I did it again now.'

I was horrified at this suggestion.

'But is it in any danger?' I asked. 'It's an island block, so how can a fire get either into it or out of it accidentally?'

'A grass-fire might get into it,' said Uncle Jim, 'same as it got out into the grass.'

'But the only grass is on the south side,' I pointed out. 'There's a road and ploughed land on the other sides, and a south wind usually brings rain and cool weather.'

'Yair,' agreed Uncle Jim vaguely. 'Anyway, it needs burnin' orf. 'Asn't been done for three years.'

I made one last attempt to save what had seemed to me such an attractive little piece of real Victorian bush.

'But how can the young trees ever grow if you keep burning them down?' I protested. 'There are millions of young mountain ash, messmate, and bluegum seedlings coming up all over the place in there.'

'Yair?' said Uncle Jim, digging his spoon into a large slab

of steamed pudding. 'What's the use of seedlings? You can't sell 'em. I don't know one from the other meself.'

I looked at him incredulously. But I soon realised that Uncle Jim, although he had lived at Rock Mountain all his life, knew very little about trees, apart from the technicalities of cutting them down and selling them. In Uncle Jim's mind native trees were divided into three categories—large, sound trees provided by a kind of Providence for man to fell and sell; fully grown but rotten or imperfect trees, to be ignored; and seedlings and saplings, to be treated as inflammable rubbish and burnt.

My final remark, to the effect that the fire-prohibition period had not yet ended, met with the information that it would end that night, and the next day I could help him with the 'burnin' orf' if I liked.

An ominous north wind was already blowing when I got up next morning, but 'Can't do no 'arm' was Uncle Jim's verdict. So we set off, Uncle Jim lightly armed with a box of matches. I took a fern-hook and hoped for the best.

'I got a photo of a wallaby in there yesterday,' I remarked, pointing.

'Did y'?' Uncle Jim marvelled. He cogitated for a time. 'Pity I didn't bring me gun.'

We lit about fourteen fires along the south edge of the trees so that the fire would burn back against the wind, and immediately had to set to work beating out grass-fires around the potato-paddock fence-posts. By the time we had them all safe the fire was roaring away merrily on a solid quarter-mile front, but just moving steadily, owing to the north wind blowing it back all the time.

There wasn't much to do but stand and watch, and at eleven o'clock we left it to go inside for a cup of tea.

When we came back the wind had changed to north-west and part of the fire had got away through Uncle Jim's east fence into Ted Angus's cow-paddock again.

We scrambled through the fence, of which two posts were already ablaze, and spent the next hour beating back the grass-fire while Ted got out his plough and ploughed a break around his haystack. Then he ploughed a break across the paddock so the fire could go no farther, and we all went off to lunch. I marvelled at Ted Angus's philosophical attitude, but Uncle Jim seemed to think he had no cause for complaint.

''E can't talk,' said Uncle Jim. ''E's a real firebug 'imself. Always settin' somebody's fence alight. Nearly burnt down 'is own 'ouse last summer.'

The ten-acre block was now just a smoking ruin, with not more than fifty green heads showing through the smoke.

'She'll be safe fer another coupla years now,' remarked Uncle Jim with satisfaction.

'Safe from what?' I asked rather bitterly. 'Timber thieves?'

This piece of impertinence was passed over in silence.

Suddenly Aunt Emily leaped from her chair and pointed dramatically through the window.

'Look!' she cried. 'That fool Ted Angus lighting the park on a day like this!'

Ted Angus was sauntering across the road, and just behind him, on the south side of the road, a flame shot up through the bracken. Uncle Jim responded with an extraordinary burst of profanity.

'I said 'e was a firebug!' he panted as we rushed towards the flames. I still had my fern-hook, and Uncle Jim had paused to seize a gum-bough.

The wind had veered again to due north and was blowing about fifty miles an hour, so the fire had spread over several hundred square yards before we could get there, and the undergrowth was so thick we couldn't get to the other side to stop it.

A snake shot out from under a log and wriggled right between my feet. After a leap into the air which any Australian Rules footballer might have envied I quickly destroyed the snake, and then looked around to see what Uncle Jim was doing.

He was quietly rolling himself a cigarette and gazing at the blaze thoughtfully.

'Reckon we'll 'ave to get the brigade out fer this,' he said finally. 'We can't do much with it on our own.'

I was pleasantly surprised at this display of civic interest, as I didn't suppose he would have considered the park any of his concern. But the next remark dispelled my illusions.

'The fire's 'eading straight fer Dick's place,' he explained. 'So you better go an' warn 'im an' Mary while I go an' get me truck out an' rustle up the brigade.'

I remembered then that Uncle Jim's younger brother Dick had married since my last visit and had built a home on the far side of the park.

The park consisted of forty acres of natural forest with a look-out commanding a magnificent view, a picnic-shelter and fireplaces. No resident of Rock Mountain ever took the slightest notice of it.

As I drove past the pretty little log shelter-shed and down the winding track flanked by tall tree-ferns and trailing clematis I wondered what it would all look like when I returned. Already the birds were clamouring shrilly overhead.

Dick was out felling timber somewhere, and Mary at first was incredulous. But when I showed her the cloud of smoke rising above the trees at the back she squealed in dismay and began to pack clothes in gaily-striped suitcases.

'There's no need for that yet!' I said sharply. 'Stop being hysterical and come and help me clear your backyard. This house makes me think of a bomb on the end of a fuse.'

And so it did. The park trees, with dense undergrowth, came right to the back fence, and from there bracken, dried grass, weeds and all kinds of rubbish continued without a break to the back wall of the big wooden shed which served as garage for the truck, workshop, toolshed and general junk-store. From the side of the shed nearest the house timber was stacked untidily, and about two tons of dry firewood was heaped near the back porch. The house itself was weatherboard.

'Is the house insured?' I asked Mary.

'I don't think it is,' she whimpered.

I made no further comment. But I drove Dick's truck up to the porch and told Mary to load the wood onto it while I made a break through the bracken beyond. Mary was an ex-typist who still wore high heels and red fingernails. With a little brutal encouragement I soon had her loading firewood, energetically but tearfully.

I hastily cut a small break all round the backyard, then set it alight and pranced like a dervish raking escaping tongues of flame back into the central bonfire. I was soaked in sweat after the first five minutes, but I had a fifty-yard strip of scorched earth between to the fence and the house at the end of half an hour.

Mary was still loading firewood, and the smoke from the fire in the park was rolling over us like a blanket.

I had just finished tossing the odd lengths of timber back into the shed when Dick came rattling up in a friend's truck. Dick and his friend leaped out in great excitement.

Dick abruptly asked what in the name of blazes Mary was doing with the firewood. He told Mary to go inside and pack, and she shot me a look of triumph as she disappeared.

'Thanks for burning this break,' he added more graciously. 'It gives me something to start from.' Dashing across to the fence he set light to the undergrowth in the park.

I sat down wearily on the step of the truck and asked friend Dave, 'What's that for?'

'It'll burn back to the fire that's already coming forward,' explained Dave.

'Oh,' I said. 'What for? So as to trap the chaps fighting in there?'

Dave spat contemptuously.

'Nah!' he said, 'I guess they can go back the way they came. They had the fire well under control when we came round.'

'If they had it well under control, why start it again?' I asked, honestly puzzled.

'I wouldn't have bothered meself,' conceded Dave. 'But I suppose Dick thinks it's best to be on the safe side.'

'And what about the Ranger's house?' I asked.

The Ranger's house was on the south-east corner of the park, and was therefore likely to catch the fire from two directions.

Dave considered this for a moment.

'Yair,' he agreed, as he thoughtfully gnawed a cigarette. 'The Ranger's in there fighting with the others. Reckon I better go round and warn him about this one Dick's started.'

So off he went, and in another hour the fire was within a hundred yards of the Ranger's north fence and within two hundred yards of his east fence. Twenty of us were converging in a semicircle round his place when a new recruit, known locally as 'Mad Mike', rushed up, armed with the usual weapon, a box of matches, and set fire to the bracken to the south of the house.

When the scarlet-faced Ranger asked him what the unspeakable so-and-so thought he was doing Mad Mike pointed out, with the aplomb of a general explaining a complicated tactical manoeuvre, that if the wind changed that would make a useful break.

'And what if the wind doesn't change for a couple of days?' yelled the Ranger. 'Your bloody break is heading straight for the house! Put it out at once!'

It took six of us half an hour to help him do it, during which time the flames were crackling steadily closer to the house.

By midnight our numbers had swelled to thirty, and the fire had burnt down the Ranger's north fence and was only a chain away from the east fence.

At dawn his wife was sitting in the middle of the road with her four wailing children and several neighbouring wives on top of all the household possessions she could move. The middle of the road was safer than the far side, because the neighbour over there had decided at 3 a.m. that he had better make his fence-line 'safe', and in so doing had burnt his fence down, and the posts were still red-hot beacons. This fire had 'got away' from his fence-line at the south-east end and was now roaring madly through a fifteen-acre block of virgin bush next door. However, it only belonged to a city bloke who was growing trees as an investment, and no one actually lived there, so the general opinion was that 'it couldn't do no 'arm'.

The Ranger's house was eventually saved, though you couldn't put your hand against the north wall, and his once attractive little garden looked like an overbaked cake.

At that stage the women on the road rushed inside and made quarts of tea, and everyone was wearily merry. I was mildly surprised to see that Ted Angus showed no sign of self-consciousness regarding his part in the proceedings, while everyone seemed to regard Dick almost as runner-up to the Ranger in importance, because his house had been in some danger. Dick told the story of my sadistic treatment of Mary, and everyone stared at me with interest.

Uncle Jim and I drove home in the bright morning, and I asked him what Ted Angus's motive had been lighting the fire in the first place.

'Aw, I suppose 'e thought the wind was going t' change,' Uncle Jim said. 'Then it would have just burnt in a little way and come back on itself.'

'But why did he want to burn the park even a little way?' I persisted. 'His own place wouldn't have been in any danger, even in the biggest fire, could it, seeing the park's on the south side of the road?'

'No,' agreed Uncle Jim. 'No, 'is own property couldn't come to no 'arm. Only the park 'adn't 'ad a fire through it for a few years, so I suppose 'e thought it needed it.'

After breakfast I went out and looked at the smoky landscape.

Uncle Jim's bush block now consisted of ten acres of blackened spars, a few of them with shrivelled leaves on top. Beyond them I could see a collection of rusty tin sheds in a neighbour's back yard which had formerly been invisible.

On the other side of the road the park was still smouldering. Some of the giant gums had escaped comparatively unharmed, but nothing under thirty feet in height was still alive, and one huge red-hot mountain-ash was tottering. When it fell it would block the road and smash through the telephone wires.

I turned to the green hill to the north, and my heart fluttered in a quick spasm of alarm. All along the horizon smoke and flames were rising above the trees.

'Uncle!' I shouted. 'There's another bushfire coming straight for us from the north!'

I heard uncle's bed creak as he sat up with a muttered exclamation. He pulled up his lowered blind and looked out.

'Aw, that!' he croaked in disgust. 'That can't do no 'arm. That's just Sandy Wallace burnin' orf!'

GWEN KELLY
(1922-   )

Gwen Kelly was born in Sydney and educated at Fort Street Girls High School. In 1944 she graduated from the University of Sydney with first class honours in English and Philosophy and the University Medal. She has worked in the public service and as a teacher at secondary and tertiary levels.

A successful short story writer, since the mid-1950s she has published stories in many journals and magazines and has won four Henry Lawson Prose Awards. She has also written four novels and, with A. J. Bennet, a volume of poems. In 1981 she won the first Hilarie Lindsay Award from the Society of Women Writers. Her novel *Always Afternoon* (1981) was made into a film in 1987.

'Mini-Skirts' is a macabre story about the sex and violence in an apparently normal suburban context.

MINI-SKIRTS

Mrs Gallery pushed subconsciously with her hand at her blue mini-skirt—aqua blue like the sea in Queensland which had always been her favourite colour when she was a little girl in Bowen which was not, after all, so many years ago. The fingers pushed, but the hem remained six inches above her knee and the bared stocking strained at the knee cap, at the varicose vein in the calf and the groping finger pressed guiltily to cover the exposed leg. Her teacup tinkled onto its saucer.

Mrs Gallery's hair rose black—she had tried all brands—above her forehead. It was lightened at the front by a golden band which had meant to be silver—only the girls in the suburbs were not really expert with hair, little more than apprentices, and so far from town out here on the outskirts.

'Personally,' said Mrs Lincoln, returning her cup absent-mindedly to her plate instead of her saucer as she took a large bite from the buttered bun, 'personally, Shirley dear, I like it. It makes me think of one of those lovely old-fashioned sunburst brooches. Or the sun on the sea at home. We had such fun, remember? And somehow it never seemed to rain. Good old sunshine state.' She patted gently the tip of her brown-checked skirt just reaching the top of her knees with self-conscious satisfaction.

'I love your aqua, Shirley. Such a gorgeous colour. I wish I had your courage, darling.' Drop of cream, smug rich cream dropped into her coffee and eddied on the surface.

Shirley tinkled her spoon against her cup—tink—tink—real china. She did like real china—and the air passing between little pieces of glass—so Eastern. All those sweet little brown children waiting on the wharf to meet the ship.

'I shouldn't worry, Audrey,' she said. 'It's just as well all of us mums don't go modern. I find the fashions a bit short myself, but of course you haven't a teenage daughter. It sort of shows you up, if you know what I mean. You look sort of dowdy beside them.'

Audrey smoothed her neatly bobbed, old-fashioned permed-on-the-ends hair. 'It must be a worry,' she said, 'having a teenage daughter. Thank God mine are all boys.' Another drop of cream—smooth, smooth—in the coffee. 'Football keeps them healthy and their minds off—well, you know what. But girls—well, girls grow up so quickly.'

Shirley's fingers resumed their pressure on the skirt. Her voice tinkled like the teaspoon which was, after all, metal. 'Cheryl's no worry, believe me. That's why I love the new fashions for teenagers, just love them. It means I keep my little girl just that bit longer.'

Audrey sipped the coffee and removed the rim of cream from her lips with the tip of her tongue. 'Little girl? I don't follow.'

Shirley ran her finger along the sunburst. 'But it's obvious, Audrey darling, obvious. Youth has revolted against the premature attempts of adults to make them grow up. No long dresses, sticky stockings or finicky feminine adornments for them. And it happened just when I was beginning to dread it. I admit it. I lowered my own hems and threw away my socks and wore lipstick—lovely bright reds, they were—by fourteen, but Cheryl seemed such a kid. I tell you again I was dreading it. No woman likes to see her little girl grow up.'

Audrey lowered her cup confidentially. 'Tell you the truth, Shirl, I never dared more than a shocking pink at first and even then I used to wipe half of it off on my hankie because Dad hated painted women.' Shocking pink on the sands of Bowen, but the palms of Eddie's hands on her body were pinker than her lips, pinker than . . .

'Then you get my point.' Press, press, finger on skirt—surely it will come down another half-inch—I never thought it would rise quite so far when I sat down—'Today's fashions are kids' fashions—straight hair on the shoulders, just like little girls, short frocks just like the ones they wore when they were seven, and lipstick—well, most of the time they don't even bother. I look at the back of Cheryl going down the drive and I think she hasn't really altered at all. You remember she was tall at seven. She's still the same little girl with long brown legs and sandals and short frocks. It's so important, their innocence, I mean.'

Audrey tucked in the last piece of buttered bun. 'You're probably right, Shirl. Anyway, it's good to know she and Bill are still steadies. If he went around with some lasses as much as he does with Cheryl, frankly I'd be worried—short skirts or no short skirts, football or no football.'

Shirley smiled and pushed the cup and spoon away. Her fingers rested peacefully on her knee. 'That's the point,' she said. 'They're kids—only a pair of kids who sucked their dummies sitting up in their prams side by side. Gosh, they were cute. Remember how they used to toddle around holding hands every Tuesday at tennis?'

Audrey stood up. 'I used to like our tennis days,' she said. 'By the way, John and I are going down to the club at five-thirty, just for a quick one. What about you and Frank joining us?'

'Just what I was going to suggest myself. Tell you the truth, Audrey, I need a bit of pocket money. Think I can make it?'

Audrey smiled. 'You were always lucky,' she said, 'even on the bandits—even when we were kids you always got the ring in the lucky dip and I got the comb.'

Shirley stood up. The aqua shone, the sun in her hair shone. 'It was great being kids,' she said. 'Such a blue, lazy sea and so much time. You know, Audrey, sometimes I think it's a pity we ever grew up . . .'

Cheryl walked along the bush track with Bill. Her frock, orange, so orange, rose gently with the full breasts, slid without an inch to spare over the rounded bottom. The line of orange spanned the top of her legs, accentuating the long lines of brown limbs and the slim long feet pressed into a pair of orange sandals.

Where the sun had not touched her, Cheryl was pale, water-weed hair undulating gently on shoulders glinting like shifting silver sand through water; pale eyes—washed grey white cloud rimmed with sky blue eye-shadow. Bill felt, without touching, the pale curve of her cheek, the pale undulation of her nose and the pink-silver barely perceptible line of lip.

From Cheryl's ears swung two long hanging loops of gold—gipsy gold. 'You bring out the gipsy in me.' One of Mum's old songs. But it fitted. Just like 'love love love' and 'yeah yeah yeah'. They both fitted. When you thought about it, they said the same thing.

He placed his arm around the orange shoulders, then ran his fingers through the pale hair melting into brown neck. His own hair fell half-blond and greasy across his forehead, down his neck, tickling his ears, and he wished the blobs of bumpy skin rash would go away. But all the kids had it. Grease from hair, they said, perhaps dandruff. However much he washed it he still had it—dandruff and rash.

They turned off the path into the scrub—their own private piece of bush, screened from the path by the tea-trees. Cheryl cuddled beside him on the fallen leaves of the trees. Severed from reality. They could be anywhere. Miles away from the city. Anywhere. She wriggled her toes out of her sandals and their feet pressed bare on the hot rock below them. 'They won't be home for ages,' she said. 'You know what it's like at the club. What's more, Mum's hoping for the jackpot.'

He laughed. 'How lucky can you get.'

At the far edge of the rock a blue-tongued lizard toasted on the hot slab. Cheryl's pale eyes gleamed and her hand pressed on his and his hand was moist and anxious. He wished she wouldn't, he wished she wouldn't. He hoped she wouldn't ask. He watched the dress across her breast rise and fall faster and faster as her breathing quickened. Her voice came to him almost in a whisper. 'Catch it, Bill, catch it.'

His hand grew moister. 'Gosh, Cheryl, let the poor beggar alone. Just this time. Just once.' Her voice tinkled like rain on glass, the tip of her tongue protruded through the silvered lips as she put out her hand and touched his.

'Why, Bill, your hand is all wet. You're scared, aren't you? What are you scared about, Bill?'

'I'm not scared,' he said.

She laughed. 'But I want you to catch it, Bill, I want it. Graham would get it for me. He's not scared.'

'I'm not scared,' he said again. 'I'll show you I don't give a damn.' He rose and slid noiselessly on his bare feet, edging bit by bit towards the lizard. Then his hand flashed and closed around its neck. The sharp brown eyes darted, the tail flailed, but the hand was iron—he knew his hand was iron—hard muscle in every inch of his body. Football star holding a silly fool lizard by the neck to please a girl—but not any girl, Cheryl.

He held his clenched hand in front of her. Her long, slim fingers, delicate, carved like her feet, stroked its tail, then she poked one finger at the palpitating throat, pushing it in and out like the keys on an organ. She laughed. 'My, you are scared.' The tongue flicked and she drew back her hand. The pale brows drew together and he watched the smooth skin wrinkle in anger. 'You vicious, slimy little beast,' she said, 'try to bite me, would you?' She broke off a twig of the tea-tree and prodded at its body, then carefully and slowly she poked out one eye. He felt the body in his hand stiffen, then wriggle with pain. He felt the nausea in his own stomach. He longed to drop it, but if he dropped it she would go away. She always had. The sickness rose to his throat, but at the same time the excitement began to spread over his body.

'Put it on the rock, Bill, put the horrid thing on the rock.' He lowered his hands, still clutching the throat. She rose like a drunken goddess, only they weren't really goddesses, one of those creatures they read about in Ancient History, mad women with streaming hair dancing in honour of Dionysus. Sacrifice and fertility, fertility and sacrifice. Funny how they went together. He pressed his hand harder on the soft neck to stop his fingers trembling.

'Fertility,' he said aloud.

'What?' she said.

'Nothing. I was thinking of history.'

'History. Don't be a pill.'

She swayed in front of him, running her fingers over the earth. Carefully she selected a rock and he watched her fingers curl around it. The hair shimmered on her shoulders.

The first blow crushed the lower body. He felt the life quiver against his fingers. The heavy lid fell over the uninjured eye. He laid the body gently on the rock and she stamped on its head, stamped it into the rock. Only a blue flick of tongue protruded like a glint of precious metal.

She caught his hands. 'Stamp,' she said, 'stamp, stamp, stamp. Stamp, I tell you.' He seized her wrists. He felt the delight of feeling her flesh yield just like the neck of the lizard and they stamped together, kicking at the fleshy remnants. They drew apart and twisted with their bodies in the convolutions of dance until he stamped the final blue gleam of life out of all existence. The flesh of the sacrifice steamed in the sun.

His arms closed around her and his hands caught the silver hair. His body rolled with hers on the bed of leaves. His fingers tore the golden earrings from her ears, lifted the orange frock from her body until she lay beneath him banded brown and white like a snake, bikini brown stomach and neck and white pale breasts and pelvis . . .

The tinkle of coins—lovely tinkle. She lifted the arm once again. Silver to spend, silver to spend. She could feel Jack's hand flick over her aqua blue rear. 'Good girl,' he said. She ran her hand across the sunburst.

Audrey sat at the table with Frank, pale-haired, pale-eyed, just like Cheryl. Her covered knee touched his under the table.

'You always were lucky, Shirl, you always were.'

CHARMIAN CLIFT
(1923–1969)

Charmian Clift was born in Kiama, New South Wales. During the Second World War she was an anti-aircraft gunner in the Australian Women's Army Service, and she edited a magazine for the Army Ordnance Corps. After the war she worked as a journalist with the Melbourne *Argus*.

In 1947 she married writer George Johnston. They lived in London and Greece for fourteen years. On her return to Australia she worked as a freelance journalist and wrote regularly for the *Sydney Morning Herald* and the Melbourne *Herald*.

Clift and Johnston collaborated on three novels. One of these, *High Valley* (1949), won first prize in a *Sydney Morning Herald* literary competition. Independently Clift published two novels and two accounts of her family's experiences in Greece. Primarily an essayist, Clift discussed with ease and wit subjects ranging from personal reminiscences to national issues. Many of her essays are collected in *Images in Aspic* (1965) and *The World of Charmian Clift* (1970).

'Other Woman' appeared in *Australia Week-end Book 4* (1945). In this carefully structured story, Clift heightens the intensity of her characters' emotions by emphasising small details.

OTHER WOMAN

When Jenny finally found the house she was surprised to find that her knees were trembling, and even more surprised to realise that the trembling wasn't caused by the cold, or the fact that her clothes were wet and clinging to her skin. It was rage—sheer, primitive rage—and she was shaking with it.

'Stop it, fool,' she told herself, 'you're not the type for dramatics. This has happened to thousands of women before you, and it will happen to thousands of women after you. You're not beaten yet.'

She squared her small shoulders with a quick, resolute gesture, and jammed her thumb down, hard, on the door bell. Somewhere behind the thick walls she could hear its raucous jangling, and she had a sudden desire to run away—anywhere into the night—before it was too late.

It was too late. Quick, light footsteps were hurrying towards the door, the sound of someone fumbling with the door latch, then the grumbling creak of the door being pulled open.

Jenny had a confused impression of a wide, high cheekboned face—a curiously foreign face—framed in soft, darkish hair. Greenish-yellow eyes widened at her in smiling enquiry.

So this was the other woman! This was Sharon! Red waves of hatred, blind, unreasoning hatred, surged and pounded inside Jenny's body. She fought desperately to subdue them. No dramatics. She couldn't permit dramatics. When her voice came it sounded queer and high-pitched; unlike Jenny's gentle voice.

'May I speak to you? I am Jenny Shane—Mrs Michael Shane.'

The green eyes flinched, wavered, then met Jenny's defiantly. The voice matched the eyes; curiously vibrant and with the same defiant quality.

'Of course. Please come in.'

Jenny followed the other woman up interminably long stairs; the woman's back was lithe and supple under a thin cotton shirt, and she swayed a little as she walked. Jenny had a sudden vivid picture of Michael and the woman walking slowly up these stairs together: Michael's eyes with a little hot flame in them and the woman swaying.

'I hate her!' Jenny thought viciously. 'I hate her!'

The other woman opened the door and stood aside for her to enter. Everything seemed unreal to Jenny now. Pellets of rain spattering on the roof; the clammy feeling of her clothes clinging to cold skin; a rosewood desk with Michael's photograph smiling at her (funny, she hadn't seen that one before); cream walls; chintz-covered divan bed (Michael must have held the woman there and whispered tender, lovely things); one picture—a Gauguin. Some aesthetic corner of Jenny's mind was oddly pleased with the Gauguin. It was so perfectly in keeping with the woman— the woman standing by the window, looking at Jenny from beneath lowered eyelids and twisting the blindcord in one square brown hand.

'How did you find out?'

'Oh—it wasn't very difficult. You haven't been very discreet, you know, and Michael has been "working back" a good deal. Besides, he's very careless about his papers. He left one of your letters on his desk. I read it.'

The brown fingers twisting the blindcord loosed their hold and the blind shot up with a startled crack. She stretched her body to pull the blind down, and her small, pointed breasts thrust rebelliously at her cotton shirt.

Jenny was shocked at the intensity of the hatred welling up inside her.

Michael had compared them, of course. Her own tiny figure— neat and unexciting—with that vital, pagan litheness. But she would dare to compete. She would dare to fight for him. The most primitive, urgent emotion possessed her. 'This man is mine!' She tried to make her voice calm and natural.

'Do you love him?'

The other woman's body tautened and curved like a violin bow. She swung round and looked Jenny full in the face. A tiny muscle in the corner of the wide red mouth quivered, and the greenish-yellow eyes were clouded with a tangle of emotions that were frightening in their nakedness. Pride, defiance, pity and triumph lashed out from them and struck at Jenny's soul. The vibrant voice rang through the room, each word terribly defined and given its full value.

'Love him? I am bearing his child!'

Something cowered, stricken, inside Jenny's stomach—and collapsed. A great humiliation and shame swept through her body, flamed in her face, and darkened her eyes with anguish. A child. She had been unable to give Michael a child.

For a second they stood there, facing each other, then—

'You win,' Jenny said dully, and went blindly into the night.

Sharon flicked a cloth over the dusty mirror resentfully. Ever-lasting housework. From the clear patch of glass her curious greenish-yellow eyes stared back at her with a hint of the old storminess.

'Heavens,' she thought, 'I'm looking exactly like a suburban drudge.'

She looked at herself closely for a moment, then remembered, with a remorseful pang, that tonight was their fifth anniversary—hers and Michael's—and poor Michael was working back again, trying to earn more money so she wouldn't have to drudge.

Darling Michael—untidy as ever. In the mirror she caught sight of his desk, littered with papers. She tidied them happily; notebook, insurance policy, letter. She glanced idly at the letter.

Something hit her between the eyes. Her inside was twisting into a hard, tight ball. Her square brown hand, fumbling frenziedly over the paper, dislodged a photograph from between the pale, scented pages.

Through a swirling haze her greenish-yellow eyes looked into the cool sardonic eyes of the other woman.

218

THELMA FORSHAW
(1923-   )

Thelma Forshaw was born in Sydney and educated in convent and state high schools and later at Sydney Teachers College. During the Second World War she served in the Women's Auxiliary Australian Air Force; after the war she worked in advertising and as a reviewer for various publications.

Her short stories have appeared in *Meanjin, Southerly,* the *Bulletin* and several other Australian and American journals as well as anthologies such as *Coast to Coast. An Affair of Clowns* (1967) is a collection of her stories about her mother's family, the problems of assimilation, and social misfits. Her vivid characterisations are done with sympathy and humour.

'The Procurer' is from *An Affair of Clowns.*

THE PROCURER

I had grown tired of waiting for my first kiss. I was fifteen, and time was flying. Of course, there had been other kisses—my mother's, and even giggling 'rehearsals' with an old school-friend (female). There had been the usual cousins, whose few years' seniority made them suddenly terrifyingly male (as they thought), and whose newfound power was exercised upon their hapless younger kinswomen, when with whoops and roars of their new, deep voices, they chased one round and round the house for a kiss, egged on by the elders' atavistic cries of: 'Catch her! Catch her!' And there was the best-forgotten, lecherous smear of a grandfather, as though a snail had left its slime upon one's lips.

These kisses I had known, but not welcomed. I could have done without them all. They came under the category of blows, teasing, or thoughtless ritual, and had nothing to do with kissing at all, as I envisioned it. The enforced kiss of a cousin was of the same order as the arm twisted up behind one's back until one agonisedly blasphemed, or the little crabs dropped down the front of one's swim-suit.

I lived in a narrow lane of rusty rooftops, where the inside walls were kalsomined, and the rooms dark, yet curtained darker, and everything kept clean, but appallingly shabby if you compared it with most other places. It was my good fortune not to make this comparison for some time to come, so that, as far as I was concerned, we lived like everyone else, and hot water from the copper felt as good in our chipped and rusty bath as it did in better ones, and we ate well off our inelegant tables, and curled up perhaps cosier in ancient, battered armchairs than the people who sat up like Jacky on their touch-me-not furniture.

My mother went out to work, and I had started my first job,

while my little brother learnt the ways of a spiv, unsupervised, in the lanes and grimy concrete streets around us.

Three nights a week we had free music, when the great dance-hall that towered over our tiny terrace blared out its Old Time and Modern to the whispering shuffle of dancers' shoes that sounded like wind-blown leaves rustling over the floor.

We were hard by Parramatta Road and, on Friday nights, the Band of Hope warred against the dance-music from the Palais with dauntless tambourines and voices loud with conviction. Opposite them, a spinning-wheel clattered rowdily round its circle of lucky numbers and, with the incessant whine of trams, it all sounded like a carnival in full swing. To me it was poignant and alive and exciting, and I breasted the noise on Friday nights up-the-road as joyfully as I breasted the surf at Bondi.

Although we lived where we did, and as we did, I was born without a sense of my proper place, and see now that I must have appeared rather peculiar. I pasted up articles on How To Be A Lady, studied outmoded manuals on etiquette found in the 'sixpenny box' of a bookshop, and soaked up a knowledge of the cosmetician's art that would have made me a much sought-after undertaker had I turned my talents to that business.

Compulsively self-improving, I groomed myself as though for some 'fine lady's' place in the world. Under my uncouth Australian accent I began to cultivate another, more mellifluous. I sat up, stiff as a poker, at all times, and I exercised my bit of mind by winning the limerick competitions in the local newspaper until the editor tersely informed me he was calling it a day as I was the only entrant.

Dedicated pupil of my own finishing-school, I had no friends, save frail bonds with three girls who had left good old St Fiacre's at the same time as I had, and to whose love-talk I listened when we met up-the-road, or at the beach on Sundays. They suffered me, rather than included me as one of themselves. I seemed tremendously stuffy, I suppose.

Among the boys of that rugged neighbourhood, my cygnet was looked upon in much the same light as the original ugly

221

duckling. The three girlfriends—well, acquaintances—boasted of being tripped up in the park at night, and having to struggle for dear life. *They* had been kissed long ago—real man-and-woman kisses—and described for me in minute detail the feelings and sensations that accompanied them. I felt sad and envious. Slapdash girls got kissed, why not I—precise exemplar of the cosmetician's art, priestess of self-improvement?

With me, boys stood off, eyeing me curiously, even dourly. I was found wanting in some way. At the Palais they danced with me—that is, when some specially repulsive fellow was dared—as if I were a tree, and did not come back a second time. It seemed I was encumbered with a Taboo.

Just the same, I steadfastly evaded the overtures of more seasoned lovers. Hoary-seeming bosses, with leathery skin and tufted nostrils, who were willing to try what youth viewed with sullen or amused suspicion. I did not want their skill, their thoughtless reflexes. My father had been a ladies' man. I knew all about that.

Misguidedly, I paid ever more attention to my appearance and manner, which, being culled from books, had a formal, old-world air.

When I strolled up the dusty side-street to the shops, no Hollywood starlet, out to catch a producer's eye, watched her deportment more carefully, held her head just so and, of course, there was that peculiarity of the young belle—the cold hauteur, the utter indifference, that air of superiority *bound* to win all hearts!

'I care not a fig! Not *that*!' she seemed to say as she glided with royal mien past the pool-room on the corner where the lairs squatted, smoking and yarning, on their haunches in the sun. Past the milk-bar where the boys clustered, swiping at each other. The lairs' lips only curled, and the boys looked, then looked away, and looked back, wryly amused. ('Hey, what is it?')

Self-improvement intensifies—what else is there to do?—and soon my thirteen-year-old brother notices that I sit at home night after night, often cemented in some horrendous 'mask' that would scare even a body-snatcher, but which is said to ensure a flawless complexion.

One evening he says racily, 'Say, sis, howja like me to get yer a bloke?'

The perfectionist's head lifts from its 'improving' book. The bleak eye that conceals an inferno looks him up and down.

'*You* get—*me*—a boyfriend?' But it is more a question than the derision intended.

'Sure thing.'

Street life has developed in him a cocky swagger. Already he has the earmarks of the spiv. He is always 'finding' things. Once he brought home a horse he had 'found', brought it right up to the front door, so that when the door opened my mother gave a terrible wail of fright. He runs about for our local bookie; he sells bottles, newspapers, and 'arranges' work for me in the milk-bar on dance nights. He is here, there, and everywhere that something wants doing or getting. He will, it seems, do anything for a bob, though he is not a Boy Scout. I keep concealed from him a passionate affection.

He says characteristically, 'Say if I do, now—what's in it for me?'

I am bored with my book, so I lean on my elbows (which are stuck in two halves of a lemon for softening and whitening purposes), and say to the squirt, just to pass the time, 'What do you want?'

'How about a go on yer typewriter?' He adores the mysterious machine which is taboo to all but me, and which my mother picked up at the local auction for thirty shillings. It goes—in a way—sufficient for me to practise, so that I can eventually take an office job and leave the clothing factory where I wrap dresses in tissue paper all day.

'Absolutely no! You'll only muck it up worse than it is.' And I turn back to my book, a battered volume about Carnarvon finding Tutankhamen's Tomb, brought home from the auction in a five-shilling box of junk.

'Ah, all right, lousy! What about giving me a bob then? I

could have a fly at winning a pair of ducks on the spinning-jinny and sell 'em for a quid, after.'

'All right. But, first of all, who is he? I don't want any babe-in-arms, and no old grand-daddies either.'

He does not say, 'Beggars can't be choosers', even if he thinks it, because he is a nice boy, mild, good-natured, some think charming. I used to fight all his battles on the way home from school. (As well as being a 'lady', I am also something of a pugilist.) He grins faintly, so perhaps he is remembering the times when my blood-curdling snarls and windmill tactics put to flight some half-dozen louts. For all my exalted aspirations, I recognise that there are situations only a pugilist can handle.

'Well, how about it?' he says reasonably. 'Will you be in it for a bob?'

'Okay,' I say, and slap down the shilling I have fished out of my purse. 'Done! Now about that feller—fellow—'

'He's a decent bloke, don't worry,' says my kindly brother. 'He saw you up the street one day and thinks you're good-oh. I told him you only look stuck-up when you're out. I didn't tell 'im you swear, though.' He greatly admires my colourful private cursing, but realises it is a purely idiosyncratic taste.

Though my spirits lift, 'Uh!' is all I say to that. Then, 'What's his name, anyway?'

'We all call him Lugs.'

'God! Lugs!'

'His ears are a bit on the big side, that's all. But he's a good bloke.'

'How old is this—this Lugs?'

'Sixteen and a half.'

'Lugs is?'

'Yeah.'

'Hasn't he got another name?'

'Dunno. He's always been Lugs as long as I've known him.'

'What's he bother with a kid like you for?'

'Crikey, turn it up! What's this, a third-degree? He's me mate's brother, that's all. Anyway, he's young for his age. He gives us a game of marbles sometimes if he's got nothing else on.'

'Lugs does?'

'Yeah. He's a good bloke. Nothing stuck-up about Lugs.' He giggles.

I look black. 'Go on—what's the rotten joke?'

'Nothin'. I was just gunta say "only stuck-out"—like his ears—get it? Not stuck-*up*, but—'

'Yes yes yes. I get it, Bob Hope.'

Thoughtfully I toy with the idea of demanding my shilling back, or, at least, haggling for a reduction in fee. But I am in no position to parley. I want very badly to be kissed like the girls I know, and to find out what 'happens'.

My procurer arranges for Lugs to pick me up on Friday after tea, and I prepare myself as if for a bridal, which I do, anyway, at the drop of a hat. The well-groomed 'lady' emerges from the bobby-pins, the egg-mask, the rinse with oatmeal-water to make the skin velvety. My hands tremble so much that, after I have tinted my nails, I spend some time scraping the dried varnish off my fingertips with a vegetable knife. My lips are meticulously outlined with an orange-stick, as the book tells. I am scenting myself discreetly with Californian Poppy, when my brother calls, 'Hey, sis, Lugs is here!'

Ah, Lugs is *here*!

The 'lady' moves into her cool, haughty glide, as I emerge through the faded curtains that divide our tiny dark hall from the lounge-room, my brother casts a rapid eye over me and says reassuringly, 'It's okay, sis. You don't have to bung on any side with Lugs. He come all the way from Balmain for yer! There y'are, Lugs—not a bad sort, is she, eh?'

His sales-patter gets results—of a sort.

'Oh boy—get the vision in blue!' quoth Lugs, like a masher born.

I dart a look at him and am all dismay. It is a face with a knobby forehead, eyes so rudimentary that there is room only for pupils, and a long, clown-like mouth that resembles the slot of a letter-box. The lugs are there all right, to the extent that the so-called face happens, incidentally, to be between them. His head is like a vase with handles, which may sound like the Song of Solomon, but is strictly modern realism.

The sale apparently clinched (how much did Lugs pay?), my brother says jovially, 'We call him Red Sails in the Sunset, sometimes.'

'Ah, turn it up, will yuh?' Lugs grins, and it looks as if someone has tried to cut his throat and missed the target. He closes the gap as though he has just snapped up a fly. Then he gives me a look of great kindliness not unmixed with superiority, that is, if a barracuda can be so expressive. True to his youth, he has taken me at my own evaluation, and my diffidence, blushing and dismay inform him that I am a wall-flower and damn' lucky to be going out with him. He is pretty shrewd at that.

He crooks his arm invitingly. 'Hook on,' he commands with incredible aplomb. Meekly, I do so and we sail off, not into the sunset, wafted by his 'red sails', but into a mild evening which he considers 'grouse for a trot through the park'.

He by-passes the local Reserve with its spoil-sport lighting, and takes me on a tram trip to University Park, about four stops away. I am too confused, and too meek to enquire why we are going to the park at night. Besides, silly questions get silly answers. But my wits are about me to the extent that he has a great deal of trouble finding a bench I will agree to occupy. Finally, we discover one directly under a lamp, near a path where people might be expected to pass, and this suits me fine.

We sit there, looking blankly at the gloomy, reed-fringed lagoon that sometimes figures in my nightmares. Lugs says nothing. I say nothing. Yet, I am determined to be kissed. I do not want to waste time, anyway, on idle chatter, even if there was any, which there isn't.

Lugs's arm inches round my shoulders and, after adjusting it by some indicatory shrugs to a proper position, I happen to look at him the same moment that he looks at me. I wonder if my face appears as ghastly-blue under the lamp as the cadaver that grins back at me. He has those little squiggly eyes. I particularly loathe such eyes. His face draws nearer, and his breath smells mannishly of tobacco. I don't see how he can kiss me, grinning. Still, anything can happen.

I clench my teeth and compress my lips tightly together to reinforce my stamina. Horrible as this situation is, I intend to see it through to its logical conclusion. If only he didn't look so *blue* . . . There is a slight skirmish as we wordlessly try to arrange our noses, in much the same way that two people keep colliding in a doorway, saying, 'After you.'

Finally, noses correctly aslant, it is only a moment till the lips—ah, the letter-box!—meet mine. Our teeth clash together and a jarring shock runs through my jaws. (Hell's bells! My precious teeth! Are they cracked?) Then follows a tentative, even wary pressure of mouths and . . . The dentist says, 'It's out! And you didn't feel a thing, did you?'

Too bloody true!

'Ah, how about sitting on my coat?' says Lugs, very pleased with *himself.*

I will not sit on his coat. I have been given the drum about sitting on coats. I would like to go home.

'Gee, the night's only a pup, but.'

That may well be, but I've got what I came for, and it's home for me. Lugs and I board another tram on Parramatta Road, and he nods as I alight at my stop. 'I get out further on,' Lugs says. 'You be all right? Hoo-roo!'

He does not wave, and neither do I. Only adults are so false. I stalk past the dim doorway of the pool-room, round the corner and into the lane where I live under the shadow of the dance-hall. I feel myself to be a terrible failure.

There and then I begin to cancel from memory the tepidity, the nothingness of that great experience, the First Kiss.

Surely the kisses of his bought red mouth were sweet—my foot!

I hope Lugs develops a delayed-action passion for me, as he ought, considering his all-round deficiencies. I badly want a chance to knock him back.

But my brother says through a mouthful of Weet-Bix at

breakfast a couple of days later, 'Lugs don't wanna make another date with you, sis. He reckons you're a bit on the cold side for him. I had to give him half his dough back. He says he done a bob on you as it is.'

I am too mortified to demand half *my* dough back.

In the meantime—on with self-improvement, and this now takes the form of the erasure of the 'patrician' and the careful reinstatement of the mores into which I was born, and which can never be mistaken for coldness.

It is not very long after that I land a local football-player and win my first bruise in the lists.

DOROTHY HEWETT
(1923-   )

Dorothy Hewett was born in Perth, and spent her childhood in Western Australia's wheat belt, where, until she was twelve, all her schooling was gained through correspondence lessons. Later she studied at Perth College and at the University of Western Australia. She has worked as a journalist, an advertising copywriter, and as a tutor at the University of Western Australia. Although she has often returned to Western Australia, Hewett's home is in Sydney.

Hewett's career as a writer is an impressive one. She has been writing for nearly fifty years. When she was seventeen she had poetry published in *Meanjin*. Hewett has published one novel, many short stories, five volumes of poetry, eight plays, and has had at least another six plays produced but not published. Her novel, *Bobbin Up* (1959), was based on her experiences as a textile worker, a resident of an inner-city suburb, and a member of the Australian Communist Party. It was immediately popular and was translated into many languages. It has recently been republished. Since the 1970s, drama has been the field in which Hewett is probably best known.

Her awards include the ABC National Poetry Prize (1945 and 1965), the Australian Writers Guild award (1974 and 1981) and the Australian Poetry Prize (1986). In 1986 she was made an Officer of the Order of Australia.

Hewett has also received awards for her short stories; these include second prize in the *Women's Weekly* Short Story Competition and the Mary Gilmore Award twice. 'On the Terrace', which appeared in *Summer's Tales 3*, examines the way men idealise women, thus denying them the right to their individuality.

ON THE TERRACE

They met on the Terrace one late afternoon in summer, with the sea breeze blowing the girls' skirts like flower-bells growing out of the glittering asphalt.

She saw him coming towards her out of the office crowd going home, with the light playing across the small hard bones of his cheeks, his neat body set deftly into the wind.

'Well, Emily,' he said. 'I've been looking for you. I heard you were over here. What happened to the marriage?'

And she knew that ever since she'd come back to the West she had been waiting for this moment, perhaps even before she came, knowing that Tim was living here, and yet doing nothing about it, waiting for time to bump them together somewhere. It was as if an invisible gauze curtain slowly rose up into the shining air and left them staring at each other among the tapping typists' heels, and the newsboys shouting, the golden light falling from the high buildings in steeple shadows across their faces. She laughed, remembering from Sydney his trick of asking blunt, embarrassing questions. But she could match him there, with her answers.

'I left him,' she said. 'He was a paranoiac.'

'Aren't we all?' he said lightly. 'Aren't you?'

The fragile shell of self-justification she had built around herself trembled, and the terror came out lumbering round the street corner, like the middle-aged mongoloid who used to chase her after school.

She teetered for a minute on the edge of the safety fence around this particular abyss, and was afraid of his probing, hostile, masculine mind, always, automatically, on the man's side.

But he held her arm disarmingly and smiled down at her. 'When can I see you?' he said. 'Let's see each other soon?' Like a child asking, and she was reassured and absurdly happy, like a young girl with her first tentative love affair. She gave him her mother's address.

'I can't stop now,' he said. 'I'm late for work already. I'm on the *West*. Journalism again. I swore I'd never go back but you've got to eat.'

He waved and left her standing in the street with excitement pumping away like an electric motor in the pit of her stomach, and she was glad that she was still lovely, and her thirty-six years sat so lightly on her.

'You don't look a day over twenty-eight,' her old friends told her. It was as if she'd shed a chrysalis and come out like a new being, or was it only the old childish being she'd simply put on again with her broken marriage; the girl who lived at home with her mother, even the same bed in the sleep-out, the unfinished course at the university taken up again, as if she was a perpetual adolescent, never to break free from the locust's wing, the only difference the two sandy little boys scuffling in the bed on the other side of her.

Tim and she had met occasionally, in Sydney, in another world. She had shared stew, and plums and custard with him and his wife, a young, lovely, stuttering girl in an old peeling room in a two-storeyed terrace off Hyde Park, with the electric light shining on her hair all day, and the Archibald Fountain splashing darkly from verdigris marble outside.

She could still taste the sourness of the plums and hear his tart, impatient voice castigating the girl for her bad cooking, and the girl going quiet, not even stuttering any more. Emily hadn't liked that, but she had liked the girl. Tim sat glowering over the plum stains on the tablecloth. He was working as a gardener in the park and trying to finish his novel. It was as if he had borrowed something of the darkness of the park trees, some quiescence from his spade in the rain-sodden soil, and the small dingy city sparrows picking and squabbling under his boots among the sour Moreton Bay figs.

'Tim gets very impatient with me,' the girl said, as she showed

Emily out onto the landing. 'I'm ... I'm n-not a g-good cook.'

Emily had heard later that Tim's stuttering girl had followed him to Perth, only to run off with an Italian musician.

Tim turned up on the Saturday in a Volkswagen and charmed Emily's mother, who was wary and sceptical of all men since Emily's divorce, just as if she'd turned back the ticking clock over the stove, and Emily was a teenage virgin again.

'He's a bit glib,' Emily's married sister said. 'But very charming. Oh! I give you that. He's a real Lothario. But I wouldn't trust him as far as I could see him. It's those eyes.'

Tim whisked Emily and the two little boys into the Ranges to visit his artist friends who were building houses out of sweat and pisé among ragged gums and blazing granite ridges.

'These are Emily's children,' Tim said proudly, introducing her, as if he was saying: Imagine. Emily is a real woman! She looked at him curiously, startled. Had all his women been infertile, somehow sexless, like beautiful dolls, shielded with contraceptives?

'She's just written a book that's been threatened with banning for dirty language. And look at her, just look at her.' He doubled up with laughter on the granite ridge. 'Look at her face.' He took it between his hands and pinched her cheeks. 'Like a child,' he said. 'Such innocence. And that mouth. Where did you learn dirty words, Emily? Like a parrot? You're like one of your own children,' and Emily was not allowed to protest, to cry out her maturity, but had to sail with false pretentious innocence, a kind of mother-wife symbol, out to a vine-trellised terrace, and drink tea from crooked shiny brown mugs baked in the kiln behind the house.

Tim and Emily walked down the track to the car. 'I can't stand their attitude,' he said, waspishly, 'pretentious arty talk about saving the trees while they sit on their hilltop and the world blows up, cups with crooked handles, when the ones you get in Woolworths for a deener work much better.'

She thought how unkind and intolerant he was. 'I liked the cups,' she said simply. 'And trees need saving. Certainly they're a bit out of this world, but they're good and innocent and talented and they love you.'

They drove through the sunset with the shadows lying across the road and a strange red light seeping into the car from the sky.

They took a sandy white road winding between blackboys like grotesque, arthritic banksias, and the prickly ancient scrub of the coastal plain.

Tim drove in silence, his knuckles sinewy white on the wheel, and she noticed that he drove well, confidently and deftly, as he did everything physical.

'Let's talk about you and me,' he said at last. 'We've both been through the mill. Have we learned anything? Could we be good for each other? Learn from each other?'

The engine purred and the car wheels shushed through the sand. She felt confident and no longer wary. It was the closest they would ever be to each other.

'Maybe,' she said, commonsense telling her to be quiet. She glanced at him and smiled, feeling warm and maternal and beautiful, as all women do when a man finds some kind of an answer in them, even if it is only fleeting. But the look of his profile outlined on the red glow from the sky, disturbed her again. It was driven. Above the wheel and the glare off the road his cheeks and nose stood out like white bone, hard, psychopathic, warped like some kind of maimed animal driving through the dark, wrapped in his own ego as tight as a cocoon. She moved away and the wind blew off the blackboys and banksias like darkness.

Why do they find you, so unerringly? the small, merciless analytic voice said in her ear.

Why do you always attract the misfits, the psychos? Where are you going with this man you hardly know, with the children of another psychopath asleep in the back of his car? You are all they've got between them and the dark outside. Their only roof-tree is you. You've been burnt once, and the scars are still egg-shell thin. Don't push your luck too far, Emily.

233

But to be loved again, to matter to somebody, to share the delight in words and books, to have the burden of loneliness taken away. But it was all an illusion. It was she who loved, who couldn't stop herself, who was irresistibly drawn towards the maimed, challenged to make whole with love, fascinated by the strange roads through the bush of the mind, as if this landscape and the pale moon that began to ride it now, was the self that sat beside her in the fleeing car. Was it a just question?

'Aren't you a paranoiac? Aren't we all?' . . . we, the deviates; the burnt, the maimed, the incomplete? Or are we the sensitive, the seeing eyes?

They stopped outside her mother's house and she had no answers to her questions. She only knew she was in already, deeper than she should be, and rapidly forgetting how to swim out in time.

The little boys woke grizzling and demanding. 'C'mon Mum,' they said belligerently, but Tim put his arm out, barring her in.

'Wait,' he said, a child's imperiousness in his voice, too. Emily felt the wills of the two little boys, and the man in the front seat, clash and hang in the car.

'I want to talk to your mother,' Tim said. 'She's got *some* rights, you know.'

Have I? Emily thought sardonically, but then she leaned towards him, quiescent and female, giving herself up to the strident maleness in him, guiltily abandoning the little boys to their fate.

'I can see you again next Saturday,' he said. 'I've got the day off. Will we go for another drive, take the kids somewhere?'

Emily made her first mistake. She rebelled at the role he'd written for her.

'No,' she said. 'I'd like to go out without the kids for once. I'm tired of being just a mother.'

He stiffened, and she felt him withdraw. She had pushed the pace too fast, demanded a man-woman, not a mother relationship. She stopped, half understanding, but he rallied.

'Okay,' he said. 'I'll call for you Saturday night,' but she knew

234

that she had already disappointed him. He had wanted a slow, secure build-up, with the children as a buffer.

On Saturday night she wore a deep blue dress embroidered in gold thread, and black openwork stockings. She had to be 'mod' and sophisticated to carry this off, so she dressed like an adolescent. After a moment's hesitation he took her to his two-roomed flat on the Terrace; a concrete cell with only the bare necessities of divan, kitchen table and two chairs, the only luxury an expensive record-player in the middle of the floor. He brought out the claret, put Beethoven on the record-player and told her to sit on the divan. He sat at her feet. The stage was set for the usual seduction. She knew he had done it many times before, and felt cynical about him. She kept on talking and smoking nervous cigarettes she didn't want.

'Wouldn't you be more comfortable lying back on the pillows,' he said, and she smiled sardonically. She bent forward for a light and he reached up to her lips. It was all done so quickly, tactfully, tenderly, that she scarcely knew how she lay naked in his arms, with his hips pressing down on hers, as hard and skilful as she had known he would be, reducing her to a child, breaking her defences, leaving her quite naked and crying out in love, on the bed in the dark cell of the room, like a second womb, with Beethoven's fifth plopping down in the record-player like punctuation marks to each stage of love. She was so hungry, so insatiable that she threw caution out of the bed, and lost control. But he went to the cupboard and got out his contraceptives, under his clean handkerchiefs and underpants, where he kept them.

Afterwards she lay in the crook of his arm, while he smoked, stretching like a big heavy cat, feeling her body and cheeks burn and shake with the memory of it.

'Haven't you had anybody since your husband?' he said.

'No,' she said, abruptly.

'You lazy girl,' he said, slapping her gently. 'Anyone as lovely as you are and as enthusiastic, should have no trouble.'

She was hurt but she said nothing.

'Tell me about it,' he said, sensing that he had hurt her, and she told him about the humiliations of her marriage, the utter failure, sex used as blackmail to bring her to heel, the ignominious return to her mother's house, the loneliness, holding the pillow against her breasts pretending it was a man.

'And now it's over,' he said. 'Out of your system. Don't think about it any more. Don't let it cripple you.' He looked down at their bodies lying locked together in the bluish street light coming from outside. She was big-hipped with small breasts, and heavy strong legs.

'We'll have our photo taken,' he said laughing. 'Send it to one of those highbrow literary magazines. Australian writers get together. That'll make their hair curl.'

She giggled and loved him now. 'What's the matter?' he said. 'Why are you so quiet? You liked it enough, I know!' And he laughed at her again.

'I think I'm in love with you,' she said, sitting up in bed.

He lay with his arms behind his head, watching her. 'Don't say that,' he said harshly. 'Love! It's too difficult.' He pulled her down and made love to her, methodically and passionately, using his strong neat slender body like an instrument, and she cried out again and again, till he put his hand over her mouth.

'Why do you do that?' he said angrily. 'It offends me, offends my fastidiousness. It's like making love to an animal, not a woman. We've got minds, we're not mere bodies.'

'I don't know how else to make love,' she said humbly, and afterwards when she went naked to the toilet, and came back walking happily through the dark room with the lights of passing cars on her body, he lay looking at her with disgust, as the cistern wheezed and gurgled through the flat.

'I hate those bloody toilets,' he said. 'Haven't they got any finer feelings, these jerry-building architect bastards? It offends me. Here; put your clothes on. It's late. I'll make you some coffee and take you home.'

She stood desolately beside the bed.

'Don't make me go home,' she said. 'I can't leave you ever again.'

236

He shook her arms. 'You've got to go home, Emily. Be sensible.' She dropped her head on her breast. 'I can't be sensible any more,' she said. She went down on her knees. 'Please Tim, please don't send me away.'

'Get up,' he said roughly. 'You're a grown woman. Stop behaving like a hysteric. This is only the first night. We'll have plenty of others.'

She dressed slowly while he made the coffee and they drank it sitting side by side on the floor.

He turned and looked at her. 'I would have liked it to have been slower,' he said, 'a real courtship. But maybe it was inevitable this way. Maybe it's just as well. We couldn't afford to waste much time.'

'What happened to your wife?' she said. 'The girl that stuttered. Why did she run away?'

'Elizabeth? That had to happen,' he said. 'I never loved her. She was only nineteen. We got married in Melbourne because she wanted it and I didn't care. I could never love her enough, never give her anything except tolerance, and even that wore thin. She deserved something better.'

'You were unkind to her,' Emily said. 'In that flat in Sydney. I heard you.'

'Was I?' he said, surprised. 'Not actively unkind, surely. I just didn't care at all. But women are always accusing me of being unkind. My first wife said I was rude and unkind. I walked out on her because she was more interested in politics than in me. Then I lived with a Jewess in Melbourne who had a homosexual husband and a spoilt son. She paid too much attention to the son, so I left her. She was beautiful, black-haired, like a tigress, but it was him or me. I want my women all to myself.' He stood up and looked out of the window. The street lights switched off and the room became utterly black.

'Women are always falling for me,' he said. 'I don't know why. I'm not much to look at. You know Eleanor Cuffley, the Melbourne poetess? We used to go around together. As far as I was concerned it was quite platonic. When I caught the boat to Sydney she came into my cabin and threw her arms around my knees and told me she loved me. Begged me to stay. I got her up off the floor and tried to get rid of her, gently. But she had no pride. She never forgave me. But in *love* with her! Jesus! Nice enough, but ugly; and those thick ankles. Poor Eleanor!'

'You shouldn't tell me these things,' she cried out.

He dropped down beside her, taking her face in his hands. 'Jealous, darling?'

She struggled out of his hands, shocked at his cruelty, his vindictiveness towards these other women, seeing him discussing her in some cell-like room in some city late at night, with another tousled girl.

'When I first saw you,' he said, 'you were pregnant. I was sitting in a writers' meeting in Sydney, and you walked in. You were beautiful, calm and serene, and I looked at you and said to myself: That's one woman I couldn't teach anything to.'

Emily laughed wryly. 'And now you know how wrong you were,' she said, and by his silence knew she had shattered the last illusion of herself as earth-mother, the one who would make him whole.

'Why do you say these things?' he said angrily. 'You're deliberately perverse.'

'Why not, if they're true?'

'Because you must leave people with some illusions,' he said. 'A woman shouldn't walk naked.' She looked at him sadly, knowing that this was the rock they would founder on. 'A woman must have secrets,' he said, 'she must have mystery. You're not a real woman, because you've got no mystery.'

Emily stood stiff and ungainly in the middle of the room, with tears in her eyes.

'Don't you find me attractive? Not even sexually?'

'Yes, I do, very.' He smiled, hastening to assert his own virility, but she knew, instinctively, that he saw her nakedness as both brutish and repulsive.

He had wounded her at the centre of her femaleness and left her defenceless.

238

'For God's sake, Emily,' he said. 'Try to *understand* me!' He put his arms around his knees and rocked on the floor in a gesture that was characteristic.

'One day,' he said dreamily, 'I'm going to travel the world searching for the meaning of love. Someone, somewhere, must have found the answer. Do you know the answer, Emily? Surely, with all your experience?'

'No,' she said harshly. 'I don't know it,' and thought what a fool he was to travel the world for an answer that was in the room with him now.

'The psychologists say people are crippled by their parents,' he said. 'I never told you about my parents, about my father. He was a big, generous, handsome man. We loved him and my mother adored him. We had everything, a big house in Randwick, racehorses. He was a company promoter. Then suddenly, one day it was all gone. He was in gaol for embezzlement, and we were the kids whose old man was in Long Bay. The fights I had. Jesus it made me tough. We lost just about everything and ended up in little rooms on top of a school shop in Paddo. It always smelt of boiled lollies. Mother kept the shop. Oh yes, she kept us together. Maybe it would have been better if she'd let us go to hell. And then when he came out she had a place for him to come to. She did her duty and she hated him. He had his own room and there he stayed. He looked diminished, somehow. He always wore carpet slippers and he didn't work any more. He had a stroke at last and died in my arms, and she was glad. There was only one thing he asked of her in all those last years, a decent cup of tea. And mother couldn't make tea. It was always weak, with tea-leaves on top. When I was home I made it for him.'

Emily moved to him and held his hand, but he didn't see her. 'Funny thing,' he said bitterly (he told such a good story), 'I had a letter from mother the other day, she's taken a job making tea for a factory round the corner. They always compliment her on her tea-making.'

They drove back through the deserted streets, past the silent

239

Terrace offices, across the bridge, with the lights extinguished in the black, flowing river. They held hands and felt close together and sometimes she dropped her head on his shoulder.

'It's very late,' he said. 'Take off your shoes and creep in. Use some caution. What will they think?'

'That I've been in bed with you at your flat,' she teased.

He bent and kissed her slowly. 'You're very sweet and honest,' he said. 'I'll ring you, darling, but if you want to see me very badly ring me at work on Tuesday.'

She rang him on Tuesday, and his voice on the phone was sharp and efficient. 'Meet me for a drink after work,' he said, and rang off. It's his newspaper voice she told herself and caught the trolley-bus into the Terrace through a mass of great clouds piled pink and heavy as marble behind the thin black factory chimneys suspended upside-down in the river. She ran up the marble steps of the Palace Hotel feeling like Cinderella, and there he was sitting in the lounge with a big, genial middle-aged man, drinking beer and laughing. 'This is Ted,' he said. 'An old mate of mine from Kalgoorlie,' but he never looked at her face, never spoke to her directly.

He's shy, she thought. He doesn't want this Ted to know anything about us. And she watched him surreptitiously across the rim of her beer glass, loving the way he held his small hands and the sound of his voice.

But when Ted had disappeared into the dusk and they walked arm-in-arm up the Terrace for a meal at the Greek's, she knew something had gone wrong. He kept his body stiff and alien and they talked commonplaces. He made a fuss when the girl in the restaurant brought the wrong order. People turned to stare at them.

'What's wrong?' she said. 'What do you want to tell me?'

He dropped his eyes and then looked up at her. 'I can't love you, Emily,' he said softly. 'And I don't want to hurt you. So I'm telling you now. It won't work. You're not my kind of woman at all. There's nothing wrong with you. Nothing. Maybe it's me that's wrong. But I couldn't face you, Emily. You're brutal and

240

honest and strong and naked. You'd swallow me whole. One of those women with opinions. You can't shut up.'

Emily sat quite still and smelt the grease from the restaurant. People were talking incessantly and so was he. 'Please shut up,' she said. 'You've said enough. Just shut up now.'

He leaned forward. 'Emily,' he said, 'look at me. I've hurt you terribly, haven't I?'

She looked at him, unblinking, until the tears hazed over her pupils. 'Yes, terribly,' she said simply.

'I'm sorry. But there's nothing I can do about it. I had to be honest, didn't I? You'd want that?'

'Yes,' she said, and her voice cracked.

She stood up. 'Please take me out of here,' she said. 'Before I make a fool of myself,' and they went down the street, he hanging on to her arm, mortally afraid she would make a scene, this naked woman who had no fastidiousness, no breeding, no finesse.

She began to talk quickly, laughing and half crying, her fingers digging into his arm, dragging the threads of her dignity together. 'It's such a pity,' she said. 'We could have had such a wonderful time, you and I. If only you could see. I'd be so good for you, and now you'll go through life looking for the perfect woman, this woman that doesn't exist, this Utopian mate of yours. Why must you punish all women for your mother?

'I can see you getting older and older,' she said cruelly with her chattering, face-saving tongue. 'Searching the four corners of the earth, getting more and more bitter and unsatisfied, sleeping with woman after woman, none of it any good, till you can't get a woman any more. You're nearly fifty now. It can't last much longer.'

He winced. 'I'll find what I want somewhere,' he said, 'but keep on if it makes you feel any better.'

They stopped on the Terrace corner. 'We could see each other occasionally,' he said. 'I could ring you now and again. We could be good friends, at the risk of sounding corny.'

The street light fell on his face and she thought she would die, watching him. People brushed past, but she didn't see them.

'No,' she said. 'I couldn't bear that. Good-bye, Tim. Good luck,' and she turned and walked away, as quickly as she could, feeling lonely and full of pride.

In two weeks she was back in the reporters' room to leave a manuscript for him to read. She had spent night after night loitering like a moll past the pubs in the Terrace where the journalists drank, looking for a glimpse of that spare athletic body, leaning over the bar.

One night she drank a bottle of wine, to give herself Dutch courage, and walked up to his flat, but he wasn't there, and when she curled up in his car under an old rug, she heard him come in late, with a woman, laughing, and so she went home.

She bought a copy of his new novel, and read it crying and exasperated in her bedroom. She wondered what the heroine, who was always dropping her kimono and sitting on the dyke with the door open, had to do with fastidiousness, and mystery. She was called Emily and she wondered if Tim had created her out of the image of this woman, a kind of Pygmalion in reverse. But she wept for this hero, who was only Tim in disguise . . . This time, they met on the steps of Newspaper House, with her brown-paper parcel in her hands and her face white.

'I was leaving this manuscript for you,' she said, pitifully. 'I wasn't going to wait and see you.'

He looked at her quizzically. 'Well, let's call it fate, then.'

'Are you taking me to dinner?' she said, smiling at herself. 'I'll pay for myself, considering I'm uninvited.'

He took her to an Italian restaurant, and complained about the steak till her cheeks burned. She thought: what am I *doing* with this bastard? Why do I forgive him everything?

'Your book made me cry,' she said, and he nodded his head and grinned.

'The critics howled too,' he said.

They walked back over the Horseshoe Bridge with the dark shadows of men and women passing arm-in-arm in the night air, the sound of the nightmare trains shunting and jarring brutally under the bridge, bellowing smoke and spark trails into their eyes.

They stood on the Terrace corner. 'I'm coming home with you,' she said. He smiled.

'Don't crowd me,' he said, taking her arm. 'Let it ride easy.' They went into the flat and took off their clothes and made love silently. He was mechanically perfect, and she broke and wept and wept in his arms.

'Stop crying,' he said. 'Nothing can be as bad as that. Listen to the music. Old Beethoven knew a lot about grief.'

He put the record on and they lay still, but she couldn't stop talking. 'Don't leave me,' she said. 'I can't take any more. I've come to the end, don't leave me.'

'No,' he said. 'There'll be other endings for you.'

'I've failed,' she said. 'What's wrong with me? I've failed with all the men I've ever loved.'

'Ssh,' he put his hand over her mouth. 'Just listen, woman, listen for once in your life, and relax.'

She stopped and knew when she was utterly beaten. The music filled the cold cell of the room and comforted her. She had wept herself dry. She said nothing even when the record finished and he told her about his new girl, only nineteen and Italian. Her parents didn't approve of him, too old, an Australian and non-Catholic.

But Maria was beautiful and virginal and obedient. Emily listened and felt the words slap against her until she was punch-drunk. Afterwards they went out into the Terrace again, and she walked, crushing the dark pulpy purple of the jacaranda blossoms under her shoes.

'Will I see you again?' she said, knowing his answer. 'We could be such good friends.' The wheel turned full circle and the irony of the words stuck in her throat.

'It's better not,' he said. 'I liked you, Emily. I didn't want to hurt you.'

'It's too late for that,' she said.

He turned impatiently and went back down the street with

his jaunty, high-stepping walk like a pony, under the fragile arch of jacarandas.

She closed her eyes and when she opened them the Terrace was empty.

He rang her once more, a year later, just after her novel came out, and was, amazingly, an unorthodox literary success. He wanted an interview.

'I didn't enjoy your book,' he said. 'I'm only a plain, simple man who can tell a good uncomplicated story. Bad language and straight sex! I'm old-fashioned enough to want to wash their mouths out with carbolic soap, and I like my young women basically virtuous.'

She went to meet him feeling sardonic, and a little afraid.

The photographer flashed his light bulb at her, while Tim fixed her head against the right light, professional and friendly.

'Let's go to the pub,' he said. 'Where I think better.' They went into the lounge of the Palace, up the marble staircase she remembered like a cruel fairy-tale. He looked at her critically.

'You're looking very well, Emily,' he said. 'Not married again yet?'

'Got any suggestions?' she said wryly.

'No,' he said. 'You know I don't know anything about you,' and Emily thought, with relief, why, that's exactly right.

He had caught her at a bad time. In her desperate need to find love she had stripped herself with obscene haste. And yet she knew there could have been no alternative. She had given herself naked into his hands and he had rejected her. He wanted the symbol of the earth-mother, without the brutal reality.

Her body would always lie between them, spread out like a grotesque animal on the divan bed, making it impossible for them to know anything about each other.

He shook hands with her outside and she watched him walk steadfastly down the Terrace, with his cocky stride, head held high like an asthmatic fighting for breath; a little man, looking somehow diminished in the late afternoon sunlight and she was free and sad and sorry for him, with enough insight to wonder how much of it was sour grapes.

NANCY KEESING
(1923-   )

Nancy Keesing was born in Sydney and she studied at the University of Sydney. During the Second World War she worked as a clerk in the navy and then she worked as a social worker at the Royal Alexandra Children's Hospital until 1951. Since then Keesing has written poetry, short stories and worked as a freelance journalist and editor. Many of her short stories were published in the *Bulletin* in the 1950s. Her work includes criticism, four books of poetry, children's novels, a biographical work and she has edited many anthologies.

Keesing has been active in literary organisations such as the English Association and the Australian Society of Authors, and edited *The Australian Author* for some time. She has been involved with the Literature Board of the Australia Council and the National Book Council. In 1979 she was made an Officer of the Order of Australia.

'It's Nobody's Business' appeared in the *Bulletin* and illustrates Keesing's understanding of human nature and her skill at precise characterisation.

IT'S NOBODY'S BUSINESS

'You *do* look depressed,' said Felicity. 'Would you prefer something stronger than tea?'

'Thank you, dear; yes, I am and I would. Any whisky?'

'Australian.'

'Oh, then with lots of ice.'

Felicity went out to the kitchen and could be heard banging the refrigerator door, running the tap and rummaging presumably for glasses, in the cupboard.

Angela kicked off her sandals, rearranged the cushions at the foot of the lounge where Felicity had lately been resting and put her feet up gracefully, spreading her full silk skirt about her legs. When Felicity came back with the tray she was languidly smoothing back her short brown hair from a white powdered brow.

'You look beautifully cool, Felicity.'

'Do I? Can't imagine why. I had two weeks' wash this morning after all the wet weather and it practically finished me. There; how's that?'

She set a small table down beside the lounge and brought an ash-tray over.

'Aren't I a nuisance! I always flick it about on carpets.'

'There's no excuse now, anyway,' said Felicity equably.

'Not drinking?'

'Just ice-water. It's supposed to be better for me.'

'Poor darling. Does having a baby make you very hot?'

'Very. But it can't be helped.'

'No? And that's just *one* reason, Angela, dear, why I feel so sorry for poor little Monica.'

'But we heard she was splendid and it was nice and cool while she was in bed.'

247

'Nevertheless, what with everything—ah, I do pity her. That's why I feel so strange, I think; when I'm sorry for people I simply *immerse* myself in their problems. My own life becomes unreal. Something like lying under a mosquito-net and looking at one's room through it. Familiar but misty—you know?'

'I see what you mean.'

Felicity squirmed in the armchair, dabbing her hot face with a handkerchief. Perspiration trickled nastily down her spine. If she lay back in the upholstery it was too hot, and if she sat forward, uncomfortable. She looked regretfully at the lounge and at Angela's slim, unencumbered form.

'No doubt it's because I'm so sensitive.' Angela sipped her drink pensively.

'But Angela, we heard Monica and Roger were so happy. After all, that's what they wanted—a son. I had a very happy note from them. She's bringing the baby over to visit me next week.'

'Ah. *Then* you'll see.'

'But the baby's all right, isn't he?'

'Oh, he's all *right* . . . I suppose. He's not *deformed.*'

'Angela, what do you mean?'

'Now, dear. Don't get excited. I'm sure you shouldn't be upset just now. Forget about it.'

'How can I forget? Monica's one of my oldest friends. Why, I've known her as long as I've known you. And if I'm to see her I'd rather know.'

Angela closed her eyes. Her beautiful mouth twisted into an expression of concern.

'You didn't see her at the hospital, did you?'

'I told you. I couldn't go. I'm supposed to rest as much as possible.'

'My dear. Actually she'd just fed the babe when I arrived, but they let me in. Oh, Monica looked wonderful. But the baby! You know they say girl babies take after their mothers and boys after their fathers? But this one! As soon as I saw him I said "Fergus!" My dear—the spit and image.'

'Fergus?'

'Yes. Fergus McAlister.'

'Did the baby resemble him?'

'That's what I'm telling you. And of course Monica had to admit the coincidence. You know that peculiar chinless look—although Monica seemed to find it attractive enough once.'

'I'm sure Fergus means nothing to her now.'

'Probably not.'

'He lives up the country, anyway.'

'I suppose he comes to town occasionally. Show-week or some such vulgar time—that bushwhacker *would* choose Show-week. In fact,' and Angela did a little sum on her white-skinned red-clawed fingers, 'if it *was* Show-week it *could* have been . . . but, no. Because . . . Well, anyway, Roger came in while I was there. Oh, so proud! I told him I thought the baby looked like Fergus. He thought it was a great joke . . . at least at first. We all laughed. And then, as I said to them, new babies are always perfectly hideous. "He'll change," I told them. But for a week or two *everyone* I spoke to was commenting on the likeness.'

Felicity drained her ice-water and moved across the room to a cane chair. It was angular and hard, but cooler than the upholstered one. Angela swallowed the last of the whisky and rattled the glass down on the little table. Felicity glanced across.

'Refill?'

'Please, darling. It's not bad—if you can't get Scotch.'

'Pete likes this, anyway.'

'Does he? Dear old easy-going Pete. How is he?'

'Very well.'

'Dying for a son, like Roger was, I suppose?'

'We don't care—so long as it's healthy.'

She carried Angela's glass through to the kitchen, walking slowly and wearily on her swollen feet. Returning, she asked, as she handed the drink to Angela:

'But Monica's son looks like any other baby now?'

'Actually, no. It's uncanny. Really, I can't *imagine* what that poor girl ever did to deserve such a thing. She wrote to me and invited me to dinner last Monday. In the letter she sort of made a little joke: something about "he's developed a chin and has grown into a proper little individual".'

'Good!'

'When I arrived Roger was holding him. Very much the incredulous papa.'

'Yes,' interpolated Felicity, 'one thing I can scarcely wait for is to see Peter. I know he'll look absolutely besotted.'

'I do hope so. I simply could not bear you people to suffer like those two. My nervous system wouldn't *stand* it.'

'I'd forgotten,' said Felicity miserably. 'I was thinking it had turned out happily—the chin and all . . .'

'Exactly. My dear Felicity, that chin! Frankly I goggled. I couldn't help it. Before I could *stop* myself I said—thinking of *his* enormous chin—"Why, Alexander!" and they had to admit, once the idea was in their heads, that that baby is *so* like that partner of Roger's who visits them such a lot—Alexander Morris, you know—it's just *nobody's* business!'

RUTH PARK
(1923-   )

Ruth Park was born in New Zealand and educated at the University of Auckland. She came to Australia in 1942 and travelled around the outback before settling in the then slum area of Surry Hills. Her experiences there during the Depression form the basis of much of her writing, including the very successful novels *The Harp in the South* (1948) and *Poor Man's Orange* (1949).

Park's writing career began in journalism, and has included all types of writing: advertising, articles, short stories, radio and television plays, travel guides, children's books and novels. Park and her writer husband, D'Arcy Niland, collaborated on their autobiography *The Drums Go Bang!* (1956). Well known for her children's series, 'The Muddle-headed Wombat', Park has written successfully for all ages. Many of her eight adult novels have become best-sellers both in Australia and overseas. She has won several awards including the Miles Franklin Award for *Swords and Crowns and Rings* (1977) and the Children's Book of the Year Award for *Playing Beatie Bow* (1980).

Park's strength as a writer lies in her believable characters, strong dialogue and sympathetic use of humour. 'The Travellers' first appeared in *Australia, National Journal* in 1947. It aptly demonstrates her understanding of children and her ability to find humour in most situations.

THE TRAVELLERS

As she walked along the platform, Budge felt as though everyone was looking at her, and nodding knowingly, as though to say: 'She's going all the way to Mount Rosa by herself. She's bought the tickets and everything, and she's only twelve.'

Her little sister Elizabeth, cantering along beside her, and chewing the elastic of her hat at a great rate, thought: 'Budge knows. Budge knows all the things we have to do. That lady has a hat like an ice cream. I went to the rest room and put a penny in all by myself. I can look at a comic in the train. Budge has the lunch in a boot box.'

And there stood the train on its invisible legs, crouched close to the ground and snuffing the air with its black nostrils in a wild, fierce delight, anxious to plunge at the hills and hurtle down into the valleys, spouting out its grey, spark-spangled breath over the shrinking grasslands.

'Chaaahhhhhhhh!' it remarked as Elizabeth trotted by. But she was not at all frightened. She smiled at it sedately, and patted its warm brown scaly side before Budge's anxious hand jerked her onwards.

When they were safely in their carriage they took their hats off and put them in the rack. Then they arranged the boot box and the string kit between them on the seat, and sat down, with a tranquil, happy excitement simmering in their breasts. Budge made sure she had the brown paper bags in her pocket, in case Elizabeth was train-sick, and Elizabeth put her face against the pane and quietly licked a round clear patch so that she might have an unimpeded view.

'Don't do that, dear,' said the lady sitting opposite. She had mottled blue beads like birds' eggs, and thin grey lisle shanks which rather got in the girls' way. Elizabeth's acorn-coloured head immediately shrank closer to the pane to conceal her crime, and Budge blushed crimson with mortification and anger that the lady had scolded her little sister.

'Oooooh, we starting!' yelled Elizabeth. She trampled heedlessly on the grey shanks and pasted her face to the window as the train gave a yip of impatience and began to slide out of the station.

'Haven't you got anybody to see you off?' asked the lady . . .

'Wheeeeee!' squeaked Elizabeth. 'Look at the bookstall and the tearooms and all the people. Look at the man with the big golden bell! They're all going! Wheeeeee! I can see them still. I can see them still, Budge!'

Then the train, giving a gigantic 'Shaaa-hhhhhhhh!' tore away from the city, crouching down on the rails and swinging its tail from side to side until everything, even the water-bottle above the seat, settled down to its restless, restful rhythm, and the music of its clacketing wheels. Elizabeth, with cheeks like plums, fell back in her place, too ecstatic to speak.

The lady rearranged the five little cases and canvas hold-alls which sat beside her. Then she said in a gentle, soothing voice:

'Didn't you have anybody to see you off? You must have some . . .'

Budge was sitting very stiff and straight. She looked everywhere but at the lady.

'The lady we've been staying with has rheumatics, so she didn't come.'

'Budge knows all about trains, don't you, Budge?' boasted Elizabeth. 'Budge could take me *anywhere*.'

'Oh,' said the lady. Budge watched with suspicion and dread a little wrinkle appearing on her forehead.

'What about your parents, dear?'

'We've only got our Mummy,' said Budge, and buttoned her lips up tight again. A great painful hate for the lady rose in her chest like a lump. She stared out the window at the flying of trees and the sheep that came and vanished in the flick of

253

an eyelid. Elizabeth's pink smile showed her two rabbity front teeth.

'Our Daddy died at the war,' she said importantly. 'I didn't remember him, but Budge did. She cried and her nose got all swollen up like a bee-sting.'

'Oh, oh,' said the lady in a soft breathy voice like the sea coming in and going out. She looked with penetrating sympathy at Budge, whose heart was beginning to burn and throb under her darned gym tunic. She was like a moth trying to get away from the pin of the lady's yearning to give tenderness.

'And now our Grandpa's dead, too, so we're shifting,' said Elizabeth cheerily. At the magic word she bounced up and down on the shiny, winey leather of the seat. Oh, how beautifully it smelled of the powder and tobacco and perspiration and hair-oil of long-gone passengers! The train swung its body around a curve, and its jubilant 'Hurrooo!' floated away with the smoky pennant. It was almost like riding a horse, so alive it was, thought Elizabeth. Suddenly her eyes sparkled. She forgot everything, and cried to Budge: 'You said we could go along to see him when the train stops. We can, can't we?'

The lady, who had been fishing in one of the bags, stopped suddenly and said: 'You mean . . . I don't . . . do you mean that . . .'

'We've got him in the luggage van with the luggage,' said Elizabeth. Overcome with excitement and importance, she kicked out and gave the grey shanks a clump that would last them for a week, but the lady did not even notice, so great was her appalled horror. Budge took her eyes off the arching, faintly smoky roof and wondered what was the matter with her. She hoped that she felt sick and would have to go to the washroom. Her eyes filled with frightened dismay as she saw the lady's spectacles become misty, and her mouth tighten and untighten. Budge looked down at her gloves, taking them off and putting them on again, but she could not keep her eyes off the lady.

'You poor, poor children,' she murmured. 'Travelling alone, and with him in the . . . oh, you poor, poor children.'

'We wanted to bring him in the carriage with us, didn't we,

254

Budge,' asked Elizabeth helpfully. 'But Mummy said no.'

'Where *is* your Mummy?' demanded the lady suddenly, straightening her lips in an angry, determined way.

Budge said timidly: 'She's at Mount Rosa getting the house ready. She went up the day before yesterday. She's meeting us at the station.'

'Oh, oh,' said the lady. She did some interesting things with her face so that Elizabeth watched with a hypnotised fascination.

'You've got a mole on your chin,' she said, 'with a hair on it.' She leaned forward and peered. 'Two hairs,' she announced triumphantly.

Budge was agonised, torn between her happiness at the lady's embarrassment, and her shame for her sister's bad manners.

She said sharply: 'Come on, you want to go to the ladies.'

'I do not,' said Elizabeth. 'I went at the station.'

'Well, it's time you went again,' said Budge desperately, poking her sister. Elizabeth folded her bottom lip under her top teeth, and her round toffee-brown eyes went pink-rimmed as she held her breath preparatory to letting out a squall.

'I don't! I don't!' she yelled.

Just then the train gave a whoop of recognition as it spied ahead a huddle of red roofs beside a glossy bend of river. It bounded forwards into the station and slithered to a halt. Now that there was silence inside the train all the jolly noises of the town came up in a wave . . . a girl ringing a bell at the tea-rooms, the newsboys baying, porters trundling trucks with rumbling wheels, and, afar off, the plaintive voices of cattle in the stockyards. Somebody shouted: 'Ten minutes for refreshments!'

'Can we go and see him now, Budge? You said!' Elizabeth was so excited her breath came in hiccups. She and Budge fell over the lady's legs in their hurry to get out. They jumped down the high step to the platform, and stood there breathing in the exotic, river-scented air of the new town.

'First we'll go and get something to eat, because we've only got the sandwiches that Mrs Withers cut,' said Budge firmly. She cast a glance at the quivering, impatient train, as though daring it to be off, and then pushed the reluctant Elizabeth towards the tearooms. There was a smell of strong tea, and all around firmly planted legs, dribbling teacups, and faces attached to thick custard-yellow squares of cake, or crushed pies, or sandwiches depressed and inhospitable.

She bought two sugar buns.

'Aw, come *on*, Budge,' whimpered Elizabeth. They broke into a run through the slowly dissolving crowd. Quickly! Quickly! Soon they were at the guards' van. They saw the red bags of mail being wheeled off and then, as soon as the men moved away they peered in.

'There he is! There he is!'

They pressed their noses to the battens of the box just inside the door. In the dusk within they could see Boodle, sitting on the stump of his tail, his back legs sticking up in a dispirited arc, his black nose sunken on his chest. Never was there a sicker dog. A sad, hopeless prisoner, he did not even have the strength to lift his eyelids when Elizabeth, his beloved, called through the battens.

'We'll soon be at Mount Rosa and then you can get out and run about, Boodle!

'And we'll have a new house with a yard, and you can chase the cat, Boodle!'

Boodle did not answer. His thoughts were fixed with horrid concentration on his stomach.

Elizabeth felt in her pocket and brought out a soft, bitten biscuit.

'Here you are,' she said lovingly. 'Here you are, little boy.'

Boodle took no notice. The train gave a little quiver, and a shriek of impatience.

'Oh, we've got to run!' cried Budge, her skin prickling all over with alarm. They pelted down the platform and fell into their carriage. Now that they were safe, their narrow escape seemed pleasant and exciting and they watched other latecomers patronisingly. The lady came in, delicately mopping tea from her lips. Budge and Elizabeth hardly noticed her. Flushed with pleasure, they opened their paper bag and put the two sugar buns on their knees. They had fine brown leathery tops, with coarse square sugar grains glued to them.

'Did you go along to the van?' asked the lady in a low, tender voice.

'Yes,' said Elizabeth happily, 'and I gave him a biscuit. *He's* all right.'

The lady stared so long, and so horridly, that Elizabeth put her hand protectively over her sugar bun.

THEA ASTLEY
(1925–   )

Thea Astley was born in Brisbane and was educated at the University of Queensland. Having taught at primary and secondary levels, she was also a Fellow of Literature and Creative Writing at Macquarie University for thirteen years. In 1980 she gave up teaching in order to write full time.

Astley has published nine novels, three of which have won the Miles Franklin Award (1962, 1965, and 1972). Other awards she has won include the 1975 *Age* Book of the Year Award, the Australian Literary Society's Gold Medal (1986) and the 1980 James Cook Foundation of Literature Studies Award for her collection of short stories, *Hunting the Wild Pineapple* (1979). In addition to her fiction, Astley has also published a critical study and some uncollected verse.

'The Scenery Never Changes' appeared in *Coast to Coast, 1961–62*. In this moving story, the main character is prepared to take on a totally different identity in her need to fit a man's idea of what the marriageable woman should be.

THE SCENERY NEVER CHANGES

At thirty-two, -three, -four—think of a number between thirty and forty but prithee not to say it, and you would have Sadie Wild, not too old, but again, not too young. Good looks had been dragging one foot off the bus since the last stop but one. In atonement, the chi-chi of frockery and hattery played two-part inventions on the still lush body, although certain disappointments that by now had assumed the bland stare of inevitability hardened her maxfactored mouth, and lay cautiously at the back of her eyes alert to anticipate the premonitory flare and flicker in the male. At each new shuffle about the backblocks into yet another staff-room, with possibilities hitching their crumpled pants before the dinner-break bell, a late spring glow widened those weary brown orbs, and parted the starlet mouth, and then she would say to herself, 'O, God, I mustn't play it wrong this time. Not this time. I'll handle it like a wren's egg. I won't look eager, sound eager, or even think eager.' But of course she did while she was still young enough not to know; and even as the years passed, and she should have learned what some precocious buds know at ten or eleven, a miscalculation of the crystal moment—seconds too early or seconds too late— would shatter it before her wincing eyes, and there she would be, brave and bright, seeing it through with a new handbag or dashing hat or a week at the Barrier, that August on an island packed from reef to peak with career women *en fête*.

Once or twice she had been in love, in those tensely young years when the disposition of a parked car or a café window or musical fragment or elusive relationship between roof and spire and park could evoke such nostalgia she would be incapable of subtlety. Their repetition these days merely feathered the surface, for tenderness is as difficult to recall as pain.

259

Consequently, each new amorous venture contained its own wry and inward assent to the dismissal that came within two or three months of that introductory and brilliant smile.

Last time it had been particularly bad. Rattling along on a rail-motor somewhere south-west of Bundaberg, recollection nagged busily and painfully. Every prop in the jerking landscape outside the window reminded: classicism of eucalypt disposition along whistle-stop branch lines to nowhere but that two-storeyed pub, the pedagogue chatter, the claustrophobia of coastal hills— all had their own heart-breaking italics for the loveless last occasion that had so nearly been it. Her quivering submission to self-designed treacly situations had not been entirely feigned. He had at first, she recalled bitterly, regarded her with the warmth of need, accepted her physical tribute, grown a little tired of her sexual zeal, and finally had held her off at blackboard pointer's length to examine the possibilities of a union.

He was nearly fifty. He was suitably divorced. He drove a large older-model car, played dull golf and lived in a rented room. That was the killer. The rented room. Descending from the shared bathroom each day, touchingly untidy flecks of lather dried on the lobes of his hairy ears, he would accept Miss Wild's late débutante gleam-paste smile and I-understand-you glance across the yellow leather eggs. They would exchange nods, world-weary, pub-weary, job-weary nods of long suffering, and their hands might brush sufficiently as they both reached for the salt.

With that speed which should always have been a warning to her, golf for one became golf for two. They inspected local tourist bait in his car. They drove dustily up and down the coast, and swam, she more coy now in her costume, for time had caused a muscle slackness and varicosity that her clothes normally concealed. She merely toyed with the water, tickled a brine-line with one salmon-pink toe, and laughed. 'I'm no swimmer!' she confessed gaily. (He was the type of man who wanted his women helpless, she estimated, but of course could not be entirely sure, as she scuttled back to the protection of her wrap and the umbrella, that this was the right thing to do.) Beer-soothed, at a later interval in another setting, unheeding the warning tuckets, he looked slyly at her above his glass rim, and said with an emphasis she liked to embroider:

'This is pretty good, isn't it?'

Like any slick-tongued starlet she had agreed. The shore, raggedly aloof below the headland slope, was all the loneliness of fifteen years of solitary pub rooms and dinner gongs and commercially travelling grogs to fill in the time. Tears, milked out of that purpling inturned tide, banked up behind the blue rims of her exotic eyelids. Out there on the lawn patch before the beach hotel with its fungus sprouting of empty tables and chairs, the drenching grey scrub north towards the headland and the ego-shrinking coolness of evening breeze, they could both believe in happy endings and knew an impulse to confess to this. An orchard of citrine bulbs fruited the main street; in the twilight, long phosphorescent parallels crept across the sea, and shattered, and rose again far out, and crept back to the pandanus cliffs and the picnic shed where sets of initials described unspeakable relationships. A bicycle squeaked along the road to collapse at the newsagency. There was about this place a deathlessness that could perceive a century of staggering bikes, and sandboys in freckles and shorts, and isolated blue-grey evening cries across paddocks or pub yards or from council-donated swings in the cliff-side park.

Impelled by timelessness such as this, and the quality of serenity these pockets of rustless regress yield, Dan had leaned across the table, and taken her hand.

'What are you doing at Christmas?' he asked.

Alert always for implication, for even the harmonics of wedding chimes, she had almost choked on her heart as it bounded up to shove gaucheries from her lips.

'I don't know yet,' she admitted, holding his eye. She hoped her own did not glitter. 'Why?'

'I've plans for once,' he said. (Look into him, her mind ordered. Hold his gaze until the trial of the moment is over.) 'But I don't know whether they'll suit you.'

'Am I involved?' It came out with shocking sprightliness that had not been her intention, so that something in the timbre of her voice frightened him a little. He pulled on his cigarette, and ran a finger down the side of his nose.

'In a way.' Twilight softened everything. Her face, his intention, outlines crumbled. 'Thought you might like to come down the coast for a bit. I'm going down for a couple of weeks' fishing south of Bega. You'd like it. Pretty restful after a hell year.'

Oh God, she thought. Wrong. But what do I say? Do I protest propriety? Do I accept on the off-chance that . . .? Why was nothing ever cleanly limned for her? Predicaments constantly presented themselves, but without timorousness. They swaggered. They strode back and forth waggling their rumps. Oh, again and again and again, it seemed forever, chances would slide away.

Her hesitation embarrassed him.

'Never mind,' he said, gulping down the last of his middy, and depleting the magic. 'It was only a suggestion.'

Frightened of putting a word wrong, she resolved on the measures of the desperate—a cool indifference coupled with a bright surface of interest in almost everybody else. But he appeared untouched by this device and was as friendly as ever, as if the abstraction of her person meant nothing. It was she who approached him in the last days of barren weather, and asked false-sunnily:

'Is that offer still open?'

It was, but not as enthusiastically, although his good nature made slovenly attempts to conceal this. But time had dealt so poorly with Princess Klein, she could sense the pea of indifference beneath layers of mattresses.

She made every effort, but that is the most that can be said for the gingham-minded nightmare of strategy to make herself indispensable. There were flurries of *bonnes bouches*, little appetisers culled from the pages of women's magazines, fluffy *mousses*, asparagus flans, anything but the full-blooded steaks he craved. She emptied ash-trays as soon as they were sullied. She talked too much. Even when she was silent he found something

262

twittering about her, although she tried to dissemble with sporty
out-door-girl cussing on the fishing trips, and noggin-knocking
of formidable duration. As the fortnight told its agonising beads
for them both, her despair carried her beyond the caution that
had kept her suspended on a maritally pegged tightrope and,
suddenly ceasing to care, revealed a loneliness and despair that
moved the man—but to pity only. Even physically his
conventionality found her just a shade too enthusiastic.

It was with the most terrible tenderness on that last dreadful
day that he told her he would not be coming back to Sydney
for another week and that, in fact, he probably would not be
seeing her at all in the new year because of a transfer. He omitted
to say that he had applied for it. Her hopelessness would not
even permit her to ask where, although her agony wondered.
They lay side by side on the sand. Her soul trickled out through
the opened pores of her ageing brown skin. Below them on the
shelving beach, wave percussion rocked and rocked to the cries
of gulls.

'I suppose I had better get back and pack,' she said.

'No hurry,' came the worst of casual answers. 'You've got
a good four hours yet. You want to make the most of this sun.'

She rolled over on her back at that and began to laugh and
laugh, creakingly, harshly. Dan put out one enormous oafish hand
to pat her shoulder.

'Come on!' he protested. 'I'm not that funny, am I?'

The laughter went on, and he repeated his words, stretching
out his arm once more to pat her; but his hand found space
and, turning, he saw he was addressing the hollow left by her
body in the loose sand. She was already halfway up the dune
where beach-grass grew in a wind-blown agony all over the crest.
Curiously he watched her graceless stride aggravated by her rage,
and observed impersonally the stringy quality of her brassy hair
glued into salty curls. For a few seconds he was tempted to call
her back, and if she had once turned to look at him might have
done so, but at last she was gone, and he dropped his face again
into the safety of his arms. When he got back to the flat every

trace of her had been removed with a scarifying fanaticism that was almost frightening, and while she examined the shrivelled pod of her pride on the station platform he dozed through the cowardly afternoon, listening to the crash of the surf.

Even now as the rail-motor took her through the most sealess of landscapes, sea burned bluely, acidly, at the back of her mind. Across this gauze, station names registered automatically and, through the pain of recollection, she noted there were still three to go before she got out. Never again, she told herself. Not ever, ever again. But she could see herself all the same. There it would all be as it had always been. The station and the back-chatting clerk. The hotel with its veranda brim pulled well down over its eyes. The dirt road. The half-dozen stores. The school with its moth-eaten fox fur of pepper-trees. Another station went by, and the absurd optimism that was her special poison began to secrete. Outside the window, tide was on the turn. The acid-blue waters were receding in direct proportion to the speed with which this rackety carriage crashed towards the town. And by the time it shuddered to a halt, and she was opening the door, her smart new leather case in her hand, the sea was nothing but the thinnest of violet lines on a horizon she could never touch. There she would be, she knew in her ashamed and humiliated heart, walking through that door on the Monday, looking around her with her bright eyes and sophisticated smile, sensing him by instinct and moving to her martyrdom like a saint.

ELIZABETH HARROWER
(1928-)

Elizabeth Harrower was born in Sydney but spent her first eleven years in Newcastle, New South Wales. After finishing her education in Sydney, she worked as a clerk. In 1951 she went to London to study psychology, but became interested in writing instead. On her return to Sydney eight years later, Harrower worked for the ABC. Later she became a reviewer for the *Sydney Morning Herald* and worked in publishing.

Harrower has published four novels; all are psychological dramas about human motivation and fears, pitting the strong against the weak.

Her short stories have appeared in various anthologies. 'Lance Harper, His Story', which appeared in *The Vital Decade* (1968), is a sympathetic story told with irony and humour about a young man and his obsession.

LANCE HARPER, HIS STORY

What's a classic? Lance Harper wondered. He was sitting in a bar watching television the night he wondered this for exactly the millionth time. And, surely, with the millionth assault on this intractable question, Lance's feeling for it could be said to have passed from passion to monomania? If so, it could account for what happened.

Sometimes he used to say to his mother, 'I don't know why I'm living, Mum.' And she, hearing that he was no more than half-joking, was proud that Lance was not like other boys, and did not even think, 'You were an accident, Lance.'

But he mightn't have cared, anyway. What was a classic? That was the point. He had hoped, when the whole question of classics presented itself to him, that as he was going on for twenty-one, five feet eleven and still growing, his last wisdom tooth almost through, that the answer was an instinctive thing like all the rest, and one morning he would wake up knowing. But he hadn't.

Now, anyone observant could have seen he wasn't well: he seldom smiled, his naturally deep-set, dark-grey eyes receded, melancholy, under his brow. But, of course, one of the facts of Lance's life was that it had never contained a soul who had dreamed of observing him. And his heavy frame, hollowed out by restless days and listless nights, looked healthy enough as he swung along the girders of one new skyscraper after another.

'He's a fabulous colour,' his mother, Pearl, told her boss, running up another red Christmas stocking on the machine. 'Fabulous tan. And his hair's all yellow with the sun.'

'Got a girl?' Bert measured off red cloth.

'No. His Mum's the only girl Lance's interested in.'

Bert paused and looked at her.

266

'That's all right! You can scoff! He's working overtime to pay off a new fridge for me, and he's trading in his car for a new one so I can be comfortable when we go out.'

'I'll get some more of that cotton,' said Bert, disappearing.

So that close hostile look of perplexity on Lance's face was never remarked. It was his habitual way of looking and was mistaken for the quizzical squint the sun gives most Australian men. Lance's dad had it, too, but with him it really was the sun. He was a builder by trade, like Lance, and swarmed over scaffolding in all weathers.

When Lance was five his mother went away one night without him, just stopping to hiss in his dark room, 'Yes, I'm going, love, Dad's sending me away. He says you both like Myra Barnes better than Mum. What? You don't? Well, someone's telling lies to poor old Mum, I'm off, anyway, Lance. Do what Mrs Barnes tells you.'

And his father said, 'What? Where's she gone? What? . . . I'll give you a good clip on the ear if I hear any more out of you. Get out into the back yard! Go on!'

About once a year after that, his mum or dad left home forever. The period of absence varied, and sometimes Lance was taken, sometimes kept, but the departures were fairly predictable and made quite a stable feature in his life.

He was invariably placed on one side of the dispute as if by some impartial referee: now he was Dad's boy, now Mum's. But sometimes, in odd moments of reconciliation, it struck his parents that Lance was a boy who kept things up too long— a moody boy, nice-looking but not nice. And sometimes they combined to chide him for his lack of friends. Not that *they* had any friends, but occasionally they felt it would be normal and flattering to them if Lance would extend himself and acquire a few.

If he did not approve of them, let him be better!

But Lance took up no challenges. His mind seemed always to be, whatever the subject in front of him, deeply concentrated on something else. He was never at a loss for thought. In the

267

house there was always something to set his mind turning: egg stuck to the ceiling where plates of breakfast had been hurled; scars on Mum's hands where she was burned while wrestling with Dad and a pot of beans in boiling water; the scar above his own right eyebrow where an ash-tray had hit him once; a broken record-player; a slashed bike-tyre.

Pearl was away when Lance had his fifteenth birthday and started work. In due course she brought home her circled eyes, her case full of shocking-pink nighties and underwear, and found a new vacuum-cleaner from Lance tied up in cellophane in the hall, and a bottle of French perfume on her oak dressing-table. And that was only the beginning. She had had no idea Lance was so fond of her. He gave presents to his father, too, at first—tools and fishing—and shaving-kits. What a generous boy!

As a family the Harpers had often been hard up. It wasn't simple to pay off the television set, piano, two transistor radios, a Model-Homes electric stove, two electric shavers, a portable typewriter, a car and furniture, all at once. But Lance worked overtime and paid his mother more than amply for his bed and food. He was a real help. She took a new notion to him.

(Their house was a wooden one and quite old, but not set in deep suburbia. The rent was small; it was close to the city and, really, very snug.)

Once when he was on night-shift and supposed to be sleeping by day in the empty house, Lance went to town and came back with a large dictionary. Looking up every second word—words like 'polemic' and 'rapprochement'—he read from cover to cover a serious-looking political weekly from London. He'd heard students talking about it one day at a railway station bookstall. It was in English. He could not, naturally, locate definitions of cartoons or the groups signified by initials alone, but at first he did find all the other words. It was the very best dictionary in the biggest bookshop in Sydney.

Apart from what he made out to be political stuff by the way the names of countries kept turning up, Lance saw that the weekly covered such topics as: Correspondence, the Arts and

Entertainment, Books, Reviews, Food and Wine and Positions Vacant. To begin with, chewing hard on a wooden tooth cleaner (he didn't smoke), Lance looked up most of the words in these sections, too. He also made a pot of coffee and drank more than he wanted.

But the definitions often turned out to be as arid and abstruse as the original terms, and Lance was obliged to penetrate so far in search of the truth of each word, chasing it through all the brand new pages, that he began to flag at the thought of the return journey to the text. There was a loss of heart somewhere in the room, or in the weather, and Lance glanced over his shoulder at the sky. 'I'm getting fed up with this,' he said aloud.

Let it be understood that Lance wasn't stupid! Ages ago in the infants' school he had often been top, or near the top of his class, without trying. Even in high school, in second year, which was as far as he went, he alone of all the forty in the room had solved a certain, very difficult, problem in algebra one day. Think of that! Lance often did.

For several hours now he linked meaning to meaning, re-writing pages of the ninepenny weekly. Then he chewed another stick of medicated wood and read his reconstruction. This was in English, too.

He couldn't understand a single sentence.

And, finally, he had to admit that it was all, all of it, even the vacant jobs, joined to a past, a present, to people, places and things, he was more ignorant of than the man in the moon. He was old enough to fight and die in a war at this time.

One evening not long afterwards, having in the meantime abandoned the dictionary in a bus, Lance was watching television, eating an apple, and painting his toenails with his mother's clear polish. The bottle happened to be on the arm of the chair he'd fallen into. Also, it was partly because (leaving aside his abstraction), he was wearing on his feet those plastic sandals, presumably modelled on Mercury's, that disfigured thousands of Sydney feet that summer, and which were called, without much splitting of hairs, 'thongs', 'tongs', or 'prongs', according to the

269

mood of the speaker. But the point is they left Lance's toenails bare, which was why he painted them when the lecturer talked on television about classics.

Lance came in at the tail-end of this programme, just as the man said, 'Now for the summing-up.' He listened quite idly at first, but it would be no exaggeration to say that afterwards Lance was a man possessed. The speaker had really smouldered with conviction, using all his force to prove that a man who knew his classics knew everything worth knowing.

'Good heavens, Lance, don't let your father catch you with paint on your toenails!'

Lance said, 'I never noticed,' and went to his room with cotton-wool and polish remover. In fact, though, he and his father hadn't spoken a word to each other in eighteen months. It wasn't likely his feet would have started them talking.

In a clean white shirt, in a new tie and suit, Lance set out for an evening class advertised in Saturday's big paper along with movies and night-clubs—the first of a course of ten lectures. He had a mushroom omelette in a restaurant near the lecture-hall, and his hand shook when he stirred his coffee. It was a pity he didn't smoke.

When he looked at his watch, a man with a briefcase sat down opposite. Lance felt his mind drop suddenly, glide, fall and swoop back to position. He said, 'You're Harold Jefferson. I saw you on TV.'

Harold Jefferson looked up. He was a remarkably handsome man and good at his job. 'Yes, I did give a talk recently.'

Then he ordered a meal and took some papers from his brief-case, not glancing up again, his equable spirit quivering at the echo of that bald address, the mental picture of that watch and suit, so spruce and naïve, and above all, at that look in the brilliant deep-set eyes of the fellow across the table. It had been an immensely stupid look of something like veneration—because *he* was a television 'personality'!

'I'd like to ask you something, if you don't mind.'

Oh, really! Harold thought. He was a nervous man of kindly instincts, but his most natural instinct now was to jump heavily

270

on whoever it was prostrated before him. This silly character (probably some would-be Elvis Presley hoping for television contacts) was humble, honoured *him*, Harold Jefferson, and for the wrong reasons! How despicable it made him seem!

'If *you* don't mind,' he murmured, not looking up. 'I'm lecturing tonight.' Harold did have charm, but he did like to discriminate a little in its use.

'Yes, I know. I'm going to be there. Mr Jefferson, you talked about the classics. You said they could make a man free, and sort of rich in himself. I liked that. I never heard anything like it before.'

Harold had to smile with pleasure and shame. He couldn't help but feel himself to be the charmed one now. These rough diamonds! You read about them and dismissed them, but they did have a certain ingenuous something.

He said, 'I'm glad you liked it,' and allowed himself the licence of comparing their probable backgrounds: there was no doubt that that fellow's would be the richer materially. Harold had gone from a Midlands town to Oxford on a government grant. In *this* fellow's background he divined quite easily (couldn't he see a more expensive suit than he had ever owned?) the latest car, the typewriter no one could use, the piano no one could play, and, probably, he thought, a large dog no one exercised.

Lance said, 'What's a classic?' And Harold grew pink, and got pinker, though his expression didn't alter. He'd been made a fool of! Either he was chatting with an imbecile or he was being taken for a fool! Probably because he was English.

But no, he realised slowly. This poor chap was genuine, all right. What a pity! But even so!

Against his will, Harold started to smile. He had been working hard, correcting examination papers, preparing lectures, trying to persuade a girl in London to come out and marry him. He was tired. He simply had to laugh.

Lance went to earth like someone mortally wounded. He put down some money and walked out into the street towards the nearest bar.

Still laughing, but half-rising in alarm to restrain him, Harold Jefferson called his apologies, dropped his briefcase, stooped to collect his papers, and lost his man.

'Mum, I've signed on a ship. I'm leaving on Friday. I'm going to the States on Friday.'

'What? Leaving me, son? You're all I've got, Lance, love.'

'*He's* still here. And I've got you a big dog so you won't be lonely.'

'A dog? How'll I feed it, Lance?'

'I don't know, Mum, with meat, I guess. I'll send you money.'

'I don't want a dog, I want you! You're all I've got.'

'No, I'm not, Mum. You'll like a dog.'

But Pearl had shut herself away to cry for several hours. He didn't change his mind, though.

Across America he picked fruit and hiked and found odd jobs. In England, a man in a Chelsea pub said two words to him he would never forget—'juxtapose' and 'machinations'. Lance often remembered that talk they had.

He spent a lot of time with women, and went quite off his mother. I'm all she's got *now*, he used to think, *now*. But he went home after two years, arriving about Christmas-time. He took his mother Scotch woollies and things, forgetting the Sydney climate in December. The temperature was about a hundred and four in the shade. But Pearl was more than happy, sobbing half the day, and showing him off to the neighbours at night. The dog had got lost. His father was in hospital.

These days Lance drank more than he used to, and talked more, too. His mother thought all this a big improvement. Her Lance was quite fascinating in a way. The way he said, for instance, (so peculiar, really, she couldn't think what he meant), 'No one could tell me what a classic was, Mum. I asked them all.'

'A classic, love? I didn't know you wanted to know.'

'Of course I did! Of course I did!' She seemed so silly to him, he thought she must be drunk. His own mother! Never mind!

That night he wandered the Sydney streets, and wound up in a bar watching television. It was here he asked his question for the millionth time. Afterwards, though he went over and over the scene in his mind, he could never be sure of his reason for throwing a bottle through the screen, and all the rest . . .

Lance got three months for this effort, and a further three later on, for assaulting a guard. That sounds worse, the last bit, than it really was. Lance and the guard were friendly; it turned out they'd both sailed on the same ship at one time, so the assault was no more than the token push they'd agreed on.

As buildings go in Australia, the prison was ancient, and none too comfortable, but it was redeemed in Lance's eyes, at least, as anyone will believe, by the fact that an eccentric, now deceased, clerk had bequeathed his quite vast collection of books, as his will phrased it 'to those unfortunates incarcerated behind stone walls'.

On the second night of his imprisonment, Lance discovered in the library shelf on shelf of a series called *All the Classics*, and accompanying the series, several copies of *The Plain Man's Guide to the Understanding and Appreciation of All the Classics.*

This useful book is now said to be, unhappily, out of print.

273

MENA KASMIRI ABDULLAH
(1930-   )

Mena Kasmiri Abdullah was born in northern New South Wales of migrant Indian parents, and grew up on the family sheep property before attending Sydney Girls High School.

She contributed short stories to several *Coast to Coast* collections and other anthologies. With Ray Mathew she wrote *The Time of the Peacock* (1965). Most of the stories in this collection are about the members of a family, strongly united by love and hope, who have to cope with the difficulties of living in a different culture. These stories are sensitively told and excellently crafted.

'A Long Way' is one of the few stories Abdullah set in India, although there is still a strong connection with Australia.

A LONG WAY

It was an ordinary jumper but no one in the village had seen it. It was Nazit's secret. It was to go a long way.

Secretly, sitting in corners, she had worked at it—knitting it from Pakistani wool. It was for her younger son in Australia.

Australia was a long way, but while she was shaping the wool Nazit felt that she and her boy were close. She knew that when he wore it he too would feel this.

She had packed her basket, putting into it three jars of chutney that everyone believed she was taking to her sister's house. But in her hands she held the soft wool jumper that was the real thing she was taking.

Her elder son's wife came to the door, and Nazit, turning quickly to hide, crushed the jumper into the basket out of sight.

'You will be back tomorrow?'

'Yes,' said Nazit. 'My sister's house is not a long way.' She half-laughed at her cleverness. She said good-bye then, and hurried from the house.

A holy singer and his two drummers were performing on the stone under the *shisham* tree. A knot of workmen had gathered to watch. Nazit avoided the crowd; Ali, her elder son, was too fond of singing.

It was not until she was out of the village, on the bank of the river under the wild cotton-trees and their spring-scarlet flowers, that she stopped hurrying. Nazit smiled; she was safe. The village and her son's fields were a long way. She followed the wide road.

At the railway station at Mooltan, Nazit showed her savings to the ticket-seller. 'Will this,' she said, 'take me to Karachi?'

'No,' said the ticket-seller, who was hot and tired.

Now she was crying. 'How far to Karachi may I go? It is all I have.'

275

For half a second the ticket-seller felt sorry for someone other than himself.

'Mother,' he began, but he remembered himself. 'Why does an old woman like you need to look outside her village?'

'I have to,' said Nazit. 'How far will this money take me?'

The ticket-seller felt tired again. It was impossible to converse with these peasants from the villages. He counted her money again, and pretended he was the teller in a European bank at Bombay. The money was hardly worth counting.

'How far?' said Nazit.

'Don't interrupt,' said the Bombay bank manager. 'I am working.' He counted the money again, and stacked it in bank-like piles. 'To Ranipur,' he said.

Nazit was frightened. 'Is it far from Karachi?'

The ticket-seller knew only that it was the station before. He handed her a ticket. 'Not far at all,' he said. He felt kind.

Nazit sat on the platform. It was full of strangers. She took the jumper from the basket, and she folded it carefully, fondling it, thinking of Yaseem her younger son, and of the Plan.

She remembered the day when the Big Man had come to the village in the big black car. He had a drummer with him, and the drummer beat upon his drum until almost all of the village had gathered. Then the Big Man stood on the great stone, and told the people that he had brought them a notice. He nailed it to the *shisham* tree. The notice told them of the Plan.

The Big Man explained that he was from the Big Government in Karachi and that there were other Big Governments in the world. They were friends that would help.

The villagers listened politely; some of the words were big, and some of them were new, and none of them meant anything at all. When the Big Man had finished they went back to their work.

But the words had meant something. Cars kept passing through the village, and Government Men, in Western clothes, stopped to tell things. One of them said that Rufi, the barber's son and Yaseem, Nazit's youngest, had worked so hard in the big school

276

in Karachi that they could have scholarships and go a long way—
to Australia.

No one wanted to understand. We have our ways, said the
villagers. They are our fathers' ways.

Rufi's father, the barber, forbade him to leave his country.
'My son has his home,' he said.

Nazit pleaded with her boy to stay. 'You are the youngest,'
she said. 'You are the one that is mine.'

Then the Begum came to the village. She was an old lady
with grey hair, but she stood very straight, and everyone knew
that she was wise and good. She explained to them about the
Plan, and they listened.

'The old ways were good, but the new ways are better. They
are a gift of goodwill. We must let our children learn, so that
they can teach others. It is not a kindness. It is a goodness.'

To her the villagers listened. Rufi and Yaseem sailed from
Karachi to Australia, and, though Nazit cried for her boy, and
the barber cried too, they knew that it was good. Their Begum
had said so.

And then Nazit had heard that the Begum was going to
Australia too.

Nazit made the jumper, and she decided to take it to Karachi
to the Begum, to ask her to give it to Yaseem so that it would
be from his mother's hands and from the hands of the Begum
who knew him.

She had to tell lies, to say she would go to her sister's and
stay there the night. Ali her eldest son would not have let her
go to Karachi alone. He might have taken the jumper himself,
and it would have been a thing not from her hands but from
Ali's.

Ali would look for her when she did not return. The man
at the station would tell him perhaps where she had gone. He
would find her, in time, and he would bring her safely home,
scolding and being ashamed that she had been alone on the road
like a woman with no family. But that would not matter.

The train came in with smoke and great noise. It frightened

Nazit a little, and the strangers frightened her too. They jostled through the compartment doorways, pushing with their rolls of bedding and their bulky bundles.

Nazit sat in the crowded carriage, jammed between people. The night came on and, though the nights were cool in all the world, they were not cool there, and Nazit felt sick with heat—suddenly, old and tired. She sat with open eyes. What if, in that carriage full of strangers, a hand had touched her basket, and the jumper had gone? What if her station came and she did not hear its name?

Dawn came, and the minute after dawn was breathless and hot, but although the train had stopped many times it was not till then, that minute, that anybody called out, 'Ranipur!'

It was a big station, and people were sleeping on it in its shade. Nazit would have slept too, but she was afraid. She knew that thieves are found on railway stations.

Suddenly, cleverly, she had an idea. Half-hiding in a doorway, she took the jumper from her basket and put it on under her blouse.

She sat cross-legged on the station, her eyes ready to close just for a minute.

A young girl was sitting near her. The girl was watching her husband approach the food-sellers—his eyes downcast, his manner timid. He was a Hindu. The sellers were Muslims. What if they would sell him nothing? What if they should give him little for his money?

They sold him four *chuppaties* and, gratefully, he thanked them. 'Even Hindu boys must eat,' they laughed at him.

He walked back to his wife looking sure and tall, showing her the food and explaining how he had cleverly managed to get so much for his money. Then she gestured towards Nazit, the hunched-up figure of an old woman almost sleeping.

A Muslim lady alone! He looked inquiringly at his wife. She put her eyes down modestly, then nodded. He went to Nazit, and touched her arm gently.

278

Starting, Nazit gazed up at him. But it was not a thief's face, only a Hindu boy.

'Mother,' he was calling her. 'My wife and I . . .' He pointed proudly to the girl, and then continued, choosing his words carefully because he knew well that Punjabi Muslims are independent and ungracious. 'I have foolishly bought too much food for us. My wife and I would be happy if you would take some with us.'

Nazit looked at the girl with her lowered head and her gentle smile. She looked at the four *chuppaties*. 'I thank you, my son,' she said. 'You are good.'

She sat with them and shared their little food. They talked like friends. They had been married a very little time. They had come the long way to Ranipur, because it was big and might give them food and work. But the girl was frightened. It was all new.

Nazit told her to have faith. 'It is all beginning,' she said. 'My son—my youngest son—he has gone a long way. He is with people he has never known.' She told them about the Plan, the Begum's promises. 'It will come true,' she said. 'Your children will learn and they will eat. They will do wonderful things.'

All this time the girl had sat with her head down—even when she was speaking—but now she raised her head and smiled. 'Our children,' said she. 'We have been married two days!' She and her young husband, and Nazit too—the three of them laughed like friends.

The sun was higher now, and the Hindus rose to leave. Nazit took one of the jars of chutney from her basket. 'A gift,' she said. 'My sons say my mango chutney is the finest in all the Punjab. It is possible they are right.'

Nazit watched them go. Then she went to the station-master. 'How far?' she said. 'How far to Karachi? Which way do I go?'

'This is the main road,' he pointed. 'If you followed it you'd come some time to Karachi. It's a long way.'

Nazit hardly heard. Already she had turned to face the road.

279

The sun climbed high and her walk grew faster. She was in a hurry to leave the town behind.

Women sat for coolness in the doorways that she passed. Some of them were churning curd to make butter. The sound of the churns echoed in Nazit's mind, reminding her of her own village and her own work undone.

She hurried—but her steps grew slower no matter how hard she tried. On every little rise she stopped and looked ahead, hoping to see the city, but she saw nothing but broad road, huts by the way, another little village to pass through.

The sun was above her head now, and she had no shadow. She was tired, and the basket had grown heavy. She was hungry, too. An old woman sat at the door of one of the village houses. She nursed a baby. 'Sister,' she called. 'You have walked a long way. Come in and rest.'

Inside the house was water for Nazit's dusty feet, a dish of *pilau* for her to eat, the baby to be looked at and the woman to be talked to. She told her of Yaseem and of the jumper that was to go such a long way. She took it off and showed it. The woman cried out at the softness of the wool.

'Think of it!' said the woman. 'Such a long way! My son too—the father of my grandchild—he is in Canada. He is learning too. Think of that! My husband and I were untouchables. But our son now can be a doctor. And his son—here with big eyes open—who knows what he can be?'

Nazit lifted the baby, and the two women wept. To them it seemed the world was flowering.

'Allah bless you,' said Nazit as she moved to go. She put one of her jars of chutney on the table. 'I have far to go.'

'*Ram, Ram.* Peace be with you,' said the woman. 'It is not far. There is one more village, and then the city. The Christian village. It is called the Biscuit Tin.'

It was late afternoon when Nazit came to the village and found the Biscuit Tin. It was a church on stilts, its roof and walls of beaten tin. There was no one to be seen. She sat on the steps in the shade, and leant on the handle of her basket.

Inside the tiny vestry the priest was dressing himself for Mass. He was trying not to remember his church in Madras, not to think of clean streets and cool buildings at all.

He had no parishioners here, only people who lived in the parish—peasants, a few refugees. Most of them Hindus, all of them polite, they thanked him for teaching their children. They came to Mass sometimes and listened. They were grateful, but his way was not theirs.

He had told the Bishop so; 'the conversion rate in this country is less than one in a million and probably none is a real conversion', he had written. But the Bishop did not or would not understand.

Tutting, he removed three oranges from the cupboard. It was typical of the visiting medical nuns to hide their little gifts in an inconvenient place. The oranges were on top of his chasuble.

He went into the church thinking of the day's business—last rites for an old woman surrounded by crying family. Now they, and all the village, were out burning the wretched woman as though she were a pagan.

The church offended him. An old table for an altar—that was an insult to God, but he comforted himself with the thought that the Mass he was to say was the same as the Bishop's, the same as the Pope's.

Afterwards, carrying the oranges, he made to leave the church, but the sun in the doorway glared into his eyes. Even the evening sun here was distastefully irreverent.

He moved to descend, and Nazit turned and looked up at him. He saw into her eyes. He dropped the oranges into her basket, and moved down the steps past her. Nazit watched him go, wondering what one said to a strange white man. She put the last of her jars of chutney on the step, and, taking the oranges, she walked over to the irrigation channel. She sat by it and bathed her feet as she ate the oranges. This was the last village, not far from Karachi; this must be her last rest.

But it *was* far. The road went on and on, and Nazit followed it. At every turn, after every clump of trees, she hoped for the city, but it was not there. Her eyelids kept closing as she walked.

281

It was dark now, but the night was still and hot, and the sky seemed close and heavy on her back. She was sweating. Her eyes were running, almost as though she were crying, but she could not stop. It was tomorrow the Begum was to go.

The road wound round a hill, and suddenly, on the turn of the road, there were people everywhere—in tents and shelters, in poorest huts, people who cooked by open flame, children who ran naked between the fires, people who wore rags. They were refugees.

'Praise Allah!' said Nazit. 'I am in Karachi.' She went to a clump of guava trees, and took the jumper from her basket. Again she put it on and hid it under her blouse.

It was early morning when she woke. The first breath of the day moved on her face. She wondered for a moment where she was and why. 'Laila,' she murmured. That was her daughter-in-law's name. Why wasn't she near? Why wasn't she cooking? All around her were little fires, the smell of curry. Then she remembered.

'Eh, mother,' said a gnarled old man near her. 'You don't belong here. You're not used to being on your own. Would you like some water?' He held an earthenware jug towards her.

Nazit took it from him. He was black as a Bengali, but he was smiling at her. 'You are kind,' she said.

'I'm just a man who one day will be old.'

Nazit smiled at him. 'I am older than you, and I have come a long way,' she said. 'And I am wiser than you, because I know that everyone is kind.'

The man laughed at her. 'Where are you going, mother?'

'Where I am now—Karachi.'

'This isn't Karachi. This is the refugee camp, miles from the city.'

'But—' Nazit faltered. 'The ship,' she said. 'I have to be there when it sails, before midday. Is there time?'

'Yes,' he said. 'You come with me. I am going in my cart to the markets. I sell pots, jugs, anything that earth can make. Are you catching the ship?'

282

'No,' said Nazit. 'But I am going to see the Begum.'

The Begum stood by the ship's rail, and looked at the crowd that filled the wharf. Her son Selim stood by her and talked. Everything he said annoyed her. He was educated and Englishy and arty. Her two old friends—Dr Haroon, of Karachi Hospital, and Professor Shah, the philosopher from Lahore University, talked too, with jokes and laughter. But the Begum hardly heard them, did not want to hear them.

Her daughter had been in Australia for some time. She wrote home often, but recently the letters had been full of worries. The Plan might fail, its good work be undone.

There were critics who said that it was silly, wasteful, that the country had causes of its own, that its people needed houses, and that its people's money was being thrown around overseas. What, they asked, have foreigners to do with us?

What, indeed? The Begum could understand it all. What had foreigners to do with her? Australians need have nothing to do with her people unless they wanted to be friends. And did they want to?

She clutched at her handbag irritably: it was full of notes for her Australian lecture tour—UNO reports, health reports, hygiene reports, soil reports, irrigation reports . . . what do reports mean?

Someone touched her arm and she turned. 'Nazit!' she said. 'You come to see me off, to wish me well! But where is Ali, Laila?'

'I have come alone,' said Nazit.

'Alone?' The Begum and her friends stared at her. Nazit was very old and a Muslim. The Begum held her away and looked into her red-rimmed eyes.

'I came in the train to Ranipur, and then I walked. But last night I slept. A kind man drove me here today.'

She swayed and almost fell as she spoke, but the Begum held her. 'Sister,' she said. 'You could have sent your wishes. Why did you come?'

Nazit handed her the jumper. 'It is not a good jumper,' she said. 'But I made it for Yaseem, my youngest who is in Australia. Give it to him for me, from his mother's hands.'

'I will find him and give it to him,' said the Begum. 'I will tell him to love it. But you must now do exactly as I say.'

'Exactly as you say,' said Nazit. She suddenly felt very old and useless, wanting Ali and even Laila with all her irritating household ways.

'Selim,' said the Begum. 'You will send a telegram to Ali. You will tell him that Nazit is with you, in my house, safe. And then you will—'

'Mother!' said Selim. 'I am an adult. I have graduated. I know what to do. You are not supposed to lecture *me.*'

The whistle was blowing. The voices all around were louder. Hands were beginning to wave. 'It is time for us to go,' said the professor.

'God be with us all,' said the Begum, thinking her own thoughts.

'All,' said Nazit. 'They all of them helped me. Everyone is kind—the Muslim, the Hindu, the Untouchable, the Christian, the Potter. They didn't know me but they loved me.'

They all looked at her, but it was Selim who spoke—Selim who was educated and wrote poetry and was irritating. 'Mother,' he said to Nazit, 'what else should they do? They are your people. The world is your people.'

The ship moved from the wharf, and the streamers broke. A cry went up from the crowd, and the Begum waved. My people, she thought. Selim, the professor, the doctor, Nazit, the man and the woman, the babies in arms. Our people.

On the wharf she saw the few wealthy and well-fed, the many thin and poorly dressed. She stared at them, seeing a thin-legged child who was running through the crowd gathering streamers, to roll and sell again; a pregnant woman who was leaning on the custom-house wall.

The ship moved from the bay.

In her mind the Begum saw the refugee camps, the hungry and the poor, the beaten and the lost. They are all our people,

284

she thought, no matter who we are or what, no matter where they are or why.

She took the notes from her bag, tore them slowly into four and dropped the pieces onto the water. She watched them sink. Reports, she thought; statistics, numbers. I will find the people, and I will tell them. I will go to the houses, the streets, the parks. I will tell them how Nazit came to me a long way and how I too have come to them a long, long way.

The ship moved on, towards Australia, parting the sea, going quickly on its long, long way.

SHIRLEY HAZZARD
(1931–   )

Shirley Hazzard was born and educated in Sydney. She has travelled extensively in the Far East, New Zealand and Italy. For ten years she worked at the United Nations but resigned in order to devote her time to writing. Her non-fiction work, *Defeat of an Ideal* (1973), is an account of the United Nations' failures and weaknesses. Married to American writer Francis Steegmuller, Hazzard has become an American citizen.

Hazzard has published three novels and two collections of short stories. In 1966 she was awarded a grant by the US National Institute of Arts and Letters. *The Transit of Venus* (1981) won the US National Book Critics' Award for the best novel of 1980. Many of her short stories have appeared in the *New Yorker* and she has won a first prize in the O. Henry Short Story Awards.

'A Sense of mission' appeared in *People in Glass Houses* (1967), a collection of satiric short stories about a bureaucracy like the United Nations.

A SENSE OF MISSION

'Carry your bags, miss?'

It was the first remark addressed to her by those she had come to serve.

'A taxi?'

She nodded, reluctant to begin by speaking English, startled to find her language apparent. She spoke to the porter slowly in Italian, the lingua franca of this island. Someone was to have met her; they hadn't come. Yes, she would go to the hotel. Which hotel? Well—what hotels were there? A Bristol, a Cecil? A Majestic, perhaps?

The porter smiled. What she wanted was the Hotel of the Roses.

Only hours since she had stepped into the plane from the winter night of a northern city, Miss Clelia Kingslake was breathing mild morning air by the Aegean. The sun streamed down on valley, rock and green hill, and the driver leant against his taxi in his shirtsleeves. Miss Kingslake's pang of ecstasy was not a bit the less for her having recently entered her fortieth year—quite the reverse, in fact. All the same, when her baggage was aboard and they drove off, she became distracted from her new surroundings, wondering if she could possibly have missed her as yet unknown colleagues. She was to have been met at the airport; so she had been assured before leaving Organisation Headquarters the night before. There had been no one the least colleague-like in the waiting-room, and in any case they would have approached her. It didn't matter—she could manage for herself and they had more important things to do. For the time being, the entire region was dependent on their vigilance. After all, wasn't this an emergency mission?

The taxi rattled through a fertile valley towards the sea. When they reached the corniche, the driver slowed down, pointed out a row of Turkish houses, asked her why she had come to Rhodes.

She explained, on an assignment for the Organisation.

'*Ah sì. La NATO.*'

Oh no, no. NATO was a military organisation. Hers was a peace-keeping one.

The driver shrugged at this subtlety. He could not be bothered splitting hairs, and lost interest. Did she see those mountains across the sea? That was the coast of Turkey. And here, as they swung around a curve, was the city of Rhodes.

Clelia Kingslake had a glimpse of golden walls, of white shipping, of a tower, a fortress. She was revisited by ecstasy. A moment later she found herself in a driveway.

The hotel was formlessly vast, and brown—a dated wartime brown suggestive of inverted camouflage, as if it had been wilfully disguised as a military installation. Upstairs, however, unlatching the shutters of a charming, old-fashioned room, she looked down over terraces and a pebbled beach to the sea and, once more, out to the blue Turkish coast. The open French windows formed, with their outside railing, a narrow balcony. She pulled up a chair and, leaning her arm on the rail and her chin on her arm, sat there in the winter sunshine, happy.

Clelia Kingslake was happy because, first of all, she was a Canadian. Fished out of the Annual Reports Pool at Headquarters, where she held a superior clerical post, flown to Rhodes at one day's notice, arriving there to sunlight and sea, to trees in leaf, flowers in bloom, to the luxury of finding herself beside the Mediterranean—all this by itself might not have been thoroughly enjoyable to her strict northern soul had she not come to assist in a noble undertaking. She had been sent to serve the peoples of the Eastern Mediterranean in their hour of need, and it was this that sanctioned her almost sensual pleasure in her surroundings as she sat gazing out from the Hotel of the Roses.

She was, in however modest a degree, the instrument of a great cause: in this setting redolent of antiquity she even risked to herself the word 'handmaiden'. A dozen years earlier, in Toronto, she had diligently studied Italian in order to take her elderly mother to Rome. In the end, that summer, they had settled for Lake Louise, but she had kept up a little with the language. And this dormant ability had posted her now, miraculously, to an emergency mission newly established in the Mediterranean as an antidote to an international crisis.

An employee from the hotel was opening coloured umbrellas on the stony beach below. One or two hardy guests were bathing, although the sea looked neither calm nor warm. Apart from occasional shouts of *'Herrlich!'* from the swimmers, the only sound was the rhythmic crunching of waves up the pebbled shore. 'Sophocles long ago heard it on the Aegean,' quoted Miss Kingslake to herself, and the consummation of the familiar line in an actual experience, combined with fatigue from an overnight plane journey, brought a rush of tears to her eyes.

The telephone rang and she jumped up to answer. It was the concierge. Yes, he had put the call through to her office. No, no one wished to speak with her. However, there was a message: a Signor Grilli (the concierge permitted his voice a faint smile, for the name meant 'crickets') would come to see her at eight this evening.

She put the phone down. She had expected to be called to work at once and was disappointed. It was considerate of this Grilli, who was in charge of the new mission, to give her a day's grace, but she was anxious to take up her duties. She thought she would rest before unpacking and walking out to look at the town.

'Grilli. Downstairs.'

'I'll be right down.' She sat up, replaced the receiver, tried to think where she was. It was after eight. She sprang off the bed, pulled on her dress, combed her hair, alarming herself by muttering 'My God' as she fumbled with buttons and looked for her shoes.

When she came out of the elevator there was no one to be seen. The concierge directed her to one of the lounges. It was a large room beside the bar, decorated with graceful murals of the seasons, and the one person in it was paring his nails beneath the harvest. Miss Kingslake realised that, because of the name, she had been expecting a slight brittle figure, whereas the man who glanced in her direction, put away his nail file, and made a minimal effort to rise was a big man, a fat man, too young a man to be completely bald. His Sicilian ancestry—from which he had inherited the knowledge of the Italian language that had brought him on this mission—was not apparent.

She shook hands and sat down with an apology for keeping him waiting. 'It must be the journey.' She smiled. 'I was in a deep sleep.'

He glanced at her a second time, looked away. His hands quivered with the suppressed need to fidget. He said, 'You haven't come here to sleep.' When Miss Kingslake said nothing he went on, 'I've been here three weeks. The first week I didn't sleep at all. No time. Kept going on coffee and cigarettes. Just as well you weren't here then, if you need so much sleep.'

'I was assigned here only yesterday.'

'And if you don't work out, you're going back just as fast.'

The waiter came up. Grilli ordered fruit juice, Miss Kingslake a sherry. The drinks were put down, with a big dish of peanuts, and Miss Kingslake asked, 'When may I come to the office?'

'Tomorrow, Sunday. A car will pick you up here at 7 a.m. I'll be in it.' The flat of his hand smashed down among the peanuts, a massive displacement that scattered them as far as Miss Kingslake's lap. He brought his fist back to his mouth and eventually continued. 'Give Noreen a day off. If nothing else. Noreen's been here from the beginning. Work! You ought to see that girl work. A truck horse. You know Noreen at Headquarters?'

'Perhaps by sight.'

'She's in our department there—Logistics. Not one of your fancy do-nothing departments. She's been in most of these emergencies—Suez, Lebanon, Cyprus, now here. If I had to go on another mission like this, I'd say give me Noreen.' Another peanut spun into Clelia Kingslake's lap. 'Rather than any six others.'

'Can you give me an idea of what I'm to do?'

'We all pull our weight here. I don't know what you do at Headquarters and I don't care. Here you'll do anything that comes to hand. Cables, letters, typing, accounts—'

'I can do any of those things.'

'You'll do all of them. You'll be in with the Cap.'

'The Cap.'

'Captain Moyers. He's been seconded from Near East Peace Preservation. Assigned to us as Military Observer, but he's turned his hand to everything during the crisis. A Canadian like yourself. But a great guy.' The eyes were wandering again, contentiously raking the walls, lingering suspiciously on Primavera. 'A rough diamond, but a great guy. He'll be here any minute. He went out to the airfield to meet Mr Rees.'

Miss Kingslake pondered. Rees was head of the Logistics Department at Headquarters. 'He's here?'

'Three-day tour of inspection. Oh, all the big brass have been through here this month—the Director-General himself came through, you know, on his way to the trouble spots. Mr Rees was too busy to come before.'

He pronounced it as if it were all one word, Mysteries. Miss Kingslake, her own gaze wandering, noted that the murals were by Afro. 'I don't want to keep you.' She allowed herself to add, 'I'm sure you need your sleep.'

Grilli was leaning forward, his hands splayed over the chair arms. All at once he changed colour. He hoisted himself up, vast and padded—it was as if the armchair had come to its feet—and shot out between the glass doors into the lobby.

Mysteries, surmised Clelia Kingslake, signing the bill. She followed. Grilli was bowed over a little cricket of a man, while a military figure strode about the lobby roaring orders in English. When Miss Kingslake came up, Grilli introduced her.

'Mysteries, this is Miss Kingslake, the newest member of the mission.'

Rees shook hands. He looked Miss Kingslake in the eyes and held her gaze. 'Miss Kingsley,' he said quietly, 'I want you to know that people like you are continually in our minds at Headquarters. Sometimes staff members in the field tend to feel forgotten. Believe me, they couldn't be more mistaken. I want you to know that it's fully appreciated, the wonderful work you are doing here.'

'Thank you.'

'Believe me.'

The three men were to dine together. Miss Kingslake was grateful that no suggestion was made that she should join them. While Grilli accompanied Rees up to his room, the Captain came over to Miss Kingslake, cap in hand, and introduced himself.

The Captain was also a fleshy man, though short. His face was red and puffy. He wore heavy dark glasses with square dark frames. The regularity of his black moustache suggested an inept disguise—another case of bad camouflage.

'We're sharing an office, I think?' said Clelia Kingslake, when they had exchanged names.

'So that's his idea, is it?' The Captain shot her a necessarily dark look. 'More room in his office than in mine. What-have-you and so on. Could have requisitioned another office from the locals.'

Miss Kingslake said, with a helpful air of making light of things that was one of her more difficult characteristics, 'Oh well—it's an emergency mission.'

The Captain slapped his cap against his leg with annoyance. 'Emergency, bah. I've been in the Eastern Mediterranean five years. Seen nothing but a lot of so-called emergencies. Let them kill one another—best thing that could happen, what-have-you and so on. Or drop an atomic bomb on the lot of them.'

Miss Kingslake stared. 'The Organisation—'

'Organisation!' The red face inflated with facile rage. 'A lot of clots, that's what they are, this Organisation of yours. A lot of clots.'

Miss Kingslake turned away. The Captain followed her to the elevator. 'And the Arabs. Don't talk to me about the Arabs.'

She made no attempt to. The elevator arrived.

'Vehicle at 0700 sharp. What-have-you and so on.'

Just before seven Clelia Kingslake came down to the hotel lobby. A second sleep, a bath, and a new day had made a difference to her spirits. Waking in the dark that morning she had thought the situation over. Was it not true, after all, that she—through no fault of her own—had come belatedly to a mission where others had been under strain? That she had encountered them, yesterday evening, at the end of a fatiguing day spent in the faithful performance of their duties? Miss Kingslake's heart brimmed with understanding as she climbed into her claw-footed bathtub.

How much she had to be thankful for, she exclaimed to herself as she climbed out. In all her time with the Organisation, she had longed to go on such a mission. Not that she discounted for a moment her two years spent in the field with the Survey of West African Trust Territories, a rewarding experience in useful work and heartening *esprit de corps*: but SWATT, an economic mission, could hardly compare with a dynamic political mission such as this one. It was the immediacy that took Miss Kingslake's breath away.

Twice before she had been assigned to a peace-keeping mission, only to be forestalled at the moment of departure—once by a bloody revolution in the country of her destination, another time because of a slipped disc. Now it had all come to pass. Even a lag in the Reports workload had helped to facilitate her sudden departure: only two days before, she had completed proof-reading on appendices for the World Commodity Index.

Environment would always have been secondary to Miss Kingslake's wish to serve—adverse conditions, in fact, would merely have challenged her to make light of them in her helpful way. Almost guiltily, then, having fastened her skirt, did she cross to the windows and look out on the Anatolian sunrise as she buttoned her blouse. She had no right to expect that the fulfilment of her desires would take place in so much comfort.

She dwelt again, indulgently, on the encounter with her new

colleagues. Grilli, a young man, evidently insecure, had been abruptly elevated to a position of unnerving responsibility. When Miss Kingslake's industry, her goodwill, made themselves apparent to him, his manner would change. And had he not himself described the Captain as a rough diamond? A display of diamantine qualities would soon put the Captain's opening remarks in perspective. *Pazienza*, thought Clelia Kingslake to herself, smiling in the glass as she put on the jacket of her best blue suit.

A black Chrysler was waiting in the hotel driveway, and Grilli was in it. Miss Kingslake greeted the Rhodian driver who handed her in, and asked his name.

'Mihalis,' he told her. 'Michele, Michel, Mike.'

Grilli said, 'The others are late too.'

'You aren't at this hotel?'

'Managed to find a modern place.' He jerked his head inland. 'Brand new. Air-conditioned. Music piped in.' They sat in silence. He looked steadily at the folds of her skirt, then reached out and took her sleeve between thumb and finger. 'Buy this out of your *per diem* advance?'

Pazienza, Miss Kingslake said to herself. She thought, This man is afraid of women. But she harboured the knowledge unwillingly and had not the faintest idea of what to do with it. The mere realisation in itself suggested something unsporting, an abuse of power.

The driver opened the door. Rees appeared, carrying a camera and a briefcase. Grilli made an attempt to stand up inside the car.

'Sorry to keep you busy people waiting.' Rees settled himself on the other side of Clelia Kingslake. 'I overslept, I'm afraid. The plane journey, change of hours—it's quite an adjustment.'

'Certainly takes it out of you,' Grilli agreed sympathetically.

'I hardly remember where I was, this time yesterday. Malta, was it, or Herakleion?' Rees smiled benevolently at Miss Kingslake. 'How do you do.'

'Clelia Kingslake,' Grilli said. 'She's the latest arrival. I think you—'

Rees shook hands, turning to her full face. 'Miss Kingsland,' he said gravely, 'I know from experience that staff members in the field tend to feel forgotten. It's natural, being so far from Headquarters—natural, but mistaken. Believe me. You people, and the wonderful work you're doing, are in our thoughts at Headquarters every day. I want you to know how much you're appreciated and remembered.'

'I do know. Thank you.'

Grilli moved uneasily. His hands shifted back and forth over his knees. 'Here's the Cap.'

The Captain strode from the hotel, got into the front seat, turned and nodded curtly. Something had happened to him in the night. He was redder and flabbier, out of sorts and breath. The driver jumped in beside him, closed the door, reached for the starter.

'Well, get going, man!' cried the Captain impatiently.

The car rolled out of the hotel driveway. To their left, through a screen of eucalyptus leaves, they glimpsed an enclosure of long, leaning markers.

'A Turkish cemetery,' exclaimed Miss Kingslake, leaning forward.

The driver slowed down. 'It is the cemetery for civil servants.'

They passed through an agglomeration of Mussolini's architecture, and came within sight of the harbour and the ancient city. At this hour the walls of the Crusaders were tangerine, their splendid order pierced here and there by a gleaming tower or a minaret. Clelia Kingslake sensed, again unwillingly, that an expression of interest would not be welcome. Nevertheless she said, 'How marvellous.'

'A façade,' Grilli said, 'that's all this is, a façade. This place is poor as hell. Without the big powers to back them up, they'd be nothing.'

On the far side of Miss Kingslake, Rees beamed. 'I'd like a picture of this.'

'All right, man, you can stop here. *Momento,* what-have-you and so on. Not here, you fool, have a bit of sense, pull over to the wall.'

'If we pulled out of here, all this would fold up tomorrow.'

'The walls,' said Miss Kingslake, 'are in some places seven centuries old.'

'Not getting out, Miss Kingsford?'

Having left the car, Grilli turned back, hung his fingers over the open window. 'Take my advice, girlie. Don't try to be a wise guy.'

Alone with the driver, Miss Kingslake asked, 'Where do you live, Mihalis?'

He pointed, 'Over there, on the façade.'

They followed the road Miss Kingslake had travelled the day before. Rees was to pay a courtesy call on the commandant of the airfield, whose name he read out several times from a slip of paper. Grilli would leave him there and return for him. (Later Miss Kingslake was to discover that Grilli, self-conscious about his inherited Palermitan accent, declined to deal with purer-spoken officials—a complication that had not been foreseen at Headquarters.) Grilli and Moyers spoke of invoices, of supplies and equipment; and Miss Kingslake, considerately leaning back to facilitate their discussion, was reassured by this talk of tonnage and manpower. Was it not all this, ultimately, that mattered on an emergency mission?

When the car drew up, Grilli escorted Rees into the airport. The Captain also got out and scrambled into the back seat, where he heavily and patriotically exhaled Canadian Club.

'That's it. What-have-you and so on.'

'What?'

'The office. The mission. HQ Rhodes. For what it's worth.'

Following the direction of his jabbing finger, Miss Kingslake discovered a large stuccoed cube alone in a rocky field.

'You mean, right here? At the airfield?'

'Converted military post. Lent to us by the locals. Supposed to be gratis, but they'll want their pound of flesh, just wait, what-have-you and so on.'

Some minutes had passed in silence before Miss Kingslake enquired conversationally, 'How far is it from here to Lindos?'

The door opened. 'You didn't come here for sightseeing.' Grilli climbed inside.

Having followed her companions up a short flight of steps, Miss Kingslake presently lost them in a maze of connecting rooms. The offices were high and wide, and floored with huge black and white tiles—hot weather rooms that were fringed with cold at this season. In the centre of each stood a new electric stove attached by its cord to some far-off outlet. These cords went rippling and wiggling beneath desks, under double doors, out into corridors; those that had not lasted the distance had been extended with others. The whole establishment was swarming, a nest of vipers.

Clelia Kingslake made herself known to the mission accountant, a Dane, and to the radio operator, a Pakistani. With a new, urgent perception, she saw that both were of crushable substance, and her heart sank though she said some cheerful words. A room containing the local recruits, boisterous with laughter when she opened the door, at once fell silent. Half a dozen messengers and drivers sat on the edges of tables speaking Greek, and on the single chair a little old man was fitting a roll of paper into an adding machine. She enquired for the Captain's office and they showed it to her, pointing out its particular black cord writhing down the hallway.

Following this, Miss Kingslake went to meet her Minotaur.

She found herself alone in the room, and sat down at what was apparently her desk, at the lightless end of the room. She uncovered the typewriter, unlocked the drawers. A sheet of instructions had been left on the blotter and was signed Noreen. Miss Kingslake switched on her desk lamp and began to read. 'Two pink flimsies Beirut, one white flimsy Addis—'

Mihalis came in with something in his hand.

'It's a light meter.' She took it from him and put it on the desk. 'I suppose it belongs to Rees.'

Mihalis lingered.

'Thanks. I'll see he gets it.' She picked up the list again.

'Headquarters all yellow flimsies.'

Mihalis leant forward. Miss Kingslake looked up.

'It takes one hour to Lindos.'

She smiled. 'Thank you, Mihalis.' With the best will in the world, she could not help feeling as if a code word had been slipped to her in prison.

The Captain's boots, having metal on them, were very loud on the tiled floor. 'What was the driver doing here?'

'He left this.'

'I'll take charge of that. Slack, that driver. Needs bracing up.'

'Really?'

'Like the rest of them. Go into that room of theirs down the corridor, they're acting up all day long. Good mind to report the lot of them, what-have-you and so on. Not the Europeans, of course, just the local staff.'

'The local staff *are* the Europeans.'

'Paid far too much of course.' The Captain was at that moment drawing an allowance from the Organisation in addition to his Army pay. 'The way this outfit of yours throws money around. Not theirs, of course, so they feel free.'

Miss Kingslake lifted out the contents of her In-tray.

'Don't talk to me about drivers. Had a series of drivers in Kashmir, biggest lot of clots, what-have-you and so on. Rented a villa there, awkward driveway, narrow entrance between two concrete posts. Just room for the car, inch or two to spare. Made it a condition of keeping the drivers—they had to go through without slowing down. One scratch and they were washed up, through, no reference.' The Captain laughed and crashed his mailed feet delightedly on the tiles below his desk. 'They snivelled at first, of course, but they needed their jobs and they made it their business to learn.' He tipped his chair back, rummaged in the desk drawer for cigarettes. 'Don't talk to me about drivers.'

Clelia Kingslake was setting out the incoming cables, like cards for solitaire. She could see the concrete blocks looming, feel the sweat on her brow and on her hands gripping the wheel.

SHIRLEY HAZZARD

And to think that only yesterday she had wept over Matthew Arnold.

The Captain spoke out on a variety of subjects, always exhorting her not to talk to him of these matters. He was unused, he divulged, to women in his office. He liked his own office, with at most a corporal in attendance. He was a man who lived among men. (Four years earlier, although he did not say this, he had abandoned a wife and child in Battleford, Saskatchewan.) He was accustomed to working with men throughout the day; to returning in the evening to BOQ.

This, though Miss Kingslake could not know it, was Bachelor Officers' Quarters.

'BOQ, that's the place for me.'

'I'm sure.'

When Rees looked in to retrieve his light meter, the Captain brushed away his thanks. 'Delighted to be of service, sir.'

'Sorry to disturb you busy people.'

The sun came round to the front of the building, and the Captain went out and stood in it. He could be seen by Miss Kingslake from where she sat, planted with his back to the window and his feet wide apart. He had taken off his sun glasses for the first time.

Miss Kingslake got up from her desk and brought a mirror out from her handbag. Walking over to the light, she touched the discreet contours of her hair with an accustomed hand and took the opportunity to put on face-powder. When this was done, she held the mirror up and made a face into it. In a high voice, as if mimicking a child, she said *'Pazienza.'* After a moment she added, also out loud, 'What-have-you and so on.' Standing there in a square of sunlight, she rocked back and forth on her sensible heels.

She put the mirror away and came back to her desk. She made up a large number of cardboard files, feeling ashamed of herself.

Miss Kingslake sat in a chair by Grilli's desk, a notebook in

299

her lap, while he spoke on the telephone. Grilli talked loudly in order not to be afraid, like a person in the dark. If he does a good job, she reasoned, why should I be concerned about his personality? She wished she were less exacting. She wished she were more—

'Outgoing.' Grilli dictated a cable, turning loose sheets on his blotter all the while. He drafted a short letter to his section at Headquarters. 'Date that today,' he said.

'Yes, of course.'

'I mean Sunday. Not "20th"—but *"Sunday* 20th", get it?'

He slapped down a handwritten list on the desk by Miss Kingslake's arm. 'Mr Rees is throwing a party for the government officials here. Invitations to go out today, champagne party at the hotel, Wednesday, six o'clock.'

Miss Kingslake placed the list on her knee, under her notebook. 'Any special wording?'

'Yeah.' Grilli read from the reverse of the paper on which Rees had written the commandant's name. 'To express heartfelt gratitude, profound appreciation for cooperation, etc., you fix it.'

'Shall I put "RSVP"?'

'RSVP? Christ no. If they don't want to come and drink champagne they can go to hell.' His quivering hand passed unimpeded over the top of his head. 'What a day.'

'You've been busy?'

'Nothing to what it was before, of course.'

'Of course not.'

'The first couple of weeks. Just me, Noreen and the Cap. Kept going on coffee and cigarettes. The Cap's a great guy, don't you think? A rough diamond.'

'They don't make them like that any more.'

'Knows this region like the back of his hand. You should hear him. Not much of a talker, but when he gets going.'

Miss Kingslake said, 'He has a singular verbal tic.'

She could not tell whether she had said something unspeakable or merely incomprehensible. Grilli stared at her. 'I'm trying to get him recruited into the Organisation. A senior post, of course.

He's wasted in the Army. I've spoken to Mr Rees about it. The Organisation, that's the place for him.'

Miss Kingslake said, 'He seems so at home in BOQ.'

Grilli returned to his papers. 'A lot to do. Been a big strain, this job. Not the work, even, but the responsibility.'

As long as he does his job. Miss Kingslake's pencil was at the ready.

'Being on your own, that's what gets you. Anything goes wrong, you're responsible.'

'That's what I imagine.' She lowered her pencil again.

'Dealing direct with the big brass. They want something—they want it now, like this.' He snapped his thumb and forefinger twice.

'Frightening, sometimes.'

'I can handle it.'

'Naturally.'

'Can't talk all day. I've got a job to do.' He tipped his chair back and locked his hands behind his head. He looked expansive—not only in the physical sense, for his face assumed a contented anticipatory smile. 'A letter. For today's pouch.'

Miss Kingslake poised her pencil.

'One flimsy.'

'Just one.' She made a note.

'White.' Grilli gazed upward, his eyes—half-closed in the act of composition—rotating over the motionless ceiling fan. His lips moved once or twice before he actually spoke.

'Dearest Mom,' he began.

IRENE SUMMY
(dates unknown)

Very little is known about Irene Summy. A few short stories by her appeared in *Southerly* and *Overland* in 1968–69. One of her plays, *Man of the Mountain,* was published in *Six One-Act Plays* (1970).

It would be interesting to know what has happened to a writer with the potential reflected in the few excellent short stories we could find.

'The Secret', which appeared in a 1968 *Southerly,* is a powerful story in which Summy writes with great insight into the sadism and masochism that are especially manifest in children's games.

THE SECRET

Sandwiched between her parents on the front seat of the car, Tina looked out at the falling night.

'Dear God,' she prayed in the silence of her own cathedral, 'don't let them leave me alone with Brownie.'

But even while praying she knew there was no escape. The grown-ups would want to talk and instantly upon arrival relegate her and Brownie to play checkers on the floor in the back room that smelled of dirty clothes and cats. 'My room,' as Brownie called it and made fun of Tina, because she still slept in her parents' bedroom. 'Do you like to hear them making noises?' Brownie had asked, which was silly, because her parents didn't make any noise, except that Daddy sometimes snored. But then Brownie said and did a lot of things that Tina didn't understand and would have liked to tell her mother . . . like the secret for instance. Especially the secret. But telling the secret would not change the way she felt about it or about Brownie, and that she could not ever tell her mother.

It had started accidentally as a game, then suddenly one day it wasn't a game any longer, but a dark terrible secret . . . like stealing or lying, only worse, because you could not tell anyone, not even God, or say that you were sorry and promise never to do it again, because you couldn't help it . . . you didn't mean to do it . . . it just happened. Though sometimes Tina thought that Brownie started it and knew how Tina felt and wanted her to feel that way. And that was the worst part of it—that and not being able to tell her mother from whom she had never before had any secrets at all.

'You aren't falling asleep, dear, are you?' asked her mother and shook her gently. 'We're almost there.'

The car was slowing. 'Please Daddy . . . please Mummy . . . please God . . . don't leave me alone with Brownie.'

303

When the door had closed behind the adults, and their steps and voices had faded down the hall, the two children stood facing each other in the gloomy, untidy room where Brownie slept. The checker board already was on the floor.

'Shall we play?' asked Tina nervously.

Her cousin smiled. Hands on hips she stood with her back to the door—a sturdy nine-year-old with brown eyes and curly brown hair framing a round, mischievous face. 'I know what you're getting for Christmas.'

'No!' cried Tina, covering both ears with her hands. 'Don't tell me. I don't want to hear.' Her pale blue eyes in the thin, triangular face circled the room as if hunting for a place to hide.

Brownie laughed. Coming closer she took hold of Tina's hands and forced them down. Tina struggled, turning her tiny wrists to free herself from Brownie's grip. 'Don't . . . please don't.'

Abruptly the older cousin released her, pushing her back towards the unmade bed. 'Why don't you want to know?'

Tina stumbled, and recovering her balance said breathlessly: 'It's better not to know.'

'Why? Why is it better not to know?' Brownie came closer again, blocking Tina's path. 'Sit down.'

'Not tonight. Brownie. Please. It's Christmas.'

'So what?' With the palm of her hand Brownie kept forcing her back. 'Sit down.'

The edge of the bed cut into Tina's thighs. Panicky she stepped aside, ducked, and Brownie's hand shot out, her fingers clutching Tina's hair. Slowly, very slowly, she started pulling. 'Sit down.'

Tina briefly closed her eyes as if listening for something. Reluctantly she sat.

'Now stay there,' said Brownie, releasing her hold. She crouched, groped under the bed and produced a skipping rope with yellow handles.

Her eyes on the rope, Tina moistened her lips. 'Let's play checkers . . . please.'

Brownie unbuckled her belt. 'A puppy,' she said. 'That's what you're getting.'

'A puppy?' Tina smiled, her eyes widening in disbelief and wonder, then clouding again. 'You shouldn't have told me. You spoil everything. Why do you want to spoil it?'

'A boxer,' continued Brownie, her lips drawn back, her eyes two narrow slits of brown malice. 'It's in a box outside. And I'm giving you a collar for it. With a little bell. And . . .'

'Please . . . don't tell me any more,' Tina pleaded, almost crying, thinking how happy she would have been, if Brownie hadn't told her, and now already in her mind she had seen the dog and held it in her arms and wouldn't be surprised but would have to pretend so as not to disappoint her parents or rouse their suspicions. 'You spoiled everything,' she cried and rose, forgetting the rope and her fear. 'I'm going to tell my mother.'

The belt lashed out and hit her smartly across her thin, bare legs.

'Sit down,' said Brownie, her tongue showing briefly between her thick, pink lips.

Tina sat again, as if someone had pushed her. Swiftly Brownie knelt and tied her ankles with the belt.

'Is it too tight?' she asked.

Tina shook her head. 'You haven't locked the door,' she said and swinging her legs off the floor lay down on the bed. Her voice was toneless now, a little weary. For a second, quite strongly, she could smell the cat—an acrid unpleasant smell, that was also somehow strangely pleasurable.

'I don't have to,' said Brownie. 'Dinner won't be ready yet for half an hour.' She waited. Their eyes met briefly, then slowly Tina raised her arms until her fingers touched the end of the bed. Looping the rope around her cousin's wrists, Brownie tied them securely to the wooden bars.

Maybe it wasn't the cat . . . maybe it was Brownie who smelled like that, thought Tina, breathing it in, repelled and yet intrigued.

'What am I getting?' asked Brownie.

'I don't know.'

'You're lying. What are *you* giving me?'

'I'm not saying.'

'Tell me.'

'Never.' Tina almost smiled, hugging her knowledge of Brownie's present, protecting it against her cousin, and somehow, obscurely, protecting her cousin too . . . shielding her from disappointment and from the wrath of adults. I'll never tell, she thought fiercely, steeling her will. Whatever they do . . . I'll never tell. I'll never cry. I'll show them how brave I am. Nobody can make me cry. Already things were getting confused and unreal, like in a dream.

Brownie gave a gurgling little sound, like she was laughing in her throat. She put one knee on the bed next to Tina, then swung the other leg across her like straddling a horse, and began to tickle her cousin.

Tina giggled, squirmed and suddenly began to struggle. 'No more . . .' she gasped, the laughter turning into panic, because it hurt to breathe.

Brownie did not seem to hear. Her eyes, gazing into Tina's, were glazed, her lips half parted in a peculiar smile that made Tina feel giddy. She gasped again, frightened because she couldn't breathe and frightened of Brownie who didn't look like Brownie any more, and her legs, tied at the ankles, moved frantically from side to side in a desperate attempt to throw off the weight of Brownie's body.

'Tell me,' said Brownie, bearing down, the muscles of her legs straining to keep the other still. 'What are you giving me?'

'I won't . . . I won't . . .' hissed Tina, her lips scarcely moving, her being rising in a fierce determined effort to break the other's will, to crush her power.

Brownie shifted one hand to Tina's hair and pulled. Tina instantly ceased moving and lay still. Closing her eyes she felt as if her blood, her heart and stomach, every little part of her was slowly being drawn to her head and through her hair into Brownie's hand to float away and disappear. It was almost pleasant lying there, helpless and unable to move, trapped between Brownie's legs with her body soft and heavy like a pillow on her chest. Tina suddenly felt drowsy and wanted to sleep . . .

to sleep in Brownie . . . drown . . . become a part of her. The pull in her hair began to slacken. She moved her head a little like a kitten, begging to be caressed. And now Brownie was stroking her hair or combing it with her fingers.

'You're crying,' she said, touching Tina's cheeks. 'What are you crying about? Did it hurt?'

'No,' said Tina. 'I'm not crying. I never cry.' Opening her eyes, she said vengefully, spitting the words into Brownie's face: 'A bike, that's what you're getting. A bike. A bike.'

From far away, in a different world, a door was heard slamming. Brownie jumped to the floor, untied her cousin's hands and legs. Speaking in a loud, clear voice, she said: 'It's your move, Tina. Come on. Move.' Pushing the rope under her bed she hastily buckled her belt.

'Hurry,' she whispered. 'Hurry.'

Drying her eyes with the edge of her dress, Tina got off the bed. She wanted to know what Brownie thought, how Brownie felt, but didn't dare to ask, didn't dare even to look at her.

Footsteps sounded in the hall outside, and the two little girls, carefully avoiding each other's eyes, sat down on the floor to play checkers.

OTHER TITLES IN THE IMPRINT SERIES

ECLIPSED

Two Centuries of Australian Women's Fiction

Edited by Connie Burns and Marygai McNamara

This anthology presents the range of Australian women's writings from the first white settlement to the present, and includes pieces by both established and newer writers, as well as pieces by writers who had previously been 'eclipsed' by their male counterparts.

Editors Connie Burns and Marygai McNamara have chosen works by authors such as Catherine Helen Spence, Caroline Woolmer Leakey and Miles Franklin, and combined them with contemporary writers such as Helen Garner, Sally Morgan and Margaret Coombs to produce a book which is not only representative of the rich tradition of writing by Australian women, but one that is also innovative and highly entertaining.

PERSONAL BEST

Thirty Australian authors choose their best short stories

Edited by Garry Disher

In most short story anthologies, an editor decides upon an author's best or most representative story. But what do the writers themselves think?

Personal Best breaks new ground in inviting thirty Australian writers to select and explain their best or favourite story. Here are early stories, new stories, famous stories—and a host of unexpected choices. Furthermore, in discussing the stories' origins and how they were made, the contributors to *Personal Best* give a fascinating glimpse of the writer at work.

This anthology represents the best: our best authors choosing their best stories. Contributors include: David Malouf, Elizabeth Jolley, Frank Moorhouse, Kate Grenville, Peter Carey, Barbara Hanrahan, Gerald Murnane, Beverley Farmer, Robert Drewe, Glenda Adams, Helen Garner . . . and many others.

Absorbing and entertaining, *Personal Best* is the ideal introduction to contemporary Australian short story writing.

CLEAN STRAW FOR NOTHING
A CARTLOAD OF CLAY

George Johnston

Clean Straw for Nothing and *A Cartload of Clay* are the second and third novels in George Johnston's powerful *Meredith Trilogy*. In *Clean Straw for Nothing*—set against the backdrop of a Greek island—David Meredith re-evaluates his worth, his relationship with his wife, his sense of frustration at his inability to find the answers he craves. *A Cartload of Clay* sees him return, subdued and depressed, to Australia, where he rediscovers his affection for his native land, a land he had previously turned his back on. It is an affection, however, that acknowledges the country's deep faults and failings as well as its virtues.

These two books, the sequels to *My Brother Jack* and published for the first time as a single volume, are classics to be read, re-read and treasured.